To Wed
A Texan

Also by Georgina Gentry

Cheyenne Captive
Cheyenne Princess
Comanche Cowboy
Bandit's Embrace
Nevada Nights
Quicksilver Passion
Cheyenne Caress
Apache Caress
Christmas Rendezvous
Sioux Slave
Half-Breed's Bride
Nevada Dawn
Cheyenne Splendor
Song of the Warrior
Timeless Warrior
Warrior's Prize
Cheyenne Song
Eternal Outlaw
Apache Tears
Warrior's Honor
Warrior's Heart
To Tame A Savage
To Tame A Texan
To Tame A Rebel
To Tempt A Texan
To Tease A Texan
My Heroes Have Always Been Cowboys
To Love A Texan

Published by Kensington Publishing Corp.

To Wed
A Texan

GEORGINA GENTRY

ZEBRA BOOKS
Kensington Publishing Corp.
www.kensingtonbooks.com

ZEBRA BOOKS are published by

Kensington Publishing Corp.
850 Third Avenue
New York, NY 10022

All Kensington titles, imprints, and distributed lines are available
at special quantity discounts for bulk purchases for sales promo-
tion, premiums, fund-raising, educational, or institutional use.

Special book excerpts or customized printings can also be created to fit specific needs. For details, write or phone the office
of the Kensington Special Sales Manager: Attn. Special Sales
Department. Kensington Publishing Corp., 850 Third Avenue,
New York, NY 10022. Phone: 1-800-221-2647.

Zebra and the Z logo Reg. U.S. Pat. & TM Off.

ISBN-13: 978-0-8217-7991-0
ISBN-10: 0-8217-7991-5

First Zebra Mass Market Printing: March 2008

10 9 8 7 6 5 4 3 2 1

Printed in the United States of America

This story is dedicated to the memory of
four great women writers of the West:

To Helen Jackson,
author of A Century of Dishonor,
the earliest exposé of the cruel way our country
mistreated American Indians.

To Mari Sandoz,
who, in her many books about the West,
such as Cheyenne Autumn,
wrote in an even more poignant way.

To Oklahoma's own author, Angie Debo,
who exposed scandals in this state about
prominent whites stealing from the Indians
in her book And Still the Waters Run.
Ms. Debo was considered a troublemaker for her exposé.
Very late in her life,
Oklahoma finally recognized her truthful
integrity and honored her.

And finally to my favorite woman writer of Western fiction,
Dorothy M. Johnson,
author of The Hanging Tree,
The Man Who Shot Liberty Valance,
and A Man Called Horse.

Because I was inspired by these four brave,
talented women, I write about the Old West.
I hope I do them proud.

Prologue

The story you are about to read is based on an actual incident in Texas history.

The year was 1895, the middle of the so-called "Gay Nineties." America was both powerful and prosperous, and would soon be involved in the Spanish American War and building the Panama Canal.

The new heavy-weight boxing champion of the world was "Gentleman Jim" Corbett, who had just defeated the well-known John L. Sullivan for the title. A Texas promoter decided he could make a lot of money by staging a fight in Dallas between the new champ and the up-and-coming challenger, Bob Fitzsimmons.

Prize fights were against the law in most states, including Texas, but there was nothing Texans loved more than gambling and fighting, so the promoter thought it was a shoo-in. What he didn't count on was having to battle the indignant ministers' alliance, outraged ladies, four governors, and the presidents of both America and Mexico. Before it was over, this event became a media circus involving the well-known gunfighter Bat Masterson, the infamous Judge Roy

Bean, John L. Sullivan, the Texas Rangers, and the Mexican police, the *Ruales*. Oh, and did I mention there was a big African lion and a goat in the mix?

If all this seems ridiculous to you, you don't know Texans. To them, it was just par for the course. Get ready for the countdown as our handsome gambler/promoter, Jack "Cash" McCalley, comes up against widowed Mrs. Bluebonnet O'Neal Schwartz Purdy, president of the Lone Star Ladies For Decency and Decorum, who is determined to stop all these uncivilized, barbaric she-nanigans. Let round one begin!

Chapter One

The Cattlemen's Hotel, Dallas, Texas, early summer, 1895

Mrs. Bonnie O'Neal Schwartz Purdy was in a very good mood that late afternoon as she walked up to the hotel desk to check in. Unfortunately, that was about to change.

"You have my room ready?" She pressed her small frame against the desk, too warm in her black dress as she made ready to sign the book.

"Ahh, Mrs. Purdy, we seldom see you in Dallas. How's the town of Shot Gun?" There was perspiration on the man's pasty face and she could hardly hear him over the crowds bustling through the hotel and into the dining room.

"Just fine," Bonnie nodded and smiled, weary after her long train trip. "It appears we'll have a large crowd for our convention."

"That's the problem, ma'am," the clerk took out a hankie and wiped his gleaming face. "There's so many ladies and so much confusion."

Bonnie blinked, sensing his discomfort. "Is there a problem? I asked for a suite."

"I, ah, can't find your reservation and the hotel is full."

"What? But I sent my reservation in weeks ago. Surely there's a reservation for the president of the Lone Star Ladies For Decency and Decorum."

He mopped his brow again. "Perhaps at another hotel—"

"No." She shook her head; tired and a little impatient. "That would be too inconvenient."

"I know, ma'am." He wiped his face again, very nervous this time.

She could probably get him fired, but maybe he had a family and needed the job. She sighed and lowered her voice. "Look, surely you have some rooms saved back? I'll not be choosey and I can do without a suite."

"I don't think . . ." He wiped his face again, obviously well-aware Bonnie could get him fired. Abruptly a light seemed to break over his face as he studied his books. "You know, now that I think of it, I might be able to give you half a suite."

"Half?"

"Well, a gentleman keeps a suite here permanently, but he's out of town and possibly we could give you one of the two rooms."

Bonnie thought a moment. She'd like a reasonable solution and she didn't want to cause problems for this poor clerk. "There's a door between? Is this gentleman liable to return unexpectedly?"

"No, no," the man shook his head, reassuring her. "Besides, there's a sturdy lock on the door between and I'll see you get the only key."

Bonnie hesitated. She could raise a fuss and maybe get others tossed out of their rooms for her convenience, but she was always fair. "Are you sure that's all you've got?"

The clerk began profuse apologies again, offering her the keys.

She was a bit upset but there didn't seem to be any alternative. Most of the meetings of the state-wide ladies' club would be held in this hotel and she didn't relish trying to manage with a room across town. "Very well, it will do."

As she signed the register, the clerk rang for a bell-hop. "Take Mrs. Purdy's things up to 203B."

The Mexican boy looked perplexed. "Si, but that's Senor Cash's—"

"It's Mrs. Purdy's room now," the desk clerk snapped.

The bellhop shrugged and started to say something else, but Bonnie caught the warning glare in the clerk's pale eyes. Well, none of that was her business. She turned away from the desk, paused. "Oh, by the way, I'd like room service every morning, breakfast and the newspaper." It was one of the few luxuries she allowed herself. Having grown up very poor, she would always be thrifty.

"Certainly, ma'am."

"I take one scrambled egg, ham, biscuits and a small pot of coffee." She looked toward the noisy dining room as she took her keys, handed them to the bellhop. "I think I'll have some supper and then go up. Big day tomorrow." She reached into her reticule for a tip. "I'll be in the dining room if any of my district leaders need to find me. You can return my keys there."

The Mexican boy grinned at the size of the tip, touched his cap before turning toward the stairs.

"We're much happy to have all these hundreds of ladies in town, Senora."

She nodded and smiled. "We're looking forward to a good convention." She turned, lifted the hem of her black skirt and strode toward the busy dining room.

Once there, she decided since she'd had a big steak dinner on the train, perhaps she would have only some iced tea and a small salad. The dining room was crowded and bustling and the waiter guided her to a small table near a window and handed her a menu with a flourish.

Cash McCalley strode through the front door of the Cattlemen's Hotel, smoking a cigarillo and grinning as he approached the desk. The place seemed to be full of females and not the kind he liked—these all looked strait-laced and respectable. Not that he couldn't charm some of them out of that, but Fifi might be in town soon and she really knew how to please a man. To the desk clerk, he said, "Howdy, Earl, my usual suite, please."

The man paled and rubbed his mouth. "Uh, Mr. McCalley. We thought you were out of town—"

"I was, but as you can see, I'm here," Cash grinned. "Been back East; just made a big deal."

"Good for you, sir. Perhaps now, you might, er, catch up your past bill?" Earl's voice was timid.

Cash gave him his most engaging grin. "By thunder, Earl, you know I'm good for it. Now when this deal works out, I'll be able to catch up all my old debts."

Earl chewed his pale lip. "Uh, I think the manager—"

"What would you think about a world championship boxin' match right here in little old Dallas?"

"Sir?"

Cash rubbed his hands together with enthusiasm and winked. "I just have to tell someone. It'll be in the papers tomorrow mornin'. Hear this: I've just arranged a fight between Champion Gentleman Jim Corbett and an up-and-comin' fighter, Fightin' Bob Fitzsimmons."

"I thought John L. Sullivan was the champ?" the clerk asked.

"Nope, got beat some time back by Corbett. Why, men will flock to Dallas to see this fight and as the promoter, I stand to make a pile of money."

"So then you'll pay your bill?"

"Of course, now gimme my keys." Cash was suddenly a bit annoyed. All the money he'd saved over the years, he'd lost in the Crash of '93, but things were looking up for him now. He hummed a bit of "Camptown Races" as he signed the register and accepted the key, started to turn away, then paused. "You only gave me the key to 203A."

Earl pulled out his hankie and wiped his pale face. "Uh, you see, sir, there's a big ladies' convention in town—"

"Don't I know it?" Cash snorted. "Train was full of them, righteous lookin' old biddies."

"Well, sir, I had to give one of them the adjoining room to yours."

"What!" Cash whirled around, trying to control his Scots-Irish temper. "But that's my permanent suite—"

"Well, she was most insistent, sir, and your bill is long overdue and you were out of town—"

"I told you I'd pay it as soon as this big deal comes off, and as you can see, Earl, I'm back in town."

"I—I wasn't sure if you'd really need the other room—"

"Don't I usually have a lady or two with me?" Cash snapped.

The clerk mopped his face again. "Cash, you know if it was up to me, I'd have saved it, but with your past due bill and this being an important woman—"

"By thunder, you're insultin' me. Cash McCalley always pays his bills. I'm just a little short now, that's all. Miss Fifi LaFemme may be arrivin' in town."

Earl leaned forward, very interested. "Isn't she the one that does that cancan dance?"

Cash nodded and grinned. In his mind, the long-legged Fifi kicked her heels high and showed her lace garters. "That she is. I was thinkin' it might be convenient for us to have adjoinin' rooms."

"I am so sorry, Mr. McCalley."

"Oh, forget it," Cash muttered. "Maybe the old hens will only be in town a couple of days." He held out a coin to the Mexican bellhop. "Take my bags up. I'll be in the bar if anyone needs me and then I'll be in the dinin' room." He turned and humming, strode toward the bar. He was in too good a mood about his coming success to let a mix-up like this ruin his day.

After two good stiff drinks of bourbon, he felt even better and headed for the dining room. Standing in the doorway, his mood began to sour. To the headwaiter, he said, "By thunder, Joe, who are all these women? They chatter like hens and flutter about. Can you get me a good table away from the noise?"

The tall waiter smiled. "Glad to see you back in town, Cash." Then he looked about at the crowds. "Pretty busy. You'll have to wait or share a table."

"What? I don't want to share a table." Cash

grumbled, "Unless you can find a pretty miss to sit with, and just lookin' around, these are the most strait-laced, homely bunch of old biddies I've seen in a coon's age."

"It's the Lone Star Ladies For Decency and Decorum," Joe whispered, "their annual convention."

Cash groaned aloud. "More days of all this noise and confusion? I'm hungry enough to eat a sheep." He paused and thought. Well, no, no Texan was ever *that* hungry.

"If you'd share a table, Cash, I think I can seat you right away."

Cash took a deep breath. The scents from the kitchen made his mouth water. "I'm tryin' to decide if I'm that hungry." He thought about it. "Hell, yes, I am."

The waiter gestured. "I see a lady eating alone over there near the window. I can ask if she'd mind sharing."

Cash took a critical look at the woman the waiter indicated and did not like what he saw. The diminutive lady was maybe in her late twenties or early thirties and wore a rather dowdy black dress and hat. *A widow,* Cash thought, *and a rather plain and poor one at that.*

"Cash, would you like me to ask her if she would share her table?"

Cash groaned aloud. He was hungry as a wolf, but sharing a table with that prim brunette put him off. Oh, hell, he could stand anything for a few minutes. "Go ahead."

The waiter went to the table and leaned down, speaking to the woman. She frowned and looked toward Cash with evident distaste. Clearly, she did not like the idea any better than he did. Damn, he was hungry. He tipped his Stetson to her and then doffed it, smiled his most engaging smile. She seemed to hesitate. She did have big blue eyes, but a thin, disapproving mouth and her hair, under her black hat, was pulled back in such a severe bun that it must hurt her face. He smiled again and tried to look charming. She said something to the waiter and frowned again. Evidently, she didn't find Cash too appealing. That hurt his pride; he'd never met a woman who didn't find him utterly fascinating.

The waiter returned. "Mrs. Purdy is a little hesitant, but I told her you were a perfect gentleman."

"She's worried I might be a masher?" His voice rose in indignation. "By thunder, that plain, prim little—"

"Cash, lower your voice," the waiter gestured. "She might hear you and change her mind."

"Oh, hell, lead on." Cash took a deep breath and followed the waiter across the crowded dining room.

Bonnie watched the pair threading their way through the crowd toward her. Already she regretted having made the offer. This tall, broad-shouldered Texan was just the kind of man she had always avoided. He was a little too handsome and dressed too flashy in a scarlet vest and a silk necktie with a diamond stickpin. No doubt, he was probably a gambler like her second husband.

He reached her and gave a deep bow with a flourish of his Stetson. "My lady, thank you so much for your generosity. I don't often meet such a charming woman—"

"Oh, just sit down. I am not the kind of woman who is taken in by fancy compliments." She pointed to the seat across from her. From here, she could smell the fine cologne. She tried not to look at him because there was something dangerous about those gray eyes that surveyed her under a shock of curly dark hair.

"Oh, but a lovely lady like you should be complimented." He took his seat and reached for his napkin with a flourish. "Allow me to introduce myself, kind lady. I am Cash McCalley."

His voice was a deep baritone with a West Texas accent.

"Cash is not a name, sir."

"Well, actually, my Christian name is Jack. And you are?"

"Mrs. Purdy." She snapped and began to eat her salad faster, eager to get away from this obvious rascal.

Cash sighed and turned to the waiter. "The biggest steak you have and potatoes and biscuits. You know how I like my steak."

"Yes, sir, Cash." The waiter scribbled on his pad and left.

The chatter of women swirled around them as Cash turned his attention to the lady. "Lovely day, ain't it?"

She merely nodded and reached for a cracker.

Poor thing, she couldn't have too much money or she wouldn't be wearing such a dowdy dress and eating a small salad. He felt a little sympathy but he dare not offer to buy her dinner; a respectable lady would never allow a stranger to do that.

"I've just returned from an excitin' trip back East," he said to break the silence. "And you?"

"I'm a librarian," she said, not looking up, "and I'm in town for a convention."

"Oh, really? How interestin'." Of course it wasn't interesting at all. Mrs. Purdy looked like a librarian, very prim and proper, although, when she looked up, she did have startling blue eyes. He'd never been in a library, nor was he even sure what a librarian did, although now that he thought of it, he might have seduced one or two. The strained silence returned and he was more than grateful when the waiter brought his food.

The steak was so large, it lapped over the china plate. Cash took a deep breath of the scent and cut into it. It looked juicy and delicious. He put a bite in his mouth and chewed slowly, closing his eyes. Ah, just right. When he opened them, the lady was frowning at him.

"That meat is so raw, with a little bit of help, that steer could recover."

"By thunder, just the way I like it." He frowned at her then realized she was staring at his plate. He glanced at her small salad. Probably the poor thing couldn't afford a steak but he could not offer her a piece of his. That would be too intimate and insulting.

"Mr. McCalley," she lowered her voice and now it had a nice, musical tone to it, "I don't think you can eat all that. May I trouble you for the scraps?"

"What?" Her request caught him off-guard.

Her delicate face turned deep pink. "I—I don't want you to think me forward, but I'm feeding a stray cat."

Uh huh. So she was hungry. "Certainly, dear lady. Would you like some potatoes, too?"

She looked puzzled. "I'm not sure cats eat potatoes."

He didn't want to embarrass the poor little thing. No doubt she would eat the meat up in her room later. "Well, I'll have the waiter box up potatoes and bread, too, just in case cats like them." Actually, he had planned to save the scraps for the old cat he'd been feeding down at the train depot, but there'd probably be enough for the lady and John L. too.

For the first time, she smiled at him and she was more attractive than he had first thought. "Thank you, Mr. McCalley, you are indeed kind." She had a Texas accent, he thought.

"Purdy," he mused as he ate, "I used to know a Purdy; Clint Purdy."

"Probably not the same one." Bonnie kept her eyes on her plate, not wanting the stranger to see her face. Clint Purdy. She was embarrassed at the memory. How could she have been fooled so badly?

"I didn't think that was a common name," Cash persisted, watching her as he ate. "Clint, old 'Ace High' Purdy."

Cash had a gambler's keen eye at reading people and he saw the way she started and her face reddened and tears came to her eyes. So she'd been taken in by that handsome scoundrel. Strange, she didn't seem like the kind to attract a rascal like Purdy. Most gamblers liked flashy, wild women. Cash thought of Fifi LaFemme and sighed. Hell, even if Fifi did return to town, she wouldn't be sharing his suite.

"Gracious, I—I really need to go now." The lady checked the small watch pinned on her bodice.

"Certainly." Cash signaled the waiter and said to him, "Take the scraps and divide them up in two little bundles."

"Sir?"

Cash frowned. He was too much of a Texan to embarrass the prim lady. "Mrs. Purdy and I are both feedin' strays."

Bonnie eyed him suspiciously. He didn't look like the type to feed stray anything, except maybe saloon girls. Oh, this varmint was the kind who would attract saloon girls, all right. "You're a gambler, Mr. Mc-Calley?" she asked before she thought.

"Well, more of a promoter." He leaned back in his chair and reached for a cigar in his silk vest, seemed to realize he was with a lady, and put it back.

A promoter, she thought, that was a fancy name for a gambler, wasn't it? She wasn't sure. She took another whiff of his expensive cologne and moved uneasily in her chair. There was something very virile and male about him that made Bonnie nervous.

About that time, the waiter returned with the two little bundles of food.

"Thank you," she said to the waiter and got up.

Immediately, McCalley jumped to his feet and bowed. "So nice of you to share your table, Mrs. Purdy."

He was so masculine and intimidating that a warning bell went off in her head. She backed away in confusion. "Thank you for your scraps."

"Have the waiter get you some butter for those potatoes."

"I don't think cats eat potatoes," she said again, mystified.

"Oh, shucks, I forgot."

He nodded to her and smiled. Stuttering in confusion, she grabbed up her reticule and the steak scraps and fled out of the dining room.

Cash stood staring after her. What a funny, prim little creature. Well, he hoped she enjoyed the steak. As poor as she appeared, she must be really splurging to be staying at the Cattlemen's Hotel.

The waiter presented him with his bill. "How was the dinner, Cash?"

Cash grinned and waved it away. "Excellent. Joe, I'm headed to the bar for a drink and a cigar. Have the doorman send down to the livery for my horse, would you?" He gave the waiter a hefty tip that he couldn't afford, told him to put his dinner bill on his tab, picked up the other package of scraps and strode out. If his big deal went through, he'd be rolling in money again like he was back in '93 before the panic wiped him out.

Outside the hotel, Bonnie waited for the buggy that the doorman had called for her.

"Ma'am, do you need a driver?" The liveryman stepped down.

"No, I can handle a horse." Holding onto her little bundle of scraps, she let him help her up into the buggy and then she drove to the train station. Dallas was getting to be a very large town, she thought. She liked it better back in Shot Gun, but duty had called and she had come. Tomorrow, the Lone Star Ladies convention opened and Bonnie was determined that she would be the best president the group had ever had. This was rather a snooty group and with her impoverished background, she didn't feel like she belonged and especially not as the new president.

The charming rascal of a Texan crossed her mind again. Oh, he looked like he could be as dangerous to women as a coyote in a chicken coop, but after two marriages to rascals, she was not about to get mixed up with one ever again, especially not a Texan. They were the worst kind.

She drove out to the depot and reined in.

Most men would laugh at the idea of making a trip

to feed a stray cat but she had sensed that randy gambler had not. Gracious, what on earth did he think she was doing with the scraps? Hopefully, she wouldn't see any more of him while she was at the hotel. She climbed down and walked up on the platform. It was nearly sundown and there was almost no one about. "Kitty?" she called. "Here kitty, kitty, kitty."

After a few minutes, a ragged orange cat stuck his head out from under a sidelined freight car and regarded her suspiciously.

"Come here, Kitty Tom, I've got something good for you."

The big cat watched her but did not move.

"Oh, you poor wild kitty, I'm not going to hurt you. Here." She laid the scraps out on the platform and backed away.

The cat's battle-torn ears moved and he sniffed the air, seemed to decide the steak was worth the risk and scampered over to the food. He gobbled, all the while watching Bonnie with suspicious yellow eyes.

"You poor thing," she murmured. "You know, if you'd trust me, I could offer you a good home when I leave here. Wouldn't you like to have a home?"

The cat only eyed her and gobbled the food. Perhaps if she could only pet him . . . she moved closer and the cat took off in a flash, running back under the freight car. Bonnie sighed. "I'll leave and you can finish your dinner," she promised the wild stray. "You've got to learn to trust somebody or you'll never have a home."

The cat watched her from under the freight car and Bonnie turned and walked back to the buggy. When she glanced over her shoulder, Kitty Tom had returned to the steak scraps.

Bonnie took the buggy back to the hotel. As she was alighting, Cash McCalley came out of the hotel and across the walk. He smiled and nodded, tipped his hat. She caught a distinct scent of bourbon as she returned a polite but cool nod. At the door, she turned and watched him mount a spirited gray stallion the doorman held for him. Then he turned and rode away, tall and superior in the saddle.

Headed out for a night in the saloons, Bonnie thought with distaste. She could only imagine what happened in those dens of iniquity. No doubt, he danced with those loose women and no telling what else. She felt the heat rise to her face just thinking about it. Not that she knew anything about that. Her first husband had been elderly, so there wasn't much intimacy. Mostly he had needed a housekeeper, so he'd married her, and the second one . . . well, she didn't even want to think about how she had been fooled. She had loved three men and they were all dead now. Tears came to her eyes and she dabbed at them. She must stop caring and put the past behind her.

The next morning, she was barely dressed when room service knocked at her door. She took the tray over to a table and poured herself some coffee with plenty of thick cream while she read the paper from the tray. The front page made her almost drop her steaming cup in her lap. The headline read: PROMOTER TO BRING BIG FIGHT TO DALLAS.

"What?" She blinked as she read:

Local promoter and well-known man about town, Cash McCalley, has just returned from New York with plans

*to put on a world championship prize fight right here in
Dallas. . . .*

All three of the men she had loved had been killed
in fights and she felt duty bound to see to it that no
more women suffered as she had. Bonnie slammed
her cup down with a resolute gesture. "I knew he was
a scoundrel. A bloody, savage fist fight here in Texas?
When respectable people are trying to civilize this
state? Not if the Lone Star Ladies For Decency and
Decorum have anything to say about it!"

Chapter Two

Hurriedly, Bonnie finished her breakfast and got dressed in her frumpy black dress. She sighed, looking in the mirror and brushing a wisp of brown hair back into her severe bun. Maybe she really ought to buy something new while she was in Dallas. Why? Staying in widow's weeds protected her from men like the late Clint Purdy. That made her think of Cash McCalley. "Humph. There are more important things to worry about than a dress right now."

Today was Saturday and in less than two hours, she would be calling the general session of the Lone Star Ladies to order. She was nervous and unsure of herself at chairing this first important meeting; knowing she had so little background for it. She didn't want to make a fool of herself. Still there was a lot on her agenda for respectable women to consider since Texas men could be such untamed hooligans.

Pouring a second cup of coffee, she reminded herself that she must get some scraps over to that poor stray cat sometime today.

That made her think of the steak scraps and once again, the rascal she'd met last night. If she'd had any

inkling that he was involved in bringing this despicable
prize fighting to Dallas, she wouldn't have allowed him
to share her table. She hated any kind of violence,
having grown up in a shack with a drunken father who
threw things and beat all the children when he was on
a toot. She had escaped when she was sixteen after
Danny . . . she would not think of her dead brother now,
it hurt too much. Bonnie gritted her teeth and returned
to her newspaper.

> *Local promoter, Jack McCalley, better known to the
> sporting set as "Cash" assures this reporter that the pre-
> sent champion "Gentleman Jim" Corbett, and a top
> challenger, Bob Fitzsimmons, have signed contracts to
> stage a fight here in Dallas, time and place to be an-
> nounced.*

Gracious, what a sleazy rascal. Bonnie slammed her
cup down so hard, it rattled. She'd known there was
something about that man last night that had unnerved her, but she'd thought it was his masculinity.
Well, this fight was indeed a topic for her morning
meeting. If it were up to respectable women, there'd
be no match and as for all the low-life it would attract,
Texas had enough problems with unruly males without adding this to the mix. What Texas needed were
less male brutes like Cash McCalley and more men
like Herbert Snodgrass, her fiancé. Now Herbert
might not be tall and good-looking like that rascal,
but he was just the kind of man civilized women
favored—steady and predictable as a grandfather
clock. And about as exciting.

"Bonnie, you should be ashamed of yourself," she
sighed. "Herbert is an upstanding citizen while that

Cash character would probably steal the gold out of a lady's teeth."

And kiss her so skillfully while he was doing it, she wouldn't notice. "Bonnie Purdy, what are you thinking? Get your mind on the mission of this convention. The ladies elected you to help bring civilization to Texas and you must not fail them."

Thus bolstered, Bonnie gathered her reticule, pinned on her red, white and blue convention ribbon and marched down to the lobby, ready to do battle against anything that seemed wild and uncivilized. In effect, almost everything that Texas males so enjoyed.

Down in the crowded lobby, she ran into Herbert Snodgrass. He might have been nice-looking except that his hair was thinning and he was a bit plump. He also had allergies. "Why, Herbert," she said, surprised. "I wasn't expecting you'd be in town."

He sneezed, wiped his nose. Then he took both her hands in his soft, pink ones. "My dear, I was in Dallas for the Chickie Best account and thought I'd drop by to encourage you on your first day as the new president."

Herbert was an accountant and salesman for chicken feed across the state. Not very exciting, she thought, but dependable. Much better and more respectable than being a so-called promoter.

"You're so sweet," she nodded and pulled her hands from his with a sigh. Herbert sniffed and reached for a hankie. He was so civilized and tame; just what she was looking for in a husband. Not at all like that tall varmint who'd shared her table last night. "I've got to go. The opening session begins in the ballroom in a few minutes."

"Perhaps we can get together for lunch today?" He

sniffed. Herbert always sniffed. "You know, we need to talk about setting a date—"

"Not now, Herbert." She glanced at her tiny lapel watch. "There's just too much to deal with this week."

"But you've been putting me off for three years."

Bonnie sighed. "We'll meet in the hotel dining room for lunch." She gave him a vague nod, her mind busy with her day's projects as she turned to go. She hadn't quite decided what to do about Herbert. He might be a little dull, but he was safe and predictable. There was no danger or challenges in the man at all. Now that Cash McCalley was as wild as that stray Tom cat she was feeding. "Good-bye, Herbert. Hope you do well at Chickie Best this morning." She smiled, turned and walked away.

Minutes later, she stood in front of the crowd in the ballroom, listening to the chatter and excited buzz. Could these elegant ladies see that she had no background, no fancy schooling and that she'd taught herself to read and write?

She took a deep, nervous breath and banged her gavel for order. "Ladies, ladies please! Let's have the opening ceremonies and get our meeting started."

She and her fellow officers sat to one side of the stage and the members took their chairs as the Texas and American flags were carried down front.

Minutes later, Bonnie returned to the podium to warm applause. So far, so good; they seemed to be accepting her. She looked out at the hundreds of women gathered in the ballroom. They were respectable women, the backbone of Texas civilization and God knew Texans needed civilizing. "Ladies, if you have read the morning's papers, you know we have a serious challenge facing this group."

A murmur ran through the crowd as those who had seen the front page related the events to those who hadn't.

Bonnie banged for order again. "I think keeping organized bloody fights and the gambling and all that goes with it out of Texas should be a high agenda for those who favor decency and decorum."

"Hear! Hear!" shouted a number of ladies.

Thus encouraged, Bonnie warmed to her topic. "This rascal who is called Cash McCalley is planning a huge fight right here in Dallas, main headquarters of the Lone Star Ladies For Decency and Decorum. That's adding insult to injury."

A murmur of dismay ran through the crowd, and near her the plump vice-president Ethel Wannamaker pulled out her smelling salts and began to gasp.

"Yes, I am shocked, too," Bonnie nodded.

"Madam President," a homely housewife in an ugly pink dress stood up in the audience. "Did I not see you having supper with Cash McCalley last night?"

"Indeed you did," Bonnie fumed righteously. "I offered to share my table since there was none available. But immediately, I could sense he was a rascal and a rogue—"

"But a mighty handsome one," Ethel Wannamaker sighed.

"I didn't notice," Bonnie snapped and realized she lied. "Worse yet, the scoundrel is a Texan born and bred."

"Them's the best kind," another lady noted.

"I think not," Bonnie snapped. "I feel it is our duty to bring civilization to wild, undisciplined Texas men and turn them into respectable husbands and fathers."

"It'd be sure fun to try to tame that one," Ethel murmured and Bonnie turned and glared at her.

"Madam Vice-President, you are out of order. Keep your mind on the mission of this organization."

"Hear! Hear!" shouted the ladies again.

"Now," Bonnie said, "I understand by the newspaper that the sleazy Mr. McCalley is meeting with the city fathers this afternoon to ask their blessing and support for this questionable project. I feel we should attend as a group and protest, speak up for the respectable people of Texas."

The ladies cheered again.

They approved of her. Smiling, Bonnie rapped for order. "I think we should also ask our members to contact their church pastors to add pressure to the council and mayor."

"But the paper says the mayor supports the prize fight," a lady in a huge hat announced.

"We will see about that," Bonnie said. She was nothing if not determined, now that she was certain the members were supporting her. "Now ladies, let's break into groups and discuss strategy. First, I would like to make a motion that after lunch, we should gather out front and march to city hall to protest."

"I second the motion!" called the lady in the ugly flowered dress.

"The motion has been made and duly seconded." Bonnie nodded. "Is there any discussion?"

Plump Ethel held up her hand and Bonnie motioned with her gavel.

"Madam President, will we get to see Cash McCalley?" The hopeful tone of her voice annoyed Bonnie.

"No doubt," Bonnie snapped. "I imagine every gambler, hooker, pickpocket, saloon owner and anyone else who wants to make a dime off this infamous event will be there."

The lady in the big hat said, "I call for the vote."

Bonnie smiled at her and nodded. "All in favor signify by saying aye."

There was a mighty roar of ayes from the audience.

"Any nays?"

None.

She had met with approval from these upper-class Texas ladies. Bonnie smiled and rapped her gavel. "The motion is passed. We will meet in front of the hotel at one o'clock. I will ask Ethel Wannamaker to contact local pastors this morning. Now we will break into discussion groups by county to discuss other items of importance to the betterment of Texas."

Bonnie stepped back, satisfied and relieved as the ladies stood up and began to scatter about the ballroom. From what Bonnie could hear, there was a great deal of talk about recipes and new fashions and not as much about bettering Texas by civilizing the wild male population, but then, the organization was fairly new.

She turned to Ethel, the plump local housewife. "Gracious, Ethel, must you sabotage what I'm trying to do?"

"I didn't mean to," Ethel said, "it's just that I saw that Cash McCalley and there was something about him—"

"Never mind," Bonnie said in her coldest tone, feeling guilty herself about how she'd been attracted to the rascal. "Remember, he is the enemy."

"Then where do I go to surrender?" Ethel sighed.

"You are a married woman!" Bonnie reminded her.

Plump Ethel flushed. "I—I just wondered what it would be like to—"

"Ethel!"

"Uh, I mean—"

"I know what you meant. Now go contact the ministers' association," Bonnie said. "We want them with us on this."

Ethel scurried away. Now Bonnie was more sure of herself after the warm reception the members had given her. For the next several hours, she went about the various groups, listening and redirecting some of their efforts.

Several hours later, the groups broke for lunch.

With regret, Bonnie remembered that Herbert would meet her in the dining room. It was crowded of course, with all the ladies in town for the convention, but her plump fiancé waved to her from a table. He stood up as she approached.

"Dear Bonnie," he tried to kiss her cheek, but she turned her head.

"Really, Herbert, this is a public place. It's just not respectable."

"But we're engaged, aren't we?"

"I suppose."

"Suppose?" He sniffed and reached for a handkerchief. "Honestly, my dear, I don't know what's gotten into you."

She gave a dismissing wave of her hand. "Please, Herbert, I have a lot on my mind right now. I do so hope to be the best president Lone Star Ladies ever had. You know, I was just barely elected, and only then, I think, because of the—"

"Of course," Herbert nodded in understanding. "I know you're under a lot of pressure to prove yourself."

She was only half listening as she looked back at him. It was odd how the light on his head made his thinning hair so noticeable.

The waiter came and Bonnie ordered a big steak.

"My dear," Herbert said with disapproval, "are you sure you ought to eat all that red meat? It seems so—so primitive. You know, I never eat that heartily."

Primitive. In her mind, she saw Cash McCalley attacking a huge, rare steak with gusto. She sighed. "Herbert, don't patronize me."

"You are certainly different today," Herbert said with a sniff. To the waiter, he said, "I'll have the creamed vegetable soup and some tapioca pudding."

That was Herbert all right, bland and colorless as tapioca. *What is wrong with me?* she scolded herself. She had been drawn to Herbert because he was so safe and predictable and now. . . .

The waiter left and while the crowds of convention women swirled in and out of the dining room, Herbert went on and on about landing the Chickie Best account this morning while Bonnie nodded and only half listened.

When he finally paused in talking about himself and the chicken feed business, Bonnie asked, "Did you see this morning's paper?"

"Yes, the price of grain is way up, so our profit margin—"

"That's not what I meant. I meant about the rogue, Cash McCalley, who's going to put on this big prize fight?"

"Oh, that." He shrugged his narrow shoulders. "Well, from what I've heard about that rascal, I'm not surprised."

Bonnie spread her napkin across the lap of her

black dress. She didn't want to ask, but she couldn't help herself. "What have you heard about him?"

Herbert sniffed and pulled out a big hankie, wiped his nose. "Very scandalous."

Now she really did want to know. For a moment, she seemed to smell the woodsy scent of Cash's cologne. Herbert always had a faint aroma of medicine. "The Lone Star Ladies intend to challenge this affront to civilized behavior, Herbert, so perhaps you should tell me what you've heard. Forewarned is forearmed, you know."

"I don't know about challenging that scoundrel," Herbert sniffed again and reached for a hot roll and the butter. "Around town, they say he's a good man with fists, women and cards and a pistol, too."

"What do you mean 'with women'?" She felt like Ethel Wannamaker, but she couldn't help herself.

Herbert colored and stared at her. "Bonnie, you would probably have no idea what I meant. Why, he's seen about town with some of the wildest, most notorious dance hall girls. I can't imagine what they see in that rascal."

Bonnie remembered Cash sitting across from her and sighed. Yes, there was something dangerous and enticing about the Texan. But of course, not to a respectable widow like herself.

"Besides, they say he escorts Fifi LaFemme when she's in town."

"I'm not sure I know who that is."

He gave her an annoying, patronizing smile. "But of course a lady wouldn't know that name. Fifi LaFemme is the star cancan dancer at the Black Lace Saloon, or so I hear."

"What is a cancan?"

He hesitated. "A dance. They say the girls wear such short skirts, their legs show and when they kick up their heels, their lace underwear is quite visible and . . ." He colored and didn't finish.

"Gracious. What else do people say?"

Herbert stared at her with his watery eyes. "It's just gossip among men; not fit for a lady's ears."

About that time, the waiter brought their food. Bonnie cut into her steak while Herbert frowned in disapproval. It was a big, juicy steak with lots of gravy on a mound of potatoes, with excellent hot rolls. "Believe me, I only asked because our ladies' group has decided to protest this fight McCalley's planning."

Herbert's eyebrows went up in his chubby face. "That's a very ambitious project, Bonnie. I don't think Cash McCalley is someone to cross."

"Well, I'm stubborn, too, and the ladies thought it was a great idea. Besides, it is for the good of the state."

Herbert laughed. He had the most annoying, high-pitched laugh. "Honestly, I doubt if many Texas men would see it that way." He paused. "But of course, I'm in complete agreement with you, my dear."

"Then you'll be happy to join our protest this afternoon at city hall?" She looked at him point blank.

"You mean, confront Cash McCalley?" His face turned pale and his pink hand that held his soup spoon shook a little.

"There will be hundreds of us. And besides, you know what the Texas Rangers say about 'no one ever stopped a man who was in the right but kept right on coming.'"

"I am not a Texas Ranger," Herbert said. "I am from

Des Moines. Besides, I hear that rascal carries a pistol and knows how to use it."

"You don't think he'd start shooting at a bunch of ladies? No Texan would do that."

Herbert snorted. "I think this thing about Texans being chivalrous is a bit overstated."

Bonnie glared at him. "I assure you it is not. Texas men may be the last real men left in this world. Now they might be a little wild and rough around the edges—"

"A little?" Herbert scoffed.

Suddenly, Bonnie didn't like him very much. She remembered suddenly that he was after all, a Yankee from Iowa, even if he was a perfect gentleman. "Then if you're so sure I might be in danger, I know you'll want to accompany me in this protest."

"Me?" Herbert squawked and touched his chest with his soft, pink fingers. "Why, they say that rascal is a big bar room brawler! And if I should get hit in the nose . . . well, you know how much trouble I have with my allergies."

"Of course, I understand." Bonnie said and resumed eating.

Herbert sniffed again. "Rather than taking on some dangerous rascal like McCalley, I think you ladies should focus on disgraceful subjects like working women and young girls wearing short skirts while riding those newfangled bicycles. Why, you can see their ankles. Disgraceful!"

Bonnie frowned at him. "You don't have to look at their ankles, Herbert." She decided not to tell him she had recently bought a bicycle because it looked like so much fun, but she had not learned to ride it yet. She wasn't at all sure it was a proper activity for the state president of the most dignified women's club in Texas. "There's a really cute song about it." Without thinking, she began to hum the first few bars of "A Bicycle Built For Two."

Cash McCalley strode into the dining room just then. As he was shown past her to a table, he smiled, and nodded. "Good to see you again, Mrs. Purdy."

Bonnie stared after him. She noticed so did every woman in the room.

"*Again?*" Herbert said. "What did he mean by that?"

For some reason, she dreaded to tell him, although she'd done nothing wrong. "Well, nothing much. We shared a table at supper last night."

"What?" Herbert paused with a spoon of tapioca halfway to his thin lips. "Why didn't you tell me that?"

"Gracious, Herbert, don't carry on so. It didn't seem important."

"My fiancée has supper with the most notorious womanizer in the state and doesn't think it's important?"

"I didn't know who he was and the dining room was crowded and he was hungry."

"I'd sooner have dinner with a wolf or a bear," Herbert grumbled.

"Oh, hush, Herbert." She wiped her lips with the linen napkin and tried not to stare at the back of Cash's head. He was entertaining a whole table full of women who might not be ladies. They seemed to be hanging on his every word. So were all the women at the tables around him.

"Did you tell me to hush, Bonnie?"

"I—think I did. I'm sorry, Herbert."

"Ladies never tell anyone to hush, Bonnie, especially their fiancé."

She gritted her teeth. What she'd really like to do was tell him to shove that spoon down his throat, but she didn't say that. She signaled the waiter to their table. "Please sack up my steak scraps. I'm feeding a stray cat."

"Yes, ma'am, Mrs. Purdy." The waiter bowed and took her plate away.

"Is it wild?"

Bonnie nodded.

"Wild things are dangerous," Herbert shook his head in disapproval.

"I think I can tame it. Taming wild things is always a challenge."

"I really prefer goldfish," Herbert said.

"You would," Bonnie said.

"What?"

"Nothing. Herbert, I must go up to my room and get my notes. The protest will be organizing at one o'clock. I'll expect you to march right by my side to show the upstanding men in this state are as opposed to this bloody thing as the women are."

He winced. "Please don't use the word 'bloody' when I'm eating."

"I keep forgetting you're not a Texan," Bonnie said as she stood up.

Herbert scrambled to his feet. "I'm proud to say I'm not. I don't like most Texans. They are boastful, arrogant and think they are superior to everyone."

"They can't help it," Bonnie said. "Remember, we were our own nation for ten years before we let the rest of the states join us and we'll never forget that."

The waiter returned with the small package of meat scraps and she took it. "I'll see you out front for the protest, Herbert."

"But—" he began to sputter. However, Bonnie was already sailing out of the dining room. She had to pass Cash McCalley's table as she left and she smelled his cologne and saw the expression on the women's faces at his table. They looked like deer caught in a lantern light, just mesmerized by the charming rascal. *How could they be so stupid?*

Cash was in a rare good humor as he ate his steak with gusto. The drab little widow from last night brushed past his table as she left the dining room and he nodded to her, but she did not acknowledge him as she left.

The women at his table now were some of the girls from the Black Lace Saloon and the respectable ladies in the large dining room were craning their necks with curiosity. Indeed the dining room was full of respectable women, all wearing small red, white and blue badges of some kind. Oh, yes; something about a convention.

When he had come in just now, he had seen the petite widow seated with a very dull, drab man. Well, that suited her. Mrs. Purdy certainly wasn't Cash's type. He liked his women loose, wild and passionate. He smiled at the thought and wondered how he would explain to Fifi that the hotel had given away her room. With a few kisses and caresses, Fifi would forget. He smiled as he thought of the tall blonde with the full curves. After his afternoon meeting with the town businessmen, he was looking forward to some fun and a little bouncing on a mattress with one of these girls from the Black Lace. At this moment, he was glancing around the table, trying to decide which one would be the lucky lady. Of course none of them were ladies.

He was in high spirits because the mayor had already assured him there would be no trouble with the city council over the prize fight. Most of them were in favor because of the money it would bring to town. And Cash had already charmed old Mrs. Pendigast. Soon as he had an affirmative vote from the city council, the old lady would lease him enough land to build the big arena. Her pasture just north of town would be perfect for his event. In fact, it was probably the only land big enough and convenient enough that was available for this fight. There would be a lot of money in this for him and the event would also be good for Dallas. Yessiree, his biggest problem now was did he want a blonde or a redhead to enjoy after the council meeting was over? Or maybe one of each?

"Ladies," he smiled as he finished his steak, "I've got business downtown. Afterwards, I'll come by the Black Lace and we'll have a drink or two."

The girls giggled with delight as he stood up and bowed. He managed to convince the waiter to add the tab to his overdue hotel bill, put on his Stetson and went outside where his gray stallion waited. Yes, he thought as he mounted up and rode away, it was going to be a great afternoon.

It took Bonnie a few minutes to get her ladies organized after lunch. It was sort of like trying to herd chickens, she thought. Herbert had joined them, along with a few husbands, but none of the men looked too eager to be here.

Ethel Wannamaker rushed up to her. "Did you see him in the dining room?" she gushed. "He had a whole table full of women."

"I saw him." Bonnie kept her voice cold. There was no point in even asking who she was talking about.

"And I imagine he could handle them all."

"Ethel!" Bonnie felt her face burn even as her mind pictured the possibilities. Evidently, the plump housewife was picturing it, too. She licked her lips and sighed.

"Did you check with the ministers?" Bonnie asked.

"What?" Ethel started. Evidently, her mind was still on what Cash McCalley might be able to do with half a dozen women.

"The ministers," Bonnie said patiently.

"Oh, yes," Ethel nodded. "Too short a notice, but they'll get involved. They are spreading the word now."

"Good. Now let's get to City Hall. Ladies!" She clapped her hands together and raised her voice like she did when rowdy students made too much noise in the library. After a moment, they quieted. "All right, Mrs. Wannamaker has just assured me that the ministers' organization intends to join us in this endeavor."

The ladies cheered. "Hear! Hear!" Indeed, Bonnie wasn't sure that most of them even knew what they were cheering about, but it was enough to be part of something that involved excitement and making decisions on their own. For some of them, this might be the first time they had been to anything more interesting than a quilting bee.

"Now, ladies," Bonnie brought herself up to her full but petite height and then climbed up on a hitching block. "City Hall, where this meeting is to take place, is only two blocks away. We will organize into lines and march in protest."

"Bonnie," Herbert said, "get down from there, you might fall."

She decided to ignore him. After all, he wasn't her husband yet.

"But women can't vote," a lady called out, "so why should the city council care what we think?"

"Good question," Bonnie nodded, "and perhaps we can involve the suffragists in our project later."

"Bonnie," Herbert said in a hoarse whisper, "you sound like a liberal. Surely you aren't in favor of letting women vote?"

"And you aren't?" She felt a little shocked. Perhaps she didn't know Herbert as well as she thought. "Here's the answer, ladies. Good women can influence their husbands, sons and brothers to vote against a city council or any elected official who goes against common decency. If we can get backed by the preachers of this area, and indeed, maybe all of Texas, there is no end to what we might accomplish."

A passing cowboy yelled, "Why don't you women get back in your kitchens and stop meddlin' in men's business?"

Several men passing shouted in agreement.

"If it concerns Texas, it is our business!" Bonnie shouted back and she heard Herbert sigh with disapproval. "Now ladies, let's march!"

The ladies cheered and stern Mrs. Olsen yelled, "Perhaps we could sing hymns as we march on City Hall."

"Good idea!" Bonnie said as she made her way through the crowd so that she stood by Herbert, Ethel, Mrs. Olsen and the other officers and proceeded to lead the ladies out into the street where startled horses reared and whinnied at the disorderly battalion.

Emboldened by the members' warm acceptance of

her, Bonnie raised her hand. "Ladies, forward! For a civilized world and a better Texas!"

A cheer went up and Mrs. Olsen began a slightly off-key chorus of "Marching to Zion" as the women started up the street. More startled horses reared at the noise and men turned to stare, open-mouthed.

Oh, but this felt good, to be accepted and to do something positive for the future of Texas. Since she was short, Bonnie had to take long strides to stay in the vanguard and she didn't know all the words to the hymn, but she tried.

Inside City Hall, Cash had just passed out some mighty fine Havanas and poured drinks all around as the gentlemen smiled and nodded. Oh, yes, this was going to be as easy as stealing hot pies off a window sill. The city council and the mayor were all for his prize fight. What real man didn't like the idea of watching other men beat each other bloody?

An alderman said, "Mr. McCalley—"

"Cash, please. We're all just friends here." He winked and gave him his best "old buddy" smile.

"Well, Cash, it's against the law to stage boxing matches in Texas—"

"A lot of things that are fun are against the law in Texas," Cash winked again at the man and the others laughed and nodded in agreement. "But the mayor is in full agreement with us and we haven't heard of any organized opposition."

An off-key sound drifted through the open window on the warm air. Cash paused. "What in the name of thunder is that? Sounds like someone stepped on some cats' tails."

The men paused in sipping their aged bourbon, looked puzzled and listened as the sound grew louder.

"Sounds like a revival or something." The mayor's bushy eyebrows went up.

"Distractin' anyway." Cash sighed in exasperation and strode over to the window to close it. He paused and stared. Coming down the street was an unorganized parade of some sort; women, wearing red, white and blue badges and waving banners. "A bunch of old biddies comin' this way. Maybe a suffragette protest, Mayor?"

"Oh, hell, not again." The mayor came to the window and looked out. "I don't know what it is with these women that they expect equal rights with men; even wantin' to vote."

"Them liberals has been stirrin' them up again," an alderman griped.

Now all the men brought their bourbon and cigars and came over to the row of windows to stare out in idle curiosity at the crowd of stalwart women marching down the street.

"Sounds like a hymn," Cash said. "Maybe they're advertisin' a revival."

"Maybe so," said the mayor, "but I'd swear they're coming here."

"Now why would they do that?" Cash took a swig of bourbon. He was more than a little annoyed. Here he almost had this thing wrapped up, only needing the final vote and then important businessmen to offer financial support. Cash certainly didn't have the money to fund a big event like this himself.

"Ain't that some reporters trailin' them?" Mr. Wannamaker, the owner of a big hardware store asked.

"They must be expectin' something interestin' to happen then," another complained.

"Damn," muttered Olsen, the owner of a local dry goods store, "I believe the old biddies are coming in here. I hope my Mildred ain't mixed up in whatever it is."

"I hope it ain't a prohibitionist group like that crazy Carrie Nation's bunch in Kansas."

"In that case," said another, "we'd better get rid of the evidence quick."

"I'm all for that," Cash said and drained his glass. He wasn't quite sure what was going on that had riled the ladies, but it didn't seem like it was his problem.

Then for the first time, he noticed the group's leader. She was a small woman in a dowdy black dress but today she wore no hat and her brown hair was pulled back in a severe bun. *Mrs. Purdy.* Cash groaned aloud. If the righteous little librarian was involved, somehow, he was sure it boded no good for him or any other rowdy Texas male!

Chapter Three

Two policemen tried to stop the ladies from entering City Hall, but Bonnie faced them down. "How dare you?" she shouted over the off-key hymn. "We are law-abiding citizens and have a right to speak to the mayor."

"The mayor is in conference on important business," a fat policeman drawled.

"Yes, and we know what it's about," Bonnie shouted back.

"Let's leave," Herbert pleaded, grabbing her arm, but she shook him off.

The ladies had now changed their song to "When we all get to heaven, what a great rejoicing there will be. . . ."

A reporter pushed forward to speak to the officer. "Am I to understand that the mayor will not see the Lone Star Ladies after they have gathered here in Dallas? What do you think our readers will say about that?"

The fat policeman seemed to reconsider. He wiped sweat from his beefy face and shrugged, pointed to the stairs.

"Forward, ladies!" Bonnie waved her troops on. "We are about to confront sin but be of brave heart. Goodness will triumph!"

The ladies let out a cheer and then they pushed forward, marching up the stairs. Bonnie paused on the second floor, momentarily confused by the many doors. Then her keen nose picked up the scent of cigars and bourbon and she threw open a door and marched into a very large office followed by her ladies. The gathering of men looked both bewildered and a little afraid. All except that big bruiser, Cash McCalley; he looked downright annoyed.

"Which of you men is the mayor?" Bonnie demanded.

A short, bearded man hesitated, then stepped forward. "Ladies, as you can see, we're holding an important business conference."

"I can just imagine," Bonnie sniffed, waving her ladies to silence, "I can smell the bourbon from here."

"Bourbon?" Mrs. Olsen pushed through the crowd and confronted a cowering male. "Elmer? Aha, yes, I see you in the back there! You know what your doctor said about liquor and your liver. You should get back to the store."

Elmer sighed, put his glass on the desk. "Yes, Lovey, I'm going." The crowd parted and Elmer, his shoulders slumped, brushed past the women and out the door.

A buxom lady in a big-flowered dress looked about, frowned. "Harold? Is that you? How dare you get mixed up in this scoundrel's schemes. You ought to be ashamed of yourself."

Slight, balding Harold hesitated then shrugged

helplessly at the other men, pushed though the crowd and fled like a rat leaving a sinking ship.

Bonnie smiled with triumph and the mayor didn't seem to know what to say. He turned and looked toward the big Texan. In turn, Cash gave her a charming smile. Oh, he was such a rascal, he probably got women to swoon and do anything he wanted by looking at them like that. Well, he had met his match with Bonnie; after all, she'd had experience with a rascal before. Behind her, she heard several of the ladies sigh as he walked over.

"Now ladies," he almost crooned as he tried to take Bonnie's hand and kiss it, "you know men are just weak creatures who can't resist a little whiskey. Why, it's mother's milk to a Texan."

Gracious, his hand was big, completely enveloping her small one. She jerked out of his grasp. "Sir, we are not here to deal with you. We came to talk to the mayor and the aldermen about this bloody fight you are planning to bring to Dallas."

She thought she heard Cash groan but he recovered nicely. "Gentlemen, let's get these ladies some chairs so they can listen in on what I'm proposin'."

"But—" protested an alderman.

"Ahem," Cash shot him a warning look. "I'm sure that after they hear me out, the ladies will be reasonable and go back to the hotel."

"You are being snide and condescending," Bonnie snapped and the other ladies murmured approval.

"My dear lady, we can certainly tell you're a librarian, usin' big words like that." He gave her that smile. Mixed with the scent of fine cigars and bourbon was that heady aftershave wafting from his big frame. "Bein' your average Texan, I don't even know what them big words mean, but I have the greatest respect for your opinion, Mrs. Purdy. Now ask your ladies to sit down."

What else could she do? The men were already bringing chairs. She took one and glared at her cowering escort. "Herbert, aren't you going to say anything?"

"Uh, I—I don't know what to say." He retreated to a chair and began to blow his nose.

"Now," Cash said, striding up and down before the crowd, "we will let the lady speak first and tell us why Texans shouldn't be allowed to watch a good fight. After all, is there anything more American or more Texan than two men goin' at each other with their fists?"

The men cheered.

One shouted, "Remember the Alamo!"

"Let's drink to that!" an alderman yelled, then slunk back under the glare of indignant women.

Bonnie stood up and took a deep breath. She was really a shy person but when the situation called for it, she could stand her ground. "Gentlemen," she said, "think about what Mr. McCalley is proposing. If this fight comes off, there will be thousands of rough fellows pouring in here on trains, wagons and horseback, over-running the fair city of Dallas. Why, loose women will be everywhere and money will be thrown about on gambling and liquor. Is this the kind of town you want?"

She realized the men were all smiling faintly if not wistfully at the picture she painted. Maybe she had failed somehow. Tired but not defeated, she took her seat.

"By thunder, I couldn't have said it better myself,

dear lady. Why, I believe you are on our side." Cash stuck his fingers in his silk vest and smiled at her.

"I am not!"

He rubbed his hands together as he strode up and down before the businessmen. "Yes, the lady is right, gentlemen. Dozens of trains will be arrivin' as thousands come to see this great sportin' event. These big crowds will need hotel rooms, meals and entertainment. All that will be provided by the businesses of Dallas. We're talkin' about a great deal of money coming to town, gentlemen, to be spent in your hotels, shops and restaurants."

The men all smiled and sighed with pleasure at the picture Cash painted.

Oh, he was a smooth talking devil, all right, Bonnie thought. She jumped to her feet. "Gentlemen, would you put profit ahead of ethics?"

Cash looked at her and grinned. "Now what do you think?"

Some of the men laughed.

She realized that she would have to take a different tact. "Come, ladies, we are wasting our time here." She signaled her troops to leave.

"Ahh," Cash nodded, "you are now seein' what is reasonable and you won't—"

"We are simply regrouping, Mr. McCalley," she snapped. "I'm a Texan, too, born and bred in the Big Thicket country and I never run before a fight."

"Then may the best Texan win." That infuriating man held out his glass to her in a toast.

"I do not intend to lose!" she vowed and nodding to her ladies, she headed out the door. The ladies struck up "Onward Christian Soldiers" as she led them from City Hall, with the reporters following and scribbling furiously.

What she would do next, she was not certain, but this was becoming a personal matter. She would not let a cheap, sleazy rascal like Cash McCalley make a fool of her and her organization. "Herbert, I really expected you would step in instead of sitting there like a ninny."

"Against Cash McCalley?" he squeaked. "Bonnie, I love you, but I'm not crazy. That ruffian would wipe up the floor with me."

"I reckon he would at that. Come, ladies," she gestured, "let's go back to the hotel and make some plans. Later we will have backup from the preachers. Remember the Alamo!"

The ladies cheered and Herbert sniffed some more. "Now what's that got to do with anything?"

"Gracious, Herbert, don't you know what the Alamo is?"

"I don't know, an old church or something."

"Herbert, the Alamo is the most sacred shrine in the whole, entire world, every child in the Lone Star state knows that. Haven't you seen our flag?"

He shrugged his narrow shoulders as the group walked up the street. "It's just a flag."

"With the lone star and the scarlet bar across the bottom to represent the bloody ground that Texans have fought and died for."

He winced. "Honestly, Bonnie, I wish you wouldn't use the word 'bloody.' I just had lunch."

Bonnie sighed. She reminded herself again what a civilized man he was and that was why she had said she might marry him. Well, she would not think about that now.

* * *

The Lone Star Ladies held an organizational meeting back at the hotel ballroom. More sure of herself now, Bonnie rapped her gavel for silence. "Fellow members, you can see which way the wind is blowing and we need to call up the reserves."

Little Miss Piggsley, the old maid school teacher from Waco, said, "What will we use for reserves?"

"Well," Bonnie said, "there must be a few men who have some conscience about bringing all this sinful circus to Dallas."

Ethel sighed, "Men are such weak, foolish creatures."

Mildred nodded. "They certainly are. Why, they all need good women to show them the right way to live."

Bonnie didn't say anything for a long moment. She didn't think of Cash McCalley as weak or foolish. He was as cunning as a coyote, but when it came to wine, women and song, he was probably the worst of that whole lot. Wild and reckless, he might be one that could never be tamed. Which made her think of Kitty Tom. As soon as this meeting broke up, she must go feed the orange stray.

"Here is the motion I am putting forward," she said to the assembled group. "Most of you will be leaving by the middle of the week, so I'll have to call on the Dallas and Fort Worth chapters to keep up the battle, bring in new members and whatever respectable men we can find to help our cause."

Mrs. Olsen nodded. "Don't you have to go home, too, Mrs. Purdy?"

"I have resolved to stay as long as it takes to win this battle!" she said with great spirit. After all, she did have Bill to keep her place running and the make-shift library was shut down temporarily while the new building was built. "Those of you members from the surrounding area, ask your pastors and churches to unite behind us. I make a motion that we invite local preachers to meet here with our officers tomorrow after Sunday dinner."

"I second the motion," Miss Piggsley said.

"We have a second," Bonnie said. "Is there any discussion?"

Silence.

"Then I call for the vote!"

Ethel Wannamaker shouted, "I move we accept this motion by acclamation!"

The ladies shouted "yes" in a way that shook the room. A cheer broke out through the crowd and the delegation from Lubbock began to sing "The Eyes of Texas Are Upon You!" and started marching around the room. They were joined by the delegation from Gainesville and the ladies from Lufkin. Soon the women of El Paso and Victoria had joined the parade.

Bonnie rapped her gavel but the ladies were having too much fun marching and singing. She rapped for order for five minutes before things quieted down again and she managed to get everyone back in their seats. In the meantime, plump Herbert stood on the sidelines sniffing and frowning.

"Ladies," Bonnie raised her voice, "the motion has passed and we will be asking the pastors of this area to join us in our struggle to keep bloody fist fights, dubious trash and loose harlots from rolling into this city by the thousands. Do I hear a motion to adjourn?"

"I so move!" shrieked the lady in the ugly flowered dress.

"All in favor?" Bonnie said.

A roar of approval.

"Done!" Bonnie shouted with a smile. "We are adjourned until two o'clock tomorrow. Now spend your afternoon recruiting more good women to our cause."

Miss Piggsley said, "I was hoping to do some shopping while I was here in Dallas."

Bonnie frowned at her. "Shopping? When there's a crusade like this to conduct?"

"Well, I saw a pair of shoes in a store window that was having a sale—"

"Sale? Where?" shouted a dozen women.

Bonnie sighed. Women would be women after all. "Never mind. If you must go shopping, try to spread the word among all the clerks as you go. After all, if the men are going to spend all their money on fight tickets and gambling, there won't be as much spent on ladies' shoes and clothes."

That really seemed to alarm the delegates.

"Hear! Hear!" the ladies cheered and began to file from the ballroom.

Bonnie was abruptly very tired. It had been a hot walk to City Hall. Yet she still had the duty of seeing about that poor, homeless stray.

"Herbert, I've got to go see about a stray cat." She tried to dismiss him.

"Oh? I thought we might have an interesting afternoon playing checkers until dinner." He tried to take her hand.

She shook her head. "I've got so much to do with all the planning."

"Then maybe I could go with you to see about the cat," he sniffed.

"Don't you have some important accounts to meet

with across the state this coming week?" She was eager
to get away from him.

"Well, I could delay them."

"Gracious, Herbert, I would never keep you from
something so important. Go on now."

He sighed and left. Bonnie checked to make sure
she still had the meat scraps in her reticule and asked
the doorman to call for a buggy. At home, she sometimes defied convention and even put on men's pants
to ride astride, but of course here in Dallas, she must
maintain proper decorum.

When she got to the train station, she tried to coax
the big Tom cat to come closer, but he only eyed her
suspiciously and refused to venture near. She finally
gave up, left the scraps for the cat and after a moment's
thought, went into the station where she approached
the telegrapher. She had a feeling she was going to have
to be on her toes to defeat the crafty Cash McCalley and
she intended to plan ahead for any possibility.

It was almost dark when she returned to the hotel
and had supper with some of the ladies in the dining
room. Those who had been hesitant were now buoy-
ant with enthusiasm under Bonnie's leadership. They
all seemed to be looking forward to tomorrow's meeting with the churchmen. She was a successful leader.
Danny would have been so proud. That thought
almost choked her and she swallowed hard and went
out into the lobby. It was bustling with people and she
spotted Cash about the same time he seemed to see
her. He had a blond hussy on his arm and he turned
away as if hoping Bonnie wouldn't notice him.

Humph, isn't that just the kind of woman he would

choose? Bonnie thought and wrinkled her nose in disgust. The woman was younger than Bonnie, dressed in a flashy, low-cut scarlet dress and hanging on Cash's every word.

With Cash's back turned, it was easy for Bonnie to go up the stairs to her room. Perhaps she would read a book or go over her notes for tomorrow afternoon's meeting. Growing up in a moonshiner's poor shack, Bonnie had had to teach herself to read and she had never gotten over the magic of the printed word. She settled into a chair with a copy of *Helpful Hints For the Modern Woman in A Man's World.* She had planned to lead her ladies into passing a resolution supporting suffragists this term, but stopping the bloody fight had taken her foremost attention. After a few minutes, she was yawning and wishing she had something more entertaining. There must be lots of exciting things to do in a big town such as Dallas. Outside her room, a man passed by humming a popular tune of the day: "After the Ball."

"After the ball is over, after the break of morn, many a heart is broken . . ."

She had only been broken-hearted when Danny had been killed. Bonnie laid down her book. Indeed, she'd never really been in love, no, not with either of her husbands. She was guilty and ashamed of the realization. Elderly Hans had offered a refuge in a hostile world to a young, scared girl and she'd been grateful and fond of him, but not in love. She had thought she was in love with Clint Purdy, who had passed himself off as a respectable businessman and had swept her off her feet in a whirlwind courtship. She smiled wryly. Why had she not realized it was not her person that attracted that charming scoundrel?

No, he had been after something else. Now that she
thought about it, her second husband had been a lot
like Cash McCalley, but not nearly so handsome or
charming.

As far as the ball, she'd seldom been to a dance.
Probably there was a dance going on at this very
minute somewhere in Dallas. That Cash McCalley
probably had that blond hussy in his arms right now.
He'd have more in mind than dancing. She sighed
wistfully. Nothing much went on in her little town of
Shot Gun and everyone was too busy with cattle and
horse ranches to fool with frills. In fact, she had
offered to be the temporary librarian because no
one else volunteered. She loved having all those
books to read.

Footsteps passed by out in the hall, and a woman
laughed at something a man said. Bonnie's ears
perked up as she recognized Cash McCalley's deep
baritone voice. He was saying something almost in a
whisper and the woman laughed again and said, "Oh,
Cash, honey, you're such a naughty boy!"

She'd just bet that was true. Bonnie put down her
book and stood up. It was dark outside now and she
turned up her lamp, went to her door, put her ear
against it and listened. She heard the distinct sound
of the Texan's key opening a door and entering. It
dawned on her that Cash McCalley had the room
next to hers, so she had the other half of his suite.
How annoying. Here she wanted to stay as far away as
possible from that man and now he was next door.
Worse yet, he was actually bringing that woman to his
room. Scandalous!

Bonnie paused, trying to decide what to do. Next
door, a scratchy phonograph wax roll began to play

"Camptown Races." Now how did he expect respectable people to get any sleep with him and his floozy cavorting about? She ought to complain to the desk clerk. Of course, since it was only about seven o'-clock, there probably weren't many residents asleep yet.

Then she noticed her handkerchief had fallen out of the keyhole of their adjoining doors. Gracious, she certainly didn't want that rascal peering in at her. She leaned over to pick up the hankie to put it back in the keyhole and hesitated. Of course it was not ethical to peek through, but it was too irresistible not to look. Besides, suppose that rascal had lured some respectable lady into his lair and might be about to seduce her? It would be Bonnie's duty to bang on the door and save the naive innocent. She pressed her eye against the keyhole.

It wasn't some innocent. The blonde in the bright red dress clung to Cash, dancing so close, red dye might come off on his expertly tailored jacket. He whispered something in her ear and the girl threw back her head and laughed like a hyena that Bonnie had once seen in a travel book.

"Oh, Fifi, honey, I'm so glad you're back in town. I missed you so." Cash stopped dancing and kissed the girl. My, did he kiss her. Bonnie gasped at the way he took the blonde in his arms and kissed her deeply, thoroughly while his big hands roamed up and down her back. "Oh, Fifi, you know what I want, don't you?"

Gracious. What did he want? Bonnie's imagination ran wild. Probably something erotic that Bonnie didn't know how to do. Bonnie gasped at the sight of the clinging pair, feeling suddenly very warm. The temperature must have gone up in the building; after all, it was summer.

Now he had his mouth against the girl's ear, nuzzling there and she giggled and said, "Oh, Cash, you're so naughty!"

He laughed too and ran his hand over her red bodice.

No man had ever kissed Bonnie like that. Her kisses from her two husbands had been quick, dry pecks. Probably that smooth rascal next door knew how to kiss a woman and make her beg for more like that blonde was now doing.

Bonnie suddenly realized she was trembling and perspiration had beaded on her forehead. It was from sheer shock and outrage, that was all. Why, the very idea of that rascal bringing a saloon girl up to his room in a respectable hotel. She was fuming as she forced herself to tear her gaze away from the keyhole and stuff the hankie back in. She was also more than a little ashamed because peeping into keyholes was not something ladies did.

Maybe Bonnie should rescue that errant girl next door before Fifi succumbed to that rascal's kisses. Yes, that was Bonnie's duty as a respectable woman. However, putting her ear against the door, it didn't sound as if the girl wanted to be rescued. She was begging all right, but what she was begging for set Bonnie's face ablaze. The very idea! And in a respectable hotel, too.

Indignant, Bonnie strode out of her room and went downstairs to find the house detective. He was plump and wore a dirty gray suit.

"I am Mrs. Purdy," she said. "I'm here with the Lone Star Ladies convention."

"Ma'am?" He moved his soggy cigar to the other side of his mouth.

"There is something scandalous going on in room

203A. A man has a girl in there and I fear he means to harm her."

The detective straightened. "You mean, kill her?"

"No, I—I mean seduce her."

He grinned and looked interested. "What's the room again, lady?"

"203A. You'd better hurry. Scandal would be very bad for the hotel."

"Yes, ma'am." He headed for the stairs with Bonnie right behind. However, as he knocked on Cash's door, Bonnie slipped into her own room, put her ear against the adjourning door and listened.

"Go away!" she heard Cash yell. "I'm very busy now."

Oh, I'll just bet you are! Bonnie thought in a huff.

The house detective knocked more insistently. "Cash, is that you?"

"Hell, yes! Is that you, Murphy? I'm busy. Go away."

"I'm sorry, Cash, I got to insist. Open the door."

She heard grumbling as the rascal strode to the door, and threw it open. "What the hell you want, Murphy? Things are just about to get interestin' in here."

She heard the house detective walk into the room. "Oh, I'm sorry, Miss LaFemme, but there's been a complaint. Lady must have seen you goin' into Cash's room. Why don't you two go back over to Fifi's place?"

"Never mind," Fifi's voice sounded very annoyed. "I ain't in the mood no more. I'm leaving."

"Naw, don't leave," Cash sounded desperate. "We only needed five more minutes—"

"For you maybe," Fifi snapped. "I'm outa here."

Bonnie heard light footsteps and cautiously opened the door to the hall. Fifi LaFemme was striding down the hall, adjusting her wrinkled red dress.

Bonnie closed the door and smiled.

The two men's voices drifted through the door. "Murphy, who in thunder complained?"

"Some mousy little widow; very respectable."

The very idea. Bonnie fumed. She wasn't mousy, was she? She turned and took a good look in the bureau mirror.

On the other side of the door, Cash groaned aloud. "I reckon I know who that is. Reckon she saw me down in the lobby with Fifi and guessed the rest. It ain't enough she meddles in my business affairs, she's got to snoop in my private life."

How dare he? She was not snooping, she was only helping keep this hotel respectable.

Murphy said, "You going over to Fifi's place?"

"Hell, no, you heard her just now. Reckon I can forget that fun for tonight."

"All the boys is real excited about you bringing that big fight to Dallas."

"Yeah, tomorrow afternoon late, I've got to go over to old Mrs. Pendigast's place and finalize that deal. Right now, I think I'll go down to the bar and have a drink. You want one? I'm buyin'."

"Don't mind if I do," Murphy answered and the two of the men left the room. Their steps echoed down the hall.

Mrs. Pendigast. The old lady was a good friend of Bonnie's from years ago. Whatever the deal was, maybe Bonnie could put a stop to it. For the next hour, she worked on some convention business and tried to read the newspaper, but couldn't seem to get past the article about the dashing promoter and his bloody fight.

Two hours later, Bonnie heard Cash come back into

his room. He was probably mad as a rained-on rooster. Thank God he didn't seem to know she had the room next to his.

Bonnie made sure her door was securely locked and got ready for bed. She lay sleepless for a long time, listening to Cash pace the floor of his room. He hadn't gotten what he wanted from Fifi and he must be restless.

She lay there staring up at the ceiling of her darkened room and tried to make plans about tomorrow, but she couldn't keep her mind on it. She kept picturing what she had witnessed earlier, the way Cash had forcefully taken that girl in his arms and kissed her thoroughly.

As she drifted off to sleep, Bonnie dreamed she was the one in Cash McCalley's arms and he was kissing her like no man had ever kissed her, deeply, thoroughly, his big hands molding her against him. His mouth was hot on hers, his tongue caressing her lips as he reached up and loosed her hair in a cascade of brown curls. He tangled his fingers in her hair and turned her so that she could not escape his devouring kisses. His big hand stroked her bodice, then slipped inside. His fingers touched and caressed her breasts and she shivered with anticipation, wanting him to explore even further.

Was she insane? Bonnie came awake suddenly and sat up in bed, breathing hard. The room was hot, but not as hot as her skin. She flung off the sheet, went to the window and threw it open, listening to the night noises of the small city. She had never had such an erotic dream before and it unnerved her, especially since the man in her dream was that scoundrel. Why, she wouldn't let him hold her hand, much less . . . she remembered what Fifi had been begging for and felt the hot blush rush to her cheeks. Bonnie tiptoed to the adjourning door, put her ear against it and listened. There was no light under the door and after a long moment, she heard Cash's gentle snore. Why had Bonnie cared so much who the rascal slept with? Except sleep wasn't what Cash had had in mind for the floozy and this was a respectable hotel.

Bonnie smiled. So she had ruined his evening and tomorrow she would ruin his sleazy business deal. The local pastors could surely be persuaded to bring pressure to bear to stop this bloody prize fight. If Cash Mc-Calley thought he was stubborn, just wait until he came up against Bonnie Purdy. Oh, did he have a rude awakening coming! She smiled at the thought.

Chapter Four

Bonnie enjoyed her room service breakfast early Sunday morning, attended a prayer session in the ballroom for the out of town conventioneers and later, joined some of the ladies for a light luncheon in the hotel dining room.

Cash McCalley came into the dining room with several cohorts. He started when he saw Bonnie and her friends, then seemed to recover. As he passed them, he bowed. "Good Sunday to you, ladies."

Several of the women sighed and turned to watch him as he sauntered to his chair. "Oh, my, what a charming man!"

Bonnie frowned. "He's a rascal. You should have seen the hussy he had up in his room last night."

"Oh?" They all leaned in. "What happened?"

Bonnie didn't approve of gossip. She glanced across the room at Cash McCalley. The rascal winked boldly at her. The very idea. She was fuming. "Never mind. Now ladies, remember, we have a meeting with the pastors in about an hour."

She glanced at Cash McCalley. As usual, he seemed to be enjoying a large steak with gusto while he talked to the men who shared his table. Businessmen he was adding to his scheme, no doubt. Somehow, this had become personal for Bonnie. She smiled as she imagined his face when he found out about the pastors' association coming into the fray.

Right after lunch, she and her officers met with the pastors at one of the local churches. There was probably twenty of the gentlemen there.

"Now, Mrs. Purdy, what is this all about?" The tall, thin one peered at her over his gold-rimmed spectacles.

"I dare say some of you have heard of Jack McCalley? His nickname is Cash?"

A preacher nodded. "Seems I've had several young ladies come confess their sins in which Mr. McCalley played a large part."

"I wouldn't doubt that one bit," Bonnie fumed, remembering last night's episode with Fifi. "I think he is to some women what catnip is to kittens."

"Praise the Lord!" said a short, fat man with a very pink face, Reverend Tubbs, by name. "It's good to know there are a few women of good morals who don't find the randy rascal attractive."

Of course she didn't. Bonnie remembered the wide shoulders, the scent of his aftershave, the overwhelming male virility of Cash. He made her as nervous as a long-tailed cat in a room full of rocking chairs. "Today's problem is not about Cash McCalley and his many women," she waved that thought away. "As you men know from reading the papers, the rascal is bringing a world champion boxing match to Dallas."

"Oh?" Two of the preachers who had appeared to be dozing came awake, obviously interested. "Fights?"

"Yes, bloody, savage fights between two supposedly civilized men."

"Well, dear Mrs. Purdy," the oldest preacher said, "Texas men fight all the time; I think it's in their blood."

"This will be for money," Bonnie said. "Perhaps most of you don't know I have had tragic, personal losses because of fist fights."

"Oh?" Reverend Tubbs asked, but she didn't like to talk about it. Hans and Clint had indirect connections, but Danny—

"It's too painful to talk about," she said.

The pastor clucked sympathetically and the others murmured regrets.

Bonnie nodded. "What bothers me is that there will be thousands of people rolling into Dallas for this fight; gamblers, pickpockets, loose women."

"Ah, at last some excitement." The tall preacher said brightly.

Everyone turned and looked at him.

Bonnie asked, "Where did you say you were from, sir?"

"Born in Gainesville, moved here lately."

"Ah, that explains it," murmured a man in the back.

Gainesville was in northern Texas, almost to the Red River, which almost made the man a Yankee or at the very least, a liberal.

Bonnie played her l card. "Pastors, give thought to this: if you do not help us, tons of local money will be bet on this bloody event and going to buy fight tickets. That's a lot of money that won't go into your collection plates."

She had struck home with that thought. Many of the pastors' faces turned ashen.

"Praise the Lord!" whispered a fat preacher. "We

must do what we can to keep this Godless boxing match from happening."

"Amen!" echoed the others. "Mrs. Purdy, what do you want us to do?"

"Could you join our ladies in a protest march to City Hall?" Bonnie asked. "And bring your congregations?"

The old one cleared his throat. "I'm afraid some of the men from our churches will be planning on attending that fight."

"Then bring the ladies," Bonnie argued. "You know they'll be against anything that involves loose women, gambling, drinking and playing hookey from work. But surely there are a few men who will join our protest."

"You're right!" Reverend Tubbs declared. "Our ladies are against anything men do that might be considered fun. I say the pastors' association ought to help Mrs. Purdy and her organization."

"Hear! Hear!" shouted several.

In the end, the pastors voted to join Bonnie's group in a protest march to the city council on Tuesday afternoon. Plans were made and the meeting broke up.

Bonnie was pleased as she took her rented buggy and headed for the railroad station to feed the cat. When she got there, she noticed a little dish of meat scraps over by a rail car. That puzzled her. *Was someone else feeding the stray?* Kitty Tom stuck his head around a corner and watched her suspiciously. "Kitty, kitty?"

The cat didn't come closer. When Bonnie tried to advance, he backed away. She said, "I wish I could make you understand that as soon as I put a stop to this bloody fight, I'll be leaving and you'll probably starve. If you'd just trust me and give up your wild

ways, you'd love it. I've got a big house with lots of
room to roam back in Shot Gun, and a pretty lady cat
named Spottie."

The orange Tom only turned and scampered away.
Some wild things just can't be tamed, Bonnie thought with
a sigh. Cash McCalley came to her mind and she
frowned. With that scoundrel, who would even want
to try? Wait until he found out some of the surprises
Bonnie had planned for him. Right now, he was dismissing her as a mere, unimportant woman, but she'd
get some respect from the rascal yet.

She smiled as she got in her buggy and headed out
for an afternoon visit with old Mrs. Pendigast. Bonnie
would show that Scots-Irish lady-killer a thing or two.

Cash was in a good mood as he rode out to old Mrs.
Pendigast's home on the edge of town. The old lady
had at least eighty acres she said she would think
about leasing to him to build an arena and parking
for all those buggies and wagons that would be
coming to the big fight.

In the meantime, he'd lost a few of his male supporters who were afraid of their wives, but most were
still supporting him. After all, as Cash kept assuring
them, by mid-week, all those militant housewives
would have gone home, including that annoying Mrs.
Purdy. He shuddered at the thought of her. Why, she
was almost as stubborn and opinionated as he was
himself. Cash much preferred dealing with women
like Fifi who never questioned any decision he made
and were just happy to be in his company.

Cash rode down the drive of the big white house,
enjoying the late Sunday afternoon warmth. Soon

Texas would be hotter than hell with the lid off, but today, the weather and his mood were just right.

Uh oh. He had spoken too soon. Whose buggy was that tied up out front? Even as he reined in and dismounted, tied his stallion to the hitching post, the one and only Mrs. Bonnie Purdy walked down the steps and out to the buggy. From the dour expression on her face, she wasn't any happier to see him than he was her.

"Oh, hello, Mr. McCalley. Nice day, isn't it?" She didn't smile.

"Well, it was." He took off his Stetson and bowed. He could barely be polite to this woman who had become such a pain in his a—side. "I didn't know you knew old Mrs. Pendigast."

She smiled without mirth. "Mrs. Pendigast and I are old friends."

Uh oh. "Well, so are we. You're just leavin'?" He didn't want her to turn around and go back inside.

"What does it look like I'm doing? Of course I'm on my way out. I had a lovely visit."

Now he did smile and made a sweeping bow. "In that case, ma'am, let me help you." He came to the side of her buggy.

She looked at him as suspicious as a baby chick eyeing a crouching fox. "I'm perfectly capable of getting into a buggy. I probably handle horses better than you do."

He gritted his teeth. By thunder, he'd never met such an opinionated female. "I doubt that, ma'am. I used to be a cowboy."

"Oh? When did you leave a respectable job for your present vocation?"

Cash hesitated. He wasn't sure what the word

meant, but as a true Texan, he could not trade insults with a mere woman. "I was only tryin' to be of assistance to a middle-aged widow. I meant no—"

"Middle-aged?" she fumed. "I'll have you know I'm only twenty-six!"

Oh hell, he'd blown it this time. Was there any way to make amends? "A thousand pardons, ma'am, it's just that with your hair and clothes, I wasn't sure . . ." He stumbled into confused silence.

"My hair? What's wrong with my hair?" Her voice rose.

"You—you have beautiful hair, Mrs. Purdy." He was almost stuttering in confusion. "It's just so—so—"

"Never mind." She blinked rapidly and her face reddened. "I am a respectable widow, not a floozy, and so my appearance is conservative. But I reckon you don't know about respectable women."

He drew himself up proudly. "My mother, God rest her soul, was a respectable woman."

"I imagine she is presently spinning in her grave."

He would not let her get his goat. Instead, he merely smiled. "No doubt."

"Good day, sir." She was evidently annoyed and in a hurry to leave. When she hiked her skirt and tried to get up in the buggy, she caught her heel and would have fallen had he not reached out to steady her. "Unhand me, you brute."

By thunder, the woman was impossible. What had he done to deserve this? "Mrs. Purdy, I assure you I was merely tryin' to keep you from fallin' in a most undignified manner. I'm sorry if you saw me as a masher."

Her face reddened and she stammered with

confusion. "Then I'm sorry, too. I'm afraid I've been impolite."

"No, it is I who have not behaved like a Texas gentleman." He touched the brim of his hat and bowed. "Here, may I be of assistance?"

She paused, looked nervous as a kitten balanced on a shaky tree limb. "If you would be so kind."

When he looked into her face, he realized she did have big blue eyes and yes, she was younger than he had first thought. He put his hands on her small waist and lifted her up into her buggy. She didn't weigh as much as his Winchester rifle and she didn't stand shoulder high on him. Her grim mouth suddenly looked very soft and vulnerable. He stepped back. "Well, good day, Mrs. Purdy."

She looked baffled and utterly undone. "G-good day, M-Mr. McCalley." She was stuttering. Bonnie Purdy suddenly seemed small, fragile and vulnerable.

"Nice to see you, Mrs. Purdy." He bowed again and abruptly she snapped her little whip and her startled horse took off at a trot, leaving a trail of dust behind.

"Hmm." He ran his hand through his wavy hair and smiled to himself. She was beatable and he knew just how to do it. If there was one thing Cash was an expert on, it was women.

Still remembering the faint scent of her delicate cologne compared to the heavy perfume Fifi used, he got the box of chocolates out of his saddlebags and walked up on the porch, rang the bell.

In a moment, white-haired Mrs. Pendigast answered the door, smiling to see him. "Why, Mr. McCalley, do come in."

"So nice to see a charmin' lady again." He gave her

his best smile and handed her the candy. "Sweets for the sweet."

"Aren't you nice. Do come in."

She ushered him into a parlor full of faded lace curtains and dusty bric-a-brac. It smelled faintly of moth balls. "The maid will bring us some tea."

"I'd love some." Tea? He hated tea. What he wanted right now was some good bourbon or at least some coffee made to a Texan's taste; strong enough to float a horseshoe.

They both sat down on the Victorian furniture and the old lady opened the box of candy.

Oh hell, it was melted. He'd spent too long palavering with that annoying Mrs. Purdy. "I'm sorry. It was perfectly good when I brought it."

"Never mind." She smiled and leaned closer. "You just missed meeting my dear friend, Bluebonnet Purdy. She doesn't get to Dallas but once in a coon's age."

He managed to keep from grimacing. Now what was that conniving, stubborn little wench doing out here? "Oh, we met as she was leavin'. A really likable lady." He glanced about, a little nervous that God might suddenly hit him with a lightning bolt for lying. Nothing happened. God must agree with him.

"Isn't she, though? She's had such bad luck with men, widowed twice, you know."

They must have both died to get away from the strait-laced little cuss, he thought, but he only clucked sympathetically. About that time, the maid brought in a tray of iced tea, put it on a butler's tray and left.

Mrs. Pendigast winked at him. "I know how Texas men like their tea." She reached behind the couch cushions and came up with a flask of bourbon. She poured a generous shot into each glass.

"My dear lady, you are a woman after my own heart."
He took a big drink and suddenly felt very generous,
even to the annoying Mrs. Purdy. After all, she was a
helpless little thing, a struggling widow in a man's world.

The old lady warmed to her story, leaning closer.
"Yes, Bonnie has had bad luck with husbands," Mrs.
Pendigast shook her head. "She married a much
older man at sixteen to get away from her Pa's beat-
ings, and Hans got himself killed in a fight. The
second one got killed only a couple of hours after
their wedding."

How lucky for him, Cash thought, but he only shook
his head. "Poor soul."

"Yes," the old lady tasted her drink, thought a
minute, added some more bourbon. "Since Purdy's
been dead four years, she should be out looking for
another husband. Don't know why she insists on
wearing widow's weeds."

"Maybe she loved him madly."

"Well, now," the old lady leaned back in her chair,
"it was a whirlwind courtship. She might have cared
about him, naive as she was, but I don't think the
rascal gave a tinker's dam about her, from what gossip
said."

That sounded like Clint Purdy, Cash thought. But
why would the gambler marry the drab little widow?
Clint liked saloon girls. He must have been drunk
when he said "I do."

Cash had been on the scene when the other man
died, so maybe he knew things the naive Mrs. Purdy
didn't. Yep, old "Ace High" must have been very, very
drunk to marry the strait-laced lady, Cash thought,
but he only said, "Too bad."

They sipped their bourbon and tea in silence.

After a while Cash decided it was time to approach the old woman about the reason he had come. He reached inside his jacket for the legal papers. "Dear lady, I came to bring you the documents to sign about the fight."

"Ah, the fight," she nodded and blinked. "I do like you so much, young man."

Something about her demeanor made him pause, holding out the papers. "And I like you, too, Mrs. Pendigast."

She sighed. "That's what makes it so difficult."

Uh oh. He began to have a feeling that he was going down like the Texans at the Alamo. "Is there a problem? I thought we had worked all this out."

"Yes, but you see, Bonnie has been explaining to me what a bloody thing it would be."

By thunder, that little rascal had done him in. "The men would be wearin' boxin' gloves, Mrs. Pendigast. I don't think it would be bloody at all."

"That's not what Bonnie said. She made a special trip to warn me about what a bad thing it would be for Dallas."

If he had known then what he knew now, he would have shaken little Mrs. Purdy 'til her teeth rattled rather than help her gently into her buggy. "Is it possible that Mrs. Purdy is exaggeratin' for reasons of her own?"

She peered at him with pale eyes. "Are you calling the president of the Lone Star Ladies a liar?"

It sounded so ungentlemanly. "Oh, no."

"I'm a charter member of the Lone Star Ladies myself, you know."

"No, I didn't know." He sank back in his chair and sighed, the legal papers dangling from his fingers. That petite brunette wasn't so naive and helpless after all. Bonnie Purdy would make a helluva poker player, although he was certain such a genteel lady didn't play poker. "Mrs. Pendigast, think of all the people and money that will be pourin' into Dallas for this event."

"Loose women, pickpockets and scoundrels, Bonnie says and she's probably right. Now that I think about it, Mr. McCalley, a boxing match doesn't seem to be something a Lone Star Lady should support."

He let his hand fall to his side with the papers in it. "I thought we had a contract. I don't have any place else to hold this event, Mrs. Pendigast."

She shrugged and sipped her tea. "I really am sorry, but after talking to Bonnie, I just don't think I can let you use my land. Sorry."

In vain, he argued, begged and pled, but in the end, he walked out of the big house with no signature on his contract. He strode out and leaned against the hitching rail, talking to his horse. "Well, Dusty, now what in hell am I to do? The fighters will be arrivin' to set up trainin' camps and I don't have any place to stage the fight. Worse yet, I'm runnin' low on money."

Maybe he could raise more backing from the businessmen who hadn't been scared off by the little widow. Anyway, the whole shebang of do-gooder ladies would surely be gone in a few days and with it, their influence. He still had time to charm old Mrs. Pendigast into changing her mind—if he could keep her away from Bonnie Purdy.

"You little wench, I ain't ready to holler 'calf rope' yet," Cash vowed. To holler calf rope meant to surrender in Texas lingo. Mounting his gray stallion, Cash rode back to the hotel.

Chapter Five

Meanwhile, back at the hotel, Bonnie took a good look at herself in the mirror, remembering McCalley's comment. Even though she disliked the man, his remarks had wounded her.

How dare he think I am middle-aged? She stared at her image, really seeing herself now as he might see her and blinked. Her brown hair was drawn back so tightly in a severe bun that it pulled at the sides of her face. Her widow's dress was more than dowdy; the black silk was turning a putrid green. She looked exactly like a mousy librarian. Gracious, wasn't that the look she had cultivated the last several years and deliberately at that, to protect herself from more men like Clint Purdy? And yet, her pride had been hurt by Cash McCalley's remarks.

Bonnie had never thought herself pretty, so she hadn't been too vain about clothes and her appearance. Now she stared hard at her reflection and a little vanity emerged. She would never be as pretty as that Fifi LaFemme, but she wasn't exactly coyote bait, was she?

Maybe it wouldn't hurt to do something to her hair.

Bonnie had thought at one time that she had pretty hair. Now as she took it down and shook her head, staring at her reflection, she saw herself as that promoter saw her and was annoyed. She'd show him. She called down to the desk for the maid to bring up a curling iron.

After she washed her hair, she began curling the sides and turning the back into a fall of ringlets when she heard a man's boots stomping down the hall. She heard him open the door next to hers, go inside and slam the door so hard, the building seemed to rattle. She could hear him marching up and down, swearing. Cash McCalley was evidently furious.

Bonnie smiled. So Mrs. Pendigast had stayed true to her word as a Lone Star Lady. And the oh-so-charming scoundrel wasn't used to women bucking him. He certainly deserved that comeuppance. Besides insulting her, he had made Bonnie feel like a foolish schoolgirl, stuttering and stumbling when he had stood too close. She took a deep breath and remembered he wore the most wonderful aftershave. She hadn't realized how big and powerful the man was until he'd put those strong hands on her waist and lifted her into the buggy.

From the next room echoed more cursing and pacing. He must have kicked a heavy footstool or a bedpost because there was a loud thud, then a muttered curse and the sound of him hopping about on one foot. Bonnie held her breath. She'd just as soon he not find out she was next door, at least until he cooled off about being bested by a mere woman. Finally he seemed to be washing; she could hear the splash of water and wondered what he looked like without a shirt. That she would even think about such a thing shocked her. She had a terrible urge to pull the hankie from the keyhole in the door between them and peek, then was horrified at the thought. "Bonnie," she scolded herself, "you have always been an ethical person. Do not stoop to that rascal's level."

Still, the thought was tempting. Even as she listened, she heard him go out his door and close it. His boot steps echoed down the hall. Probably going out to a saloon or over to visit some tart like Fifi. For some reason, that annoyed Bonnie and she was upset with herself. "I don't care what the scoundrel does personally as long as he doesn't create havoc in this nice town with his uncivilized fight."

Smiling to herself, she continued curling her hair. Finally it was pulled back in a mass of curls at the nape of her neck and tied with a ribbon. She stared at her reflection, feeling a bit giddy and foolish. At least she looked different now; maybe even younger. Satisfied, she went downstairs to supper.

As she stood in the dining room doorway looking about, she saw Cash sitting at a table. Following the waiter, she tried to hurry past that table, but Cash stood up, reached out and caught her wrist. "Why, Mrs. Purdy, how good of you to join me for dinner." He wasn't smiling.

She tried to pull away. "Ah, I see some of my fellow members waiting across the room. I believe they are saving me a place. Turn loose of me, you villain."

"Spoken like little Nell bein' tied to the railroad tracks." He turned and looked toward the ladies, gave them a nod and a most charming smile. They all smiled back and seemed to sigh. "You see? They think you lucky to be havin' dinner with me. Do sit down."

The waiter had turned and was looking from one to the other uncertainly. "Is everything all right, ma'am?"

Cash still held her wrist. The dining room was crowded and people seemed to be watching. She wasn't going to create an ugly scene here. It was one thing to cause a ruckus for a worthy cause, but she shied from personal scandal. "Yes, it will be all right."

Cash grinned. "I'm so glad you see it my way." He pulled out her chair and after a moment of hesitation, she took it. He stared at her. "By thunder, you've changed your hair; very becoming."

"I—I had been planning to do it for some time."

He took his seat, not speaking, but leaned on his elbows and surveyed her. "Yes, much better."

She felt like he was almost leering at her with an approving nod and flushed. "If I had known you would like it, I wouldn't have changed it."

He smiled. "Cantankerous, but spirited. Pretty, too. Yes, indeed, Mrs. Purdy, I think I underestimated you."

She met his gaze without blinking. "People often do because I'm not very tall."

"I noticed when I lifted you how slender you are."

She felt herself flush. "I—I don't feel at ease discussing such personal items."

He smiled again. "I didn't mean to make you blush, Mrs. Purdy. I presume you would think me bold if I called you Miss Bonnie?"

"I would. Only Herbert is allowed that liberty."

"Oh, yes, the chicken feed salesman." McCalley reached for a menu, frowning.

"He is a respectable gentleman, unlike present company. Someday, I expect to marry him."

He looked at her, so at ease, so sure of himself. "You've been stallin' him a long time."

"Now how would you know that?"

He winked. "I asked around town."

She couldn't keep from wiggling uneasily in her chair. "My personal life is none of your business, sir. Please talk about something else," she snapped and picked up her menu.

"All right, let's talk about the boxin' match."

"I didn't mean that; I—I meant something like the weather."

"The weather?" he shrugged. "Okay, it's warm outside. Soon it will be a typical Texas summer, hotter than hell with the lid off. Now let's talk about something really important."

"I don't know that we have anything to discuss." She shook her napkin out and spread it across the lap of her black dress.

"Mrs. Purdy," he said in a slow Texas drawl, "this afternoon you attempted to destroy me financially by cuttin' me off at the pass, so to speak."

"I don't know what you're talking about."

"Don't try to look innocent! You are a very poor liar. I'm talkin' about Mrs. Pendigast. Please tell me what I have ever done to you to deserve this."

She felt her hand shaking. She glanced away from his gray eyes, now dark as an approaching storm. "Sir, I have no interest in your financial affairs although I suspect they are a little, no, more likely, a *lot* shady. I fear you are just like my last husband."

"So that's it."

She hadn't meant to reveal that much about herself. She turned her face down to her menu and did not look at him. "Clint was a rascal, just like you, and like you, charming enough to cause women to do stupid things."

He leaned forward and smiled, lowering his voice. "You find me charmin'?"

"I said you were a rascal."

"You said I was charmin'." He leaned toward her, his voice low.

"I did not mean it the way you think." She moved uneasily in her seat, looking around for the waiter. The sooner she got her food, the sooner she could leave.

He shrugged. "Mrs. Purdy, I can sympathize with you. I knew your late husband."

"I don't believe you." Her voice rose and she thought about getting up and running out of the dining room, but people seemed to be watching them.

"No, in fact, I was there the night he died."

"What?" She struggled to hide her surprise. "Frankly, I doubt that. I was watching from that upstairs hotel window and I didn't see you."

He lowered his voice still more. "I was in the saloon when Ace High got caught palmin' a card. A fight started and those *hombres* chased him out into the street. I followed to see what would happen."

"Are you accusing my late husband of cheating? You're a cad, sir." She started to get up, but he motioned her back down.

"You're a poor liar, lady," he whispered. "And you know as well as I do that Ace High Purdy would steal the butter off a sick beggar's biscuit. I watched the fight and saw him run."

"Fighting!" She was livid. "That's what got him killed. My first husband, too."

"Mrs. Purdy, fightin' didn't get Ace High killed, he ran out into the street and got hit by a beer wagon."

She felt her face flush. "Well, if it hadn't been for the fighting, he wouldn't have run out into the street and got hit."

He raised one eyebrow. "I do extend my sympathies, ma'am, but old Ace High has been dead for more than four years and he wasn't much to begin with. You seem too smart to have married a slick *hombre* like that."

She felt her face flame. "How dare you!" She got up from the table and walked out of the dining room, head high and proud. Yes, Cash must have known Clint all right. She was ashamed that she had been taken in by the dead gambler and had vowed it would never happen again. She had been both stupid and naive to think greedy Clint had really loved her when really, all he was after was . . . never mind. It was because of what Clint had said to her moments after the wedding that she still wore mourning. It kept possible suitors from approaching her. After Clint, she didn't trust any man to love her for herself. Her brother, Danny, was the only man who had ever loved her and it was her fault he had been killed in the boxing ring.

She went back to her room, had a tray sent up and made her plans. Now she was twice as determined to stop Cash McCalley. He made her feel too vulnerable as if he could see into her very soul. That made her angry and afraid. Of course, she assured herself, this conflict was not personal, it was for the good of Texas.

Certainly the Lone Star Ladies had other important business to take care of, but Texas could never become really civilized and progressive as long as the men flocked to events like brutal fights. Of course that was her only reason, she reassured herself as she read her notes for tomorrow's meetings. She was too ethical to let this become a personal battle between her and that slick scoundrel. With the ministers' group lining up behind her with their protest parade, that ought to finish Mr. McCalley's bloody project.

After awhile, Bonnie got ready for bed but she couldn't sleep. For some reason, she kept reliving the afternoon and how Cash's hands had felt on her waist when he lifted her into that buggy. She had never felt so small and vulnerable. That made her dislike him even more. As she turned over and over, attempting to sleep, she smiled as she pictured the look on his rugged face when the protest parade began.

Dimly she heard the sound of boots staggering down the hall. She heard them stop at the room next door and then the sound of the door creaking. A man sang, "Oh, camptown ladies sing this song, doodah! Camptown racetrack five miles long, oh, doodah day. . . ."

Gracious, Cash McCalley was drunk, she thought with disgust. Well, that certainly didn't surprise her. There was no telling where he had been the last couple of hours. The face of that cheap blonde came to her mind. Yes, he'd probably been with her. Disgusting. Bonnie didn't even want to think about what they might have been doing. Thank goodness Bonnie's own beau, Herbert, was an upright and respectable person. If he were a little dull, that was the price one paid for wanting a dependable beau.

She craned her neck, listening. Cash McCalley seemed to stumble around his room a little, then she heard the creak of the bed as he fell across it. She imagined him lying there, probably half dressed. Her own bed seemed very large and lonely. Yes, she needed to set a wedding date with Herbert. And she would . . . sometime.

The next day dawned bright and clear. Bonnie was in a cheery mood as she dressed, enjoyed her room service and saved a bit of ham for the orange Tom cat. Then she got dressed to attend her meeting. There was no sound from the next room. When she pressed her ear against the door, she heard snoring. Good, Mr. McCalley was out like Lottie's eye as they said in Texas. Lottie Deno had been a legendary saloon girl who lost an eye in a brawl. Every Texan knew the story. Anyway, his drunken slumber gave Bonnie a headstart.

Just before she left the room, Bonnie stood in front of the big mirror, looking at her black dress critically. Did she really look frumpy rather than respectable in the plain black dress? Maybe it was out of style and a little frayed and discolored. In a way, the arrogant McCalley was right, Clint had been dead for over four years. No one would fault her if she changed from black to soft dove gray, denoting light mourning, or left mourning all together. It wasn't as if she had been married to Clint for more than a couple of hours; why, he'd never even bedded her, preferring instead to head for the nearest saloon and gambling hall and another woman.

So let this drunken rascal, Cash McCalley, sleep while she outwitted him. Humming softly to herself, Bonnie went off to her meetings. There was a lot of planning to do to get hundreds of protestors out to join the preachers in flocking to the city council meeting.

* * *

Cash woke with a groan, rolled over and picked up his big gold pocket watch off the table next to the bed. Four o'clock? Morning or evening? Then he realized the sun shown through the drapes. Good God, how long had he been asleep? He vaguely remembered a card game, Fifi perched on the arm of his chair, and some whiskey. A lot of whiskey. He needed to wipe out the annoyance of that stubborn little widow. She was attempting to cost him a lot of money and the men of Dallas a lot of fun. Or course, that was respectable women for you; always trying to curtail a man's freedom and tame him into dullness. By thunder, that wasn't going to happen to Cash McCalley.

He realized he was still partially dressed. Cash stumbled to his feet, pulled off his rumpled clothes and washed up. He felt like an Indian war dance was stomping around in his head, but he dressed and slapped on a little bay rum. What he'd really like to do was crawl back in bed, but the city council was meeting at six o'clock and he had to be there. Once he got his permit, tight-laced Mrs. Purdy and her uppity group of respectable club women could go suck a raw egg.

Or maybe the Lone Star Ladies had lost interest in his little bit of rough-hewn sin and were now concentrating on something women should do, like maybe planning a bake sale. Now there was something Cash could approve of. Soon their annual meeting would be over and all those housewives would go back to their kitchens where they belonged and the annoying Bonnie Purdy could return to her library.

His head throbbed as he went into the dining room,

which was almost deserted this late in the afternoon. He paused in the doorway and looked around like a coyote checking for hunters. Good, there were no upright, righteous women wearing little badges anywhere. Taking a seat, he ordered a glass of tomato juice with a raw egg and some Worcestershire sauce in it, to be followed by a big steak. Then he leaned his head on his hands and groaned.

He managed to get the food down but he wasn't sure it was going to stay down. To the waiter, he said "Joe, be a good *hombre* and bring me a double shot of bourbon."

The balding waiter grinned. "The hair of the dog, Cash?"

"Yeah."

"Maybe coffee would be better."

"Maybe later," Cash said. "Bring me the bourbon." He looked around. "I haven't seen a single Lone Star Lady since I came downstairs. Are we lucky enough that their convention has ended?"

"Don't think so; they were all here for lunch." The waiter shrugged, then went to get the drink. He brought it back and Cash gulped it.

"Ah!" Cash savored the bourbon and sighed. He was feeling a lot better. He'd make his speech to the city council, most of whom were old friends and gambling buddies of his and they'd give him the permit. The boxers and their people were already packing to come to Texas to set up training camps. Cash rubbed his hands together, thinking of all the money he was going to make on this deal, and then thought about all the details and arrangements.

He realized he was having a difficult time thinking over the noise. Noise? What noise? He turned his head irritably as he finished his drink. There seemed to be some kind of racket outside. He swore he heard cheering crowds and hymns. He called the waiter over. "Is there a revival in town?"

The balding Joe looked as puzzled as he felt. "I don't know, but you know Texans, they dearly love a parade."

"Used to when there was a parade, it revolved around a lynchin' or runnin' someone out of town," Cash muttered. "Now it's usually something more respectable like a revival."

The racket seemed to be moving closer to the hotel. With his headache, Cash found it very annoying. The off-key singing drifted from the street. "When the roll is called up yonder, when the roll is called up yonder, when the roll is called up y-o-n-d-e-r, I'll be there. . . ."

With a sigh, Cash finished his drink, got up and followed the other stragglers out the front door to see what the noise was about. Out on the sidewalk, huge crowds had gathered to see the parade.

Cash elbowed his way through to the street to watch. "What's the parade for?"

The man next to him shrugged. "I dunno, seems to be a bunch of preachers."

"A revival," Cash grunted, noting the forward line of ministers carrying a giant banner that read: DALLAS PASTORS ASSOCIATION. IT'S SIN WE'RE AGIN.

Cash grinned and turned to the fat man behind him. "We're all agin it, but it sure is fun."

"Ain't that the truth?" the man agreed. "Now what are those ladies doin'?"

"What ladies?" Cash turned and craned his neck to see the street. The parade was bigger than he had thought. A line of determined-looking women with their little red, white and blue badges marched behind the preachers. The ladies carried a big banner that read: KEEP TEXAS CIVILIZED, SAY NO TO DEBAUCHERY.

He wasn't even certain what debauchery was. Cash blinked as he recognized Bonnie Purdy in the middle of the front line, marching along in her dowdy black dress carrying her share of the banner.

When she saw him, she nodded at him.

"Oh, I knew it was too good to be true. I thought they'd left town," Cash groaned as a straggly, makeshift band brought up the rear of the parade with their cymbals and drums. The ladies sang: "We're marching to Zion, beautiful, beautiful Zion," and the drums went boom! Boom! Boom!

Boom! Boom! Boom! went his pounding head.

The fat man said, "Boy, that's the biggest parade I ever saw. Now where do you suppose they are heading?"

Cash began to have a horrible suspicion as he watched the huge crowd of women marching past, the curious crowds along the sidewalk getting bigger and bigger. The parade seemed to be headed straight toward City Hall. "Oh, no, she wouldn't dare!"

But of course she would. Cash pushed through the crowds, trying to catch up with the parade. That little wench and her respectable club was taking her protest to the city council meeting and somehow, she'd managed to involve all the local preachers and lots of other people. She had outmaneuvered him. If he hadn't been so furious, he would have admired her cunning. He bet she'd make a good poker player, but she probably didn't even play bingo.

Now he had to get to City Hall and confront the

protestors before they got into the council meeting. It was difficult to weave his way through the curious crowds.

"Onward Christian soldiers," sang the protestors, "marching as to war . . ." and the drums went boom! Boom! Boom! The banging didn't do anything to help either Cash's mood or his headache.

Bonnie Purdy was as tricky as he was himself. He couldn't let her get into City Hall. Why, with dozens of preachers and all those hundreds of righteous, indignant women, the city council would think twice about voting for anything that was shady and sinful, even if all the men in the county were in favor of it.

"I'd like to wring her little neck!" Cash threaded his way through the crowds, moving down the congested sidewalk toward City Hall. He got there about the same time as a bunch of reporters who scribbled furiously on their notebooks. The parade stopped out front and a fat, pink-faced preacher held up his hands for silence, climbing up on a box. At least the drum stopped pounding. "As Mrs. Purdy says, we have a chance to save Dallas from this savage and sinful event, God willing. Now we will pray and go inside to confront the council members."

Cash thought he might could deal with a few preachers and some irate ladies, but he didn't think it was fair to stack the deck by bringing God into it. Now the crowd moved toward the doors. Cash pushed through the crowd at the same time as Bonnie Purdy. He went through the door first.

She turned her head and saw him. "Well, you're no gentleman or you would have held the door for me."

"Mrs. Purdy, I'd like to slam you in the door. Why don't you infernal women go back to your kitchens where you belong instead of interferin' in men havin' a little fun?"

"Mr. McCalley, you are a male Chauvinist pig."

"I haven't the least idea what that is, but I know what a pig is."

"Enough said then."

The crowd pushed them together and he was more than aware of her warmth as he pressed against her. For a moment, he forgot what a pest she was and was almost tempted to pinch that round bottom under that swaying little bustle, but he didn't. The staid Mrs. Purdy would certainly set up a howl of indignation that would cause him to get beaten with a dozen parasols from outraged ladies.

The crowd flowed up the stairs, carrying Cash along with them. They still sang and waved their banners. They entered the council chambers and quickly filled all the seats, the others standing with their banners, singing.

The mayor banged his gavel in vain, attempting to establish order. "What is the meaning of this outburst?"

The preachers shouted in unison, "It's sin we're agin!"

"Amen!" echoed the Lone Star Ladies For Decency and Decorum.

The mayor looked puzzled and banged for silence.

A councilman protested, "Now folks, Texans have always been a mite easy on sin—"

"We're talking about a bloody fight!", Bonnie shouted, "And if we let it happen, there's no tellin' what kind of Sodom and Gomorrah will follow."

Cash was fuming as he shouted, "Lady, you ought to be ashamed for exaggeratin' like that."

The council members looked even more puzzled. One of them said, "Is this a revival or what?"

Cash pushed through the crowd to face the council. "All this ruckus, I think, is about that little boxin' match I want to put on—"

"That bloody fight!" Bonnie protested, confronting the council. "It's bad for Texas and a bad image for Dallas."

"Lady," Cash sighed, "Dallas ain't exactly like a Sunday school."

"Think!" Bonnie was so short, not everyone could see her. She climbed up on a chair. "We want respectable people moving to Dallas to buy homes and groceries and dry goods. The time of gamblers and fights in the streets and brawlers like Cash McCalley is over."

"Hear! Hear!" The ladies cheered and the ministers started another off-key chorus of "When the roll is called up yonder, I'll be there."

Cash waved for silence as he took his spot next to Bonnie Purdy. "Folks, this fight will bring in thousands of spectators and maybe new residents who'll like what they see of Texas. They'll need hotel rooms, meals and a million other things."

The mayor, who was a friend of Cash's and who owned a restaurant, smiled at the thought. "The man has a point."

Bonnie looked about. "Would you men choose profit over ethics?"

Cash snorted. "You're talkin' to a bunch of Texans, Mrs. Purdy. Now what do you think?"

The Methodist minister stepped to the front. "Council men, need I warn you that the ministers of this city can preach sermons of hell and brimstone and get all the men out to vote?"

"Gamblers and sinners will vote, too, gentlemen," Cash reminded them, "and I think we outnumber the righteous."

"Yes," Mrs. Purdy shouted, "but your crowd is usually too drunk to vote."

"You have a point there," Cash was forced to admit.

The preachers and the ladies broke into another chorus of "Onward Christian Soldiers." The newspapermen scribbled furiously.

The council members looked toward Cash and the mayor shrugged his shoulders as if powerless. He rapped for order again. The preachers stopped singing but the ladies waved their banners and protest signs. "Maybe," suggested the mustachioed mayor, "maybe we could set up a committee to study this problem—"

"Oh, no, you don't!" the little widow protested. "You're just trying to stall until we leave town."

I can only hope. Cash's headache grew worse. The drum seemed to pound louder and louder while the righteous sang. He wanted to grab up the little widow and turn her over his knee, but of course he couldn't do that.

The mayor seemed sad as a hungry hound. Cash knew the man had planned to buy front row seats to the big fight and put a little wager down also. Now he looked toward Cash. "Mr. McCalley, we are bound to represent the majority."

The ladies and the preachers cheered.

"Now just a damn minute!" Cash roared. "You know there's more sinners than righteous folks in Dallas and they'd enjoy a good prize fight."

Mrs. Purdy climbed up on a chair to address the

council. "Think before you vote," she cautioned the uneasy men. "Think about Dallas' future and all the generations to come."

"By thunder, I can't see that one boxin' match will create much trouble for future generations," Cash argued.

"Drunkenness, wild women and gambling," Bonnie raised her voice. "Do you really want those kind of people mixing with your women and children?"

The preachers cheered again. "Sin! It's sin we're agin!"

"It's just a boxin' match!" Cash yelled. "I can't see nothin' too sinful about that."

"Men beating each other bloody while a crowd of hoodlums cheers, drinks, and bets on the outcome!" Bonnie shouted. "Is that what Dallas is about?"

"No!" yelled the Lone Star Ladies and the preachers and they began to march around the council chambers, singing, "When the roll is called up yonder, I'll be there."

Cash struggled to be heard over the singing. "Texas has always been about fightin' and gamblin' and drinkin'. Why should we change now?"

Bonnie frowned at him and the reporters scribbled furiously.

The little widow was still on her chair. Over the singing she shouted, "Council members, you'll have to answer to your wives if you vote for this. Why, some of your wives are in this very crowd."

Cash groaned, seeing the council members' faces turn pale as frog bellies. The idea of having to deal with nagging wives was hitting home for the gentlemen. "A good fight is what Texans are all about. Remember the Alamo!" Cash shouted.

That got a cheer from the crowd because all Texans remembered the Alamo.

"Think, gents!" Cash challenged. "You think Crockett, Travis and Bowie would have knuckled under to women?"

"They would if they knew my wife," a man muttered.

Bonnie now waved a Texas flag. "Yes, remember the Alamo, people. Those brave Texans died so we could build a state free of sin!"

"Yes, sin!" shouted the preachers. "It's sin we're agin!"

Cash decided it wouldn't do any good to point out that many of the defenders of the Alamo were from out of state and most of them wouldn't have passed the litmus test for being free from sin anyway. "Gentlemen of the Council, won't you put off this vote for a few days?" If he could just outwait the Lone Star Ladies, he'd be home free because even preachers, being Texans, liked a good fight.

Mrs. Purdy waved her flag and started a chorus of "The Eyes of Texas Are Upon You" to the cheers of the crowd.

He'd like to spank that little bustle, but of course, he couldn't do it. She wasn't his to spank and she'd probably bite his knee and scratch him while he tried anyway.

"Gentlemen," Mrs. Purdy shouted, "call for a vote now!"

The crowd cheered and in vain, the mayor banged his gavel but the lady would not be silenced. In the end, the council voted that no, a boxing match would not be held anywhere in this county. Then they slunk out of the chamber like coyotes deserting a steer carcass.

Cash was too stunned to do anything but blink and glare at the little leader of the pack of protestors while reporters crowded around him. "You got anything to say, Cash? You gonna keep goin' with your boxing match?"

"This ain't the only town in Texas," Cash declared. "I'll find another place to hold my contest. Men run things in Texas, and that ain't gonna change." With that, he strode out of City Hall. Damn that stubborn woman, she was almost as conniving as he was himself. Maybe when the ladies convention broke up, he could ask the city council to reconsider their vote. Otherwise, he wasn't certain what he would do. The fighters would soon be arriving in Texas to set up their training camps. There was an arena to be built, tickets and posters to be printed and Cash had stretched his credit and his money to the limit.

Worse yet he'd been outmaneuvered by a little female not much taller than a shotgun. "Mrs. Purdy," he vowed to himself as he strode through the evening back to the hotel, "this is only round one. I'll win this thing yet because I'm tricky as a coyote and I got another card up my sleeve!"

Chapter Six

When Bonnie left the council meeting, she was pleased that she'd kept the bloody boxing match from corrupting Dallas. Well, Dallas wasn't all that innocent, she conceded. And no more young men would die as Danny had died. Her convention would be over soon, but she'd better stay on a day or two. She didn't trust that slick rascal not to wait until the ladies were gone to change the city council's mind.

It was almost dark, but gathering up some food scraps at the hotel, she took a buggy to the train depot. As she alighted, she almost bumped into Cash McCalley coming out of the station. "Ah, Mr. McCalley, are you leaving town?"

"No," he said, "dare I hope you are?"

Annoyed, she shook her head. "I'll be staying on a few days. I came down here to feed a stray cat."

About that time, Kitty Tom stuck his head out from under a rail car. "Here, Kitty Tom, I've brought you some food."

"That's *my* cat," McCalley sounded annoyed. "His name is John L."

"He's obviously not your cat, he's a stray and I call

him Kitty Tom." She walked over and spread the meat scraps for the cat who eyed her cautiously from under the rail car. "I intend to tame him and take him home with me."

"I've been feedin' him and I'll have you know John L. can't be tamed. Besides, he likes bein' wild and free."

"We'll see about that," Bonnie said. "I think he'd be perfectly content lying in front of the fire at my house with my lady cat, Spottie."

"Women!" The scoundrel snorted and started off the platform. "That cat is a Texan and Texas males can't be tamed."

"Humph!" Bonnie fumed, watching him mount that big gray horse and ride away toward the hotel. Could that rascal have any other reason for being at the station?

She needed to get back to the hotel before it got any later. Ladies did not go out unescorted after dark in a city like Dallas. Still she went in to talk to the telegrapher, a lanky boy with a big Adam's apple. "Was Mr. McCalley just in here?"

The boy nodded. "Yep, gettin' a telegram."

"Oh, from whom?"

"Nope, not from whom, from the mayor of El Paso," the boy said.

Bonnie reached into her reticule. "I don't suppose you'd like to tell me what it was about?"

"Can't." The boy shook his head, "Not allowed to."

Bonnie considered. Bribery was wrong and beneath her dignity, but then, when dealing with a slippery villain like Cash McCalley, she'd had to do things she wouldn't usually do. Bonnie laid a silver dollar on the counter. "It'd be worth this to me."

The boy hesitated, looking around. "I don't reckon it would hurt none." He reached to take the coin.

"Well?" Bonnie prompted.

"He was gettin' a reply from the mayor of El Paso about if'fen he could come down and see him about puttin' on a boxing match. The mayor wired back right away; said 'you bet.'"

Bonnie chewed her lip and thought. El Paso was a wild and wicked border town, where anything went. Every Texan knew that. What a tricky coyote McCalley was. "When is the gentleman taking the train?"

"Tomorrow afternoon. Train leaves at four, ma'am."

Bonnie smiled. Her convention ended at noon tomorrow, but the battle must not be lost. "I'm buying a ticket," she said.

The boy's sandy eyebrows went up. "You goin' with Cash?"

"Perish the thought!" She rolled her eyes. "Oh, here's another dollar. If anything comes up, don't tell Mr. McCalley I'm going to El Paso. I want to surprise him."

The boy nodded and took the money. "Reckon he'll be surprised, all right."

"I need to send a couple of telegrams myself," Bonnie reached for a pen. "And I may be gone for a day or two. I'll pay you to feed that stray cat for me."

"That's Cash's cat," the boy informed her. "He's been feedin' him for weeks now."

"Kitty Tom is not McCalley's cat," Bonnie said, annoyed. "Or he'd take him home."

"Cash says John L. is wild and likes it that way."

"We'll see," she said and continued writing. There was a small chapter of the Lone Star Ladies in El Paso and certainly a ministers' alliance. If Cash McCalley thought he'd put something over on her, he was in for a big surprise.

She wrote her telegrams, sent them, bought her ticket and walked out to her buggy, very pleased with herself. It was dark as she drove back to the hotel. If Cash McCalley thought he could trick her, he was in for a big shock. After all, she was a Texan, too.

The convention ended the next day with Bonnie encouraging the ladies to get involved in suffrage and women's rights, which some whispered made her too liberal. She also cautioned the Dallas-Fort Worth chapter to stay alert as that rascal of a Texan might still try to set up the boxing match after he figured the ladies had dispersed. Then she went up to her room to pack.

She ran into Cash McCalley out in the hall. He looked puzzled as he bowed low. "Mrs. Purdy, are you lookin' for someone?"

"Ah, no, she—I think she's already checked out." She didn't want him to know she was in the room next to his.

He grinned and nodded. "Your convention is over?"

"Yes, but don't think we are letting our guard down, sir. If you should go to the city council again, some of our ladies will be there."

"Oh, I expect that. Don't worry, Mrs. Purdy, I've learned my lesson." He nodded and walked off down the hall.

That scoundrel. If he only knew she had learned about El Paso. Maybe she could avoid him on the trip and he would be the one in for a surprise when he stepped off the train in that border town.

Smiling to herself, she packed up and went downstairs.

At the desk, the manager said, "Did you have a good stay, ma'am?"

"Excellent. In fact, I may be back in a couple of days. Would you reserve that same room, please?"

"That's usually Mr. McCalley's suite." He sounded uncertain. "Sometimes he has ladies—"

"Spare me the sordid details," Bonnie snapped. "But anyway, if the gentleman is leaving town for awhile, he won't need rooms, will he?"

The clerk scratched his thinning hair. "I reckon not."

Bonnie paid her bill and checked the lapel watch on her black dress. She still had time to do a little shopping before she caught the train.

Now she walked to a fine dress shop and stood outside a long moment, staring at her reflection. Much as she hated to admit it, Cash McCalley was right. Her dress was dowdy and out of style and after one year, much less four, convention dictated that she no longer had to wear black; especially if she were interested in marrying again.

God forbid, she thought as she went inside. She'd wed two Texans and she didn't intend to wed another. Herbert was a safe beau who didn't seem to expect much. *Herbert.* She'd forgotten about him. Gracious, the train to Shot Gun left the station a little after the one to El Paso and Herbert had said he would be at the station to see her off. Somehow, she wasn't looking forward to that, not when she was trying to sneak aboard the El Paso train without Cash McCalley seeing her.

It was an elegant shop. The clerk inside looked her over critically as if judging whether Bonnie could afford to shop there.

"I am Mrs. Clint Purdy from Shot Gun, and I think I need a few things." She handed the girl her card.

"Oh, yes," the snooty young clerk seemed to recognize that name on the card. "Do come in, ma'am," the girl was suddenly eager to please. "What can we show you today?"

"I haven't much time, I've a train to catch, but I'd like a complete new outfit, something conservative in plain gray or dark navy."

"Of course." The girl nodded. "Although, you know, with your blue eyes, I have several in light blue and especially a fine silk in a mist blue that would be perfect for you. Latest style, big leg o' mutton sleeves. The bustle is disappearing, you know."

She didn't know. Bonnie had never been interested in high fashion. She hesitated, then nodded. "Show me some."

The silk dress was spectacular, Bonnie thought as she ran her hand over the full skirt. It had the new leg o' mutton sleeves, a tiny bustle, much lace at the throat and the color was the same blue-gray shade as early morning mist in the Texas hills. "It's beautiful. I'll try it on."

"It's more than a little expensive, but I don't suppose that's a problem for you, now is it?"

She didn't like the girl's snooty assumption, but even then, Bonnie hesitated. Growing up poor had made old, thrifty habits hard to break. "Of course not."

She bought more than she intended; the silk dress, a baby blue riding outfit, a crisp blue and white gingham dress, dainty underwear from France and fine kid high button shoes. The clerk brought out an elegant little hat with feathers that matched the color of the riding outfit and blue ribbons to pull back Bonnie's brown curls. When Bonnie looked in the mirror, she was surprised and pleased. She not only looked stylish, she looked much younger than she had in the severe black dress.

"I think I'll wear the riding outfit and hat." She glanced at her lapel watch again. "I must hurry, I've a train to catch. I'll take some of these things with me; deliver the rest to my room at the Cattlemen's Hotel."

She paid the sizable bill, gathered up a few purchases and headed for the station. She almost groaned aloud as she saw Herbert waiting for her there.

"Dear Bonnie." He tried to take her hand, but they were full of parcels, which she dumped in his arms. "You—you look beautiful. Such a change! I'm so flattered you've done this for me. You must be considering my offer of marriage."

Now that she thought of it, she wasn't certain why she had bought the fine new clothes. Herbert hadn't entered her head as she'd shopped. She looked up and down the track. "Uh, no, Herbert; at least, not yet."

"Then I dare hope?" He leaned closer as if to kiss her cheek, but the parcels blocked him, and then he began to sneeze. "The feathers," he gestured toward her new hat and sneezed again.

"I'm so sorry. I didn't think." This gave her an excuse to back away from him. She was as nervous as a baby calf in a roping pen and she didn't want to discuss matrimony.

Several tracks away, the train to El Paso waited,

smoke coming out of its stack. Now another train pulled slowly into the station, belching smoke, right next to the platform. "Here comes my train, Herbert. You may go now. I can get myself on board."

"Honestly, I wouldn't hear of it! I'll at least carry your luggage aboard."

Now what was she going to do?

The train screeched to a halt amid a flurry of black smoke and clanking bells. It blocked her from the train to El Paso. What to do? Herbert gathered up her things and led her onto the train to Shot Gun. "Maybe I should stay and wave good-bye to you," he said.

"All right," she sighed.

They boarded and stood in the aisle. Through the window, she could see the other train. If she weren't such a lady, she'd curse. Here she stood in a train that would soon depart for the town of Shot Gun when she wanted to go to El Paso. She peered out the window.

Herbert frowned and sniffed. "Whoever are you looking for, my dear?"

"Uh, no one." If she did manage to get off this train before it left the station, she didn't want to run into Cash McCalley. Even as she turned and peered toward the station, she saw Cash McCalley alighting from the hotel buggy. On his arm was the blonde, what was her name? Oh yes, Fifi LaFemme. Miss LaFemme wore a bright red dress and it was cut very low. What a hussy. Was he taking her to El Paso? Probably he'd want all the comforts of home on this trip.

The engine whistled a warning.

"Gracious, Herbert, you'd better hurry, this train is leaving." She almost pushed him down the aisle.

"Nonsense," he sneezed and wiped his nose. "I wish you'd remember my allergies when you buy things."

"I'm so sorry, Herbert. Maybe you need to get away from these feathers."

His pale eyes watered. "There's a few more minutes yet and we've much to talk about."

Oh Lord. "Herbert, why don't you come to dinner at my house in a few days and we'll talk then."

"Well, I'll be in the area handling a new feed store account, so I guess I can do that."

"Great! I'll have the cook fix something special."

"Do I dare to hope?" He grabbed her hand. His hand was soft and sweaty.

"About what?" She pulled away and peered toward the other train.

He sighed and sniffed. "What ails you, Bonnie? You know about what."

"Uh, yes, maybe, I don't know." She looked out the window again.

"Honestly, Bonnie, what has gotten into you?" He sounded annoyed.

"I—I'm just afraid you won't get off the train in time."

"That's not too bad. Think of all the time we could spend together talking about our future as we rode toward Shot Gun. That is, if you'd take off that hat."

The train whistled again and shuddered a little.

"Herbert, the train is really leaving. Get off!" She pushed him down the aisle to the exit.

"All right, all right, I'm going." He sounded irritable as he stepped off onto the platform and stood looking up at her. "Honestly, you've changed, Bonnie. You don't seem the same at all. The last couple of days, you've been very flighty and confused and now you've changed your look and the way you act. . . ."

If only he would just go away.

"Good-bye, Herbert," she waved her hankie at him. "Don't stay to see the train off, I'm fine."

"Well, if you think so—"

"I think so," she insisted.

He was grumbling under his breath as he turned and walked away. She could see Cash McCalley standing on the platform, holding the hussy's hand and looking earnestly into her eyes.

The train rumbled a little. Quick or she'd be on her way to Shot Gun. She grabbed a porter who was passing by. "Quick, get my luggage. I—I'm on the wrong train!"

She ran to the end of the car with people staring at her strangely. Bonnie clambered down from the coach and ran to the other train as the one to Shot Gun pulled out slowly in a shower of smoke and ashes. She paused and peered out the window toward the station. Cash McCalley was still saying good-bye to that Fifi LaFemme, kissing her boldly right there in public while she clung to him, obviously almost swooning with pleasure. Had the hussy no shame? Now as Cash picked up his luggage, the hussy grabbed him for one last kiss. His kisses couldn't be that good, could they?

Bonnie was fascinated by the spectacle. Then she realized that any minute, he'd be coming aboard and she'd better move fast. Maybe this wasn't such a good idea after all. He'd be furious when he found out she was on the train. Well, maybe he didn't have to find out until they reached El Paso. She smiled at the thought, knowing who would be waiting in the station.

She had opted for a compartment so she fled there now and tipped the porter who was waiting with her luggage and parcels. He left with a big smile at the generous tip and she slammed the door and leaned against it, breathing hard. Through the window, she could see Cash McCalley striding across the platform with Fifi waving a lace hankie and blowing kisses. The cad didn't even look back at the blonde. The train whistle sounded a warning. Bonnie reached to pull the shade so he couldn't see her.

The train blasted a warning again and then shuddered as it made ready to leave. She went to her door and put her ear against it. She heard Cash laughing with the conductor as he passed by her door.

He said, "Where's the club car? I need a drink."

Of course he did. What was it about Texas men and alcohol? Of course, if he got drunker than a boiled owl, she wouldn't have to worry about him finding out she was aboard.

The train pulled out of the station, chugging and hissing. It picked up speed as it left. Bonnie pulled up her shade and looked out. Fifi LaFemme still stood on the platform, waving her hankie and weeping. She froze in place as she seemed to see Bonnie and now the girl was running down the platform, screaming. She looked furious. No doubt she had recognized Bonnie and thought Cash was rendezvousing with her on the train. At least Fifi couldn't alert him now and Bonnie didn't care what the girl thought. Bonnie and a scoundrel like Cash McCalley? What a ridiculous thought.

Bonnie collapsed on her bunk with a sigh of relief. Finally she was on her way to El Paso. She had no idea how long the trip took. It probably stopped in a number of stations to pick up passengers and freight. Because of her telegram, the ladies in El Paso would know when to expect her. What a reception was waiting when they pulled into the station. She smiled just picturing it.

She thought about having the porter make down her bed, decided she'd wait. Outside her window, the fringes of houses and buildings were slipping away until she saw farms and ranches on the wide plains. She remembered Fifi's rage when she had spotted Bonnie on that train. For once, the ladies' man was innocent, but when he got back to Dallas, there'd be hell to pay. Bonnie smiled at the thought. Fifi would never believe he had traveled alone. However, when she considered again, Bonnie was annoyed. How dare that hussy think Bonnie would have any interest in even talking to a rascal like Cash, much less . . .

Bonnie checked her little watch again. Could she get a tray brought to her compartment? It would be nice to slip into something comfortable and take off her shoes and the little feathered hat. Yet she really wanted the full service of the dining car. Cash McCalley would stay in the club car, gulping drinks for a couple of hours, no doubt. It was possible she could get an early supper and be back in her compartment asleep before he ever finished guzzling whiskey.

The train chugged along, rhythmically clacking as it headed south. She tried to make some plans about what she would do in El Paso, but all she could think of was the image of the big Texan on the station platform almost bending that blonde over backward for his embrace, then the confident way he strode toward the train. She could almost smell the masculine scent of his tobacco and shaving lotion. She wondered what he would think of her stylish new clothes.

That thought shocked her. "Gracious, what do you care whether he likes them or not?"

In a few minutes, she heard the porter coming down through the train with his little chimes. "Supper, first seating. Supper now being served in the dining car."

Bonnie hesitated, not wanting to risk colliding with Cash McCalley in the aisle. Who was she kidding? No doubt he was already on his third drink and had gotten a poker game going.

Gingerly, she opened her door and peered out into the hall. Nothing. She checked her appearance in the little mirror on the door and went out and down to the dining car.

Cash lingered in the club car over a drink with two drummers he met who were unlucky enough to get into a poker game with him. By the time he got up from the table and headed for the dining car, he had enough money to live comfortably for a few days. Lord knew he was running low on funds because of that stubborn do-gooder. He wished now he'd taken Fifi with him, but there would be willing women aplenty in El Paso; dark, passionate Mexican girls. He grinned to himself. "No use takin' coals to New-castle."

The porter came up behind him as Cash entered the dining car. "Hot enough for you, Mr. Cash?"

Cash laughed. "Texas is always hotter than a brandin' iron, I reckon. If you can't take the heat, you move out of Texas."

"Ain't that the truth?"

Cash looked ahead of him. A petite woman had just

gotten up from her table at the far end of the car and hurried out the other door. Somehow, she looked vaguely familiar. A horrible suspicion crossed his mind but he shook his head as he settled into a chair. No, there was no way Mrs. Purdy could be on this train. Besides, that woman had been wearing a stylish feathered hat and a baby blue dress almost the color of early morning mist over the Davis Mountains out in the Big Bend country. He'd never seen the widow in anything but dowdy black.

He reached for a menu and smiled. A good steak, a cup of coffee, then maybe a fine cigar out on the rear platform before retiring for the night. He had a full day ahead of him in El Paso tomorrow.

If Bonnie hadn't heard Cash's familiar voice as she finished her chocolate cake, she wouldn't have had time to scurry out of the dining car. She paused outside the door and stood on tiptoe to peer in. He looked happy as a dead hog in the sunshine; probably drunk, she sniffed. What was she to do? She couldn't reach her compartment without passing through the dining car. Then she had an idea; she would go out and stand on the platform at the end of the last car, enjoy the breeze of the warm night until he finished eating and went back to the club car.

The train swayed rhythmically as she stood there, holding onto the iron railing. Texas was beautiful even in the darkness with the stars shining down on the vast expanse of flat plains. Somewhere, a coyote sang, but it was barely heard over the click-clack of the moving train.

Cash enjoyed his dinner immensely and finished

with a bowl of wild sand plum cobbler, topped with thick cream, and a cup of coffee. His troubles didn't seem so important now and at least that annoying girl had gone back to wherever she came from. *Shot Gun*, he remembered, *Shot Gun*. He wasn't certain he'd ever been there but he knew it was beautiful rolling land in the middle of the Texas Hill country, famous for its fine ranches. He sighed as he stood up. He'd been saving for a ranch himself when the Panic of '93 had wiped him out. He hadn't given up on the dream, but he was getting discouraged.

He decided he'd have a final smoke before he retired and wended his way through the swaying cars toward the back of the train and the platform of the last car. As he opened the door to go outside, he realized there was a woman on the platform already. The lady had her back to him and she started as he came out on the platform. "I'm sorry, ma'am, I didn't mean to startle you. I was just comin' out for a cigar."

She murmured something and kept her back to him. In the starlight, he recognized the hat and the light blue dress. She was small and slightly built and wearing some delicate scent that made him take another breath; a deep breath. Under her hat, her brown hair was pulled back in curls that shone in the moonlight. She must be quite pretty, he decided, and moved closer. Pretty women were a commodity he never got enough of. He cleared his throat. "I say, there's something familiar about you, Miss. Have we met before?"

She muttered something softly and shook her head.

Shy, he thought. He liked that in a woman, probably a real lady. "It's a lovely night, isn't it?"

She murmured agreement.

"I think I should introduce myself," he said in his

most charming manner. "I'm Jack McCalley from Dallas and you are?"

She murmured something unintelligible.

Cash was truly puzzled. He was interested in the pretty lady, but he didn't want to be accused of being a masher. Keeping her head down, she turned and tried to brush past him, headed for the door back inside the car.

The moonlight shone on her face and a chill went through him as he recognized her and blinked in disbelief. "Mrs. Purdy?"

"I—I was just going in," she said, but he reached out and grabbed her arm.

"What the hell are you doin' on this train?"

She tried to pull away, didn't look at him. "Going home to Shot Gun, of course. The convention is over."

He whirled her around, looking down into those big blue eyes. "This ain't the train to Shot Gun."

"It isn't?" The big eyes widened. "Gracious me, I'm on the wrong train! I reckon in the morning, I'd better catch another train back."

He was annoyed that she was here, that before he'd realized who she was, the lady had aroused desire in him. "I'd call this an emergency," Cash said. "Maybe I should pull the brake cord and stop the train."

She shook his hand off, confronted him, no longer the shy miss. "Are you loco? There's no town around here for miles. I'd be stranded here hoping another train would come along."

"Exactly." He backed her up against the door, glaring down at her. "Tell me you aren't goin' to El Paso?"

"El Paso?" The long lashes blinked. "This train is going to El Paso?"

He sighed. "Mrs. Purdy, you are a very poor liar."

"That's because I haven't had as much experience as you have." She tried to slip under his arm but he put his hands on each side of her head, trapping her against the swaying car. He looked down at her in the moonlight. The plain little librarian was pretty. Pretty? *Cash, my boy,* he warned himself, *you must be drunk.* He hadn't had anything with his meal but strong coffee. No, he was not drunk. The annoying wench was suddenly pretty.

Bonnie looked up into his face. She didn't doubt one bit that he might pull the emergency cord and put her off the train out here on the wide open plains.

"Mrs. Purdy, why are you going to El Paso?" He thought he knew the answer already. Was there no losing this pest? She was worse than a cotton boll weevil.

He was standing close, too close. She could smell the faint scent of some woodsy aftershave and see the outline of his square jaw quite plainly. She retreated against the car as much as she could, but he leaned closer still.

Her heart began to hammer. "Sir, if you do not back off, I shall scream."

"I'm not sure anyone could hear you over the roar of the train." He was annoyed both with her and with himself for being drawn to her. He might as well get even. He smiled slowly. "Mrs. Purdy, I have been hypnotized by you since the first moment I laid eyes on you; like—like a magnet to steel, like Romeo to Juliet."

She felt perspiration break out all over her slight body and she wasn't quite sure why. "My dear Mr. Mc-

Calley, I doubt if you even know who Romeo and Juliet were."

He leered down at her. "Ah, always the librarian. Weren't they lovers?"

"Uh, yes." She didn't like the way he was looking at her. She felt like the heroine in a melodrama except the handsome rascal staring down at her didn't have a mustache.

He leaned closer. "Your beauty intoxicates me."

"No, Mr. McCalley, it's the whiskey you drink."

"You make it very difficult for me to be romantic," he said and one of his big hands toyed with the lace of her collar.

"I intend to." She could feel the heat of his fingers. "Mr. McCalley, need I remind you I am a respectable widow?"

His fingers were now caressing her throat. She felt as nervous as a baby bird in a wolf's mouth.

"Yes, so respectable. But inside, I sense a wild thing tryin' to get out."

"I don't think so." She tried to edge away but was blocked by his arm.

"You've changed your dress," he murmured so close, she could feel the heat of his breath. "I thought that might signify you were ready to leave your widowhood."

"I—I saw a sale and couldn't resist," she stammered.

"I don't think it's that at all," he whispered. "Mrs. Purdy, Bonnie, is it possible we are soul mates that the universe has finally brought together?"

"What?" she stammered. "Mr. McCalley, you are talking nonsense. We are adversaries."

"But we need not be." He leered again and bent his head closer. "It's just that I am drawn to your beauty."

"Mr. McCalley," she said matter-of-factly, "if you think I am like all those other women and that you can charm me into giving up my crusade—"

"Yes, Joan of Arc, that's what you are, savin' all us rough men from our sinful ways," he said and leaned forward to kiss her.

"What?" For a moment, she was so caught by surprise, she couldn't do anything but freeze in position. At the last moment, she bent her knees and slipped under his arm so that he got a mouthful of the feathers on her hat. "Sir, I think you have gone loco. I am not Fifi LaFemme."

"Fifi?" He blinked and looked confused as he turned toward her, still coughing and picking feathers from his mouth.

"Mr. McCalley, don't try to look innocent. You don't know how," Bonnie snapped. "I saw her swooning away in the station. Really, sir, that was a shameful display."

"Why, you snoopy little—"

"I wasn't snooping, a hundred people saw you two pawing each other."

Now he looked sheepish and taking a deep breath, he stepped away from her. "Well, now, Fifi insisted on comin' to the station. Excuse my behavior just now, Mrs. Purdy. I—I don't know what came over me."

She didn't know what had come over her either. She had wanted that kiss, wanted it like some harlot; wanted to be kissed like no man had ever kissed her before. Her own reactions unnerved her. Bonnie liked being in control of her emotions. She took a deep breath and came to her senses. "Mr. McCalley," she said in her coldest, most no-nonsense voice, "your behavior was less than gentlemanly. I'm going to my compartment."

She whirled, still a little dizzy at the sensations he had invoked in her and strode through the door and down the narrow aisle with him right behind her.

"A thousand pardons, dear lady," he murmured, dogging her footsteps. "I was just so carried away by your beauty."

"Just minutes ago, you were going to throw me off the train," she snapped over her shoulder and kept walking.

He followed closely behind her, begging. "Please, ma'am, I didn't mean to be so forward. I just couldn't help myself." Actually, he was more than a little surprised at his own reaction. He'd started out to intimidate her for daring to follow him to El Paso, then he had had to fight the urge to sweep her into his arms and overwhelm her with a hundred kisses. She was so dainty and vulnerable and somehow, so innocent.

"Stop following me!" she yelled back over her shoulder.

"Bonnie, I have to follow you, my car is down this way, too."

"Of yes, of course." She stopped in front of a compartment door. "You may not call me Bonnie; it is not proper. I'm going in now."

"Don't go; stay here with me or let me come into your compartment."

"You must be joking!" She whirled away, went inside and peeked around the door. "Oh, by the way, Miss LaFemme saw me through the window as we pulled out. She looked really mad."

"What?" he roared but she had slammed and locked her door.

"Come out here, you little rascal! You'll have gotten me in a whole lot of trouble with Fifi!"

He banged on her door but she simply smiled and sat down on the bed the porter had readied. "Go away!" she commanded.

"By thunder, Bonnie, you come out here!" He felt arousal and anger. This woman was one he could not seduce or intimidate and he wasn't used to that.

About that time, a conductor came along and grabbed his arm. "Mister, I can't help it if you're having trouble with your love life, you got to be quiet a'fore someone complains."

Well, damn. Cash leaned against the door and wondered if he'd lost his touch. Not only was she not going to back down on her damned crusade, she had created a big mess with Fifi LaFemme. The blonde would never believe he wasn't meeting Mrs. Purdy on the train. Besides now he was going to have to return to his cheap seat and try to sleep there.

With a defeated sigh, he started back toward his car, wondering. How could a poor little librarian afford a compartment? Oh, of course, the Lone Star Ladies must provide their president with funds. He didn't believe for one minute that she'd gotten on this train by mistake. No, it wasn't enough that she had hounded him in Dallas and blocked his big plans, she intended to do the same in El Paso. Well, she was just one woman, what could she do to stop a boxing match in a wild border town? That rough town would probably laugh at her and send her on her way. He smiled with relief.

Or maybe not. Mrs. Purdy seemed to be stubborn enough to get what she wanted. Well, the librarian would surrender before he did. Worse yet, he'd so been looking forward to the passionate reward he'd get when he got back to Dallas and instead, Fifi would probably brain him with a whiskey bottle.

Cash returned to his hard, cramped seat and tried to sleep, but all he could think of was that annoying girl sprawled in a big comfortable bed in a luxury compartment. In his troubled dream, he opened the compartment door and looked down at her. Her brown curls spread out on the silken sheets and she wore some delicate, pink nightgown. "I thought you'd never come, Cash, darling," she whispered and held out her arms to him. "You want to put on a boxing match, poor little me won't try to stop you if you'll just make love to me."

"Oh, honey," he murmured and tried to cuddle closer.

"Stop that, partner!"

He opened his eyes to stare at a bearded old goat in the next chair. Cash had laid his head on the old man's shoulder.

He pulled back. "Sorry, *hombre,* I didn't mean a thing by it."

"You do that again, I'll blow your damned head off."

Cash held up his hands in a placating gesture. "All a big mistake," he smiled weakly and tried to get comfortable in the hard seat, which was impossible. He got no sleep that night as the train rumbled toward El Paso.

Chapter Seven

Bonnie passed a sleepless night on the train going to El Paso. She was tired and the big bed was comfortable, but all she could think of was how close she'd stood to Cash and the heat and scent of the man. He'd almost kissed her. Was she sorry she'd moved away?

Gracious, are you loco, Bonnie? she chided herself. *What kind of slut would let a man she barely knew kiss her?* She remembered the way he had kissed Fifi and sighed. Bonnie had never been kissed like that.

Of course that rascal was only trying to charm her into dropping his opposition to the boxing match. He had no real interest in her. Like with Clint Purdy, she was only a means to an end. Well, she wouldn't be fooled again. "Just you wait 'til tomorrow morning, Mr. McCalley," she vowed through clenched teeth. "I'll make you wish you'd never gotten into a contest with me."

She was almost ashamed to admit even to herself that this had degenerated to more than a squabble over a bloody boxing match—it had become a personal conflict between the two of them. *Very* personal.

No doubt that rascal was not above attempting to seduce her to get his way. Women seemed to faint at his touch and fall into his bed. Well, not this woman.

After awhile, the rhythmic swaying of the train lulled her to sleep.

She awakened just before dawn and dressed in last night's outfit as she heard the porter coming down the aisle, ringing his chimes. "Last call for the dining car. Last call for breakfast."

She was hungry and no doubt Mr. McCalley was asleep in his chair in a forward coach after a sordid night of gambling and drinking. She put on the perky hat and hurried toward the dining car. Even as she stood in the doorway, she saw the car was full of diners. The black waiter said, "Sorry, ma'am, we are crowded this morning. Would you mind sharing a table?"

"Not at all, I'm hungry. When will we be getting into El Paso?"

"About an hour, ma'am." He turned and led her through the busy car toward a table at the far end. She was halfway into the chair before she realized the man seated across from her was Cash McCalley.

To the waiter, she said, "Please find me another table."

But the man had scurried away.

She slumped back into her seat, not looking at the rascal who leaned on his elbows and smiled at her. "Ah, so we meet again."

"What a coincidence," she said and cleared her throat, uncomfortable to be here.

"Actually not," he grinned and leaned back in his chair, obviously sure of his charm. "I bribed the waiter to seat you here."

"I should have expected this and bribed him, too."
She tried to stand up again but he reached out and
grabbed her hand. His was strong and big, covering
her small one. She could either sit down or make a
scene. "Let go of me, you polecat," she whispered
through clenched teeth.

He leered at her. "Go ahead, make a scene," he
challenged. "I dare you."

She imagined thirty people staring as she created a
ruckus and after a moment, settled back into her
chair. Bonnie's staid reputation and respectability
meant everything to her. As the president of the Lone
Star Ladies, she was expected to be above reproach at
all times. "You win this one, you masher, but I'll get
even later."

He threw back his head and laughed, turned loose
of her hand and picked up his menu. "You know,
maybe I shouldn't say this, but I find you challengin'
and entertainin.' I don't know when I've enjoyed a
trip so much."

"And I find you crude, rude and egotistical. Believe
me, Mr. McCalley, there are women in this world who
don't find you irresistible."

"Not many." He winked at her. "I didn't expect such
spirit from a librarian."

"I'm a Texas girl, raised in the Big Thicket," she reminded him and picked up a menu. "Texas women
can give as good as they get."

"Then I'm lookin' forward to the contest."

"No, you're not," she snapped. "You'd like to throw
me under this train."

"Ah," he sighed, "if only it were possible. I will admit
I was tempted to put you off the train last night, but I

was afraid you'd raise a howl and the conductor would let you back on."

"You're all heart," she said.

"Nice hat," he said. "Missing a few feathers, though."

She gave him a glare cold as blue ice. "Some loco idiot tried to eat them."

He smiled. "I wouldn't have if you'd stood still."

"And let you kiss me? Ha, I think not."

"You don't know what you missed. Now," Cash said and picked up his menu, "may I suggest the Mexican omelet? That is if you like things spicy?"

"Not as much as you do, no doubt," she snapped.

The waiter came by just then and Cash signaled him. "I'll have the Mexican omelet with ham and biscuits," he said, "and the lady will have?"

"Steak and scrambled eggs and some coffee please."

The waiter nodded and left.

Bonnie gritted her teeth. "I can't imagine why you would ask that I be seated at your table."

"Until last night, I hadn't realized what a charmin', attractive woman you are." He almost purred as he smiled at her.

"I don't believe a word of it!" she retorted. "Saloon girls may lap those lies up, Mr. McCalley, but I doubt an honest word ever comes out of your mouth."

"One or two," he shrugged. "But by thunder, I wasn't lyin' when I said I'd just realized what a beauty you are."

She felt her face burn. "Your flattery will not stop my crusade."

He looked directly at her with those gray eyes, gray as a thunderstorm. "I wasn't flatterin' you, Mrs.

Purdy. You are suddenly the loveliest woman I have ever met."

"I don't believe you."

He shrugged and sipped his coffee. "Suit yourself."

Their food came and she picked up her fork. "Aren't you furious with me?"

"Why?" He stared at her over his cup. "For accidently getting on the wrong train?"

"Surely you don't believe I got on the wrong train?"

"You said you did and I don't reckon a lady would lie. After all, they say if the president of the Lone Star Ladies says a flea could pull a train, go ahead and buy your ticket. Her integrity is above reproach." He began to eat, adding pepper sauce to his omelet.

She felt herself color. "I—I admit I am ashamed of my duplicity."

"Mrs. Purdy, you may be a librarian, but I'm just a poor cowpoke from West Texas. I don't even know the meanin' of that word."

"If you're a cowboy, what are you doing in such a sleazy business in Dallas?"

"Tryin' to survive." He shrugged sheepishly. "My ma was a ranch cook and my pa was a wrangler killed in a stampede. West Texas land is so poor, it takes three people to raise a fuss."

She nodded. "I hear it's flat and dry."

He laughed. "Dry? It's so dry, all the Baptists had to become Methodists; not enough water to dip anyone."

She tried not to smile. He was charming, she admitted that to herself even though she was determined not to let her guard down. She poured thick cream into her coffee and began to cut her steak. It was juicy and the steaming scent made her mouth water. In addition, there was a platter of light, fluffy biscuits, blackberry jam and butter. "How's your omelet?"

He was eating with gusto. "Hot and peppery, just like my women."

She frowned. "Spare me the sordid details." She took a bite of the steak and sighed. She hadn't realized she was so hungry.

He paused, fork halfway to his lips. "Does the chicken feed salesman know you were goin' with me to El Paso?"

"I was not going with you and don't refer to Herbert that way." She continued eating. The biscuits were hot and tasty. She reached for the jam.

"No tellin' what old Herbert will think, us spendin' the night on the train together."

"With about two hundred other people," she reminded him and sipped her coffee.

"If I was old Chicken Feed, I'd be a mite upset to think my woman was on a train with Cash McCalley." He leaned back in his chair and wiped his mouth.

"We are not *together*, and besides, Herbert trusts me," she said loftily as she ate her meal. "He would never believe I could be doing anything unethical."

He knew something about Herbert Snodgrass, but decided not to tell her. She wouldn't believe him anyway. Cash looked deep into her eyes. "If you were my woman, I'd beat hell out of the man who tried to kiss her on the rear platform."

She choked suddenly on her coffee. "If you tell him that, he will not believe you. Besides, Herbert is too civilized to resort to barbaric fisticuffs."

He shrugged and pushed back his plate. "I was only tellin' you what I would do. I reckon the chicken feed salesman is too lily-livered to fight over a woman."

She felt herself flush. He was so male; so primitive, so aggressive. "You are out of line, sir. And you will not distract me from my mission with your attempts to be Sir Galahad."

He threw his napkin on the table. "Miss Librarian, you know this old Texas boy don't know who that is. And about our conflict; this has become more than about a boxing match with you, hasn't it? It's become personal."

She didn't look at him. "I—I would never stoop to letting it become personal. I—I just think a bloody professional fight is bad for Texas, that's all."

"Lady, Texans beat each other senseless in saloons every day. These men will be wearin' boxin' gloves."

She bristled. "I hate fighting of any kind. Both my husbands were killed because men wanted to settle their differences with their fists."

He stared into her eyes with his steel gray ones. "I know about Ace High; what happened to the other one?"

"Hans was killed in a fight."

"Ohh," Cash nodded as if in understanding.

"I—I was very young and running from a drunken, abusive home. My papa was a moonshiner; can't get much lower than that." She colored and looked at her plate, avoiding his eyes.

"That ain't your fault," Cash said gently.

"Anyway I went to work in that elderly rancher's house as a maid; cooking and cleaning was all that I knew. When people began to gossip, Hans married me."

"Was he killed in a boxin' match?"

"Sort of; a fist fight," she stammered. "He had

gotten himself into a brawl on Main Street in our little town. The other man threw a punch and Hans fell."

He looked as if he didn't believe her. "And?"

"His head hit a horse watering trough as he went down and he died."

"Not a very dignified endin'."

"Fighting is never dignified," she snapped and concentrated on her coffee.

"So because both your husbands got killed in brawls, you intend to keep followin' me around and stop me from settin' up this boxin' match?" He glared at her.

"No, something else." She glared back, fighting to keep the tears from coming as she thought of Danny.

There was a long pause with only the click-clack of the train along the tracks and the chatter from the other tables.

He said, "Aren't you gonna tell me?"

She shook her head and frowned. "None of your business. I hate bloody boxing matches; young men dying because they desperately need money and to entertain brutish crowds."

He looked at her, raising his eyebrows as if to read what was behind her words; then shrugged. "I'd better warn you; I'm very stubborn," he said and leaned back in his chair.

"So am I, Mr. McCalley. You haven't met anyone as stubborn as I am."

"Excuse me for sayin' so, but can the Lone Star Ladies afford to keep fundin' you while you run about the country stickin' your nose in my business?"

"That's hardly any of your affair. If it concerns decency and decorum, my organization feels they must get involved. I dare say my financing will outlast yours."

"By thunder, that's for damned sure," he growled. "But maybe businessmen will be willin' to help finance me; I'm not gonna let you win this."

"Then I accept the challenge, Mr. McCalley." She kept her tone resolute, "And may the best man win."

"Mrs. Purdy, you are not a man, you are a headstrong, dainty little woman; a pretty one, I'll admit, but El Paso is a wild, wicked town. You'll be laughed out of the city council."

She smiled a little too sweetly. "We'll see."

He swore under his breath and got up, threw down some money and left the table. Bonnie smiled to herself as she enjoyed the rest of her breakfast. He was right about one thing, this contest had become personal and she was as determined as he was to win.

As she sat sipping another cup of coffee, the conductor came through the dining car. "El Paso! We'll be in El Paso in ten minutes. El Paso coming up!"

Bonnie left money on the table and hurried back to her compartment. Because she had wired ahead, Bonnie thought Cash would be in for a big surprise when they pulled into the station.

"El Paso!" yelled the conductor, hurrying through the train as it slowed, "coming into El Paso!"

Bonnie directed the porter in gathering up her luggage and then she went to stand at the exit near Cash McCalley and a dozen others as the train braked and slowed. She peered out a nearby window. There was a crowd on the platform at this early hour. Good, her telegram had gotten through.

As the train stopped and the conductor opened the doors, a brass band out on the platform struck up a song.

"What the hell?" Cash muttered, "We got a dignitary on board?"

Others shook their heads and looked bewildered. He looked at Bonnie suspiciously, but she only shrugged and tried to look innocent.

The band played "Onward Christian Soldiers" as the crowd stepped down from the train. A large group of very respectable ladies waited on the platform and a group of older men held up a banner that read: EL PASO PASTORS' ALLIANCE. IT'S SIN WE'RE AGIN. The ladies rushed forward to surround Bonnie as she stepped from the train.

"Oh, hell," Cash snarled behind her, "not again!"

"Why, Mr. McCalley, don't be so profane." She smiled sweetly at him. "I'll see you at the city council meeting later this afternoon and I'll be sure and tell all the citizens you think their town is wild and wicked."

He groaned aloud as Bonnie trooped along with her local members of the Lone Star Ladies, marching away from the railroad station.

He bought a paper from a little boy outside the station. The headlines read: RELIGIOUS FERVOR SWEEPING TOWN IN THE MIDST OF A SUMMER REVIVAL. QUESTIONABLE PROMOTER HOPING TO BRING BLOODY FIGHT TO EL PASO.

"By thunder, who had managed to contact the paper?" Reckon Cash didn't need to guess.

He went about town, talking to businessmen and trying to build support for his big fight but not meeting much enthusiasm. Later that day, he headed to the council meeting.

"That woman!" Cash raged as he went into City Hall, "That dainty little annoyin' woman!"

The room was packed with protestors, many waving

banners that read: "Say no to bloody fights!" "El Paso is not a wicked town!"

The first three rows of seats were filled with prim, respectable housewives wearing their red, white and blue Texas flag badges. Yes indeedy, El Paso had a local chapter of the Lone Star Ladies For Decency and Decorum.

He didn't stand a chance and he knew it. He gave the best presentation he could. Then brave and plucky little Mrs. Purdy tore the men's hearts as she stood in front of them and wept, describing about how a boxing match would corrupt their young men and how the sleazy gamblers who came to town would take their hard-earned money and seduce their daughters. In the end, she jumped up on a chair and waved a Texas flag, which brought everyone to their feet with a roar of approval. "Remember the Alamo!" she shouted.

Oh, there was not a dry eye in the house as her brass band struck up "The Yellow Rose of Texas."

In vain did Cash try to point out that this boxing match had nothing to do with the Alamo, and that it might bring a lot of money to town. That brought a gleam to many a businessman's eye, but after all, most of them seemed to be married to staid members of the Lone Star Ladies.

As one of the older businessmen said, "I fought on the front lines at Gettysburg and was wounded, but I ain't brave enough to go up against my old lady on this."

When it came to a vote, Cash went down to defeat like Custer at the Little Big Horn. It seemed El Paso wasn't as wicked as he thought it was.

Tired and disgusted, he checked into a hotel to

rethink his plans. He had one more ace up his sleeve. He walked down to the train station to send a telegram.

> *To the honorable president of Mexico: I would like to talk to you about arranging a profitable boxing match in the town of Juarez, right across the border. Stop. Awaiting your reply here in El Paso. Stop. Sincerely, Cash McCalley.*

Then he went back to the hotel, had dinner, a few drinks and played poker in a rough saloon whose customers didn't seem to know that El Paso was now in the midst of a religious and cultural revival. They broke up some furniture and a big mirror later in the night when there was a dispute over an ace up someone's sleeve and the fist fights broke out.

Bonnie, very satisfied with the events at the city council, took a buggy later to the railroad station and bribed the telegrapher to give her a copy of Cash's telegram.

"Mmm." She studied it a long moment, then sent a wire of her own, before returning to spend the night with the president of the local chapter of Lone Star Ladies, an old maid school teacher with four cats.

The next morning, Cash had breakfast in a sleazy Mexican dive since the furniture at last night's place was too broken up to open for business. His knuckles were bruised, but he'd had a great evening. There was nothing a Texan liked better than a good brawl, yet now they were all trying to act civilized and horrified at the thought of a little boxing match.

Then he lit a cigar and walked down to the depot. "Any telegrams for me?"

The grizzled old Mexican shook his head. "No, Senor."

"Well, let me know when a message from President Diaz comes through."

He played poker all afternoon and won several hands while he waited. About supper time, here came the old Mexican telegrapher. "Here's your answer, Senor."

Cash tipped him and frowned as he looked at the message.

Dear Senor McCalley. Stop. I regret I cannot allow a bloody fight to take place in our Juarez bull ring. Stop. Mexico is too civilized for such savagery. Stop.

"What is he talkin' about?" Cash grumbled to himself as he paused in his reading. "It's a bull ring. They spill bull and matador blood every week there, but my boxing match is too savage and bloody?"

Cash read the final paragraph of the telegram:

Senor, I regret I cannot cooperate, but you see, I buy fine horses from a ranch owner there in Texas who assures me this would not be a good thing. Stop. If I allow the fight, the rancher will no longer sell me horses. Stop. Sincerely, President Diaz.

Cash crumpled the paper in a rage. So some Texan who was afraid of his wife, who was no doubt a member of the Lone Star Ladies, had put the pressure on the president of Mexico. Bonnie Purdy had to be at the bottom of this. Right now, he'd like to pitch her into the bull ring, right under the hooves of some enraged bull.

What was he going to do now? No doubt the two boxers and their entourage were already on their way to Dallas. Cash was running low on money and he probably couldn't lure any more wealthy businessmen into becoming sponsors unless he had a place to hold the match. He had to return to Dallas and make some new plans.

He ran into Bonnie as he got back on the north-bound train. "Don't even talk to me," he growled. "You are like an annoyin' little cockleburr: I can't get rid of you."

"My exact thought!" She snorted and stuck her nose in the air.

They managed to avoid each other the whole trip until the train approached Dallas and they were again standing next to each other, ready to alight.

"Dallas! Coming into Dallas!" yelled the conductor as the train slowed, puffing into the station.

Bonnie leaned forward, peering out a dusty window. Oh, gracious, Herbert stood on the platform, looking anxious. The voluptuous Fifi LaFemme, wearing a tight purple dress, also waited on the station platform.

"This ought to be interesting," Bonnie said to Cash.

"What are you talkin' about?" he asked, but she only shrugged.

The train's brakes squealed as the engine clanged to a halt and the conductor began to unload the luggage. Bonnie stepped off the train just ahead of Cash McCalley.

Herbert rushed to meet her. "My dear, honestly, I've been worried to death about you!"

"Why? I'm a grown person. I can take care of myself."

He began to sneeze and his eyes watered. "I wired Bill and he said you weren't on the train to Shot Gun. What were you doing in El Paso?"

"Wipe your nose, Herbert. I certainly didn't expect you to worry Bill. I had to go to keep that fight out of El Paso."

He had turned and stared behind her. "Honestly!" he said with great disapproval. "Honestly!"

"What?" Bonnie turned and saw Cash McCalley. When the rascal saw her looking at him, he winked and tipped his hat.

"I enjoyed our time together," he drawled and bowed.

"Well, honestly!" Herbert said again, and began to sneeze.

"Stop saying that, Herbert. You know how I loathe that sleazy promoter."

"He wasn't looking at you like *he* loathed *you*," Herbert bristled and his eyes watered.

Bonnie sighed. "I suppose you intend to fight him for my honor?" she asked, remembering Cash's words.

"Fight him?" Herbert sniffed, "Honestly, you know I wouldn't do that, Bonnie. What's come over you?"

Cash had evidently overheard. He grinned and winked again. She could kill him; she could just kill him . . . as long as it didn't involve fisticuffs.

About that time, she saw Fifi pushing her way through the crowd to greet Cash.

Bonnie heard the girl screaming, "I saw that prissy gal gettin' off the train. You said you was goin' alone."

Cash made a placating gesture. "Fifi, I *was* alone."

"You think I'm blind or somethin'? I saw her get off

that train ahead of you. Knowing you, I can't believe you wasn't havin' a cozy fling on that train."

Now Bonnie whirled to face Fifi. "Miss LaFemme, I resent the fact that you would think I'd sully my reputation by taking up with such a sleazy character as Cash McCalley."

"Sleazy?" Cash's voice rose, "You callin' me sleazy?"

Herbert almost seemed to tremble before the taller, stronger man as he wiped his drippy nose with a shaky hand. "Bonnie, let's get out of here before there's a scene."

Fifi shrieked at Cash, "You Casanova, you think you're stayin' with me after bein' with Miss Prissy on the train, you're mistaken!"

"He wasn't with me," Bonnie snapped at her, "and if you don't stop saying that, I'll make you wish you hadn't."

Herbert pulled in vain at Bonnie's arm. "Dear, let's go. We're creating a scene here."

"A scene?" Bonnie's voice rose. "It's not me, it's her. Miss LaFemme," she confronted her, bristling, "if I were going to sully my reputation, I can assure you it would not be with a sleazy gambler like Cash McCalley."

"I am not a gambler," Cash protested. "I am a promoter."

"Ha! Same thing," Bonnie declared.

"You two ain't foolin' me," Fifi took a deep breath, almost popping out of her tight purple dress. "I know what's goin' on here."

She turned and strode away, nose in the air.

"Fifi," Cash yelled, "it ain't like that. You think I'm desperate enough to take up with this prim little widow?"

However, Fifi kept walking.

Cash whirled on Bonnie. "Now see what you've done."

"Serves you right, I'd say," Bonnie kept her tone haughty. "If you didn't have such a reputation as a ladies' man, she wouldn't be so suspicious. Herbert, get my luggage, I'm going to the hotel."

"Hotel?" Cash yelled. "I was hopin' you were catchin' the next train to Shot Gun."

"Of course not, did you really think I'd yell 'calf rope' and quit?"

"I could only hope," Cash sighed.

Herbert squared his thin shoulders. "Sir, do not address my fiancée in that rude way."

"Oh, shut up and go sell some chicken feed," Cash said.

Herbert turned to Bonnie, sniffing. "Did you hear that? Did you hear what he said? I've a good mind to—"

"No, Herbert," she grabbed his arm. "He'll mop up the floor with you. Let's go to the hotel." She turned and strode away.

Cash watched her walk toward her buggy, small frame proud and her head high like a spirited filly, trailed by that ridiculous little chicken feed salesman from Des Moines. Surely she was too damned pretty and proud to waste herself on a twerp like Herbert. On the other hand, they deserved each other.

In the meantime, he had bigger problems than dealing with the stubborn little librarian. Like a very low bank account. The boxers and their entourages were due in on a train from back East anytime and Cash dare not tell them he'd found no place to host the big boxing match. By thunder, what was he gonna do?

Chapter Eight

Bonnie checked back into the Cattlemen's Hotel, making sure she got the same room again. She was afraid Cash might be coming in right behind her and would discover what she was up to, but he didn't check in. No doubt he had gone to a saloon to play cards or over to Fifi's place for some mattress fun. The thought of that made her fume because—because it was so sordid and not at all respectable. She told herself that over and over as she paced her room. "Respectable? Ha! I laugh when I even think of that man and that word together."

And she paced some more.

As much as Herbert wanted to take her out for dinner that evening, Bonnie managed to avoid him and went down to the hotel dining room alone. Afterward, the waiter got her some meat scraps from the kitchen.

Kitty Tom seemed to be waiting for her when she returned to the train station.

"I didn't forget you," she crooned as she spread the meat. "Now why don't you let me tame you? I can't stay in Dallas forever, you know."

The cat wiggled his ragged ears and eyed her suspiciously, but kept his distance until she retreated. Evidently, he was used to his wild, vagabond life and didn't trust her enough to give it up.

Then she went into the telegrapher and laid a dollar on the counter. "Mr. McCalley got any new messages?"

The skinny kid took the dollar and nodded. "I was just gettin' ready to take it to him. You know where he is?"

Bonnie snorted. "Try the nearest saloon and gambling hall. What's the message?"

The boy handed it to her to read.

Boxers on their way from back East. Stop. Arrive tomorrow morning. Have reporters there. Stop. Arena ready? Stop.

She handed it back to him. "That's fine. You can deliver it now." Bonnie wrinkled her forehead in thought. So he hadn't let the fighters know he didn't have an arena set up for their match yet. No doubt tomorrow morning's newspaper would trumpet the arrival so there'd be big crowds of sporting men to meet the train. She'd alert some of her supporters too. McCalley might be in for a big surprise.

The day dawned bright and warm. Cash was in a great good humor as he looked around the hotel dining room and finished his breakfast. He had seen nothing of Mrs. Purdy. Maybe she had rethought her plans now that her convention ladies had all left town.

Maybe she had packed up and gone back to Shot Gun. He could only hope.

There was still no sign of her as Cash drove to the train to meet the boxers and their entourage. As he neared the station, he saw a throng of men. He reined in and stepped down from the buggy. As he tied up to the hitching rail, half a dozen reporters crowded around him. "Big day, huh, Cash?"

He nodded, tucked his thumbs in his vest and grinned. "You can quote me as sayin' this is a big day for the state of Texas. A heavy-weight boxin' match will really put us on the map."

They tossed questions to him as they all moved out onto the platform and turned to look north. In the distance, a train chugged toward them.

"Cash, what about those ladies who were protesting?" A scruffy one asked, his pencil poised.

Cash shrugged. "Well meanin' but misguided. They ought to stay home and not stick their noses in men's business."

All the men guffawed. "That's tellin' 'em, Cash."

"Besides," Cash said, "that female convention is over and they've all gone home."

"Including Mrs. Purdy?"

He made a wry face. "I don't know about Mrs. Purdy. Let's hope she's back in her town library by now, censorin' kiddie books. She's no more problem to me than a worrisome little mosquito."

The men all laughed again and the reporters scribbled furiously. The crowd of men gathering to meet the train was growing. The mayor rushed over to shake Cash's hand. "I brought along a band to play a welcome."

"Fine. Mayor," Cash said, "would you like to make a few remarks?"

Was there ever a politician who didn't? Cash thought as the mayor puffed out his chest and looked toward the train chugging toward them.

The mayor said, "Sure. I'll wait until our important guests arrive and welcome them to Dallas."

All the men peered up the track toward the approaching train. It clanked and puffed and whistled. The mayor turned and waved at his small brass band. It struck up "The Yellow Rose of Texas."

Funny, Cash thought he heard a faint hymn over the train's roar and the little brass band. Surely the mayor's band hadn't changed to hymns. The off-key song grew louder. Puzzled, he turned and looked toward the street and groaned aloud. "Oh, no, she wouldn't!"

But of course she would. He shouldn't have been naive enough to think that the petite widow would simply fade away in defeat. Marching toward the station came a parade of ladies wearing red, white and blue badges and carrying Texas flags. They were followed by stern men waving Bibles and carrying their PREACHERS' ASSOCIATION, IT'S SIN WE'RE AGIN banner. Behind them marched a big brass band playing "We're Marching to Zion."

All the men on the platform turned to gape at the oncoming parade. The mayor's little band tried to play louder but was quickly drowned out by the approaching band.

One of the reporters said, "Cash, I thought you said the opposition was over?"

He gritted his teeth. "I reckon I underestimated her."

"We're marching to Zion" wafted on the warm air

as the protest parade approached the station. The train slowed and puffed as it neared them.

"Quick, Mayor," Cash said, "get your band to play 'For He's a Jolly Good Fellow.'"

The mayor signaled his band and they struck up the song as the train pulled into the station. However, the protestors' band was larger and drowned out the mayor's musicians. The train's hissing and clanging could barely be heard above the "Marching Onward To Zion" refrain. Cash spotted Bonnie Purdy, in her mist blue dress, leading her troops and waving a Texas flag.

The reporters immediately deserted Cash and rushed to meet the petite brunette, crowding around her as she led her ladies and preachers onto the platform.

Cash sighed. He could just wring her neck. He'd never met such a stubborn, determined woman. The mayor looked baffled and the sporting crowd slinked away in the confusion as if embarrassed to be seen with the pro-boxing forces.

About that time, the conductor put down the steps and tried to shout something, but he was drowned out by the ladies and preachers who were now marching up and down the platform. The conductor took off his cap and scratched his head, began to take the luggage off. The protestors' band continued playing even as the mayor stepped forward to meet whoever was about to get off the train. Cash pushed forward too. There was a lull in the noise and then a loud roar that could be heard even over the two competing brass bands.

Both bands hesitated and their music dwindled off

even as a large African lion stuck his head out of the train and roared again.

"A lion! It's a real lion!" A lady screamed and people began to run. The brave sportsmen were trampling ladies and preachers in their rush to escape. The lion padded down the train steps nonchalantly, stepped onto the platform and roared again.

Cash heard Bonnie scream. Without even thinking, he pulled his derringer and stepped over to protect the women from this savage beast, all the while knowing that the tiny pistol wasn't going to be of much use. That's when he noticed the lion was old, a bit motheaten and slightly cross-eyed.

A big, brawny man stepped down from the train. "Don't panic, folks. It's just Nero, Mr. Fitzsimmons' personal pet. He won't bite."

There was a sigh of relief through the crowd as Nero lay down on the platform and looked around. Cautiously, the reporters crowded close to the train. Cash stepped forward and signaled the mayor to move, too.

Cash recognized from the sporting section of the *Police Gazette* that now coming off the train was the world's heavy-weight champion, Gentleman Jim Corbett, tall and muscular, followed by some of his people. Right behind him had to be Fighting Bob Fitzsimmons, a lanky red-headed Irishman and his group.

Cash strode forward to shake hands with all the newcomers, carefully stepping around the bored lion. "A big welcome to Texas, gentlemen. I am the promoter, Cash McCalley, and here's our mayor who will say a few words."

The mayor cleared his throat and stepped forward.

Fighting Bob looked around at the diverse crowd. "You got ladies interested in boxing?"

Bonnie Purdy faced him. "Sir, we bear you no ill will, but we are here to protest boxing in Dallas."

"What?" asked Gentleman Jim and the lion roared again.

"Friends and honored guests," the mayor began, "most of us are thrilled to welcome boxers to Dallas."

As Cash watched, Mrs. Purdy signaled her troops and the band began to play louder. "We're marching, marching, marching onward to Zion . . ."

The ladies and the stalwart preachers sang the hymn as they strode around the platform. The mayor tried to continue his speech, but was drowned out by the protestors' band.

The train crowd looked baffled and the lion yawned in boredom. The reporters scribbled furiously.

And to think he'd rushed forward to protect her from the lion. Right now, Cash had an urge to pick up the petite widow and toss her to Nero. Except the fat, sleepy old lion didn't look as if he could eat anything with bones in it.

Cash elbowed his way through the protestors and shouted in the mayor's ear. "I think we'd better get our fighters to their trainin' camps."

"What about my speech?" shouted the mayor.

"I don't think the ladies are gonna let you give it!" Cash shouted back.

"But I worked for hours on this," protested the mayor.

Cash made a helpless gesture with his hands. "You think you can out-shout 'Marching to Zion'?"

"Oh, very well," the little man huffed in defeat.

Cash stepped forward to the fighters and shouted, "I think we'd better get you to your trainin' camps, gentlemen."

The fighters nodded. Fitzsimmons spoke to his lion and the fighters and their big entourage started off the platform and toward the assembled carriages and wagons. The protestors and their band followed along behind while still marching onward to Zion.

The lion hopped up in the front seat of the buggy, looked around and yawned. The horse immediately whinnied, reared and tried to take off running with Cash hanging onto the bridle. He finally got the nervous horse quiet. Cash hesitated, then climbed up to the seat and tried to put as much distance between him and the big old beast as possible.

Surely, Cash thought as the entourage got in the buggies and wagons, these protestors wouldn't follow them all the way out to the country. But of course Mrs. Purdy's bunch would. They followed along as the carriages and wagons pulled out, throwing dust back on the protestors, who coughed and kept singing and waving banners. Cash deliberately speeded up his convoy and gradually, Bonnie's parade was left behind in the dust, staring after the disappearing procession.

The last thing Bonnie saw was the annoyance on Cash McCalley's face and the cross-eyed lion looking back at her, yawning. "Good job!" she shouted to her people.

All the reporters but one had gone with the boxing procession. The one approached her. "Well, the fighters are finally here. Will your people continue to protest?"

"Of course we will. I'm every bit as determined to stop this fight as that promoter is to put it on. Dallas doesn't need the kind of hoodlums and saddle tramps this bloody spectacle will bring to town."

"Amen!" shouted a bunch of preachers. "Money that should be going into collection plates will be spent on gambling and wild women."

"Sounds good to me!" grinned the reporter.

Bonnie thought about giving him a good whack with her flag, then decided against it.

"By the way," said the reporter and leaned closer, "I talked to Cash earlier and he says there'll be a boxing exhibition at the challenger's training camp at Long Pine Ranch tomorrow morning at ten o'clock. You ladies going to be there for it?"

"Wouldn't miss it, would we, ladies?" Bonnie shouted.

The preachers and the ladies roared approval. The reporter finished scribbling and drifted away.

"All right," Bonnie nodded to her troops. "You've heard where the training camp is, let's all meet there tomorrow morning." She turned and watched the fighters' procession disappearing down the road in a cloud of dust. The faint roar of the lion drifted on the hot air. She hoped it took a big bite out of Cash McCalley. "Public sentiment is opposed to this savage business and we can keep fanning the flames."

One of the ladies wiped the dust from her shirtwaist. "You think we can win this?"

"Of course we can," Bonnie nodded. "After all, so far, there's no arena to hold this fight in. Mr. McCalley has met his match. He just hasn't realized it yet."

Herbert arrived just then. He was puffing and sniffing as he stepped down from his buggy. "Bonnie, you ladies are making spectacles of yourselves. The whole town is laughing."

"That's okay, we're in the right. You know the old saying: nothing can stop a woman who's in the right and keeps right on coming."

"I believe you're misquoting what they say about the Texas Rangers." Herbert sighed and wiped his nose.

"Well, it works for the Lone Star Ladies, too." Bonnie shrugged. "Gracious, Herbert, where have you been? I would have thought you would have come out and protested with us."

"Uh, I meant to, but I couldn't get a buggy." He wiped his plump face and avoided her gaze.

She doubted that but she didn't say anything. Could her fiancé be a coward and afraid of that cheap promoter? She remembered the way Cash McCalley had jumped in front of the ladies with nothing but a tiny derringer in his hand. Now there was a brave man.

She frowned at the thought that she was admiring him. Maybe he'd been told in advance that the lion was harmless.

Her group began to break up after making plans to go out to the training camp tomorrow.

"Perhaps I could take you to lunch," Herbert suggested as the crowd wandered away. "I've wanted to talk to you about our future."

She dismissed him with a wave of her hand. "I'm hot and tired. Besides, we don't know each other well enough yet to be setting a date."

He frowned, pulled out a hankie and wiped his watery eyes. "We've known each other over three years; ever since I started selling chicken feed to the general store there in Shot Gun."

She didn't want to stand here in the road and discuss this with him. "Herbert, I'm going back to the hotel. Aren't you due to be in Waco today?"

"I changed it to be here for you." He tried to take her hand, but she shook him off. "After all, a defenseless woman in a wicked place like Dallas and dealing with the biggest rascal in the state—"

"I'm not helpless," Bonnie snapped, "and I really am quite capable of looking after myself. As for Cash McCalley, he may be a little on the shady side—"

"A little?"

"All right, a lot," she admitted, "but you should have seen him standing off that lion with just a derringer."

"Foolhardy." Herbert sniffed.

"And he's always behaved like a perfect gentleman—"

"A gentleman!" Herbert scoffed. "Why, everyone knows he's a ladies' man and a rake of the first order. That woman he sees, that Fifi LaFemme puts on a scandalous cancan show over at the Black Lace Saloon—"

"Now how would you know that, Herbert?" She peered at him curiously.

He gulped and licked his lips, not looking at her. "Well, I've heard, that's all. I wouldn't go in a place like that, but I've seen Cash McCalley in there—"

"How could you if you don't go in there?" She began to suspect there were things about Herbert she didn't know.

Sweat broke out on his pasty face. "Honestly, I—I was passing by and saw him going in, that's all. I was on my way to Wednesday night prayer meeting myself."

"Well, it doesn't matter," she shrugged. "I've got a rented buggy and I'm going back to the hotel. This battle with the wicked is not over."

"Is it really over boxing or has it become something personal between you two?" Herbert asked.

"How dare you suggest that I would stoop to that level?" Now Bonnie was upset. "This is a good and noble purpose and it has nothing to do with besting that rake."

Herbert snorted and wiped his nose again. "Why, I think maybe you're enthralled with that scandalous rascal. I can't blame you for that, dear Bonnie. You're so naive and they say he thinks he's God's gift to women—"

"I won't argue that!" she snapped. "But this is not personal. Protecting Texas from evil is one of my duties as the president of Lone Star Ladies For Decency and Decorum. As the new president, I've got to make a showing. Anyway I see nothing charming about McCalley at all. Some women are just idiots! Now I suggest you go to Waco and sell some feed. There's hungry chickens out there waiting for you."

She lifted her skirts and strode toward her buggy. Yes, that scoundrel might appeal to some women, but of course the big, grinning virile Cash wasn't her type at all and after seeing Fifi, Bonnie knew that she herself was too strait-laced and upright to be his type. Gracious, there was no telling what he and that saloon singer did while they were alone. Bonnie remembered the noise from the hotel room next door earlier in the week and sighed. Her imagination wondered exactly what it was that Cash did to get Fifi to moan like that. Certainly neither of her husbands had ever made Bonnie moan or even sigh. She remembered how close Cash had been with her trapped between his arms on the back of that train. She'd had a sudden feeling he was going to kiss her and she'd neatly avoided it by ducking under his arm. *Had she missed something?*

"Bonnie, are you loco?" she scolded herself as she drove back to the hotel. "He is as crafty as a coyote and will do whatever it takes to win; don't you be naive enough to forget that."

That evening, she had supper in a little out-of-the-way tea room so she wouldn't chance running into Cash McCalley. He certainly wasn't the type to venture into a dainty ladies' tea room. She was also thankful to avoid Herbert. She devoutly hoped he had gone on to Waco. Why had she never noticed how annoying and prissy Herbert was until now?

The next morning, as usual, she had room service deliver her breakfast and then she made ready to lead her protestors. She came out of the hotel behind Cash McCalley and stepped into the shadows so he wouldn't see her. She watched him mount that big gray stallion and trot away. He rode well and looked like he was born to the saddle. Yes, she could believe he'd once been a cowboy. A fine figure of a man, she thought with a disapproving shake of her head. Too bad he was such a wild, untamed creature. Oh, dear, that made her think about the cat.

She ran back to the dining room and got some ham scraps. When she came out to get into her buggy, Herbert was waiting there. "Dear Bonnie," he implored, "I'm sorry we had words. All I want is to look after you in a cruel world."

His glib superiority annoyed her. "Herbert, I have been on my own since I was sixteen years old, except for two brief marriages. I'm perfectly capable of looking after myself."

"Don't be upset with me, my dear one. After all, someday, we will wed." He sniffed, reaching for his hankie.

Well, he might be a little prissy, but at least he wasn't a Texan. She shrugged him off and got up into her buggy with him attempting to help her. "Now that I've thought it over, I'm not sure I'll ever marry again, Herbert. Most men seem to want to control everything and I've done very well on my own these past four years."

He climbed up in the buggy beside her without being invited. "I know that, my dear, but the two of us could run your business even better—"

"I doubt that and I'd hate to think that's what you were after. I'm doing fine with Bill."

He looked wounded. "My dear Bonnie, how could you even think such a thing? And we all know Bill should retire."

"He'll do 'til I find a replacement," she said, thinking that Herbert was not up to the job. She wasn't even certain the city boy could ride a horse. "I'm on my way out to the training camp now. Are you sure you want to go?"

He sighed and sniffed. "If you're determined to go, I suppose it is my duty as your future husband to go along and protect you."

"Protect me from what? I'm a Texan and you Yankees should remember that Texan gals can look after themselves."

"I didn't realize you held it against me that I'm from Iowa. Here, dear, let me drive." He tried to take the reins away from her, but she resisted.

"Texans never really trust anyone from north of the Red River. We're clannish." She snapped the reins hard. It startled the old bay horse and it took off so fast, Herbert was hanging onto the seat for dear life. She noted with some amusement that his knuckles had turned white.

"Honestly, Bonnie, what's gotten into you?" he shrieked and hung onto the seat as the buggy raced away. "You've changed these last few days. That Cash McCalley is a very bad influence, I'm afraid."

"He is not influencing me," she snapped. "It's just that we're both stubborn Texans who don't like to lose." She urged the horse to go even faster.

Herbert grabbed onto his bowler hat to keep from losing it. "I thought you were so staid and such a proper lady and here you are, almost racing. You really shock me, Bonnie."

She was surprised to realize she was enjoying scaring the Yankee city boy. "If you're scared, Herbert, I can drop you off somewhere."

"Of course I'm not scared," he protested, but his face looked white. "I liked you better quiet and demure."

"And dull?" she asked. "That's what I've been, dull."

"Honestly, if you think being a lady and letting men take care of things as they were meant to do is dull—"

"Herbert, you're annoying me. Please shut up." She urged the horse on.

"Shut up?" He gasped. "Did you just say 'shut up'?"

"I did," she said and was shocked at herself. Mrs. Bluebonnet O'Neal Schwartz Purdy, president of the Lone Star Ladies, had never before said "shut up" to anyone. "Maybe you're right, Herbert. Perhaps I am letting that crude, rude rake influence me too much."

He smiled smugly. "Lie down with dogs and you get fleas, I always say."

Bow wow, she thought. She fought an urge to tell him to shut up again but in her mind, she was lying down with Cash McCalley and the thought unnerved her. She must defeat him and get back to Shot Gun and her dull, safe life there. Mrs. Herbert Snodgrass. She stifled a yawn and kept driving, trying to keep her mind on the upcoming confrontation. She was surprised that she was actually looking forward to it. Until she had begun these conflicts with the handsome rake, her life had been so very dull and she hadn't even realized it. The fight scene from MacBeth came to her mind. "Lay on, McDuff, and damned be he who first cries 'hold, Enough!'"

"What?" Herbert clung to the seat and his bowler hat and blinked at her like she had lost her mind.

"Uh, it's Shakespeare; MacBeth, to be more specific. I was just thinking aloud."

"Oh, I forget sometimes about your volunteering at the library. Anyway, I don't see the point."

"Herbert," she said patiently as she drove, "when MacBeth finally confronts his enemy, McDuff, and they begin their sword fight, that's what he says about surrendering."

"Oh, well, that's about two men," Herbert's voice was smug over his sniffing, "not a man and a sweet little lady."

She resisted the urge to push him out of the buggy, even though the image of Herbert landing on his bottom in the dusty road was tempting.

They came to a fork in the drive and after a moment's hesitation, took the left fork down the lane to the ranch's big barn. "I reckon this is where the training camp is," Bonnie said. "I see a bunch of horses and some buggies tied up over there."

"I don't see any of your protestors yet," Herbert looked about nervously. "Honestly, Bonnie you don't want to go up against these ruffians alone."

"I'm not alone." She smiled sweetly as she reined in. "Weren't you just saying you'd protect me?"

His pasty face mirrored alarm. "Well, I meant, maybe bringing in the police. I didn't mean go toe to toe with a rascal like McCalley alone. They say he's quite the saloon brawler. Why once, I saw him pick up a man at a poker table and throw him . . ."

"Yes? Where was that?"

He stumbled to a halt. "I—I, at least, that's what I was told. Maybe we should wait until your protestors get here, Bonnie."

"No, let's go in and watch," she countered. "I want to see what goes on with these rough fellows."

"Cash McCalley won't like us being here," he whimpered as he helped her down.

She smiled. "Of course he won't. That's what makes it so delightful, don't you see?"

Cash McCalley sat at ringside, holding Fifi's hand. "I'm so glad you understand, doll. I truly didn't know Mrs. Purdy was on that train to El Paso."

She leaned over and kissed his cheek, leaving a big smear of bright lip paint. "I ain't mad at you, Cash, honey. After I thought it over, I realized you wouldn't be attracted to a prim, drab little thing like her. She ain't got nothin' that would interest a man."

"And you've interested a lot of men, so you should know," Cash murmured under his breath.

"What?"

"Nothin', sweets." Funny, he hadn't realized Fifi was such a cheap, stupid slut until lately. Frankly, she bored him. She never had before.

"Hey," yelled a newsman, "Cash, how about you going a round or two with the challenger?"

"Aw, I don't know anything about fancy boxin'," Cash protested. "All my fights have been in saloon brawls."

The newsmen gathered around. "It would make good publicity," one suggested.

"Yeah, I reckon it would. Okay, if maybe one of Bob's sparrin' partners can find me some trunks, I'll give it a go. A Texan is always a good sport."

With the newsmen cheering him on, Cash was led back to an improvised dressing room where he put on black tights, special shoes and boxing gloves. Then he came out and climbed up into the ring.

"Oh, Cash, honey," Fifi sighed, "you look so—so manly with your shirt off."

"I do, don't I?" He flexed his muscles and pranced around the arena a little.

"Hey, Cash," yelled a newsman, "how many rounds you think you can go with Fitzsimmons?"

"He's tough," Cash conceded and did some fancy footwork around the ring. "You'll see why he might be the next champ. When the sportin' men of Texas read about it in your papers, they'll all be wantin' to buy tickets to the big fight."

He pranced around the ring some more; a little

nervous as he saw the big Irishman climb over the ropes. Actually, Cash had never been into real boxing, but maybe he could make a good enough showing to interest the newsmen.

"Hey, Cash," one of the reporters yelled, "how about this for tomorrow's sports headline? TEXAN TAKES ON THE CHALLENGER. PROMISES GREAT FIGHT FOR THE LONE STAR STATE?"

"Great!" Cash threw some imaginary punches. "Tomorrow, we'll go out to the champ's camp. That ought to be good for another headline in the sports pages."

Nero seemed to roar in agreement. Cash glanced around. Over in a corner in the hay, the old lion chewed on a punching bag.

"Hey, Cash," another reporter shouted, "just where is this big fight being held?"

"That's what we'd like to know," a short, muscular manager said.

"I—I just haven't finalized the details yet," Cash said. Wanting to change the subject, he said, "Let's get this exhibition goin', fellas. You're gonna see the same thrill as the ticket buyers when this big event happens."

"*If* this event happens," a reporter said and the others laughed. "That Mrs. Purdy and her bunch seem pretty determined."

He winked down at Fifi who sat in the front row of chairs. "By thunder, I can deal with one little librarian."

Fifi smirked. "That's right, gents. She ain't gonna stop my man from puttin' on this fight, is she, Cash?"

Cash started to speak, then realized heads were turning toward the big barn door. *Was the lion out chasing the ranch chickens again?*

He wished it had only been the lion. Even as he stood there in the arena, little Mrs. Purdy, followed by that feed salesman, walked into the barn.

Oh, hell, and here he'd been thinking it was gonna be a great day.

Chapter Nine

Bonnie stopped dead in her tracks to stare. Cash McCalley was in the ring, bare-chested and wearing boxing gloves and black tights. The tights left nothing to the imagination. Good gracious.

"Well," Cash leaned on the ropes and grinned down at her. "May I suggest you close your mouth, Mrs. Purdy, or are you catchin' flies?"

Herbert sneezed and sneezed. "Bonnie," he said, noisily blowing his nose, "this place is full of dust and my allergies—"

"Oh, hush, Herbert," she said without thinking, still staring at the well-endowed man in the ring. "So the truth comes out, Mr. McCalley. You like to fight, too."

He grinned. "Only when I gotta."

Herbert sneezed again. "Bonnie, dear, no wonder you are shocked, seeing that rascal half-naked and in that tight black underwear."

"By thunder, then she should go home," Cash said, grinning. "I'd hate to shock a lady."

Fifi said, "I ain't shocked, Cash."

Bonnie had found her breath. "No one was talking to you, Miss LaFemme."

Now it was the blonde whose mouth fell open. "Well, I never—"

"Oh, I'll bet that's not true," Bonnie said.

"Now what do ya mean by that?" Fifi blinked and turned toward the scoundrel. "Cash, honey, am I being insulted?"

"Fifi," Cash leaned on the ropes, "I'd warn you not to get into a battle of wits with Mrs. Purdy."

"That's right," Bonnie snapped, "because you're only half-armed."

"What?" Fifi looked about, puzzled.

Cash sighed. The blonde wasn't too swift compared to the nimble-witted librarian.

Fifi stood up and advanced on Bonnie. She was taller and heavier. "Why, I'll wipe up the floor with you, you prissy little wench."

Bonnie took a deep breath and stood her ground. "I am very opposed to brawling," she said, "but if you decide to attack me, you'd better bring your lunch because it may take awhile."

"Why, Bonnie!" Herbert was evidently shocked.

Cash laughed. "Spoken like a true Texan. Sit down, Fifi, before the little lady smacks you. You, too, Mrs. Purdy. We are about to have an exhibition of the manly art of fisticuffs."

Fifi sat down, grumbling under her breath.

"McCalley, I hope you get knocked six ways from Sunday," Bonnie snapped without thinking as she took a seat.

"Tsk. Tsk." Cash winked and shook his head. "Mrs. Purdy, you don't sound like you're opposed to violence."

She smiled too sweetly. "I am, Mr. McCalley, but for you, I could make an exception."

The Irish challenger climbed into the ring. "Faith and begorrah! You two gonna exchange witty remarks all morning or can we get on with this?"

The men laughed and gathered around.

Bonnie tried to look bored and disinterested, but she couldn't take her eyes off Cash McCalley. As he danced about the ring, throwing imaginary punches, the muscles in his brawny body rippled under his tanned skin. She found herself staring at the black tights. He was all man, yes, indeedy.

Fitzsimmons pranced around, punching the air. He was taller and outweighed the promoter, but Cash looked like he could hold his own. The newsmen pressed closer, pencils poised in the air, waiting for the bell.

Herbert sneezed again and said, "Honestly, this is disgusting, Bonnie, dear. I think we should leave."

She realized she wanted to see the fight. "Uh, Herbert, we've got to wait for our protestors, remember?"

"They must have taken the wrong fork in the road and got lost," Herbert grumbled and blew his nose.

A handler rang the bell and Bonnie leaned closer, holding her breath as the two men faced each other, warily throwing punches. Cash was as nimble as a dancer, she thought, easily avoiding the challenger's punches. Probably because he'd been in so many bar room brawls, Bonnie thought, with disgust, but she couldn't stop staring. The fighters circled each other, throwing a punch here and there. The newsmen cheered them on. Sweat gleamed on both muscular bodies. Two big savage males, Bonnie thought and leaned closer. "Keep your left up, Cash," she yelled before she thought. "He's got a mean right hand!"

"Why, Bonnie," Herbert turned to stare at her, "that doesn't seem like you at all."

"Of course not, I—I'm appalled," she gulped, embarrassed that she'd gotten carried away.

No one else seemed to have noticed. The crowd of men yelled and cheered.

Fifi was on her feet yelling, "Kill the bum, Cash, honey, knock him down!"

Cash turned his head to smile at her and Fitzsimmons came through with a mean right, catching the Texan in the face. Cash staggered backward, hit his head on the ring post and went down. Blood ran out his nose. Fifi screamed while the referee began the count, then she ran up the steps to the ring and crawled through the ropes. "Cash, honey, are you all right?"

He obviously wasn't all right, Bonnie thought with alarm. Once more, she was at ringside that fatal night Danny tried to win enough money to get him and his little sister out of the Big Thicket.

Cash lay sprawled on the mat unconscious while Fifi ran in circles in the ring, screaming, "Somebody get a doctor! He's killed Cash! He's killed him!"

"Stop that screaming!" Bonnie ordered sternly as she returned to reality. Just as she had that long ago night, she ran up the steps, hiked her skirts and climbed through the ropes. The newsmen gathered around. Quickly she assessed the situation. "Okay, he's not hurt bad. I've seen cowboys out like this after a drunken fight in the bunkhouse." Bonnie strode over to the corner, picked up a bucket of water. Fifi continued to scream.

"Oh, do shut up! You aren't helping at all!" Bonnie said and threw the bucket of water on Fifi.

Fifi gasped and looked down at her dress. "You soaked me, you little—! You ruined my dress!" Her excessive makeup now ran down her face. She was a lot older than she had first appeared, Bonnie decided.

Bonnie studied Cash. He still lay motionless and bloody with members of the challenger's team gathering around him. She picked up another bucket. "Stand back!" she ordered.

As the men scurried out of the way, Bonnie dumped the bucket on Cash.

He came up gasping and choking. "What are you tryin' to do, drown me?"

"I warned you to keep that left up," she said. "The Irishman's got a mean right."

Herbert stood below her by the seats, yelling. "Bonnie, get down from there immediately! That's no place for a lady."

Fifi came at her. "How dare you dump water on me? Why, I never—"

"Best thing in the world for hysteria," Bonnie said. "Now I suggest you go home and put on dry clothes." She looked at Cash and exhaled, relieved that he wasn't badly hurt. "As for you, Mr. McCalley, I think you've just proved to these newsmen what I've said all along about boxing being bloody and dangerous."

Cash tried to sit up. "Oh, lady, do you always have to have the last word?"

"Yep. Let's go, Herbert." Bonnie hiked her skirts and crawled through the ropes. The newsmen were scribbling away. There was no telling what tomorrow's papers would say but she hadn't thought of that when she saw Cash lying there bloody and unconscious. She rejoined her beau.

"Honestly, Bonnie," he sounded exasperated, "I

never expected a lady would climb up in a boxing ring—"

"I'm a Texan," she said and headed out of the barn. "We may be a bit more feisty than Iowa girls."

"A bit?" Herbert squeaked. "I'd say so."

The old lion blinked at them as they walked past, then returned to chewing his punching bag.

Herbert helped her up into her buggy and she insisted on driving although he tried to take the reins.

"Honestly, Bonnie, I don't know what's come over you," he scolded as they drove back to town. "You were always such a perfect little lady, so meek. I think that scoundrel must be bringing out the worst in you."

She was annoyed and tired of his prissy nagging. She hadn't realized what a sissy Nancy boy he seemed to be. "Cash and I are both Texans," she said.

"Cash? You're now referring to that rascal by his first name?"

She was getting a headache. "Herbert."

"Yes?"

"Hush up."

He gasped. "You're—you're telling me, your fiancé, to shut up? I can't believe this."

"Believe it!" she snapped.

His mouth opened and closed like a fish out of water. "I realize you're probably upset at seeing all that brutal fighting and that blood," he said, "so I'll make allowances for that—"

"Don't," she said and whipped up the horse so it was almost running.

Herbert clung to his seat, white-faced. "Bonnie, you know I'm afraid of horses. Please slow down before we end up in a wreck."

She didn't slow down, but she was a little shocked

to realize she was getting a grim satisfaction from scaring the Yankee city boy. In truth, although she would never admit it even under Apache torture, she had become excited at watching the two half-naked men fighting, sweat gleaming on both muscular bodies. Cash's body had been as hard and lean as Fighting Bob's. Even now, she saw the images in her mind and took a deep breath. She couldn't shake that picture from her mind and that made her feel both frightened and guilty, remembering Danny. She had begged her brother not to go into that ring, the other man was so much bigger. He had done it for her; to give her a chance to escape a miserable future in the Big Thicket.

She returned to the hotel and sent Herbert on his way with the rental buggy, him still sneezing and scolding her for her unladylike behavior. She watched him drive away and wondered how she could have ever been slightly attracted to him. *Because he was safe,* she realized suddenly, *and so civilized.* Texas men were so masculine and unpredictable. That was why she'd sworn never to wed another one.

After she had had supper and returned to her room, she heard Cash going into his. He paced the floor a long time. She began to worry about him when there was a long minute of silence. Bonnie knelt and looked through the keyhole. His face looked puffy and bruised and he had a black eye. She watched him strip down to his underwear. She pulled away from the keyhole. A lady shouldn't be doing this, but she couldn't control her own curiosity. When she looked again, he had stepped out of his underpants and walked across the room naked, headed toward the wash bowl near the window.

"Gracious!" she said and then put her hand over her mouth, afraid he might have heard her. Cash seemed to pause, listening, then shrugged and returned to washing himself. Bonnie knew she shouldn't be peeping but she couldn't tear herself away from the sight. He was all man, all right, wide-shouldered and narrow-hipped. His muscles rippled when he walked across the room. She blinked at the sight of his maleness as he turned. She'd seen stallions back home that didn't have that big equipment. He had said he'd worked as a cowboy and she could believe it, looking at his scars.

She must stop this, it was not right at all. Grudgingly, she stuffed a hankie in the keyhole and retreated. What on earth was she doing, watching a naked man wash himself? She tried to imagine Herbert's naked body and winced. She bet it didn't look anything like Cash McCalley's.

Bonnie went to bed but couldn't sleep. When she did finally nod off, she dreamed of Cash McCalley naked in the boxing ring, dancing about, throwing punches. In her dream, she was in the front row of seats, cheering him on as he whipped the champ.

She sat up suddenly in the darkness, horrified at her dream. Thank goodness no one need ever know of this. It took a long time to drop off to sleep.

"Room service."

A bit sleepy, Bonnie grabbed a robe, opened the door to accept her breakfast, and tipped the boy who brought it. She took the tray and sat down at a little table, sighed. She hadn't had a good night, thanks to troubled images of the scoundrel next door. As she sipped her orange juice, she opened the newspaper. She read the headlines and winced, actually feeling sorry for Cash McCalley. PROMOTER GETS K.O.ED, it read, PROTESTOR THROWS COLD WATER ON HIM.

"Oh, my goodness gracious," Bonnie sipped her coffee and read the page. She was mentioned as protesting the bloodshed by throwing water on the unconscious man. Miss Fifi LaFemme was quoted as saying she was engaged to Cash McCalley and if she had known what that protestor intended, she would have pulled her hair and thrown her out of the ring.

"In your dreams, slut," Bonnie made a wry face and kept reading. Even Nero got a sentence or two. There was no doubt in Bonnie's mind that if she hadn't been there, there would have been a lot less news coverage. "You idiot," she scolded herself as she ate her eggs, "you played right into his hands, getting him even more publicity. You'd be smart to stay away and let this thing die from lack of interest."

Who was she kidding? To stay away was to yell "calf rope." Texans never surrender. "Remember the Alamo!" she said with conviction. "If Mr. McCalley still thinks he can put this boxing match on in Texas, I'll show him I'm as stubborn as he is."

Let's see, what was on today's schedule? Oh, yes, the paper said, the press would be at the champ's training camp today and so would the challenger, dropping by to visit with the press. A large crowd of admirers and newsmen were expected.

"Perfect!" Bonnie smiled. She had already anticipated this and rallied her troops for a big protest march. She saved the ham from her breakfast for Kitty Tom and waited until she heard Cash McCalley leave his room. Then she dressed in her new mist blue dress and went downstairs. Reporters saw her as she came into the lobby. Out the doors, she could see Cash riding away on that gray stallion, headed, no doubt, to the training camp.

"Mrs. Purdy," the reporters gathered around her, "what's on today's agenda? Your fiancé says you won't be going to the other training camp, that you were so undone by yesterday's blood and brutality that you almost had to have smelling salts."

"I beg your pardon!" Bonnie bristled. "I'm a Texan born and bred and Texans don't faint away, not even the women. My ancestors fought Indians, Mexicans and rattlesnakes to take this land and I'm not going to quit now."

"But your fiancé said—"

"Herbert Snodgrass is not my fiancé," she corrected. "He's just a gentleman friend. Trust me, sirs, I will be at that training camp this morning with the Lone Star Ladies and the Pastors' Association."

"You know," one of the men said as he scribbled, "this is becoming a national story. Why, they say Bat Masterson himself is coming in to cover the story for his paper."

"Bat Masterson, the gunfighter?" Bonnie asked.

"He's a sportswriter now," said a newsman.

"Yeah," said another, "and the one and only John L. Sullivan is saying he's coming down to see the fight."

"Well, they both may be disappointed," Bonnie answered as she pushed through the crowd, "because decent people will see to it that there is no fight."

"Can we quote you on that, Mrs. Purdy?"

"You certainly may," and ignoring the call for more quotes, she went out to her rented buggy.

Herbert stood there. Could he have looked any more like a tenderfoot? Why had she never noticed before how prissy he was? Bonnie sighed. Herbert wore a natty pin-striped seersucker suit, sparkling white spats, a new derby and a pink carnation in his buttonhole. All he needed was a coffin to lie in and his arms crossed over his skinny chest, she thought.

He said, "Well, I brought the buggy, Bonnie, my dear, but surely you aren't going out there and making a spectacle of yourself again for the reporters—"

"A spectacle?" Her voice rose. "Of course I am. Now if you, as a Yankee, are too lily-livered to accompany me—"

"Bonnie!" He sounded startled. "You've changed in the last few days. I—I'm shocked!"

"Oh, put a sock in it, Herbert," she snapped as she hiked her skirts and climbed into the buggy with him vainly attempting to help her. "You coming or not?"

He took two or three deep breaths, then climbed up beside her. "Honestly, I'd think after seeing those two half-naked men trying to beat each other senseless, and all that blood, your feminine sensibilities would have been so offended—"

"What offends me is you making quotes for me. I'm perfectly capable of speaking for myself."

He sniffed. "Well, where I come from, women let their menfolk handle things."

"Texas women must be a good deal feistier than they are in Iowa," she said and snapped the whip at the startled old bay horse.

Herbert grabbed onto his natty derby hat with one hand and the seat with the other as they took off at a fast clip. He didn't say another word as they drove toward the champ's training camp.

About a half mile from Corbett's headquarters, they reined in where the Lone Star Ladies and the preachers had gathered. "Good," Bonnie smiled, "I'm glad to see you all are on the right road."

The pink-faced, chubby preacher, Horatio Tubbs, stepped forward. "I'm sorry we got lost yesterday, Mrs. Purdy. We have our banners and our band as you can see."

Bonnie said, "I'll go on ahead. You form your ranks and start singing and playing as you approach the training camp so the reporters will see you. I understand there may be a big crowd as Bat Masterson himself is arriving and maybe John L. Sullivan, too."

The preacher's face lit up. "*The* John L. Sullivan? I always wanted to meet him—" He seemed to realize people were staring and frowning. "I mean, I want to get a look at this naughty pugilist."

Bonnie nodded. "We'll see you in a few minutes." She snapped her whip and drove down the dusty road toward Gentleman Jim's camp.

There were a lot of horses and buggies tied up in front of the big barn.

"Oh, goodness," Herbert sighed, "more dust and hay."

"I didn't ask you to come, Herbert," she pointed out.

"I thought you might need protection from that rascal," Herbert stepped down from her buggy.

If she needed protection, the chicken feed salesman wouldn't be much good against the virile promoter. "I don't think I'm in any danger from Cash."

"Cash? You call him Cash?" He turned to stare up at her and wipe his nose.

"I meant that scoundrel, McCalley." She stood up from her seat, preparing to get out.

Abruptly a nanny goat ran around the barn, bleating.

"What in the—?" Bonnie frowned.

About that time, the old lion tore around the barn in pursuit of the goat. Reporters and spectators spilled out of the barn to see what was going on. The goat bleated and the lion roared. That was all the sleepy buggy horse needed. It seemed to get a whiff of the lion and reared, neighing, almost upsetting the buggy. The goat ran around and around the buggy with the lion right behind. The buggy horse reared again, yanking the lead from Herbert's pink hands and causing Bonnie to drop the reins. Then the terrified old horse took off at a gallop down the road, the goat and the lion right behind it.

Thrown off balance, Bonnie fell back into her seat and dropped the reins. She screamed and made a grab for them, but they were now flapping free in the breeze. All she could do was hang onto her seat to keep from being thrown out of the buggy as the horse galloped away. Behind her, she heard the goat bleating and the lion roaring.

"Bonnie!" yelled Herbert behind her, "what can I do? What can I do?"

She glanced back over her shoulder as Herbert ran up and down, gesturing frantically. The goat and the lion were right behind her as her runaway horse galloped down the road. Boxing people and reporters stood out by the barn open-mouthed and staring. Cash McCalley had come out of the barn, too. She saw him dashing toward his big gray horse, tied up at the hitching rail. Herbert now ran in circles, screaming for help like the heroine in a melodrama.

It was going to take everything she had to keep this

buggy on the road until the horse tired and quit galloping. With a goat and a lion running along behind, that wasn't too likely. Dust flew up as the buggy raced madly. Her hair came loose and blew out behind her.

Up ahead, she caught the first faint sound of hymns. *Oh, no*.

"Look out!" she shrieked. "Runaway horse! Lion! Lion!"

The big parade didn't seem to hear her. "We're marching to Zion, beautiful, beautiful Zion, we're marching onward to Zion . . ."

"Lion! Lion!" Bonnie shrieked, but the protestors had their faces in their hymn books as they marched forward. In fact, the protestors seemed unaware of the runaway buggy coming toward them; perhaps the hymn drowned her screams and the lion's roar. Or maybe *Lion!* sounded too much like *Zion*. Bonnie clung to her seat as the buggy careened madly down the dusty road, straight toward the protestors. She could see the good people now, waving their banners as they marched in formation, while the band played loudly if not too well.

"Get out of the way! Lion! Lion!" she screamed and tried to wave at them to get off the road, but they were too busy marching to Zion to hear her. A few seemed to see the buggy coming, but looked puzzled. Fat Reverend Tubbs held the end of the long IT'S SIN WE'RE AGIN banner that flew over the parade, and a stout housewife held up the other end while the wind made it flap.

"Get out of the way!" Bonnie shouted. "Runaway horse!"

Too late the protestors seemed to realize what was happening. They collided with each other attempting to run out of the road. Some made it to the ditches on each side, some fell down. The big IT'S SIN WE'RE AGIN banner faltered and fell as her horse ran through the middle of their little parade. The falling banner startled the horse even more and it kept running, the banner now caught in its harness and being dragged along the road. Reverend Tubbs hung onto his end of the banner and was dragged through the dirt on his wide expanse of rear end.

In her terror, Bonnie heard the sound of pounding hooves and looked back. Maybe Herbert was coming to save her.

She saw the gray horse and the expert rider passing the old lion and realized who it was.

Cash yelled, "Hang on, Bonnie, don't panic! I'm comin'!"

She could only hold onto the seat as Cash leaned over from his galloping stallion and caught one of the reins. "Whoa, horse! Whoa!"

The winded old horse slowed to a trot, then a walk. The goat kept on running, right past them, but the tired old lion growled one more time in defeat and lay down in the road.

"Are you all right?" Cash yelled as he reined in and stepped down from his lathered horse.

"Of course I am!" Bonnie snapped. "I wasn't panicking, I'm a Texan, you know. All this is your fault!"

He dismounted and strode to the buggy, held up his arms. "Lady, I just saved your life and you're going to scold me?"

Without thinking, she went off into his arms and he carried her over toward the shade of a tree near the road. He was strong, she realized and quite handsome though his face was still bruised from yesterday. "This is all your fault," she said again. "If you hadn't brought this circus to town, my horse wouldn't have run away."

He grinned and plopped her down under the tree, sat down beside her. "It is kind of a circus, isn't it? Uh oh, here come your chicken feed salesman and the reporters."

"Oh, gracious, my poor ladies and the preachers." She hopped to her feet and looked down the road. The band instruments lay scattered on the road and the preachers looked very undignified. Reverend Tubbs had evidently gotten some stickers in his rear and a hole in his trousers as he was dragged along the dirt. He wore red underwear, Bonnie realized and tried not to smile. The whole protest scene was chaotic, ladies shaking dust from their skirts and running after their lost bonnets that blew along the ditches, gentlemen attempting to find their torn and battered signs and banners.

The goat had stopped a few hundred feet down the street and was now munching grass while Nero lay in the middle of the road, yawning.

Reverend Tubbs picked up his torn banner and glared at her. "Mrs. Purdy, what is the meaning of this?"

"I—I tried to warn you," Bonnie gulped, "but the singing drowned me out."

He limped off, looking for his missing banner, his wide expanse of rear still revealing red underpants.

She looked down the road. Advancing on them was Herbert and a bunch of reporters. "Uh oh," Bonnie muttered to Cash, "now see what you've done."

"I haven't done anything," he reminded her with a grin. "We were just havin' a dull news conference when you came along and stirred things up. I think you've just made for another excitin' headline, Mrs. Purdy."

"I would like to wring your neck!" she seethed, staring toward the approaching crowd.

"On the other hand," McCalley laughed, "I ought to reward you, dear Mrs. Purdy. I wouldn't have gotten half as much publicity if you hadn't showed up and created all this ruckus."

"It wasn't me, it was that damned lion."

"Tsk! Tsk!" he chided, "a lady cussin'?"

"You could make a saint curse," Bonnie seethed, "you and Nero."

Nero roared at the sound of his name, got up and padded toward them. Then he lay down next to Cash and put his head on his knee.

On the road, the protestors were still attempting to dust themselves off and reorganize. The reporters walked through the disheveled parade and straight toward the couple under the tree. "Wow, that was exciting, Cash! You're a hero!"

"Mrs. Purdy, what do you think of this man risking his life to save you?"

Before she could answer, Herbert said, "I could have saved her if I'd had a horse."

"There were horses aplenty tied up at the hitchin' rail," Cash reminded him.

"I—I have nothing to say," Bonnie stammered.

"Well, that's a first," Cash said.

The Reverend Tubbs limped over and rescued his banner from Bonnie's buggy horse's harness. It was torn and dirty. It now read IT'S SIN.

"The very idea!" the preacher fumed.

"I'm sorry," Bonnie said, "I had no idea the lion would be loose. Who owns the goat anyway?"

Corbett, the champ, strode up. "It provides milk for my baby. I imagine it'll be buttermilk after this wild chase."

Herbert sneezed. "Bonnie, I think we need to leave."

The reporters gathered around. "Oh, don't leave, Mrs. Purdy. Any time you show up, there's always a good news story."

"You see?" Herbert said, "Honestly, Bonnie, you've made yourself a laughing stock. Wait until the newspapers—"

"Herbert, shut up." She was dirty and out of sorts.

Cash grinned. "Would you like me to escort you back to town, Mrs. Purdy?"

"No, I would not," she snapped. "Herbert, dear, get the buggy and let's go." To the newsmen, she said, "You can see that whenever these boxing people get together, there's chaos and disaster. That's why we don't want this fight in Texas."

"Mrs. Purdy," Cash began dusting himself off, "you seem to be the one providin' all the chaos."

The newsmen laughed and she felt her face burn with humiliation.

About that time, Fifi LaFemme walked down the road. "Hey, what about me, Cash?"

He blinked. Evidently, he had not given a thought to the saloon girl. "Just a minute, sweet."

Sweet. Bonnie wrinkled her nose. "Herbert, get the buggy." She stuck her pert nose in the air and marched away with Herbert trailing in her wake.

Cash stared after her even as Fifi joined him, grabbing onto his arm. Bonnie Purdy might be a mite stubborn and opinionated, but hell, weren't most true Texans? When her buggy horse had run away, he'd realized in a split-second that the namby-pamby chicken feed salesman wasn't going to go to her aid. Cash had done it without thinking, just as he'd stopped a stampede or two in his earlier years. What had surprised him was how small and dainty she had felt in his arms. With her hair loose and blowing, she was almost desirable.

Desirable? The thought surprised Cash. There had been a moment when he was trying to stop her horse that she had looked up at him, blue eyes wide with fear, soft lips open. Mrs. Purdy could behave like a woman after all. There was something soft and vulnerable in her he had not seen before.

A plan began to form in his mind. The stalwart Mrs. Purdy was going to be the grit in his eggs, the burr under his saddle, the one who might stop his boxing match unless he did something to stop her.

The only option that occurred to him was to seduce her. He grinned at the thought. If there was one thing Cash knew, it was women. If he could make her fall in love with him, she'd back off and let him stage his boxing match. Then he could dump her like stale cornbread. After the ungrateful way the staid wench had acted when he'd just saved her life, she deserved it. He walked over to his horse.

"Hey, Cash, have I got to walk back to the barn for my buggy?" Perspiration ran down Fifi's face, making her makeup smear. Funny, she wasn't nearly as pretty as he used to think she was.

"Unless you want to ride behind me on Dusty."

"And ruin my dress?" she wailed.

He was abruptly weary of the saloon girl. "Catch a ride with a newsman."

Cash turned and before mounting up, he stared after the departing Purdy buggy. "Yes, lady," he whispered to himself, "you're about to become the target of my charm. Let's see how you react to that!"

Chapter Ten

She sent Herbert on his way and went into the hotel to clean up and get the dust and cockleburrs out of her tangled brown hair. She changed clothes, putting on a blue crisp gingham cotton, then read awhile. Later she went down to the dining room and enjoyed a leisurely supper, trying not to think what tomorrow's headlines would read. Thank God, she didn't see Cash McCalley in the dining room. The waiter told her Cash had eaten earlier and seemed to be in a bad mood.

She smiled, pleased she had managed to annoy him so much. She enjoyed a tasty dinner of crisp fried chicken, mashed potatoes and gravy, hot rolls, fried green tomatoes, pickled peaches, a big slice of rhubarb pie and a tall glass of cold milk. Then she took her chicken scraps, got in her rented buggy and drove to the train station. When she walked up on the platform, she surprised Cash McCalley. "Well, good evening, sir, I see you're feeding my cat."

He glared at her, the black eye now turning a little purple and green. "Your cat? Mrs. Purdy, John L. is *my* cat."

"Then why don't you take him home so he won't have to live like a wild thing?"

"He likes bein' a wild thing. Besides, I doubt I could catch him."

Bonnie squatted down and held out the chicken. "Here, Kitty Tom, here, kitty."

"That old battler is not gonna answer to a silly name like that."

However, the big orange Tom cat crept hesitantly toward her.

"Here, Kitty Tom," she crooned and held out the meat.

The cat hesitated, watching her warily, his ragged, torn ears laid back.

"See?" Cash was triumphant. "I told you he couldn't be tamed. He's a Texan and independent as a hog on ice."

She laid the meat out where the cat could see it and retreated. "He can be tamed," she said. "It just takes a little patience and trust. I'm going to take him home with me when I leave town."

"I don't reckon I can hope that'll be any time soon?"

"I hate to dash your hopes," she smiled wryly, "but the battle over your bloody event isn't finished yet."

"The Lone Star Ladies must have plenty of money in the bank to support your crusade," he grumbled as he reached for a cigar.

"Some," she smiled. He need not know she was paying her own expenses. "See? I told you." She nodded toward the big orange cat that crouched only a few feet away, eating the chicken.

He shook his head. "So he's comin' close. That don't mean you'll ever turn him into a civilized lap cat."

"We'll see," she said with a smile.

"Women!" he snorted and headed to his horse. She watched him mount up and ride away. He rode well, she thought, remembering how he had galloped to her rescue, and she admired a man who could handle a horse. He might make a good ranch manager if he could ever be tamed. "That's not too likely," she said under her breath to the wary cat. Then she went into the station and asked the telegrapher if Cash Mc-Calley had sent a telegram while he was here.

Sure enough, he had sent a wire to Austin to the governor, telling him Cash was coming to the state capital tomorrow to discuss easing the way for putting on the boxing match somewhere, anywhere in Texas.

"So the sleazy promoter is headed to Austin tomorrow," she thought aloud, knowing she'd be going, too. She couldn't ride the same train, McCalley might spot her. He was already annoyed enough with her to throw her off the moving train if he got a chance. "Is there a train to Austin later tonight?"

The skinny boy nodded. "Yes, ma'am."

"Good," she opened her purse. "So sell me a ticket and here's an extra dollar not to tell Mr. McCalley where I've gone."

Then she hurried back to her hotel to pack.

When Cash left the railroad station he rode to the Black Lace Saloon to watch Fifi kicking up her heels to that cancan dance. It should have cheered him up, but it didn't. He kept imagining the staid Mrs. Purdy in black stockings and lace petticoats, kicking up her feet to "Ta Ra Ra Boom De Ay." He bet she had pretty legs. He pictured those legs in his mind and took a deep breath. Of course the strait-laced widow would never kick up her heels for a bunch of yelling galoots like Fifi was doing right now. Men were throwing silver dollars on the stage and urging the blonde to kick even higher. They roared with approval when she turned her back and flipped up her short skirt so that her black lace drawers showed.

He turned his head to look at the crowd and saw Herbert Snodgrass throw a gold cartwheel up on the stage, yelling for Fifi to show her drawers. What a hypocrite, Cash thought in disgust as he sipped his drink. Here Old Chicken Feed was, engaged to Mrs. Purdy, and he was in the Black Lace Saloon, his eyes big with lust and his tongue hanging out like a hound dog's. Hell, it was all the staid librarian deserved, and even if Cash told her where her fiancé was spending his spare time, she wouldn't believe it.

"Ta Ra Ra Boom De Ay! Ta Ra Ra Boom De Ay!" Fifi finished her cancan to a roar of applause and stopped to gather up the money. She came off the stage and walked over to join Cash. "I'm as hot and sweaty as a hog!" she complained and yelled at the waiter to bring her a beer.

Cash winced at her lack of class. She needed someone like Bonnie Purdy to teach her how a lady behaved. Was he out of his mind? One thing was certain, the prim librarian wouldn't be up on the stage, showing her drawers to a bunch of lusty *hombres* for any price.

"Whatcha thinking about, Cash, honey?" Fifi gulped the beer, burped and wiped the foam off her upper lip with the back of one hand.

"Nothin' much." Why had he never noticed before how crude the dancer was? Cash nodded toward Herbert, who sat with his back turned at a far table. "This ain't the first time I seen him here. He come in often?"

"Yeah." She gulped her beer. "I'd tell that snotty little librarian, but it would get me in trouble with the manager. We got to protect our customers."

"I saw him toss you twenty dollars; I didn't think feed salesmen made that kind of money."

Fifi made a dismissing gesture. "He wanted to get in my bed, told me he was going to be rich soon and could buy me anything I wanted. I figured he was drunk and full of shit."

"Ladies don't use words like that, Fifi," he said without thinking.

She frowned at him. "I ain't no lady and you know it. You've changed some, Cash. Reckon you been hangin' around that prissy Mrs. Purdy too much."

He shook his head. "I can't help it; she shadows me everywhere I go. She's like a cockleburr, I can't seem to get shut of her; stubborn as hell."

She chuckled. "You're a fine one to talk. You comin' to my show tomorrow night?"

He shook his head. "Going to Austin tomorrow, see if I can get the governor to intervene."

She laid her hand on his arm. "Then maybe tonight, you could stay at my place. You ain't been givin' me much attention lately."

"No, not tonight, I got to go pack." He stood up. Somehow, Fifi didn't interest him anymore. Maybe it was just because he was concentrating so hard on this boxing match. "I got a lot at stake here, Fifi," he admitted. "If this don't come off, I'll be wiped out."

She smiled. "I got some money, sport; I'll back you."

He shook his head, not wanting the strings that

would come with the offer. "I got scruples, Fifi, about takin' money from women. Now I got to get back to the hotel; my train leaves early in the morning."

Before she could argue with him, he left and rode back to the hotel.

The next morning as he checked out, he looked about as wary as old John L. Who knew if Mrs. Purdy might be hiding somewhere close to eavesdrop on his conversation?

"You seen anything of Mrs. Purdy, Earl?" he asked the desk clerk.

"Oh, she checked out late yesterday," Earl nodded.

"What?" This was an unexpected surprise.

"Yes sir," the clerk said. "Checked out."

"Well, I'll be damned." Cash pushed back his Stetson and scratched his head. He didn't know whether to be relieved or disappointed. Somehow, he hadn't expected the feisty little thing to cut and run, yell "calf rope." He'd been sort of enjoying the daily conflict with the headstrong girl. "Hold my room, I'll be back Sunday or Monday."

"Ahem, about your overdue account," the clerk began.

"I'll be rollin' in pesos when this boxing match is over," Cash promised. "I'll pay you then."

"But the manager said—"

"Tell him I'm good for it," Cash picked up his valise and headed for the door. Now was no time to get into a fuss that might make him miss his train. Cash had put his horse in the livery stable, so he took a rented buggy to the station. The cat came out from under a boxcar and Cash threw him some ham scraps from breakfast. "You can forget about that little gal taming ya," he told the cat. "She's skedaddled back to Shot Gun, I reckon, and you and I can both stay wild and fancy free."

The train pulled into the station and Cash boarded, put his luggage in the brass rack overhead and went to the club car as the train pulled out. He didn't have enough for a room at the state capital tonight, but he was a good poker player. In a couple of hours, he'd be just fine. Cash grinned as he sat down in the club car and ordered a drink. His luck was changing with the prissy librarian giving up her opposition. By tomorrow night, he'd have convinced the governor or at least the governor's wife to side with him and that should do it. "Cash, my boy," he grinned as he sipped his bourbon, "you could talk a dog off a meat wagon with your smooth gift of gab. This boxing match is now a done deal!"

In Austin, Bonnie had settled into her lovely room at the best hotel in the capital. The legislature was in special session this hot June and she figured she'd have to appeal to the senators and representatives. She also spent the afternoon rallying the local preachers' association members and the Austin chapter of the Lone Star Ladies For Decency and Decorum.

Satisfied that she was ready for tomorrow, she went shopping for several dresses, notably an elegant baby blue silk ball gown. She knew this Saturday night was the governor's annual fancy summer ball. All the legislators and their wives would be there. She might swing a vote or two if she attended. After a moment's hesitation, she took off her wedding ring and put it

away. She had used it for protection these four years
to avoid greedy men, but she had enough confidence
now in her abilities that she thought she could stand
on her own two feet without the aid of the gold band.

After an afternoon of shopping, she had a plate of
spicy Mexican food and an excellent flan, took a bath
and went to bed. She smiled as she dropped off to
sleep, imagining Cash McCalley's face when he saw
her. He surely wouldn't be expecting her to show up
in Austin. Nor would he know the governor and his
wife were old friends of Bonnie's. When Hans had
been alive, he had often been to the capital on business and had taken his young wife with him.

Cash got off the train that afternoon and found his
way to a cheap hotel near the fancy new capitol building. He didn't know a soul in Austin, except maybe
some gamblers. He wasn't sure how he would go about
approaching the governor, but he figured he could
count on his charm and his gift of gab to get him
through. Besides that, some of those legislators were
bound to play poker. Cash rubbed his hands together
with relish at the thought. He'd learned to play poker
in the bunkhouse when he was a young cowboy, and it
had helped him out financially any number of times.

The next morning, he washed up and breakfasted
in a small Mexican cafe and headed to the capitol. He
couldn't get past the governor's prissy male secretary,
who directed Cash to the legislature where maybe the
sergeant at arms might appeal to the chief senator to
let Cash speak.

"Who is the chief senator?" Cash asked.

"The honorable Joshua Farraday from Lubbock."

"Old Josh?" Cash grinned with pleasure. "By thunder,

I haven't seen him in a coon's age. I worked on his ranch many years ago."

"Really?" the secretary looked over his wire-rimmed spectacles. "Well, he's one of the big dogs at the capitol. I imagine he'll get you into the Senate chambers."

"When the big dogs are out, the little dogs better stay on the porch," Cash said and headed for the senator's office. Once he told the clerk his name, he managed to get inside where the white-haired old man shook his hand heartily. "Why, Cash, ain't seen you in a month of Sundays."

"Good to see you, Josh. The reason I'm here—"

"I reckon I can guess," the grizzled, tanned old man sat down behind his desk and put one boot up. "Everyone's talkin' about that prize fight. I can hardly wait."

Cash breathed a sigh of relief. "I need your help, Josh. I got protestors tryin' to stop me. They say it's too bloody."

The senator shrugged. "Nothin' a real Texan likes better than a good fight, lest it's cards and wild women." He sighed as if remembering his youth. "Reckon I can get you in the Senate this morning if you want to make a speech."

"I'm much obliged," Cash grinned. "Between the preachers and the upright women, I've been fightin' a losin' battle over in Dallas."

"Dallas?" Josh sneered and reached into his desk for a bottle and two tumblers. "Them Dallas folks got so citified, they're almost Yankees."

"Don't let them hear you say that," Cash cautioned and took the glass, sighed with contentment at the taste.

"Who's leading the anti-boxing fight, anyhow?"

"Well, the preachers are involved and some women's group called the Lone Star Ladies For Decency and Decorum."

"Oh, Lordy," the old man groaned. "We got some of them women in this town, too. Seems like any time men try to have a little fun, them respectable women is out to stop it."

"Well, their leader seems to have cut and run," Cash lit a cigar. "They seem to be leaderless right now."

The old man sipped his whiskey and grinned. "You get into her drawers, Cash?"

Somehow, he didn't like anyone insinuating scandal about Bonnie Purdy. She might be annoying, but she was a lady. He shook his head. "I tried, but so far, I seem to be barkin' up the wrong tree."

"Cash, you used to be able to talk a cow out of her calf. You slippin'?"

"Oh, she ain't your average woman," Cash admitted, thinking about Bonnie, "but before she backed off, I was plannin' to try charmin' her."

The senator pulled out his pocket watch. "We better be goin'. There's an emergency joint session this morning. There'll be a big ball at the governor's house tonight. If you should want, I can get you invited."

Cash nodded. "That'd be good, Josh. Give me a chance to charm the legislators' wives into helpin' me."

The senator stood up, laughing. "I swear, you never change, Cash. Want one for the road?"

"Was Stonewall Jackson a Southern Democrat? Of course I'll have another."

Neither of them was feeling any pain as they walked over to the capitol building. In a few minutes, Cash found himself up at the podium, making ready to address the lawmakers. He looked around. It was a typical group of lawmakers, he thought. Three were asleep at their desks, one snoring loudly, two were reading, more than one was playing solitaire, two in the back were arguing and about to get into a fight, and four were slapping their legs and telling jokes.

Josh Farraday rapped his gavel for order. "Members of the legislature of the great state of Texas, this special session will now come to order."

That started a bunch singing "The Yellow Rose of Texas," which woke up the ones who were asleep. Senator Farraday made opening remarks and introduced Cash.

Cash stood at the podium and took a deep breath. "Honorable members of the legislature of the great state of Texas, I'm right pleased to be here."

"Remember the Alamo!" a tall rangy man in the front row stood up.

There was a cheer and now all the legislators were standing, singing "The Yellow Rose of Texas." Josh rapped for order in vain, and had to threaten to call the Sergeant at Arms. Cash waited patiently for the cheers and singing to die down. Obviously some of the other esteemed gentlemen had a bottle in their desk, too. He tried again. "Gentlemen, I am here today to tell you about a world class sportin' event that's gonna happen in the state of Texas."

"A coon hunt?" A legislator on the front row yelled. "I got a good dog!"

"A coyote chase?" another suggested.

More cheering.

"Something better than that," Cash grinned.

"Women and whiskey," one of the men shouted.

A roar of approval from the crowd.

"Well, maybe not quite that good," Cash admitted.

"A world championship boxin' match right here in Texas."

The men broke into wild applause and Cash sighed with relief. This was going to be easier than stealing milk out of a baby calf's bucket.

Josh hammered with his gavel again so Cash could continue.

In the sudden quiet, Cash imagined he heard the strains of a hymn. *Loco,* he thought. *You've had too much bourbon.* Even as he tried to dismiss it, the music in the distance seemed to grow louder. Men were turning around to look and a murmur ran through the Senate chambers.

"We're marching to Zion, beautiful, beautiful Zion, we're marching upward to Zion—"

Oh no, it couldn't be, Cash thought. She couldn't be here about to interfere just as he was getting help from the Texas legislature. The hymn grew louder and now men were looking puzzled and turning in their seats, heads craning to see what the commotion was.

The big doors burst open suddenly and a line of protestors, prim ladies and preachers marched into the chamber, waving their banners and singing. He knew before he saw her who was behind this. Oh, he could just wring her slender little neck. Bonnie Purdy actually smirked at him as she led her troop into the big room. Men scrambled to their feet at the sight of the ladies and Bonnie Purdy marched her troops around the chamber, waving Texas flags and banners while they sang, "We're marching to Zion, beautiful, beautiful Zion—"

The Speaker rapped for order, but he didn't get it.

The ladies marched around the room and down between the desks, waving their banners.

Now how in the hell had that woman found out my plans and gotten to Austin in time to set this protest up? He'd thought she'd cried "calf rope" and gone home. But no, she was as stubborn as he was.

Lady, he thought, *I accept your challenge. Damned if I'll let you sink me over this.*

Bonnie knew by the expression on his rugged face that she'd taken Cash by surprise like Sam Houston had taken Santa Anna at San Jacinto. Good, he hadn't been expecting her to show up. He'd thought the legislators would go for this, and being men, they probably would, but some of these legislators' wives were members of the Lone Star Ladies and the senators and representatives wouldn't dare vote against their wives. Texans were brave, but not brave enough to buck their womenfolk. Besides, some of them would soon be up for re-election and the pastors' organization swung a lot of votes.

She was having a delightful time as she waved her Texas flag and marched her ladies up and down the aisles between the legislators' desks. The preachers had taken a stand near the front with their big IT'S SIN WE'RE AGIN banner. Reverend Tubbs looked quite dignified and imposing today and he'd replaced his torn clothes. Bonnie wondered if the stout man was still wearing red underpants. That made her think of Cash McCalley striding up and down his room with no underpants at all. If he only knew. She smirked at him as she took her ladies around the room again while marching onward and upward to Zion. Cash McCalley looked mad enough to fight a bull. Well, he didn't scare her.

The whole chamber was in chaos, with the Speaker rapping his gavel for order and the Sergeant at Arms attempting to stop the parade. She'd made her point so she signaled her ladies and they marched out of the capitol building. She complimented her supporters on a job well done and told them she would see many of them tonight at the governor's ball. Then the protest broke up and she returned to her hotel, pleased with the turnout of the Austin chapter of the Lone Star Ladies.

Back in the Senate chambers, the preachers were now filing out and Cash gritted his teeth as the Speaker at the podium tried in vain to bring order to the vast legislative chambers.

"Sorry, Cash," Josh said in an aside, "I think I'd better adjourn this bunch for the day. It's almost lunchtime anyway."

Cash nodded and his shoulders sagged with defeat. The woman was not only stubborn, she was damned clever to pull this ambush off. He tried not to admire her savvy. By thunder, she might even be almost as smart as a man. Naw. "Josh, you think I can change any opinions if I come to the ball tonight?"

The old man rubbed his chin and leaned against the speaker's stand. "Might can. Bourbon will be flowin' and the men might be feelin' brave enough to go up against their wives."

"Okay, I'll try that then." They shook hands and Cash left the Senate chambers with Josh still rapping his gavel and the Sergeant at Arms still trying to bring order to the room.

Yes, he thought as he walked away from the capitol building, he'd attend that ball tonight and be especially charming to the ladies who might influence their husbands' votes. He wondered briefly if Bonnie Purdy would be there, then shook his head. A prim little librarian wouldn't know anyone important enough to receive such an invitation.

Bonnie dressed carefully for the governor's ball as the sun slid over the horizon. She put on a blue silk gown just the color of her eyes and had a hairdresser come in to curl her hair and pull it back in a mass of curls and blue ribbons. She looked in the mirror and was shocked at how low the dress was in front. It showed the rise of her breasts. Her first instinct was to pull it up, then she realized she was dealing with men and pulled it lower still. She owned a delicate blue sapphire necklace and earrings and now she put those on. Finally she sprayed herself with a dainty perfume and went downstairs. Her friend, the governor, had sent a carriage for her. She would have supper with a few select people at the mansion before the ball.

Cash cleaned up and made ready to go to the dance. He shaved and put on a crisp white shirt, polished his boots and wore his best black broadcloth coat. He looked at himself in the mirror critically and then smiled. Yep, he still cut a good figure at thirty-one. He had no doubt he could sway a few ladies into insisting a husband vote Cash's way.

He paused in the doorway, wondering where that ornery girl was tonight. Probably on her way back to Dallas, thinking her job was done.

He was wrong. When he walked into the ballroom,

he'd barely gotten himself a drink and looked around, when an official motioned for the orchestra to stop playing. The curious crowd turned toward the doorway. The official announced in a loud voice, "Ladies and gentlemen, the governor of the greatest state in the union, Texas. Please welcome him tonight."

The crowd nodded, smiled and began to applaud as the governor swept into the room with his homely wife on his arm. Right behind him came other people Cash recognized as important from this morning. A petite beauty floated in on the arm of a well-known senator. The brown-haired girl wore an expensive blue silk gown that must have cost a fortune. She was such a beauty that all he could do was stare at the creamy expanse of breast above the blue silk and the cascade of brown curls down her back. Her delicate neck shone with a fine necklace of blue sapphires. Somehow, she looked familiar.

Cash blinked. No, it couldn't be and yet the girl turned, saw him and smiled and he knew then that the staid librarian had indeed turned into a swan and come to the governor's ball. Where had she gotten such expensive things? Oh, of course one of the rich members of the Lone Star Ladies had taken pity on the poor little frumpy thing and loaned her some clothes and jewelry.

Even as he watched, mouth open in amazement, the governor approached her, then escorted her around the room, introducing her to important people. Men were lining up for an introduction. Cash didn't like the way some of them were leering at the little widow as they kissed her hand.

Cash decided at that moment he would have to

fight fire with fire. There was only one way to deal with this crafty girl—the way Cash had always dealt with difficult women. He would seduce Bonnie Purdy into falling in love with him and abandoning her crusade. *Yes,* he nodded as he strode across the floor toward her, *he would seduce her and the sooner the better!*

Chapter Eleven

Bonnie glanced across the room at Cash McCalley standing by the punch bowl. *Soaking up liquor, no doubt.* She frowned and turned away to visit with a senator's wife. She wondered who the sleazy promoter knew who had gotten him invited to the governor's ball. Not that it mattered; she had already talked to the governor and key senators at the elegant private dinner. Their wives assured Bonnie that their husbands would vote against allowing a bloody prize fight to be held anywhere in the Lone Star state.

Now Cash McCalley stood staring at her as if astounded. In fact, his mouth was open wide enough to catch flies, she thought. Whether he was shocked to see her or shocked to see her wearing something stunning and expensive, she couldn't be sure. She smiled at him as Senator Farraday walked up and asked her to dance. "Why, Senator, I'd be delighted."

He bowed and held out his arm. "You don't mind dancing with this old bachelor, Mrs. Purdy?"

She gave him a vibrant smile. "Why, Josh, you're only in the prime of life and you're the most eligible man here."

"Besides Cash McCalley," he nodded toward the scoundrel as he danced her out onto the floor.

"Oh, what a rake that one is," Bonnie wrinkled her nose. "He says he used to be a wrangler, but I doubt everything he says."

"Believe it," the senator nodded. "He was raised on my ranch. Good cowhand. He got off into promoting trying to earn enough to buy his own spread."

"Oh?" She glanced past her partner's shoulder at Cash who was now glaring at her.

She smirked at him and he put down his glass and marched across the floor. Oh, gracious, surely, he wasn't going to—

But he was. Cash tapped the senator on the shoulder. "Hey, Josh, may I cut in?"

"I don't think—" Bonnie protested, but the senator was already handing her off to the scoundrel.

"Sure, Cash, I'm sure the lady would rather dance with you than an old goat like me."

"I don't think—" Bonnie said again but by now, she was in Cash's arms and he spun her across the floor. "You rascal!" She seethed through clenched teeth, "How did you get yourself invited here tonight?"

"I might ask you the same thing," he grinned down at her. "I'm here to gather votes, I'm sure you're doin' the same. By the way, you look breath-takin' tonight. I didn't recognize you when you came in."

"I don't know whether I'm being complimented or insulted." She looked up at him. He was all man; tall and broad-shouldered and carrying a faint scent of shaving lotion, tobacco and bourbon. He was also an excellent dancer. It was a good thing she had already nailed down her votes at dinner or this charming rake would be seducing the legislative wives into pressuring their husbands to vote Cash's way.

"It's just that I noticed you've taken off your wedding ring."

"I—I decided that I'd mourned Clint long enough."

"For a marriage that lasted less than a day? I'd say so."

"Don't be fresh," she said. "Anyway, Herbert had said he felt uncomfortable with me always in mourning, so in respect for his feelings, I decided to take it off."

"Uh huh. How much do you really know about the Yankee chicken feed salesman?"

"Now how does that concern you?" she bristled defensively.

"I just think you could do better, that's all."

"I don't remember asking for your opinion." She kept her voice icy and wondered how she could escape from this scoundrel. People on the sidelines were smiling and whispering to each other.

"Are you gonna marry the Yankee?"

"What an impertinent question," she snapped. "He's my beau, that's all."

"That sounds like a no," Cash grinned and whirled her around the floor again. "That's a fancy necklace. Is it real?"

"Don't be rude," she snapped. "Gentlemen don't ask such questions."

"Seems high dollar for a little librarian."

"If—if you must know, it belongs to a rich rancher lady."

"One of the Lone Star Ladies?"

"Yes; not that it's any of your business."

"You'd be purty without any fancy jewelry," Cash

said with a grin, "and you might oughta wear pale blue more often. The color brings out your eyes."

"Thank you." She kept her voice cold. The dance ended and he walked her over to the punch bowl where Senator Farraday stood.

"Well," said the old man, "you two make a good-looking couple."

"I think not," Bonnie said.

A wealthy young rancher she knew from Grange meetings walked up just then. "Ah, Mrs. Purdy, may I have the honor of the next dance?"

"I'd love it!" she said and took his arm. They whirled out on the floor again.

Cash watched her glide away in the rancher's arms. Somehow, that annoyed him. He had liked the way the petite girl had just fitted into his embrace and he wanted to dance with her again. "What a woman," he sighed.

Josh nodded as they watched her out on the dance floor. "I'll say. You do know who that is, don't you?"

"A prim little librarian from Shot Gun," Cash grumbled, "and she's as stubborn and headstrong as I am. I rue the day she ever crossed my path."

Josh grinned. "Librarian, huh? I think you may be in for the surprise of your life, my boy."

"Why?" Cash frowned as he watched her dancing with the rancher. He didn't like the way the man was flirting with her and holding her too close.

"Never mind," Josh drawled. "I don't reckon it's important. Popular, ain't she?"

Cash watched another man cutting in on the rancher, who looked crestfallen at losing her. This one he recognized as a banker he'd seen in Dallas. "By thunder, I don't know why everyone wants to dance with her," he mumbled. "She's the most annoyin', hard-headed little thing I ever met."

"Ah," Josh said as he poured himself a cup of bourbon punch, "she's not falling for you like most women do?"

"I haven't really tried," Cash felt on the defensive now. "I'll wager if I wanted to, I could have her."

"I wouldn't bet on it," Josh said. "Half the men in the state would marry her. I think that's why she wore widow's weeds so long, to protect herself from eager suitors."

"By thunder, who'd want to marry a poor little librarian?" Cash snorted, "especially a stubborn, strait-laced gal like that one."

Josh winked. "I reckon there's a lot you don't know about Mrs. Purdy. She's really got under your skin, has she?"

"Hell, no. She's been the fly in my buttermilk since the first moment I laid eyes on her. She seems to stick to me like flypaper. Bonnie Purdy is the prim and proper lady who's trying to stop my prize fight, but I'm determined she won't."

"Ohh," the old man nodded, "why didn't you say so in my office this morning? You got your work cut out for you if you're going up against her. I think maybe you've met your match, Cash."

"We'll see." Cash put down his bourbon and strode across the floor. Bonnie was laughing and joking with some young rich dandy as they danced. "I'm cuttin' in," Cash announced.

"I don't think so," Bonnie said.

The shorter man hesitated. "Did you hear the lady? She doesn't—"

"I said I'm cuttin' in," Cash shouldered the other man out of the way and took her in his arms. He waltzed her away with the young man still protesting behind them.

"My, that was rude!"

"I'm a rude, uncouth rascal, or hadn't you heard?"

"You're causing a scene," she seethed. "People on the sidelines are whispering."

"Let them." He held her even closer.

She struggled to put space between them. "Now you really will cause talk."

"So what?" She fitted perfectly into his arms although her head was barely to his shoulder. She felt very soft and her perfume made him take several deep breaths. "I—I'm not good in a social set like this, Bonnie, I just wanted to dance with you again."

"You could have been more polite about it." She didn't want to feel complimented, but she did, knowing other women in the ballroom had been sneaking wistful glances at Cash McCalley all evening.

He grinned down at her. "It's hot in here, don't you think?"

"Yes, reckon it is. They should open more of those French doors out onto the veranda."

He looked down into her face and realized how full and soft her mouth looked. Her brown hair felt as soft as kitten fur. Her hand in his big one was small and delicate. "Why don't we go outside where it's cool?"

"I don't think—" she protested, but he was already dancing her through one of the open French doors and out onto the veranda. The moon was full and the garden smelled of roses.

"This is better," he whispered and kept dancing.

"Take me back inside this instant!" she demanded. "What would Herbert say if he knew I was out here with a rascal like you?"

"Why, doesn't he trust you?"

"Of course he does. It's you neither of us trusts."

"Bonnie, you are a lady. I always treat ladies with utmost respect." He had stopped dancing and stood looking down at her, but he didn't turn her loose.

"I've seen your choice of women," she said and tried to pull away. "I don't think you know many ladies."

"No, I don't. They might not talk to an *hombre* like me anyhow," he admitted.

"Oh, don't be modest," she snapped. "Even the governor's wife was looking at you like a hungry hound at a ham bone. I think she's hoping you'll ask her to dance."

"Let someone else dance with the old biddie. Anyway, I've been wantin' to talk to you."

"About what?" She looked up at him, eyeing him suspiciously. She had forgotten what a handsome, dashing rake he was. Her heart began to pound in a way it never had around any other man. "I—I think I'd better go inside."

He didn't let go of her. "It's cooler out here on the veranda."

"But I don't want people gossiping about me," she sputtered.

"Bonnie," and he sounded sincere, "if any man attempted to besmirch your name, I'd beat him like cornbread batter. I'd knock him clear to Mexico."

"Don't try to be gallant, you confuse me." She tried to pull away from him but he held her tightly. "I'd be impressed if I hadn't heard around Dallas that you are a rake of the first order when it comes to women."

His big hand came up and gently brushed a wisp of curl away from her face. "Folks talk, that's all."

She laughed. "I hear you're as wild and untamed as Kitty Tom. Around Dallas, they say you've left a trail of broken hearts."

"Maybe I just haven't met the right woman yet," he murmured and stood silent, looking down at her in a way that made her heart hammer. Suddenly, she was very very hot. The air seemed to crackle with electricity. The heat of his big body seemed to radiate through her clothes. She knew she ought to break away from him and scurry inside; that's what a lady should do to keep from having her reputation compromised, but she couldn't seem to pull out of his arms. She just kept looking up at him in the moonlight.

"Bonnie?" She knew he was asking permission and that she shouldn't give it. She couldn't seem to say anything, only blink and look up at that full, sensual mouth.

Then very slowly, his mouth came down on hers.

She saw the kiss coming in time to pull away, but abruptly, she didn't want to. Instead, she turned up her face and let him kiss her, tenderly, gently, thoroughly as he pulled her closer. No man had ever kissed her this way, so expertly that it made her lean into him, wanting more. Her lips parted and the tip of his tongue teased along the edge of her mouth and she gasped and clung to him, letting the kiss deepen as he held her tighter still. Every fiber of her being seemed to tense, wanting more than a kiss. Wanting more.

She forced herself to pull away. "I—I shouldn't have let you do that."

He looked puzzled and confused. "And I shouldn't have taken such liberties with a lady, but I just couldn't resist."

"This—this won't change my opposition to your bloody prize fight," she blinked in confusion, "so if you think—"

"At the moment, I don't give a damn. I'd trade a front seat in hell for one kiss from you." And he kissed her again, holding her even tighter in his strong embrace.

She gasped at the sensation of his mouth on hers, asking, no, demanding that she open her lips so his tongue could tease the inside velvet of her mouth. One of his hands came up to stroke along the swell of her breasts. She wanted that touch, wanted his hand to slip inside to caress and cup her breast. She had never felt desire before and now it terrified her. Yet she couldn't seem to pull away. She wanted him to touch her, stroke her, kiss her so deeply that she gasped for air, kiss her until she surrendered all reason and let him do anything he wanted to do with her. If he wanted to pick her up, carry her over under the shadow of the oleander bushes and make passionate love to her, she wasn't sure she would resist. She imagined the heat of his mouth on her bare breasts as the scarlet oleander blossoms fell on them both. His hands on her thighs would be gentle, yet demanding, and then. . . .

The music from inside the mansion turned from a soft waltz to a fast polka. That brought her out of her spell. She jerked away from him. "What on earth am I doing out here and with my enemy?" She broke away from him and ran back inside the mansion.

Cash stood staring after her with mixed emotions,

his virile body still pounding with excitement. He'd never been kissed like that before, innocent, yet with so much fire. He had wanted to swing her up in his arms and run away with her to where he could make passionate love to her without being interrupted. The way she had returned his kisses said she wanted it, too. Suddenly Bonnie Purdy was all woman, not a prim little librarian.

"Damn," he muttered as he leaned against a tree and lit a cigarillo with a shaky hand. This woman continued to amaze and confuse him. Well, they'd probably both be on the evening train back to Dallas tomorrow; maybe he could get her alone. She was not only desirable, but vulnerable. Seducing his biggest enemy would be like a church deacon stealing money out of the collection plate; lowdown and rotten. Cash grinned. He was looking forward to it.

Bonnie was both confused and upset as she rushed back into the ballroom. She had a sick feeling that people were staring at her, but she didn't look up.

The governor caught her as she started to exit the room. "Ah, Mrs. Purdy, I believe this is our dance?"

"Of course." She gave him her brightest smile and let him dance her around the room. Out of the corner of her eye, she saw Cash re-enter the room from the veranda. He looked upset. So that rascal wasn't used to not getting his way with women; served him right. People were correct about what they said about him. Oh, he had a way with women. Bonnie had almost been swept away with a passion she hadn't known she possessed as he held her close and kissed her.

If he had picked her up and carried her off into the

shadows of the garden to make love to her, she wasn't sure she could have said no . . . or would have wanted to. *Gracious, Bonnie, are you going loco?* No man had ever kissed her like that before, with a fire and an ardor that left her gasping. Knowing what he was and everything about him, her foolish soul had still hungered for his body pressing against hers.

Not that she knew anything about passion. After two marriages, she was still inexperienced. Hans, her doting first husband had been an old man who was impotent and barely touched her. Clint never had a chance to bed her, but minutes after the ceremony, he'd made it clear that love wasn't why he'd married her. She remembered now the pain of his humiliating remarks as he walked out of their hotel room, headed for the Black Lace Saloon. She'd been suspicious of men ever since.

"You're awfully quiet," drawled the governor.

"I—I'm just tired, that's all."

He laughed as they danced. "That was some protest your ladies put on this morning."

She looked up at him anxiously. "You don't think the legislators will change their minds about this bloody prize fight, do you?"

"Not a chance," he assured her. "Between their wives, many of whom belong to the Lone Star Ladies, and the preachers who sway a lot of votes, that promoter hasn't a chance."

"Good," she smiled and felt satisfaction. In fact, as she watched Cash standing over by the punch bowl, she almost felt sorry for him.

Cash felt glum as he poured himself a cup of bourbon punch and joined three ranchers, including Josh Farraday.

Josh said, "What happened to you? You look like a Yankee carpetbagger just took everything you own."

"It's her," he nodded toward Bonnie out on the dance floor. "I don't quite know what to make of her."

Josh peered critically at him. "You ain't fallin' for her, are you, Cash? If so, I get to be your best man."

"Don't be loco," he snapped. "She's my worst enemy; the worm in my apple. Marry? Ha! Now, Josh, be honest with me—how do you think the legislators will vote?"

The old rancher sighed and shook his head. "I'll vote for you, Cash, but I don't think many will. I think she's got you beat."

"I don't understand it," Cash grumbled. "She's smart and ornery enough to make it in a man's world; quite a woman to be just a little librarian."

"If you only knew," Josh muttered.

"What?"

"Nothin'. The lady has *savvy* all right."

"She's—she's more than that," Cash admitted as he remembered that kiss and he frowned as he watched another man cut in on the governor.

The governor strolled over to the punch bowl.

Josh said, "Governor, may I present Cash McCalley?"

The two men shook hands and the governor said, "Ah, yes, the *hombre* with the prize fight. Sorry, it ain't gonna happen, young man. The ladies and the preachers can influence more votes than you can. I got no dog in this fight, but I know a political disaster when I see one."

Cash swore under his breath. What was it with this blasted little female? He'd never met another quite like her, soft and yielding in his arms, tough as a boot heel when she needed to be. "Then Governor, would you help me contact President Cleveland? I've been thinkin' maybe I could put the fight on up in Indian Territory. That's not too far away."

"Sure," the governor nodded. "Indian Territory would probably be a good place for it."

Cash grinned. Mrs. Purdy might think she'd won and maybe she had in Texas, but Cash might surprise her with this ace in the hole.

The following evening, Cash got on the train to Dallas and ducked out of sight as he saw Bonnie Purdy coming through the station. She looked about as if wondering if he were on this train. Cash grinned to himself. "Come into my parlor said the spider to the fly. Mrs. Purdy, I'm going to seduce you tonight if I get half a chance; maybe in your own compartment that the Lone Star Ladies are paying for. As much trouble as they've caused me, it would only be poetic justice."

Bonnie looked about as she boarded, hoping Cash McCalley wasn't on this train. He'd thought he was so clever, talking to the governor about staging his bloody fight in Indian Territory. Well, the governor, being an old friend of hers, had told her about it and she'd convinced him to wire President Cleveland. The president could stop the lawless event on federally controlled land and indicated he probably would.

Somehow, she didn't feel the satisfaction she should have felt at thwarting Cash McCalley again. Then she remembered his kiss and bristled. *How dare he?* No doubt he was used to women falling into his

arms and into his bed. He'd thought he could pull
the same trick on Bonnie, but she'd show him she
wasn't dumb as a rock. Still, she remembered the kiss
and the way she had fitted perfectly into his embrace.
If he thought he'd seduce her into dropping her
protest, he had a big surprise coming. What Clint
Purdy had said to her as he left the hotel a few minutes after their wedding still stung and she never
would fall in love again; love meant trust and she did
not trust men; most especially Texans.

She went to her compartment and sighed with relief
as the train blew a warning whistle, shuddered and
began to pull out. It chugged and blew smoke as it
headed to Dallas. She watched out the window as the
landscape slipped past the window, then she settled
down to make notes about other activities the Lone
Star Ladies needed to deal with in the future. There
was just so much about Texans that offended decency
and decorum.

She couldn't keep her mind on her work; thinking
about that scoundrel. Maybe Cash was not on this
train. She didn't know whether to feel relieved or disappointed. Gracious, was she out of her mind? He was
a rogue and a threat to a quiet, orderly life. Now, Herbert, there was a settled, secure future. Make that dull,
she thought and was shocked at her thoughts. She
tried to imagine his kisses and yawned. Of course he
was respectable and Cash McCalley was wild and reckless. He made her feel like a—a slut. That both appalled and excited her.

She heard the soft chimes as the porter went
through the train announcing the first call to supper.

She wasn't all that hungry, but she was bored and
maybe there would be some interesting single lady

with whom Bonnie could share a table. She went into the dining car and the waiter seated her with a flourish.

"We're awfully crowded tonight, ma'am."

She nodded, "I understand. If there's a lady traveling alone, I'll be glad to share my table."

The waiter left and in a moment, he was back with a menu.

"Hmm," she mused, "I'll have a porterhouse steak, medium well, some fresh asparagus, a baked potato, hot rolls, a big piece of chocolate cake and some cold sweet milk."

"I'll have the same," Cash said as he slid into the seat across from her, "only I prefer buttermilk."

The waiter nodded and disappeared.

"You!" Bonnie glared at him. "I thought I made it plain to the waiter that I would share a table with a lady—"

"You did," he grinned at her. "But a silver dollar changed his mind."

"You are incorrigible."

"I don't know what that means, but I reckon you don't mean it as a compliment."

"Not hardly," she snapped.

"Well, we've got a few hours ride ahead of us, might as well be pleasant and enjoy it."

"I don't see why." She spread her napkin on her lap. "You, sir, are like grit in my scrambled eggs and I do wish you'd leave me alone."

He leaned on his elbows and winked at her. "Now you don't mean that."

"I certainly do. You are not the type of man I ever would have met if it hadn't been for your bloody business deal."

"You prefer safe, respectable men like the chicken feed salesman?"

She nodded. "I do. You are dangerous and unpredictable."

He looked at her, not smiling. "And that scares you?"

"Mr. McCalley, my ancestors fought Yankees, Indians and Mexicans for their share of Texas. As a Texan, I am not afraid of anything that crawls, walks or slithers."

"Then what are you afraid of, Bonnie? You almost run backward when I get close to you."

She felt herself flush. It was true. When this man got too close to her, it triggered such a personal reaction that it scared her. "You don't have my permission to be so personal. You are being impertinent."

"I keep forgettin' you're a librarian. You'll have to tell me what that means."

"It's an insult; look it up in the dictionary."

He merely smiled.

Was there no insulting this man enough to get him to move to another table?

The waiter brought their dinners and she concentrated on the excellent steak.

Cash watched her eat. If the truth be known, he could barely afford a meal because of his financial condition, but he was optimistic. If he could charm this woman into dropping her crusade, the boxing match would be a very profitable enterprise. *After supper,* he promised himself as he buttered a hot roll. *After supper, Mrs. Purdy, I am going to make a concentrated effort to seduce you.* He smiled, thinking the task might not be so disagreeable after all.

Chapter Twelve

They finished the excellent meal in silence.

"Now if you don't mind," Bonnie said stiffly as she stood up, "I'm going back to my compartment."

Cash came to his feet and bowed. "The pleasure has been mine, Mrs. Purdy."

"Humph!" She stuck her nose in the air and sailed out of the dining car. Once back in her compartment, she tried to concentrate on paperwork, but her mind kept drifting to the charming scoundrel. She knew what he was, knew the danger he posed, and yet, she couldn't keep him out of her thoughts. That fact unnerved her. She heard a man's boots walk past her compartment and sighed with relief. Good, he was surely back in his seat by now.

The air was too warm and close in here. She checked the little watch pinned to her crisp blouse. It had been almost an hour since dinner. And a quick glance out the window told her darkness had fallen. With that rascal back in his seat, she could chance going out on the little platform at the end of the train.

The dining car was empty as she walked through

it, wending her way to the back. Everyone on the train had settled down for the evening. Cash was probably in the club car gambling and soaking up whiskey. She opened the door on the last car and stepped out into a cool, breezy night—and almost collided with a man who was just leaving the little platform.

"Oh, excuse me, sir," she blurted and then realized it was Cash McCalley. "Oh, I thought you'd be in the club car or back in your seat by now."

"Well, that's where I was headed," he drawled, grinning down at her, "but I'll stay and keep you company."

"I'd rather you didn't," she snapped and stepped past him to hang onto the iron railing and watch the gleaming metal track slip past beneath her in the darkness.

"I'm tryin' to be polite," he said.

"You're trying to get on my good side and I'm not buying. Good night, Mr. McCalley."

He didn't seem to take the broad hint. Instead he came to stand next to her. "I almost didn't recognize you at the ball, Mrs. Purdy, you were so pretty."

She tried not to be flattered, knowing this rake could talk a dog off a meat wagon. "And before that, I was so homely?"

"Just—just plain. I mean . . . uh, I didn't expect you to be at the ball." He pulled out a silver cigarillo case. "Mind if I—?"

"Go right ahead," she said without thinking. "I like the smell of tobacco. There's something very masculine about it."

He lit the smoke and stared out at the passing landscape. "Beautiful, ain't it? No place as purty as Texas except maybe heaven."

"That's one place you may never see," she said.

"I don't care; I've seen Texas and that makes me a lucky man."

"You're pretty cheery for a man who was just defeated in Austin."

"You're that sure you've got the votes to stop the fight?" he asked.

"I am," she nodded.

"You know, lady, you're about to break me, moneywise."

"I'm sorry about that," she said, "but this is a matter of principle."

He watched her profile. She was petite and delicate in the moonlight. *Why had I ever thought her plain?* "You ain't sorry. This has become personal with you."

"Okay, so it has," she admitted. "By the way, Mr. McCalley, that's a fine-blooded stallion you own. If you really get down to your last dime, I know the owner of a big ranch who might be interested in buying the horse."

Cash shook his head. "I don't think I'll ever get that desperate. Dusty is sired by the famous Dust Devil. You know the Maverick and McBride ranch?"

"Of course. Everyone in Texas knows who they are."

"Who's the rancher who'd want my horse?"

"The owner of the Lazy S spread. Heard of it?"

He nodded. "Who hasn't? They say it's at least a hundred thousand acres. You know him?"

"The owner is well known around Shot Gun."

He smoked and thought. "I always dreamed of a big spread of my own, but haven't been too lucky. Got wiped out in the crash of '93." He tossed the smoke away and watched it hit the tracks in a shower of sparks. "If I don't pull off this fight, I'll lose what little I got saved."

"You could always go back to working as a wrangler."

"Yep, I could," he nodded. "But then I'd have to give up the dream of my own land. I'd hate to be like my Dad and Ma, worked their whole lives on someone else's place. They don't even own the little bit of land they're buried on. But then, the lot of the Scots-Irish has always been a hard one."

His sincerity touched Bonnie. "The Irish haven't had it any better," she admitted. "I'm one of a dozen kids, dirt poor. Pa lost a leg in the War, resorted to moonshining to feed us." She paused. She had never told anyone about Danny. There was no one she trusted enough. "I really am sorry I have to oppose you on this. I didn't mean to cause you financial hardship."

"Hardship?" he snorted. "Lady, much more, and I won't have a pot or a window. Not that you'd care—"

"I'm not that heartless." Without thinking, she put her hand on his arm.

"If things were different," he said gently, "and we'd met under different circumstances, who knows what would have happened?"

She felt a bit guilty. "We don't exactly travel in the same circles. If it hadn't been for this, I doubt if we would have ever met at all."

"And yet, I'm glad we did," he whispered, looking down at her.

Everything in her told her to pull back, she was standing much too close to the scoundrel; close enough to smell the shaving lotion, the scent of tobacco and suntanned skin. "We—we really ought to go inside," she said, her heart beginning to hammer uncertainly.

"Yes, we should," he murmured.

She tried to step backward, but the iron railing of the platform was behind her. In the moonlight, she looked up into his gray eyes, eyes as gray as a stormy dawn, gray as a pistol barrel. His mouth looked full and soft and she remembered the taste of it. "I—I really ought to go in," she gasped again as his big hand reached out and caught her chin, tilted her face up.

"Any time," he murmured and then he kissed her. She almost lost her balance and went off the back of the train.

"Careful," he said and caught her, pulled her to him in a strong embrace. Without meaning to, she slipped her arms around his neck and let him kiss her again. His neck under her fingers felt strong and corded; his shoulders were broad and muscular. His lips caressed hers as she gasped for air.

"I—I ought to go in," she whispered again, but she did not move.

"Yes, you should," he murmured and his tongue caressed her lips and asked for entrance. She couldn't stop herself from opening her mouth and letting his tongue tease past her lips even as his hand stroked her throat. She must make him stop that, she thought, but it felt so good, especially now that his fingers were exploring inside her blouse and the top of her corset cover. She knew she ought to protest, slap his face and flee, but it was almost as if she were hypnotized. She could not move except to lean into his powerful, virile frame and let him embrace her tightly.

"Cash, don't," she gasped.

"You really mean that?" He didn't stop what he was doing with his hand.

A long, tense moment and she closed her eyes, knowing she should protest again. Convention demanded it. "Cash, don't . . . don't stop," she murmured as his hand cupped her breast.

"I won't," he said and stroked inside her blouse, fingering her nipple.

Her knees seemed so weak, she thought they would go out from under her, but Cash held her up. Texas landscape rushed past them in the darkness, but she was only aware of the lips and the hands of this man and her own need; the need no other man had ever aroused in her.

Now his lips kissed her face, her ear, then trailed down her throat as he held her close. She arched her back, wanting him to put his hot, wanton mouth on her breast, but it would have been difficult without undressing her on the platform. "I—I'm not going to sell out the Lone Star Ladies," she murmured desperately.

"I'm not asking you to, darlin'," he whispered against her throat and then kissed her again. "I'm just wantin' to love you. You want it, I know you do. I want it, too."

His big hand slipped down her side, now pulling her skirt up an inch at a time until she felt his hand touching her lace drawers.

She felt a rush of heat, wanting him to touch and stroke her, wanting . . . *was she out of her mind?* The president of the Lone Star Ladies letting herself be pawed by this worthless scoundrel on the platform of a train where everyone they passed could see them? Never mind that the landscape looked dark and deserted.

It took all the will power she possessed to break away from him. "No!" she protested and pulled out of his arms, opened the door, fled back inside the car and down the aisle to her compartment.

Cash stood staring after her, aroused and confused. He didn't know whether to be angry with her or himself. His manhood was so engorged, it throbbed with need. He couldn't remember ever wanting a woman as badly as he had wanted this one just now. He had set out to seduce the lady and she'd foiled his attempt just when it seemed about to happen. God, how he wanted her. Maybe because the lady was so unattainable for a low-class saddle tramp like himself.

Cursing, he adjusted his clothing and took a deep breath before re-entering the car. This had been his best chance to seduce and enchant the prim widow and he'd muffed it. He didn't usually lose when he was dealing with women. He'd have other chances in Dallas, maybe, but he was running out of time. He could only stall his creditors awhile and then his house of cards and debt would tumble down around his boots.

He walked back through the swaying cars, paused at Bonnie's door. If he could just get inside . . .

He pictured the comfortable bed in her compartment, plenty of room for some wild, reckless passion. He knocked. "Bonnie, I'm sorry. If you'd let me in so we could talk—"

"Go away!" she shouted. "Or I will call for the conductor to throw you off this train at the next stop."

She sounded as if she meant it. With a sigh, he returned to his hard, stiff seat in the coach. He dropped off to sleep to the swaying of the train and dreamed he and Bonnie were once again on the platform and they were naked in the darkness, the breeze cooling their hot bodies. Her hair had come loose and blew about them both as he embraced her. Her petite body felt intensely warm and he lifted her so that he could taste her breasts. She moaned and threw her head back, letting him explore her naked skin with his lips. Then he pinned her against the swaying car and thrust up into her again and again with her moaning and begging for more and more and more. . . .

He jerked awake and realized it was only a dream and he was hot and sweaty in his miserable seat. Damn her anyhow. She lay in a comfortable bed, no doubt sleeping soundly. He sighed, got up and went to the club car, but there was no action there. That girl, that damned girl. It wasn't enough that she was wrecking his money-making plan, now she had invaded his thoughts and made him hunger for her, wanting her to beg for him to mount her again and again, digging her nails into his broad, muscular back and plunge deeper still.

He snorted wryly. "You fool! The president of the Lone Star Ladies For Decency and Decorum is not about to play the whore, certainly not for her enemy."

He spent the rest of the night sleepless and felt exhausted and out of sorts when the conductor came through the car yelling, "Dallas! We're coming to Dallas! Dallas!"

He hadn't even had time for breakfast. Well, Fifi would probably be waiting at the station and she'd scramble him some eggs.

* * *

"Dallas! Dallas! Coming into Dallas!" Bonnie heard the conductor going through the train. Not that she was asleep. She'd had a terrible night, tossing and turning, wishing she had invited Cash McCalley in. *Was she loco?* That man had tried to take her right out there in the open on the platform of that last car. There was no telling what he would have done if she'd let him into her compartment.

She pictured that possibility in her mind, imagining the muscular, broad-shouldered man lying on her bed naked. A tremor went through her slender frame. He was a stallion of a man, all right, and if she let him make love to her, it might be a thrill she had never known. "Don't be stupid, Bonnie," she scolded herself, "he's only trying to sway you into dropping your opposition to his damned boxing match. You've seen the kind of wild slut he prefers."

She thought about Fifi as she dressed quickly. No doubt Fifi really knew how to please a man and Bonnie hadn't a clue. She bet Cash McCalley knew enough for both of them. In her mind, she was back on the platform in the darkness and he kissed and fondled her until she was breathless and wanting more. Oh, this was a dangerous rascal, all right, and she'd better beware of him.

Now, Herbert Snodgrass, there was a solid citizen, a man she could trust, not dangerous at all. Not only not dangerous, she sighed with regret, he was downright dull. She tried to imagine herself in bed with Herbert and sighed again. She imagined that would be dull, too.

"Bonnie, be sensible. You're thinking like an absolute tart!" She chided herself and tried to wipe Cash McCalley from her thoughts. She had always been so practical and sensible, except when she'd married Clint Purdy and then found out he was only after—

"Dallas!" Out in the hall, the conductor came through the cars again, "Dallas! Next stop, Dallas!"

Bonnie opened her door and signaled a porter walking through, tipped him to make sure her luggage got taken off, then she went out into the car. The train slowed and whistled. Looking out a dusty window, she saw the first outline of buildings. Cash stood in the aisle near the door with his one valise and Bonnie studiously ignored him.

"Good mornin'," he nodded and smiled.

She didn't answer. This man could charm a bird out of a tree. She must forget the taste of his kiss and think about the savage boxing match. She could not let him win. This had become personal.

The train whistled and slowed, chugging into the station. She leaned to look out the window. Herbert stood on the platform, waiting. He looked a bit silly in his bowler hat and spats. Cash McCalley probably wouldn't be caught dead in a dudish outfit like that. At least, with Herbert meeting her, she wouldn't need to deal with Cash as she got her luggage and left. She also spotted Fifi LaFemme in the crowd, waiting. The saloon girl wore an ornate and too-tight red dress that left nothing to the imagination. No doubt Fifi would take care of Cash's need this morning. Somehow the thought annoyed Bonnie.

They pulled into the station, the smokestack blowing black soot. When the engineer hit the brakes, the sudden stop threw her against the big man and he smiled down at her and winked.

Bonnie righted herself with a snort, stuck her nose

in the air in case Cash McCalley tried to accost her again and got off the train.

Herbert rushed to meet her, sniffing and wiping his nose. "Bonnie, dear, I'm so glad to see you!"

"Herbert, I really wasn't expecting you to meet me. I thought you'd be on your Western route today."

He attempted to kiss her but she turned her head and got a wet, sloppy smack on the cheek. "And miss meeting my fiancée? Not a chance." His expression changed as he saw Cash coming off the train. "Oh, I see that thug was on the train. Did he make a nuisance of himself?"

"Nuisance?" She felt the blood rush to her face as she remembered Cash's fevered kisses. "He—he was trying to convince the legislators, but without much luck."

Herbert laughed. "No wonder. That rogue didn't have any idea who he was going up against, I'll bet."

"No, he doesn't know." *Or did he?* "At least, I don't think so. Let's find my luggage and get out of here."

"Oh, Cash, honey," Bonnie heard the squeal of delight behind her and glanced back over her shoulder in time to see Fifi throwing herself into Cash's arms for a passionate kiss. Bonnie remembered the taste of those kisses and was annoyed. "Look at that!" she said to her escort.

"Disgusting!" Herbert made a wry face. "Honestly, have they no shame?"

Shame? That made Bonnie remember those hot kisses on the back of the train. Cash could make a woman forget propriety and everything but his embrace. "Uh, Herbert, I've had no breakfast. Let's go directly to the hotel, shall we?"

Herbert sniffed and frowned, looking back over his

shoulder. "Honestly, the way those two are acting, I'll bet I know what he's getting for breakfast."

"Why, Herbert." She was outraged but she didn't know why.

"Oh, I'm so sorry, Bonnie dear. Please forgive me. I forgot I was in the presence of a lady."

He wouldn't have thought "lady" if he'd seen her last night with the randy rascal kissing Bonnie and running his hands inside her clothing.

"Are you all right, my dear? Your face has gone beet red."

"It—it's the heat," she fanned herself with her glove, thankful Herbert couldn't read her thoughts. *I'll bet I know what he's getting for breakfast.* Bonnie imagined Fifi naked on a table with Cash licking scrambled eggs off her bare belly, or maybe maple syrup; licking and licking while she moaned and writhed.

She made a soft, shuddering sigh, imagining it was her.

"Bonnie, what is wrong with you? You act like you're in a trance." Herbert sniffed in complaint as he put her luggage in the buggy and helped her up into the seat.

"Uh, nothing, just thinking of the next action the Lone Star Ladies need to take," she mumbled as she watched Cash and Fifi walking out to their buggy. He lifted the blonde up into the seat and slapped her round rear as he did so.

"Oh, Cash," she squealed with delight, "you're just so naughty! You shouldn't do that in public."

"I know, but I wanted to." He looked over at Bonnie as if to see whether she was watching and smirked as he climbed up into his buggy and took the reins.

Herbert frowned. "Why on earth is that rascal looking at you like that?"

"I haven't the least idea." Bonnie lied and gritted her teeth as she watched Fifi put her hand in Cash's lap and stroke there.

"Outrageous! Just outrageous what that tramp is doing and in public, too!" Herbert fumed. "She could at least wait until she got him into a bed somewhere."

"Isn't that the truth?" Bonnie said, and was furious with Cash because he seemed to be enjoying it. "Let's go, dear. We'll have breakfast at the hotel."

Herbert snapped the reins and they drove away. When Bonnie craned her neck to look back, she saw Fifi sitting so close to Cash, he had his arm around her and she still had her hand in his lap. Bonnie had a terrible urge to hit someone, whether it be the giggling blond tramp or Cash McCalley, she wasn't quite sure. That urge shocked her. Bonnie had never been a violent person. Of course dealing with Cash McCalley could drive a saint to drink.

They rode to the hotel and Bonnie checked in. "You saved the same room for me?"

"We'd planned to give you our best suite," said the balding clerk.

"No," she shook her head. "I want the room I had before, 203B."

"It's not nearly so nice as the suite," said the clerk, puzzled.

"But I want it anyway." She held out her hand for the key.

The clerk shrugged and handed it over.

"Honestly, Bonnie," Herbert said as they left the desk, "they were trying to do you a favor; give you a suite. Why would you argue over it?"

She dare not tell him about Cash's room next door and the keyhole between. "I—I just got used to that room, good view." That certainly was no lie. She tried not to flush as she remembered Cash walking around the wash bowl. Better than a good view; a *great* view.

She left her luggage for the bellhop to deal with and she and Herbert went into the dining room.

"Well," Herbert sniffed as they settled into their chairs, "what happened in Austin?"

"Nothing much," Bonnie said and picked up her menu.

"Oh?" He leaned toward her.

Could he guess how stupidly she had behaved? "Well, actually, it was a successful trip. I attended the governor's ball and influenced him and a bunch of the legislators to vote no."

He grinned. "Knowing who you are, they could hardly turn you down."

She resented his smugness. "That didn't come into play. I simply reminded them all how much influence the ministers and respectable women of this state had over male voters."

"I wish I'd been there to see that rascal's face when he realized he'd lost." Herbert smirked.

"Gracious, I'm feeling a little guilty about that," Bonnie admitted. "He's got everything he owns sunk in this fight. He'll be broke if it doesn't happen."

"So what?" Herbert sniffed. "No doubt that Fifi LaFemme will help him out financially. Her place is packed every night."

She stared at him a long moment over her menu. "Now how would you know that, Herbert?"

He seemed to choke and ran his finger around his collar as if it were too tight. "Honestly, that's what some of the men say. They say she dances that cancan and kicks so high, she shows her drawers."

In her mind, she saw Fifi wiggling her rounded bottom on the stage with Cash McCalley in the front row cheering her on. Of course Fifi would help Cash so he wouldn't lose everything. No doubt he did stud service to pay her back. That thought really annoyed Bonnie. "Let's order, Herbert. I'm very tired and would like to get some rest."

The waiter came to their table just then. Besides coffee and juice, she ordered steak and scrambled eggs with big fluffy biscuits, grits and gravy. Herbert ordered hot tea and a bowl of oatmeal which he picked at like a sparrow.

Bonnie sighed. No Texas male would be caught dead drinking hot tea and oatmeal was for toddlers. She couldn't help but think of Cash and his love of food. The man ate with gusto. In fact, Cash had a big appetite for everything—food, wine, women. At this very minute, he might be licking syrup or breakfast jam off Fifi's breasts while she writhed and squealed under him.

"Bonnie, why are you frowning?"

"What?" she started. "I—I'm just tired, that's all." She sipped her coffee, leaned back in her chair and tried not to wonder if Cash was enjoying his breakfast.

Fifi insisted on taking Cash back to her little apartment. "I really missed you!" She giggled as she made a pot of coffee and got out her skillet. "How do you want your eggs?"

"Over easy and plenty of ham," he settled into a chair and tried to concentrate on her. He wished Fifi wouldn't giggle, it really got on his nerves. Funny, it never used to bother him. His mind kept returning to last night on that train and the way the petite widow had felt in his arms. He'd almost forgotten he was only trying to seduce Bonnie so she'd back off her opposition; he had wanted her in a way he hadn't wanted a woman in a long, long time.

"Cash, honey, you're awfully quiet." Fifi sliced ham and looked at him.

"Didn't mean to be," he smiled, afraid the guilt might show on his face. He didn't want Fifi taking that big knife to his tender parts if she had any hint what he was thinking.

She finished cooking, handed him a plate and sat down, began to eat. Cash watched her. Why had he never noticed how Fifi wolfed her food and wiped her mouth on the back of her hand? Fifi ate like a hungry hog. He pictured a daintier, classier woman wiping her pretty mouth on a linen napkin.

"Cash, honey, whatcha thinkin'?" She wiped her mouth on the back of her hand again.

He winced. "Nothin'. I'm just eatin', that's all."

"What happened in Austin?" She talked with her mouth full. "You gonna be able to swing this fight?"

Why had he never noticed how coarse and crude Fifi was? "I doubt it," he sighed and started eating. Fifi wasn't much of a cook, either. He wondered if Bonnie was. "I think the little widow got to the legislators before I did, but I've got an ace in the hole."

"Oh? You're smart, Cash."

"By thunder, I don't feel very smart when I'm dealin' with Mrs. Purdy," he complained. "She's not only stubborn as a pack mule, she seems extra smart for a woman."

"And men don't like smart women, do they?" She gulped coffee and burped loudly.

"Well, I reckon they do if you want smart young'uns," he said.

"Well, you ain't wanting kids, are you, Cash?"

"Hell, no." In his mind, he saw half a dozen children playing around a ranch fireplace while he sat in an easy chair listening to a woman bustling about the kitchen. He smiled. The woman in his vision was a petite brunette.

"Whatcha smiling about?"

"Nothin'." He started and returned to his food. "If nothin' else, I'm hopin' I can move the boxin' match to Indian Territory. I talked to the governor about it. Maybe President Cleveland will step in and okay it."

"Wow! The president?"

He nodded. "That's what it would take to hold it on Indian lands. Now if I can just keep Bonnie from findin' out about it."

Fifi frowned. "You call her Bonnie?"

"Well, it's her name. Actually, it's Bluebonnet. Josh Farraday seemed to know something about her."

"Stupid name," she snorted and stuffed her mouth full.

"No true Texan would think that. It's a pretty flower. Anyway, it kinda suits her since she's got big blue eyes."

Fifi frowned again. "You're noticin' her eyes now?"

He had to change the subject. "Nothin' in a name. What's your real name, honey?"

"Gladys Stumpt. I thought you knew that. Is that Purdy woman ever going home?"

"I have no idea," he shrugged. "The Shot Gun library ain't open right now so she's got plenty of time to meddle in my business. Now quit askin' dumb questions and let me eat in peace."

She nodded and stuffed her mouth full. It occurred to him that Fifi aka Gladys never asked smart questions. He was past bored with her.

Cash finished his food and settled back for a cigarillo with another cup of coffee. It tasted burnt. Fifi might be great in bed, but he should have gone to the hotel for breakfast. He wondered if Bonnie Purdy had gone back to the hotel with that pompous chicken feed salesman. Herbert Snodgrass had looked like he was dressed for a funeral. Cash had a sudden urge to poke the oh-so-respectable businessman in the mouth. Bonnie had to be pretty naive not to see what Herbert really was.

"You ain't saying much," Fifi complained.

"I'm sorry. I'm tired, that's all."

She gave him a big smile. "Then let's go to bed. I been missing you like crazy." She leaned over and gave him a big kiss. Normally this would have been his signal to crush out his smoke, pick Fifi up, carry her to the bed and enjoy a few minutes of sex so hot it would cause the springs to squeak and the bed to fall down. He tried to remember Fifi in bed with him kissing her naked body as he had so many times in the past, but all he could see in his mind were the big blue eyes of a certain petite widow.

"Cash, are you sick or didn't you hear what I just said?"

"What?" He was jolted out of his thoughts.

"I said, let's get on with the loving."

He stood up half-heartedly.

"Well, you don't look too interested."

He wasn't, which astounded him because he always

had a big appetite when it came to loving, but right now, the thought didn't even make his heart beat faster. "Look, Fifi, I'm sorry, but I'm preoccupied right now."

"With her?" The blonde sneered.

Why have I never noticed how much face paint the tart wore? Bonnie's face was shiny clean with freckles across the nose. "Of course not, it's this boxin' thing. You know everything I got is tied up in this. I got plannin' to do and people to see, so I'd better go."

"Go? You just got here. Besides, if you need money, I'll—"

"No, no Texan would take money off a woman 'less he was married to her." He reached for his Stetson.

She smiled. "Marriage? Now I wouldn't say no to that." She attempted to put her arms around his neck, but he shook her off.

"Sorry, Fifi, I ain't very good company today. We'll get together later. Oh, get me an apple and wrap up some of that ham for the cat, will you?"

"Cat?"

"Didn't I tell you I was feedin' a stray cat?"

She shrugged. "Oughta shoot strays. I got no use for pets."

"Gimme some ham and an apple for my horse anyway."

She bustled about in her kitchen, handed it to him. "When we gonna get together?" she persisted.

"Later." He took the stuff and dismissed her with a wave of his hand. "I got to see how the boxers are doin'. That damned lion gets loose again, he may eat up someone's little baby and that's not very good publicity. Why, Bonnie would probably—"

"Bonnie! Bonnie! Bonnie!" she raged, "can't you get that prim little bitch off your mind?"

"Don't call her that, Fifi. She's a lady."

"And I ain't?"

"I didn't mean it that way—"

"Yeah, I know what you meant. You're smitten with that prissy little thing when you used to think I was just great."

"You're wrong, honey," he protested. "Why, that wench is the thorn in my paw and the worm in my apple and has been since the day I laid eyes on her. I have to think about ways to outdo her because she's so damned smart and can out-think most men—"

"You didn't used to care about smart," Fifi whined. "Now it's important."

"Look, this ain't gettin' us anywhere; we'll fight over this bone later. I got to get to the telegraph and see if there's been any word. I'll see you later." He grabbed up his luggage and turned to leave.

"Where ya going? I thought you was gonna stay with me?" She tried to block his path.

"The hotel. I got thinkin' and plannin' to do."

"You could stay with me for free."

"I'm much obliged, Fifi, but no, I think I'll be more comfortable at the hotel."

"She's at the hotel," Fifi snarled.

"So are a hundred other folks. That don't make me no never-mind. It ain't as if she's offerin' to let me share her bed—"

"And that's a challenge, ain't it? A woman that just doesn't fall on her back for you?"

"Fifi, this is loco."

"I don't think so. A gal senses stuff like this, Cash."

"Well, you're barkin' up the wrong tree. I got to go." He brushed past her and paused in the doorway. "You coming to see me dance tonight, ain'tcha?"

"No, I don't know, maybe. I got things to do. Adios." He went out the door and down to the street. Funny, he used to like spending time with Fifi. Now she just seemed bad-tempered and stupid.

He drove Fifi's buggy back to the livery stable, got the groom to saddle up Dusty. The stallion nuzzled through Cash's pockets, knowing there'd be an apple for him.

"You're a good horse," Cash patted the stallion and fed him the apple. "Wish I could afford some fine mares for you like they probably got on that big Lazy S spread." He thought wistfully of the ranch he dreamed of and would probably never own because of that damned stubborn woman.

Now he mounted up and rode out to the challenger's training camp. Fitzsimmons saw him coming and came down out of the ring. The lion yawned and padded over to lie down next to them in the sawdust. "Faith and begorrah, what happened in Austin?"

"I don't know yet." Cash looked around. There didn't seem to be any reporters or curious citizens around. "Folks losin' interest?"

The Irishman took off his boxing gloves and nodded. "Too much time has passed. Folks beginnin' to think that little Mrs. Purdy has you buffaloed."

That annoyed Cash. "I'll beat her yet, you'll see."

"Then you better think of something soon. I can't run a training camp on no money and neither can Corbett."

Cash winced. "I'll see what I can do." He got up to

leave. "Maybe not in Texas, but we'll put the fight on some place; you got my word on that."

Fitzsimmons nodded. "Aye, I still got faith in you, Cash, but I think everyone else is losing it."

"I got several other ideas," Cash said and started out of the barn. The lion yawned and closed his eyes. What a gentle big cat.

Cat. That made him think of John L. Cash left the training camp and rode leisurely to the railroad station with his little package of ham. When he went into the telegraph office, the boy looked up. "She's already been here and fed the cat."

"That's *my* cat," Cash was annoyed.

"Maybe so," nodded the skinny boy, "but you know, he'll almost let her touch him now."

"He's not a lady's pet," Cash protested. "She's got a lot of nerve tryin' to tame my cat."

"She says she's taking him home with her when she finally goes."

"I don't give a damn what she says, she ain't gonna tame old John L. He's like me; wild and free and likes it that way."

"If you say so, Mr. McCalley. Oh, here, a telegram just came for you."

"Why didn't you say so?" Cash yanked it out of the boy's hand. It was from Josh Farraday.

Dear Cash. Stop. Sorry to tell you the legislature met this morning in emergency session. Stop. Under pressure, the men decided you can't have your boxing match anywhere in Texas. Stop. I'll try to connect with the president for you. Stop.

"By thunder!" Cash crumpled up the paper and threw it down, swearing.

"Bad news?" asked the boy.

"Yeah, Wilbur, that prissy woman has outfoxed me again. I don't know what it's gonna take to defeat her and send her home. Now I got to go try to raise some money from the businessmen in this town." He turned and walked off the platform, still swearing.

Wilbur watched him go. After the promoter was out of sight, he stepped around the desk and picked up the crumpled telegram, smoothed it out. He'd take it to Mrs. Purdy; she'd give him a silver dollar for passing on this information. That lady might be prissy but Cash McCalley was right about one thing; she was smart and could outfox anybody. Everyone knew the promoter's reputation, but the lady seemed to be out-witting him at every turn. He smiled as he took off running toward the hotel.

Chapter Thirteen

Cash had changed his mind about dealing with the businessmen this morning and rode back to the hotel, dismounted and turned his stallion over to the stable-boy. He was checking in when he saw the telegraph boy coming down the stairs. The boy seemed to spot him, tried to sneak away, but Cash chased him down. "Wilbur, what's goin' on? Why you runnin'?"

The skinny kid turned pale. "I—I was just deliverin' a telegram."

Cash had him by the shirt. "So why'd you run from me?"

"I—I can't help it, Mr. McCalley, she pays me to let her know what's in your telegrams."

"What? By thunder, that sneaky little—!" Why had he been so stupid that he hadn't thought Bonnie could resort to tricks as underhanded as Cash could? So this was why she was always one step ahead of him. "From now on, Wilbur, I'll give you two dollars not to tell her what's in my wires. Better yet, I'll pay you to make up fake telegrams if I need them."

"That's against the law, sir."

"So is giving my messages to a third party. What'd you just take her?"

The boy hesitated. "She knows the governor ain't gonna let you have your fight in Texas and I took her a telegram to her from the governor. You—you can't have your fight in Indian Territory, either."

"What?"

"It's the truth," Wilbur nodded. "She got the governor to contact the president. You ain't gonna be allowed to put on your fight in Indian Territory."

"I'll be damned." Cash took off his Stetson, ran his hand through his curly dark hair. He had a mental image of turning the lady over his knee and spanking her like a naughty child. She'd probably bite him on the leg while he was doing it. "I reckon I've really underestimated the lady. Now what am I gonna do?"

"I'm real sorry, Mr. McCalley." The boy seemed only too happy to flee.

Cash watched him go. So now Bonnie knew about everything and the governor had helped her. Cash couldn't figure out how a little librarian could wield so much influence. It was the organization she belonged to, he decided. The Lone Star Ladies must swing a wide rope; more powerful than he had realized.

She was in this hotel somewhere. He had an urge to hunt her down and let her know he'd found out about the telegrams and she wasn't so smart after all.

From her window, Bonnie had seen Cash riding up to the hotel. It seemed a long time before she heard his boots coming down the hall and the sound of his key in the lock.

She knelt and looked through the keyhole. He looked tired and defeated as he flopped down in a chair. She felt shame, knowing she was to blame for his failure.

Are you loco? she scolded herself as she stood up and stuffed a hankie back in the keyhole. Boxing is a bloody, brutal sport that will bring the worst kind of thugs, prostitutes, gamblers, and pickpockets to town to prey on innocent and naive citizens.

Prostitutes and saloon girls. That made her think of Fifi. She gritted her teeth. Of course Cash looked like he'd been dragged through a knothole backward; he'd probably been bouncing on a mattress with that blonde for the last several hours. The thought so disgusted her that she renewed her vow to keep the boxing match from happening. She picked up the telegram the skinny kid had brought her.

Dear Bonnie. Stop. I have just heard from President Cleveland. Stop. He assures me that he will not allow the boxing match to take place on an Indian reservation in Oklahoma Territory. Stop. Hope to see you at the big ranch barbecue next fall. Stop. Your good friend, Charles A. Culberson, governor of Texas.

She leaned back in her chair and smiled. It might be awhile before Cash McCalley got the bad news from any friends he might have at the state capital. There would be no pickpockets, gamblers and prostitutes gathering north of the Red River for this match. Why should she care so much? She told herself she was doing the whole country a favor because boxing should be outlawed everywhere because of its brutality. Hadn't it killed her brother? Her opposition had nothing to do with a personal conflict with that man.

He was such an unprincipled rake. She remembered his embrace on the back of that train and then thought of him in the arms of that blonde. It so upset her, Bonnie stood up and began to pace. She'd almost made a fool of herself over a sleazy promoter who cared nothing for her. Like Clint Purdy before him, Cash was only interested in taking advantage of her and she'd almost fallen for it. Why, he was as crooked as a dog's hind leg.

She should check out of the hotel and return to Shot Gun. Her job as a concerned citizen was done in preventing that horrible fight here in Dallas or anywhere in Texas. From now on, the Ministers' Association and the local Lone Star Ladies could handle it. Then all that was left to do was maybe catch that stray cat and take it home with her.

She heard Cash leave his room late in the afternoon. Probably headed to a saloon or over to see that blonde. Bonnie went to the window and looked out to see him riding away. Now she, too, went downstairs, had an early supper and gathered scraps to feed the cat. It wouldn't be dark for several hours so she drove to call on Reverend Tubbs.

He ushered her into his office and offered a chair. "Mrs. Purdy, so glad to see you. How goes our crusade?"

She took the chair, smiled with satisfaction. "Well, Cash McCalley can't find a place in Texas or the Indian Territory to hold it, so I reckon he'll give up now."

"Hmm." The reverend rubbed his multiple chins. "Not like a Texan to give up easy."

"No," Bonnie shook her head, "but I don't know where else he can go with it."

The fat man leaned back in his chair and thought a long moment. "Well, there is one place I can think of that isn't so far away, a place full of gambling and scandalous happenings. Hot Springs, Arkansas."

"Now how would you know that?" Bonnie gave him a quizzical look.

His plump face turned brick red. "That's—that's what some of my parish tells me. I wouldn't know myself."

Bonnie considered. Even she had heard about the wild, wide-open resort town of Hot Springs. "I'm sorry, Reverend, but I think I've done all I can do. I need to get back to Shot Gun. Bill needs some help and I've been gone longer than I intended."

"And all decent people are obliged to you," he said.

Bonnie thought a minute. "I believe Arkansas has a chapter of the Ladies For Decency and Decorum and you could alert the ministers' alliance there. Besides, Hot Springs might not even occur to him."

"That's true." Reverend Tubbs stood up. "Well, I'm glad you were here when we needed you to help protect Dallas, Mrs. Purdy. Have a safe trip home."

"Thank you," she nodded as she walked toward the door. "And thanks for your help. It's good to know the civilized people of Texas can count on good people like you."

"Blessings on you." He walked her to the door.

She got in her rented buggy and drove to the train station, fed the cat. It almost got close enough to touch, but not quite.

"Gracious, Kitty Tom, you're running out of time," she admonished the orange stray as she turned toward the ticket office. "I'll be leaving tomorrow or the next day, so you'll have to choose whether you want to live this wild, vagabond life or go home with me where there's security and people to love you."

The big cat just stared at her.

Bonnie shrugged and went into the station. "Wilbur, I'll want a ticket to return to Shot Gun."

The skinny kid was just reading a telegram coming in over the wire. He grinned. "Cash will be glad to hear you're leaving town."

"I have no doubt about that." She snapped. "What's that telegram just coming in?"

"It's not for you, Mrs. Purdy. It's for Cash."

"Hand it over," she demanded.

The boy hesitated.

"Let me guess," she said in a grim tone. "He's now paying you not to let me see his telegrams."

Wilbur turned scarlet.

"I thought so," she nodded. "Here's five dollars to let me read it. The rascal doesn't have to know."

The boy hesitated again, then handed it over. "Just don't tell anyone."

"I won't." She read it quickly.

Dear Cash. Stop. The governor will be in Hot Springs late this week and you can talk to him and the city council. Your boxing match sounds like something Arkansas would welcome. Stop. Your friend, Ace Johnson.

So he'd been one step ahead of her.

"That rascal," she said, "he's crooked as a snake. I should have known he wasn't ready to give up." She handed the wire back to the boy. "Now you can collect from Cash McCalley, too, just don't tell him I read it."

"Don't worry, I won't." The boy looked relieved. "You still want that ticket to Shot Gun?"

She shook her head. "I've got to at least alert Reverend Tubbs and the Arkansas Ladies before I leave town. They'll need all the help they can get against an unprincipled rascal like Cash McCalley."

Odd, she felt a little excitement at not leaving Dallas after all . . . or maybe it was just that she was so annoyed with the rake for attempting to seduce her when all he really wanted was to keep her from fighting his boxing deal. He'd tried to play her for a fool and that annoyed Bonnie more than ever to think she'd weakened and let him kiss her on the train back from Austin. *How could she have been so stupid?*

She drove directly to the Reverend Tubbs' home. He was eating supper when she arrived and was ushered into the dining room. "Won't you join me, Mrs. Purdy?"

"Do keep your seat," she shook her head and motioned him back to his chair. "I just wanted you to alert the clergy in Hot Springs that Cash McCalley will definitely try to move the bloody boxing match there."

The fat man paused with half a chicken at his mouth. "What? How do you know?"

"Never mind how I got my information." She was ashamed at how unprincipled she'd become. Gracious, but one had to fight fire with fire. "I will alert the Arkansas Ladies For Decency and Decorum and ask our governor to wire the governor of Arkansas."

"Do you think we ought to be meddling in another state's business?" He wiped his mouth.

"We have to stop people like Cash McCalley," she

declared, "and we are our brother's keeper." Of course her motives were of this highest caliber and had nothing to do with her feelings toward the slick promoter, she assured herself.

"Well, then, I'll alert the ministers. Will you help organize?" He gobbled the chicken.

She hesitated. "Can't someone else take over? I was planning on returning to Shot Gun."

"But this is so important. Shall we let sin win?"

Sin. It's sin we're agin. Sin meant Cash McCalley and his poker and drinking, Fifi LaFemme with her rounded bottom showing her drawers while Cash grinned and yelled for more. "You're right, Reverend; it's the principle of the thing."

"Spoken like a true member of proper society. You are indeed a paragon of virtue, Mrs. Purdy."

She didn't feel like a paragon of virtue. If the reverend had seen her in that hot embrace with the charming Cash, her reputation would have been in tatters. She felt like a big hypocrite and it was all that gambler's fault. Damn that rake anyhow. "You're right, Reverend Tubbs, Cash McCalley must be defeated."

He wiped his greasy mouth on his napkin. "Good. We just may have to go to Hot Springs to lead the protest."

"Let's hope not," Bonnie said and stood up.

He got up and ushered her to the door. "You'll at least delay leaving Dallas for a day or two then?"

"I reckon I'll have to." She was reluctant to spend any more time in the same hotel or even see Cash McCalley. He'd played her for such a fool.

"We'll stay in touch." He walked her out to her buggy.

It was almost dusk when she drove to the train station. An older man she'd never seen was handling tickets and telegrams.

"Where's Wilbur?" she asked.

"He's gone to deliver a telegram to Cash McCalley," the older man said. "Can I help you, lady?"

Gone to tell Cash he might be able to put on his boxing match in Hot Springs, Bonnie thought. "Yes, I need to send a telegram to Arkansas."

He handed her a pencil and paper.

Now who was the president of the Arkansas chapter? Oh, yes, Gertrude Potts. They'd met once.

Bonnie wrote:

Dear Gertrude: Stop. As president of the Lone Star Ladies For Decency and Decorum, I feel it is my duty to alert you to some questionable debauchery about to descend on your town. Stop. Your local ministers' alliance will be contacting you. Stop. I may be coming to give you and your ladies some moral support. Stop. Best, Bonnie Purdy, Texas President.

She handed it over to the telegrapher and he read it.

"Debauchery?" he asked, a little too interested.

Men. They were all alike when it came to naughty fun. "Never mind. If you get a reply, I'll be at the Cattlemen's Hotel." She turned and left the station.

Later that evening, she had settled herself in a comfortable chair to read as she heard booted footsteps coming down the hall. Then she heard the sound of a key in the lock next door. She tiptoed over and knelt to peer through the keyhole. Cash looked very pleased with himself. He grinned and hummed a couple of bars of "Ta Ra Ra Boom De Ay."

That annoyed Bonnie. Of course he was in a great mood. Besides the fact that he'd probably just heard that Hot Springs might welcome him and his bloody boxing match, he'd probably been bouncing on Fifi's mattress all afternoon. The thought made her furious. And only a short time ago, he'd been charming her on the back of a train and she'd been stupid enough to almost fall for it. "Bonnie, you're such a fool. He'll do anything to get you to drop your opposition, even seduce you and you know it. Gracious, what a scheming, unprincipled rascal!"

She stuffed the hankie back into the keyhole and thought about events. She didn't really want to go to Arkansas, she needed to go home. On the other hand, she hated to see Cash McCalley win after all. It wasn't personal, she assured herself, it was for the good of the whole uncivilized male population that he go down to defeat.

She spent a sleepless night and had barely dozed off when the light tap came at her door. "Room service."

She grabbed a robe, padded to the door barefooted, barely opened it to accept her tray and tried to blink awake as she ate. What would today bring?

She needn't have asked. She was barely dressed when Wilbur rapped on the door with a telegram. "I presume you've already given a copy to Mr. Mc-Calley?"

The boy turned brick red. "Uh—"

"Never mind." She took the telegram and slammed the door, settled down to read it.

Dear Mrs. Purdy. Stop. Yes, we have just been alerted by the ministers about what terrible, sinful event is planned for Hot Springs. Stop. We need help here from someone who knows how to organize. Stop. Would you please accompany Reverend Tubbs? Stop. Best, Gertrude Potts, President, Arkansas Ladies For Decency and Decorum.

She didn't really want to go there or have to keep dealing with Cash McCalley. She got dressed, went to see the fat preacher.

"Ah, dear lady," he ushered her into his office at the church. "I, too, have had a telegram. It appears we will have to journey to Hot Springs to help our brothers and sisters struggle with sin."

Struggle with sin. Once more she was standing in the darkness with that rascal's arms around her, kissing and caressing her. The trouble was, she hadn't struggled. "I'm not keen on going," she said. Privately she thought what she didn't need to do was spend more time on a train with Cash McCalley aboard.

"Oh, but it is our duty." The fat man stood up and paced. "Hot Springs is the new Sodom and Gomorrah."

Bonnie gave him a questioning look.

"Or so people tell me," he added quickly.

"All right, if you think I'm needed. I'm so tired of dealing with Mr. McCalley."

"I don't blame you, he's such a rascal. Why, that woman he sees kicks up her heels in the most shameful manner and shows her drawers as she dances that cancan. Or at least, that's what poor, misguided souls who frequent the Black Lace Saloon tell me."

Men. Was there none of them except Herbert who could resist the lure of wine, women and song? "We must presume Cash McCalley will be journeying to Hot Springs."

"Yes, but we'll be there to organize the opposition." The preacher rubbed his fat hands together and smiled. "Hot Springs, bring on the sin!"

Bonnie gave him a searching look.

"I mean, bring on the sinners. They need our prayers," said Reverend Tubbs. "There's a weekly train tomorrow morning to Hot Springs."

"Cash McCalley will probably be on it," she said.

"Then we can pray for him as we journey. I'll invite several ladies of our church to accompany us."

At least with several ladies on the train, she wouldn't have to worry about Cash cornering her and seducing her with kisses. "All right, I'll see you at the station." She took her leave and went back to the hotel to pack. No doubt Cash McCalley would be furious when he found out she and Reverend Tubbs were headed to Hot Springs to put a stop to his boxing match. She smiled at the thought. Let him be angry—he deserved it, the rascal.

Cash was furious when Wilbur brought him word about the telegrams. Hot Springs had a reputation as a wild, wide-open resort and a good place for his boxing match. Now he knew that the big fat preacher who'd been dragged by the horse and that prim widow were going to Hot Springs to stop him. Was there no end to that woman's nosiness?

He went to the Black Lace Saloon that night and tried to enjoy Fifi's performance, but his mind was on his problem. He wondered if Bonnie Purdy knew that Herbert was sitting on the front row, watching the dancers with his tongue hanging out? If Cash told her, she probably wouldn't believe him.

Fifi joined Cash at his table after her dance. "You look as sad as a hound dog. What's the matter?"

"I'm goin' to Hot Springs tomorrow, try to set up the boxin' match there."

"Maybe I could go with you." She giggled. "We could have a good time going and coming in one of those compartments."

Cash sighed. "Fifi, with the financial shape I'm in, I'll be lucky to ride a boxcar up there."

"I'd pay for it for a chance to have you all to myself on that long ride both ways."

Once he would have jumped at the offer; Fifi was fun in bed. She should be, she'd had enough experience.

Bonnie's delicate features came to mind. She'd be on that train, no doubt about it. He remembered the kisses he'd stolen on the back platform of the train. Now more than ever, he'd have to hope he could seduce the woman so she'd stop her crusade. "I don't think you can go, Fifi. I've got too much on my mind and you'd distract me."

She turned pouty. "I can remember when you liked the distraction."

"Fifi, I got too much at stake here and I'll have to try to soft-soap that Mrs. Purdy."

That was a mistake, he knew it instantly.

Fifi's temper flared. "She gonna go to Hot Springs?"

"I'm not sure, but I reckon she will. I think there's one of them decency groups in Hot Springs, too."

"I don't like it, Cash. I seen the way she looks at you." She was seething.

"Fifi, you got it all wrong. By thunder, we don't even like each other."

"Then why am I feeling sparks when you two get close?"

"Fifi, you're loco. She's the most prudish, prim woman I ever met and she hates me."

"She'd be the first woman, then. I know you got a way with women, Cash."

He sighed. There was less and less he liked about the blonde. "I got to go so I can pack. The train to Hot Springs is in the morning."

She smiled apologetically and put her hand on his arm. "Why don't we go to my place? I'll give you something to remember me by for the next few days." She winked broadly.

Somehow, he just wasn't interested. Fifi seemed coarse and easy. She was no challenge and if he wasn't in her bed, some other man would be. Maybe he was just tired. "I got to go," he said and stood up, shaking off her hand. "When I get back, we'll get together—"

"You're turning me down?" Fifi pouted. "Why, there's a hundred men in here who would jump at the chance. All you can think of lately is that prim, prissy, strait-laced—"

"Fifi, I hate the girl. She's caused me nothin' but trouble since the first time I laid eyes on her. I'm fightin' for my life here with this boxin' match. If I can't put it on in Hot Springs, I don't know what I'll do. I've about milked my investors for all I can get out of them." He turned to go. "I'll see you when I get back."

"Remember what I got to offer," she called as he left, "more than that prissy wench has."

"Uh huh." He grabbed his Stetson and fled. With any luck, Bonnie wouldn't be on that train tomorrow and if she was, there was only one thing to do; he was going to have to charm her, seduce her and get her to drop her opposition. He grinned. He'd almost done it last time. This time, he wouldn't fail.

Chapter Fourteen

If Cash had had any plans to sweet-talk Mrs. Bonnie Purdy on the train to Hot Springs the next day, he gave it up when he saw she was traveling with Reverend Tubbs and several stalwart church ladies.

When he arrived in the resort town, Cash discovered the city council meeting had been delayed because the mayor was ill. He found himself stuck in the hotel with nothing to do. Mrs. Purdy and her party were also in the same hotel but he saw little of them because he understood from a friendly maid that they were out organizing the local church ladies to pressure the city fathers. He tried to see the governor, who said he was too busy to see Cash, but the same friendly maid let him know the governor had met with Bonnie Purdy and her church ladies. Would that woman never quit?

Being optimistic, Cash figured he might have a small chance with the local officials; at least, he had to try. With a couple of days to spare, he did some gambling and lost, which rarely happened. Cash realized his luck was not with him and being superstitious, decided to stay away from the gambling halls. He had not given up the idea of seducing Mrs. Purdy, but with the Reverend Tubbs always in tow, he didn't see how he could.

Desperate for something to do, he decided to try the healing and relaxing baths of the hot springs. He had to buy a swimming costume because he had never done such a thing. Indeed, being from dusty, dry West Texas, he could not even swim. Until he left Lubbock, he had never seen more than a gallon of water at one time except in a horse trough.

Now at one of the bathhouse big pools, wearing long woolen swimming drawers and undershirt, he stepped out gingerly into the ankle-deep hot water. He thought he heard a familiar voice and looking toward the other side, he saw Mrs. Purdy sitting on the edge of the steaming pool. He had to admit she looked quite fetching, maybe even seductive if that could be said of a woman wearing a black, ankle-length striped wool bathing dress with only three-quarter sleeves. Her hair was tied up in a black kerchief and she dangled her feet in the warm water and talked with a middle-aged lady sitting next to her. Some council member's wife no doubt, Cash thought, and she's influencing the vote right now. *Was there no place he could go to escape this annoying female?*

He ventured out knee deep and the warm water felt good. Around him, people splashed and cavorted in the water. It was a large, steaming pool with many people diving and splashing.

As he watched, Mrs. Purdy jumped from the side of the pool and dog-paddled farther out, then turned on her back and floated over to his side of the pool. He watched her. She had her eyes closed and smiled slightly as she floated. *Is this my chance to improve our relationship?*

"Hey," he yelled, "be careful, the water is deep over to your right."

Her eyes flew open and she turned toward him, frowning. "Oh, it's you. I had no idea you ever did anything but gamble, Mr. McCalley."

"You're being judgmental." He gave her his most fetching smile and motioned her closer. "I've never been here before. Are the waters really supposed to be beneficial?"

"So they say." She paused a few feet away and he wondered if she were standing on the bottom.

He ventured a little deeper, up to his waist. "Just because we're on opposite sides of the fence on one issue, Mrs. Purdy, doesn't mean we have to be enemies."

She moved toward him. "I think we have different philosophies about nearly everything, sir, which makes it hard for us to be friends."

"We could try." He gave her a warm grin and still assuming she stood on the bottom of the pool, he moved closer and discovered as he reached frantically for the bottom with his toes, that she was treading water. He went under, came up pawing and choking.

Bonnie watched him with annoyed amusement. "Oh, don't play games with me," she scolded. "Really, Mr. McCalley." She watched him sink and then come up again, splashing and grabbing at the water as if looking for a firm surface.

"Help!" he sputtered. "Help!"

"Mr. McCalley, this is not funny." She swam toward him and watched him go under and then surface again, gasping and coughing. She saw the sudden terror in his eyes and realized he was not clowning. "Hold on, I'm coming." She swam toward him, yelling back over her shoulder for a lifeguard, "Help! He's drowning!"

She saw that the lifeguard was at the far end of the pool. Cash McCalley had just gone under again. If anyone was going to save him, it would have to be her. She swam to him and in his panic, he grabbed at her. She socked him in the jaw hard and turning in the water, got behind him, began towing him toward the edge. Reverend Tubbs and three fat women ran up and down the side of the pool screaming.

Bonnie had never been both so frightened and angry. Why didn't someone do something to help her? Screaming was no help. Cash was heavy, there was no doubt about that. Bonnie began to fear he would pull her under as she struggled to reach the edge while he gasped and choked.

The lifeguard finally dove in, reached her and helped drag the limp man out of the water. There was a barrel next to the pool and the lifeguard threw him across that. "I don't know," the man muttered, "looks pretty blue to me."

"Get out of my way!" Bonnie ordered and began to roll Cash back and forth on the barrel and pounded him on the back. He coughed and choked, but lay limp as a dead steer. "Someone spread a towel!" she yelled.

"I'll pray!" Reverend Tubbs said.

"Don't pray, help!" Bonnie ordered.

The fat man looked surprised, but he and the brawny lifeguard lifted Cash and laid him out on the towels while people gathered around.

The lifeguard said, "I don't think he's breathing."

Could he be fooling? Cash appeared pale and still. Bonnie leaned over and looked into his face. He might be dying. Not if there was anything she could do about it. She leaned over and put her mouth on his and breathed hard. Nothing. To the lifeguard, she shouted, "Press on his ribs and get some air into him!" Then she put her mouth on Cash's again and breathed.

Gradually Cash became aware that a woman was kissing him while someone pummeled his rib cage. He liked the kisses, he wanted more of them. His eyes flickered open and he tried to focus on who was kissing him. No, he must have died and gone to hell because he was looking up into big blue eyes and he recognized the small, oval face as Bonnie Purdy's. He was being kissed by his worst enemy. Around his head, he saw dozens of feet and when he looked up, he saw a cluster of curious faces staring down at him. He took a deep breath, choked and began to breathe.

"He's coming around!" Mrs. Purdy declared, inches from his face.

"What the hell happened?" He only remembered that he'd been moving closer to her when suddenly, the pool had no bottom.

"He's all right." The wet girl said with a sigh and pulled back into a sitting position.

He tried to sit up, but couldn't quite manage it. The crowd of wet, curious people seemed to be growing.

The brawny young man he recognized as a lifeguard said, "I don't think we've ever had anyone drown before." He sounded disappointed.

"Who is he?" someone asked.

Bonnie Purdy wiped water from her face. "Cash Mc-Calley," she said.

An older lady said, "Isn't that something? That girl saved that big man from drowning."

He'd been saved by that wisp of a girl. What's more, his worst enemy. How humiliating and embarrassing. "By thunder, I can't help it," he gasped. "I'm from West Texas. I can't swim."

"Okay," said the lifeguard, "let's break it up." To Bonnie Purdy he said with admiration, "That was a brave thing you did, little lady, saving him."

Bonnie stared down at Cash, wondering if he faked it. "Considering who he is, I reckon I should have let him drown."

"Why, Mrs. Purdy," said the reverend, "I'm surprised at you."

She was immediately contrite. "Gracious, I reckon I can't help it; this scoundrel brings out the worst in me."

Someone in the crowd said, "The newspaper will want to know about this. The city fathers will give the brave little lady an award."

Cash groaned and sat up, wiped the water from his face.

The disappointed crowd, who had not gotten to see a drowning, began to drift away.

"Isn't it enough that you defeat me at every turn," he scolded Bonnie, "and now you humiliate me by savin' my life? How's that gonna look in Texas, a girl savin' a big *hombre* like me?"

"Okay, so next time, I'll just let you drown," she said and stood up.

He wasn't so far gone that he couldn't appreciate the view. She looked quite fetching with that black and white striped bathing costume plastered to her slim form. "It's your fault. Why didn't you warn me you weren't standin' on bottom?"

"So now it's my fault?" She smiled with smug superiority. "How was I supposed to know you couldn't swim? You could at least say thank you."

"For embarrassin' a Texan in front of fifty people?" He groused, "I could have made it to the pool side all right."

"Sure you could," she smiled, "you were just sinking to the bottom to see what it looked like."

"I didn't know any woman could swim," he grumbled. "It just ain't natural."

"You'd better be glad I could," she returned, "or they would have been picking you up off the bottom of the pool. Good day, Mr. McCalley. I suggest you stay in the kiddie pool from now on." She turned and dived off the side of the pool and swam at a fast clip across to the other side.

Cash felt everyone still staring at him. How embarrassing; to be saved by a girl who was barely shoulder high to him and probably didn't weigh as much as a roulette wheel. Cash stumbled to his feet and headed for the dressing rooms. He got dressed, went to a saloon and had a few drinks and a sandwich. Then he returned to his room. Now what was he gonna do? Bonnie Purdy would get in the newspapers as a heroine and that would swing votes her way. Would he never see the last of this stubborn, determined girl? When he slept that night, he dreamed she was the one who was drowning. He stood on the side of the pool.

"I'm comin' to save you!" he shouted.

A big, muscular lifeguard shouted, "Don't take

the chance! The water is full of rip tides and man-eating sharks!"

"A Texan always goes to the aid of a lady!" He yelled back and dove in, swimming toward the drowning girl with powerful strokes. In the background, he saw the fins of the man-eating sharks circling them both and the deadly currents pulled at him. "I'll save you, Bonnie!" he promised and grabbed her as she sank for the last time.

He caught her and slipped his arm around her petite body, then he swam toward the edge of the pool where terrified people waited and watched. The sharks snapped at him as he grabbed the edge of the pool and hoisted himself up, lifted her and carried her.

Around him, people cheered. "Hurray for the Texan! Hurray for Cash McCalley who just risked his life to save this slip of a girl!"

He made a calming gesture and nodded modestly. "It's my duty as a Texan," he said. "Remember the Alamo!"

As the crowd cheered, he laid Bonnie on a towel, knelt over the unconscious girl and put his mouth on hers. She stirred and returned the kiss, wrapping her arms around his neck. Then she slipped her tongue between his lips and arched her body up to him. He could feel every inch of her curves through both their wet suits.

"Let's go to your room," she whispered, "so I can properly reward you. My hero," she said, "you're so brave. I will no longer try to stop you from anything you want to do. Your wish is my command."

"Thank you," he smiled modestly. "I know you're offerin' your luscious body as a reward and justly so, but as a Texan, I save women every day. Remember the Alamo!"

The girl frowned up at him. "You dolt, don't you remember, I saved you! And what's the Alamo got to do with your bloody boxing match?"

Reality. Cash blinked awake and sat up in bed. Dawn shone faintly through the window. Now he remembered yesterday's events. It was true. In today's newspaper, everyone would know about it. He groaned aloud, wishing she had just let him drown. It would have been better than being embarrassed.

As he dressed, he thought about Bonnie Purdy. She had saved his life. As a Texas male, that would be a hard thing to live down. He wandered downstairs and had breakfast, then as he left, noticed the slight boy from the livery stable standing in the foyer.

"Oh, Mr. McCalley," the boy grinned, "glad to hear you're still with us; close call."

He felt himself flush. "Does everyone in town know about what happened at the baths?"

"Pretty much. I saw Mrs. Purdy being interviewed by a newspaper reporter while ago as I came to bring her horse."

"What horse?"

"She's going riding this morning," answered the boy.

"Hmm." Cash thought a minute. What a perfect excuse to be alone with her; he'd apologize for his rudeness yesterday, thank her and try to soften her up. Cash, old man, is there no end to your cleverness? "Get me a horse, too, a spirited one."

"Yes sir." The boy left the hotel at a brisk clip.

Cash stuck his thumbs in his vest and grinned. If he could ever get Mrs. Purdy alone, he was convinced he could charm her into maybe giving up her crusade against him, or even seduce her. No, this woman was the most incorruptible pillar of goodness he'd ever met.

"Watch out, Cash, my boy," he warned himself, "you want to make sure this time she does not rescue you again and make you look like a bigger fool than you already are." However unlike swimming, Cash was an expert horseman. No man or woman could handle a horse better than he could.

Bonnie had not slept well. Over and over in her dreams, she saw Cash's terrified face and realized again that he was drowning. It seemed strange that a big, muscular man could not swim, but then, they never saw much more water in West Texas than a heavy dew.

Over and over, she put her mouth on his and breathed life into him. His mouth had been soft and moist and she'd wanted more of it. That both shocked and surprised her.

In the morning, she got up and put on her light blue riding costume, complete with the cocky, feathered hat and went down to breakfast with Reverend Tubbs and some of the local ladies. They made afternoon plans to spread out over town and create a protest march for tomorrow's council meeting.

Bonnie sighed. "Then, Reverend Tubbs, if you don't mind, after what happened yesterday, I think I'd like some peace and quiet this morning."

The reverend's fat face turned sympathetic. "I don't blame you, my dear. That was a brave thing you did, saving that rascal's life."

"I would have done it for a mongrel dog," she answered. "Anyone would have done the same."

Gertrude Potts, drab and dowdy in her plain black dress, said, "You know, the Orientals say that when you save someone's life, that life belongs to you."

Bonnie snorted. "I assure you, I wouldn't want the responsibility of Mr. McCalley's lurid life. He's such a rascal."

"But a handsome one," the lady sighed and the others nodded.

"Maybe to some women," Bonnie said. "I don't find him in the least attractive." Then she winced, expecting God to strike her with lightning out of the clear warm sky outside.

The portly preacher stood and bowed to the ladies. "I'll see you later," he said to Bonnie, "at the prayer meeting tonight to pray over this evil not coming to Hot Springs."

"Of course." She looked around at the ladies; elderly widows and old maids in dowdy black or gray dresses, hair pulled back in plain buns. This was her future, she thought with dismay, and not much more interesting if she married Herbert Snodgrass. "Excuse me, ladies."

She left the table and headed for the lobby. The boy from the livery stable stood there to say there was a chestnut filly waiting for her outside.

She smiled as she went out and saw the fine blooded mount. A groom helped her up into the sidesaddle. Bonnie sighed. Back home, she preferred to ride astride as she galloped across the rolling pastures, but of course, that was frowned on in civilized society.

She followed the signs and headed out to the bridle

paths that led through the forested hills around Hot Springs. It was a warm day, but pleasant. Yesterday's events seemed far away now almost as if they'd never happened, but in her mind, she replayed putting her mouth on that scoundrel's and breathing life into him again.

As she rode around the first turn, she heard another horse behind her and turned in her saddle. "Oh, no!"

Coming fast was Cash McCalley on a fine, spirited bay horse. Should she try to outrun him? His horse looked faster than hers and Cash had already spotted her. She simply waited. "Good day, Mr. McCalley."

"Oh, it's you." His eyebrows went up in surprise, but he didn't fool her. "Well, since we're both out for a ride, I assume you'd like to have a man's protection?"

"From what?" She was more than a little annoyed as she urged her filly forward in a trot.

The rascal fell in alongside her. "Oh, I don't know; any blackguard who might do harm to a lady."

"I think I've proven I can take care of myself. Most Texas girls can."

He grinned as they rode. "But being a Texas man, I feel duty-bound to ensure that."

"I was perfectly happy with the solitude," she snapped and kept riding. Maybe he would get discouraged and ride on.

No such luck. He stayed right at her side.

"Really great trail," he offered.

"Yes, it is. I was hoping to enjoy it alone."

"Oh, but now you don't have to," he said. "It's fun to have someone to ride with."

Obviously he didn't or wouldn't realize she was

attempting to discourage him. "Mr. McCalley, we are not friends, we are adversaries."

"We don't have to be," he glanced over at her. "After all, I owe you my life."

"I'm glad you realize that," she said coldly.

"It was a brave thing you did."

"I would have done it for a drowning rat," she snapped and kept her gaze on the trail ahead.

"Well, thank you anyway. I realize I was not too grateful yesterday, but I am much obliged."

Even though she knew better, her resolve seemed to soften. "I will admit there was a few seconds that I thought we would both die. You really need to learn to swim, Mr. McCalley."

"Call me Cash, please. After all, we've shared a bond very few people have when you saved my life."

She glanced sideways. He smiled at her and her pulse quickened. Beware, she reminded herself, this man could talk a starving mutt off a meat wagon. But politely she said, "Since you can't swim, were you loco to come out in the deeper water?"

"Stupidity," he laughed. "I so wanted to talk to you and I didn't realize you weren't standin' on the bottom."

"You're wasting your time if you planned to change my mind about working against you."

"Actually," and he lowered his voice, "I was rememberin' that time on the back of the train."

She felt the blood rush to her face and kept riding. "You're no gentleman to mention that."

"I thought we had established already that I'm not a gentleman."

"We certainly have." She tapped her filly with her riding crop and it cantered ahead of the other horse.

"I didn't mean to offend you." He caught up with her. "I reckon I haven't been able to forget that night."

"I—I was foolish." She stared straight ahead.

"I was the fool," he said gallantly, "and when I almost drowned and woke up with your lips on mine, I hoped I was on the back of the train again."

"Please stop talking about that train," she snapped. "It never should have happened."

"I'm glad it did."

"Well, I am not!" She stared straight ahead and kept riding. "Good day to you, sir."

He didn't take the hint, but stayed next to her as they rode in silence for a few minutes.

Finally Cash said, "I see a little clearin' by a creek up ahead. We really should stop and rest the horses."

Reluctantly, she agreed. "But nothing else."

He feigned innocence. "My dear lady, I have no idea what you're hintin' at."

"Oh, don't you?"

They reached the clearing and reined in.

Cash dismounted, tied his horse and came around to help her. She looked down at him as if hesitating.

"You can sit up there all day if you wish." He gave her his most charming smile, "or you can come down."

She hesitated a moment, then slid off into his arms.

He was surprised at how light she was. "You don't weigh as much as my rifle," he murmured. He kept his hands on her waist and stood looking down at her. Her lips were slightly parted and he had the most terrible urge to kiss her.

"Don't," she ordered, "don't do it." She pulled away from him and walked over to sit on a stump.

Both horses moved to drink from the creek. The

woods were quiet, although a cicada whirled and somewhere in the forest, a bird called.

She should have stayed on her horse. It was not smart for any woman to be alone with this charming rascal.

"I brought a small picnic," he ventured, "but there might be enough for two."

"I'm not hungry." She stared at her small, kidskin boots and wondered how long before she could mount up and ride away.

"I've got a canteen of lemonade, and a couple of cups."

She was thirsty. She licked her lip nervously. "Now that does sound good."

"You're under no obligation," he said, "it's only lemonade."

She watched him retrieve the canteen and two collapsible cups from his saddlebags, pour and hand her one.

"Um," she said as she sipped it, "it's good and cold."

Seemingly encouraged, he dug again in his saddlebags. "I've got some cold roast beef sandwiches," he said and spread his package out on a nearby stump. "There's some pickles and chocolate cookies, too."

She watched him enjoying a sandwich with hearty appetite. No one enjoyed food like a Texan. "Perhaps I might have a little if you've got enough."

"Plenty." He smiled and held out one to her.

Their fingers touched and she seemed to feel a spark between them. Every sense she had warned her that being in a deserted forest clearing with this man was not wise. Not wise? It was downright loco. But of course, she was no young schoolgirl. She could resist his oily charm. "Of course you realize, Mr. McCalley—"

"Cash." He grinned at her.

Why have I never noticed he had a dimple near that square chin? "Mr. McCalley, your charm and sandwiches will not bribe me into softening my opposition. I do intend to speak against your boxing match at the city council tomorrow."

"Mrs. Purdy, I'm hurt that you might even suspect that I would think a pillar of virtue like you could be bribed. Perish the thought!" His gray eyes brimmed with reproach. They were magnificent eyes, she thought as she looked at him over her lemonade cup; gray as a summer storm. She tried to remember what color Herbert's were and was chagrined that she couldn't remember.

"Mrs. Purdy, I only came out today because I feel I owe you so much for savin' my life yesterday and a grave apology for the way I acted. You must realize it was a humiliatin' situation for a man, and especially a Texan."

"Oh, I reckon I understand that," she nodded and munched her sandwich. He had fine hands for a man with long, sensitive fingers. Herbert's were short and stubby. "It wasn't I who called the papers. I wouldn't have done that."

"You know," he said sincerely, "I believe you. I don't reckon you meant to publicly humiliate me."

She smiled. "I fear you did a good job of that all by yourself."

"Yes, I did and that's hard for a Texan to admit." He nodded. "Would you like a cookie?"

She took one. "Thank you. I didn't think I was hungry, but these are good."

"Would you like more lemonade?"

She nodded and he poured it.

It was quiet except for the horses munching grass.

"Almost as good as Texas," he said.

"That's blasphemy," she laughed. "No place is as good as Texas."

"True," he nodded and grinned. "Spoken like a true daughter of the Lone Star state. Remember I said *almost*. I haven't forgotten that if it hadn't been for you, I wouldn't be alive to smell the sagebrush anymore. They might have even buried me here, God forbid."

"Oh, no," she shook her head. "Even though we're at odds, Mr. McCalley, I would have insisted your carcass be shipped back to Texas."

"So the lady does have a heart after all." His voice grew soft, the stormy eyes misty.

She stared into them and tried to remember that this man was tricky as a medicine show barker. "Uh, we probably ought to be going."

"As soon as we finish the last of our lemonade. You see, I am trustworthy with a lady. Otherwise, I might have brought something stronger."

"From what I've heard around Dallas, you're about as trustworthy as a coyote in a chicken pen."

He appeared shocked. "You misjudge me, Mrs. Purdy."

Cash McCalley was the most virile, handsome man she'd met in a long time. No, ever. From here, she could smell the scent of suntanned skin, tobacco and a fine shaving lotion. "Well, perhaps it was only cruel gossip."

"Perhaps from a disappointed woman?" he winked. "I know a lady when I see one, and I would never treat you like that Fifi LaFemme. In fact, we should probably ride on now before your reputation is ruined." He stood up.

"My reputation is solid and unblemished," she protested.

"Indeed it is. Your virtue is legendary." He took the cup from her fingers with a faint smile. "Around Dallas, they say you are a beautiful, cold marble statue and no man gets to that hard heart."

"Well," she was a bit flustered from the touch of his hand. "I—I'm not sure that is true. The right man might—"

"And is the chicken feed salesman the right man?" He seemed to have moved closer.

"That's impertinent of you to ask." She tried to take a step backward, but a big tree was in her way.

"Yes, I reckon it is." He was close enough that she could almost feel his warm breath on her cheek. "It's just that men wonder and dare to hope . . . oh, never mind." He brushed a wisp of hair from her face.

"Uh, I—I think we need to be going." She felt warning bells going off in her head, but he smiled at her so gently.

"I reckon it's forward of me, Mrs. Purdy, and I wouldn't blame you if you slapped me, but I can't be sure that kiss from the train was as wonderful as I remember it. No mortal kiss could be."

She knew he was such a rascal, but he was smiling so shyly, so benign. Maybe she had overestimated his cunning. "You—you really thought that?"

"Maybe my mind played tricks on me and I exaggerated it." His face seemed even closer.

"I—I don't imagine my kiss is any better than any other girl's—"

"Oh, I reckon it is. Shall I find out?" Before she could answer, he put a hand on each side of her head on the tree trunk, bent his head and kissed her ever so gently.

It was good; good as she remembered. She held her breath as his lips caressed hers. Her toes seemed to curl up in the fine kidskin riding boots. She wanted more. Without thinking, she put her hands on his broad shoulders, stood on her tiptoes and returned the kiss.

"Why, Mrs. Purdy." He sounded shocked and then he pulled away and stepped backward.

"Oh, gracious, I—I didn't mean this to happen." She was so surprised.

"I know. My attraction for you made me forget myself and I have too much respect for you to sully your reputation." He began to gather up the picnic things.

She wasn't quite sure how she felt; maybe disappointed. She couldn't forget the taste of his lips. Surely he would at least try to kiss her again so she could slap his face, mount up and ride away.

"Mrs. Purdy, are you ready to leave now?" He had led both horses over to the log.

"Yes, I reckon so." She sighed and walked over. Cash caught her waist and stood looking down at her. He was close, too close. She could feel the heat of his big body, feel the strength of his strong hands. His mouth looked full and sensual. Suddenly, she wanted him to kiss her again before he lifted her to the horse. "It was a lovely picnic," she murmured, "thank you."

"No, thank you." He stood looking down at her and the gray eyes turned stormy. She saw the passion there and knew what was coming. She could have moved away. Instead, she lifted her face up to his.

"Bonnie," he whispered, "oh, Bonnie, you don't know

what you do to me." And his mouth, that sensual mouth, came down to cover hers. His sensitive hands lifted her to her tiptoes and without thinking, her small hands came up to his wide, powerful shoulders and pulled him closer still.

It seemed like an eternity that they kissed, with his mouth becoming bolder, forcing hers open so his tongue could taste and tease inside.

She knew she should make him stop, but she didn't want to. Instead she clung to him and opened her lips so he could kiss her deeper still. Then he swung her up in his arms and carried her back to the shaded glen and sat her on the soft grass. She looked up at him and his chiseled features were grim and his gray eyes dark with desire. "You've been a problem for me since the first moment I laid eyes on you, you heartless vixen."

The image of a heartless vixen was so romantic, not like her at all, she thought. She didn't say anything, she only held out her arms to him as she breathed hard. He was trouble—only trouble—and he was probably tricking her to stop her meddling, but at the moment, she didn't care. "Kiss me again like I've never been kissed."

He sat down next to her, took her in his arms. "Bonnie, I'm a scoundrel, you know that. I'd do anything to get what I want, I always have."

"Do you always tell women that when you kiss them?"

He shook his head. "Never. Honesty is a first for me." He began to kiss her face, her lips, her eyes.

"This will be a first for me, too," she murmured as his lips caressed her throat.

His mouth tasted the heat of her throat and now he paused. "What do you mean?"

She flushed, "I—I've not had much experience.

Hans was so old, you see, and Clint deserted me on our wedding night before . . . well, you know."

He stopped cold and looked deep into her eyes. "You—you're tellin' me the truth." It wasn't a question.

"I am," and she took his rugged face between her two small hands and kissed him so hotly that he groaned and leaned against her so that she tumbled onto her back in the grass. She closed her eyes and let him kiss her throat as he opened her bodice. He was a liar and a rascal and she was loco to want him, but she would have this moment to remember forever even though they were enemies again tomorrow.

She felt him open the lace of her corset cover and then his warm, moist mouth found her breasts. "Oh God," she gasped, arched her back and put her hands on the back of his tanned neck, pulling him down to taste and caress her breasts with his mouth and tongue.

"Bonnie, you don't know how much I've been wantin' to do this, ever since that night on the train."

"I know, I've fought it, but I've wanted it, too." She felt his hand hot on her thigh under her blue riding dress and she let her thighs fall apart so that his fingers could travel up her thigh even as his mouth ravaged her lips. Never in her whole life had she behaved like a tart and certainly not with a man she considered an enemy, but just this once in her orderly, carefully structured life, she would throw aside all caution and take this man in a frenzied, passionate embrace.

His mouth was on her breast, his fingers stroking between her thighs, pushing aside her lace drawers. He was going to take her out here in the grass like some common slut and she wanted it, no, craved it. Yet he was her enemy and she must not surrender.

"Cash," she whispered, "Oh, Cash!"

Chapter Fifteen

There was nothing she wanted so much at this moment as to have this virile male between her thighs, driving hard into her very depths. And yet, she did not trust him. She was almost feverish with want, looking up at him with a question in her eyes.

He made the decision for her. "There's someone comin.'" He said and reluctantly pulled away.

"Wh—what?" She had to have him, wanted him to finish this storm he had started in her.

He rearranged his clothing, reached down to pull her to her feet. "I hear someone on the bridle path. Let's get out of here."

She was shaking and too warm. Was she out of her mind? She had almost surrendered to the enemy. Now she could hear faint voices and the sound of horses in a slow canter. "Oh, my God, what—?"

He brought the horses without speaking, paused only a second, looking down at her. His face was tense with passion and something else, maybe a troubled confusion. "Forgive me, Bonnie."

Forgive him? When she was the one who had been lying on her back, offering her body like some wanton slut? She could only stare up at him as he lifted her to her horse. She felt her hair in a mess around her shoulders. "You lost your hat," he said and went to retrieve it.

The coming riders sounded closer now as he handed her her perky hat. How could she have been such a silly fool, knowing this rogue's reputation with women? And she'd been no better than any of them, no better than Fifi LaFemme. She was filled with a sudden fury at herself, at this charming rogue. "You—you unscrupulous bastard!" She smashed her hat down on her head, lashed her startled horse and took off at a gallop up the bridle path.

"Bonnie!" He yelled behind her, "I'm sorry! Bonnie!"

She didn't look back as she galloped up the trail. She returned to the hotel, handed her reins to the boy and hurried into the lobby.

She ran smack into Reverend Tubbs. He looked at her strangely. "Mrs. Purdy, are you all right?"

She realized she must look a mess. Damn that Cash McCalley. "I—I took a tumble, but I'm fine."

At least physically, she thought.

"Good. And the horse?"

"The horse?" She looked at him blankly.

"Was the horse hurt in the fall?" The plump man stared at her again.

"Ah, no, the horse is fine. I—I must go change." She turned and ran for the stairs, feeling that people in the lobby were all looking at her.

She got to her room and paused before the mirror. Gracious, she looked a mess. Her hair hung untidily around her shoulders, her perky hat was on backward and the feather was broken. Worse yet, there was grass and leaves all over her fine blue riding outfit. No wonder Reverend Tubbs had stared at her. Could everyone read her guilty doings by looking at her mussed clothes? "Cash McCalley, you are not going to ruin my very respectable reputation," she vowed.

She was furious with him and with herself for being so gullible when she'd known what he was. Oh, if Herbert ever found out, he would be horrified. And hadn't she sold out Danny's memory? She winced, thinking about her sterling reputation and her presidency of the Lone Star Ladies. She could only imagine the humiliation. And she'd come so far from that moonshiner's shack in the Big Thicket. It was important to be respectable, more important than anything.

She glared at her rumpled appearance and kiss-swollen lips in the mirror. "How could you be such a fool?" she scolded herself. "He doesn't care about you, he's just like Clint." She must not be fooled again. This charming rascal was only attempting to stop her from interfering in his profitable, bloody fight, nothing more.

She bathed and tried to take a nap, but found herself staring at the ceiling and remembering the feverish encounter in the woods over and over again. How could she face her group at the prayer meeting tonight? Well, she must.

In the late afternoon, she combed her hair and tied it up, then dressed in a modest pink plisse dress, got her lace parasol and went to her meeting. It was difficult to keep her mind on the discussion and she was careful not to look at the reverend, afraid her morning's mischief would show in her face. Roast beef and lemonade indeed. How could she have been so gullible?

One thing was certain, Cash McCalley had made a deadly enemy of her with his attempted seduction and she'd see him in hell before she'd let him win. There was more at stake here and if he didn't know it now, he soon would.

She did not sleep well that night. The room was too warm in the summer heat and she had torrid passionate dreams of Cash McCalley, naked and hot, his straining muscles damp with passionate heat as he took her, took her deep and hard while she writhed under him and begged for more and more and more.

She woke up gasping and drenched with perspiration. Damn him anyhow for awakening something in her that Bonnie had never realized existed. She thought about sharing a bed with a naked Herbert and shuddered. Her traitor body yearned for the rogue stallion, the one who would know how to play her like a violin, take her like a mare in heat, subdue and conquer her, leave her clinging to him and begging for more. Damn that Cash McCalley, damn him.

She would have her revenge. She would block him at every turn. Before, it had been honest opposition to his business enterprise, now it would be retaliation for what he had awakened in her that made her feel and look like a common slut, a fool. No doubt he was in some saloon at this very moment, laughing and telling an amused audience of gamblers and tarts about the elegant lady he had toyed with in the grass, had her begging for fulfillment. It was toward dawn before she finally managed to drop off to sleep.

Feeling troubled and confused, Cash had watched Bonnie ride away that morning. He had meant to seduce her, all right, but he'd never felt desire like that before. He wanted more of her and this was dangerous because this upright paragon of virtue meant nothing but trouble for him. He must forget about wanting this woman before she destroyed him and concentrate on his goal.

After she galloped away, he needed some solitude to think, so he continued his ride, still wanting her as he had never wanted another woman. Yet everything he owned was riding on this venture and the woman he was so attracted to was determined to ruin him. "I must do whatever it takes to win," he vowed. "I can't let a small female wipe me out."

It seemed that was what she planned to do. No wonder he had not been able to get a meeting with the governor. Bonnie must have already reached him. At the next day's meeting, the protestors were not only well organized, there was even a telegram from the governor, suggesting that the Hot Springs city council vote the boxing match down.

The mayor read the telegram aloud while the staid ladies and preachers with their protest signs cheered and applauded. Cash tried to say something and was drowned out. He caught the glint of vengeance in Bonnie's big blue eyes. Oh, she was out for revenge all right. No, she wanted more than vengeance—the woman wanted to peel off his hide and nail it to her door; the expression in her eyes told him that. His attempt at seducing her had back-fired and turned the vulnerable widow into an avenging angel.

The outcome was a foregone conclusion. Even before the vote, with the crowd singing "Marching to Zion," Cash knew he could forget his chance of moving his boxing match to Arkansas. Financially, he was at the end of his rope, but he was too proud to let Bonnie Purdy know that. Instead, when the vote was taken and he had lost, he took off his hat, made a deep bow to the petite widow and smiled. "The race is not to the swift but to the determined."

She smiled without mirth. "We'll see who is most determined, Mr. McCalley."

"Why don't you go back to your library and stop meddlin' in my affairs?" he snarled, losing his cool demeanor.

"It is my civic duty to stop a rogue," she snapped as the crowd began to file out.

He gave her a big, broad wink. "We both know what this is really about, now don't we?"

She felt herself flush a furious red, remembering. "How dare you?"

"I'd like more," he whispered, leaning toward her.

Bonnie resisted an urge to slap him until his teeth rattled, but she realized that would cause people to stare and ask questions. She spun on her heel, put her pert nose in the air and strode away, following after Reverend Tubbs.

Later, on the train back to Texas, she went out of her way to avoid him. She made sure she stayed away from the club car, and in the diner she sat with Reverend Tubbs who wanted to discuss his learning to read the Book of Revelations in Greek. She nodded politely, but watched the back of Cash McCalley's head as he sat at another table entertaining three ladies. She realized with a start they were three of her protestors and right now, they seemed to be having the time of their lives, giggling and hanging on every word the charming rascal uttered.

She cornered the ladies after lunch. "You realize the rascal is only trying to stop you from protesting when we get back to Texas?"

"I know," skinny Ethel Toodle sighed, "but he's sooo charming."

"I'm afraid I don't see it," Bonnie snapped.

"Oh? He said some very nice things about you."

"Did he now?" She was dying of curiosity, but she dared not ask. "He will do anything and I do mean *anything* to change people's opinion about his bloody boxing exhibition."

Plain Wilma Biggerstaff smiled dreamily. "I'm not so sure his boxing match would be all that bad."

"Wilma, how can you say that? You can't go over to the enemy."

"I reckon not," she said, but she didn't look too certain.

"Ladies, stay away from that rascal," Bonnie ordered. "He'll do anything and I do mean anything to influence you."

"*Anything?*" Ethel looked hopeful and Wilma sighed and smiled.

Mrs. Dobbs said, "Perhaps we've been too harsh on the poor boy."

"I think not. He'll play women like a cheap fiddle to get what he wants," Bonnie said emphatically, knowing she was a prime example of that.

They arrived back in Dallas. Fifi, in a tight red dress, and a whole group of female admirers were at the station to meet Cash. Some of his male supporters hoisted him on their shoulders and carried him to his buggy. "Hurray for Cash McCalley!" they shouted. "We won't have the boxing match in Arkansas, we'll have it some place in Texas."

"Not if the Lone Star Ladies have anything to do with it," Bonnie vowed as Herbert walked up.

She winced. He looked like such a Yankee dude in his bowler hat and spats.

"Humph!" Herbert sniffed as he took her luggage and kissed her cheek. "Honestly, I don't know what women see in that rascal."

"I don't either," Bonnie lied, and hated herself for it. *Why was it women always loved a rogue?*

"I heard about what happened in Arkansas." Herbert picked up her luggage.

"What—what did you hear?" She felt herself go ashen. Had someone seen her rolling in the grass with that randy rascal?

Herbert looked at her strangely. "Why, about the Hot Springs city council turning down the boxing match. Congratulations."

"Uh, of course, thank you." She felt flustered and avoided his gaze as they walked toward their buggy.

Out front, admiring females crowded around Cash McCalley. Also, the mayor and a number of men who favored the boxing match stood with him.

She heard the mayor say to Cash, "Here's someone you should meet, my boy. Bat Masterson's come to report on the match."

She turned her head to stare at the newcomer. Bat Masterson didn't look like a gunfighter, he looked like a natty sports reporter as he shook hands with Cash.

As she passed, the dapper Bat stepped up to her,

touched the brim of his hat. "Excuse me, Mrs. Purdy, would you like to make a statement to the press?"

She paused and behind Bat, Cash nodded to her and gave her a broad wink.

Gracious, had Herbert seen that intimate gesture? She wanted to throttle the Scots-Irish rogue.

"Mrs. Purdy?" Bat fingered his mustache and stood with pencil poised.

"I—I don't think so," Bonnie gulped and quickened her pace.

Herbert grumbled under his breath as he followed her. "What ails you, Bonnie, dear? That was a perfect opportunity to get your message out."

"I—I'm just not up to it," she apologized. "It was a long trip and I'm out of sorts."

Would Cash tell the whole world about cavorting with her in the woods near Hot Springs? Was he that much of a rascal? And if he did, would anyone believe him?

Out front, the hotel buggy waited. Herbert helped her up. When she glanced behind her, she saw Cash walking out to the street surrounded by an adoring group of women and trailed by the press wanting a good story. She thought she saw Wilma, Ethel and Mrs. Dobbs in that group. Oh, he was charming, all right.

When Cash caught her eye, he winked and tipped his hat to her.

"Of all nerve!" Herbert fumed, "I ought to thrash him for flirting with a respectable woman!"

"Uh, Herbert, dear, I wouldn't do that if I were you." Cash would wipe up the street with the chicken feed salesman.

"But he was openly flirting with you!" Herbert sniffed as he put her luggage in the back of the rig.

"He's only trying to stop the opposition," Bonnie said, "but it won't do him any good."

"That's right, you're not a little fool like those other women. Honestly, I don't know what they see in him."

Bonnie sighed as they drove away, remembering the taste of Cash's sensual lips and the feel of his muscular embrace. "I don't either," she said and then winced, waiting for God to strike her with lightning out of a clear summer sky.

Cash paused in his interviews out on the sidewalk and watched Bonnie drive away with that Herbert. What a rat. If she only knew . . . but even if Cash told her, she wouldn't believe the chicken feed salesman was such a villain. Funny, Herbert struck Cash as the kind of opportunist who might try to woo and win a rich woman, not a poor little librarian.

"What ya thinkin', honey?" Fifi laid her hand on his arm, bringing him back to the present.

"Uh, nothin', nothin' much at all. That's all the story, boys," he said to the eager reporters. "I'll find a way to put on the boxin' match; you've got my word on it." He lifted the blonde in her tight dress up into the buggy.

She stared at him. "You don't seem like your mind is on me or the big fight."

"Sure it is," he lied. "I'm just tryin' to decide what to do next, that's all."

He climbed into the buggy, waved to the crowd of admiring ladies and snapped the little whip at the bay horse. He drove away from the depot.

Fifi said, "Have you thought about New Mexico or Nevada for your fight?"

"I reckon I can try there," Cash said. "I reckon Bonnie Purdy will be one step ahead of me; she don't give up easy."

"You sound like you admire the little prude."

"Admire her? Hell no, she's costin' me money. Besides, she's too much like me; stubborn, determined."

"Men don't like that in a woman, do they, hon?"

"Of course not," he snapped, angry at the way he'd seen Herbert crowding closer to Bonnie on the buggy seat as the pair drove away. "Let's go back to your place, doll, and have us some fun."

"Oh, Cash, honey," she laid her head on his shoulder. "I thought you'd never ask again."

He'd show that snooty little widow, Cash vowed. He'd take Fifi back to her place and make passionate love to her.

However, when they returned to Fifi's room and got down to their underwear, nothing happened. When he took Fifi in his arms, he saw a small, accusing face and his ardor cooled. He broke out of the embrace and sat down in an easy chair. "Get me a drink, doll."

She took a deep breath, looked disappointed. "Hey, what happened to all that fun you promised me?"

He was angry with Bonnie now because her big blue eyes looking at him in his mind had thrown cold water on his need. "I'm—I'm just tired; that's all."

"It ain't like you to be tired, Cash." She walked over to a table and got him a tumbler of whiskey. "There's been times you played cards all night and rode me hard all day."

He took the drink but didn't taste it. *Rode me hard.* In his mind, he was back in the woods, about to take

Bonnie in a tumble on the grass and he had never desired a woman as much as he wanted that one. Damn her for interfering with his life and his plans. "I got to go." He stood up and began to get dressed.

"Go? You just got here." She wailed and her anger showed in her pretty, painted face. "You ain't made love to me any since this boxing thing started. You got another woman somewhere?"

"Now, Fifi," he crooned, "the only other woman on my mind is that damned little widow who's tryin' to stop me makin' any money."

"She's suddenly looking mighty pretty; new hairdo and all," Fifi snapped.

"Now what that's supposed to mean?" He paused in putting on his shirt.

Fifi put her arms around his neck. "I didn't mean nothing, Cash, honey. Just stick around and maybe later, you'll feel like it."

He had a sudden angry feeling that he'd never feel like bouncing Fifi or any of the other saloon girls on a mattress again. The girl he wanted under him, he couldn't have . . . or could he? She had stung his pride and wrecked his reputation with women. If he could only seduce her, he could ruin and discredit her, and that would clear the way for his boxing match. *Cash Mc-Calley, you are such a coyote,* he thought with a grin as he pulled on his pants. Why, you'd steal the butter off a sick cowboy's biscuit, or a staid girl's reputation and relish doing it.

"What you smiling about?" Fifi demanded.

"What?" He had forgotten she was even in the room, yet there she stood, her luscious curves only half covered by black lace underwear.

"You don't never listen to me no more," Fifi complained.

"It ain't like you to nag, Fifi." He searched around for his boots.

"It's you who've changed, Cash. Your mind is always somewhere else these days."

"I can't help it, honey, I got a lot on my mind with the battle over the boxing match. When that's over, we'll have us some good times again."

She appeared slightly mollified as she lit a cigarette. He watched her, thinking that Bonnie would never smoke, she was too much of a lady. A lady, and yet he had unleashed a tigress out there in the woods.

"I got to go," he said and reached for his coat. "The boxers will be expectin' me to report in."

"You comin' to my show tonight?"

"Huh?" Somehow, the idea of watching Fifi show her lacy rump to a hundred eager men as she danced made him wrinkle his nose with disgust. "I'll see."

With her still protesting behind him, he went out the door. What to do? He had to discredit the petite widow and do it quick. If he could destroy her lily-white reputation, neither the press nor the public would listen to her again and his project and his finances would be saved. Only one way to do that—somehow, he was going to have to seduce the enemy.

"Cash, my boy," he muttered to himself as he strode away, "you are a rat and a rascal, but things are gettin' desperate. You have to do whatever it takes to win and if that means ruinin' a lady's reputation, so be it. Besides," he grinned, remembering kissing the little brunette in the grass, "you'll have a lot of fun doin' it!"

Chapter Sixteen

Before he did anything else, he'd better go back to the train station and feed John L.

Cash stopped at a butcher shop and bought half a pound of ground beef, then he went to the livery stable, got his horse, and headed for the train station.

"Here, John L., here, cat," he called.

The ragged orange cat stuck his head out from under a freight car and peered at him.

"Come on, John L., I've got hamburger for you."

The cat merely yawned and lay down.

The skinny telegraph boy stuck his head around a corner. "He answers better if you call him Kitty Tom."

"That's a sissy name, Wilbur," Cash snapped.

"And besides," volunteered the boy, "she's already come by and fed him."

Cash was burned up. He didn't need to ask who. "You'd think with us bein' gone a couple of days, the damned cat would be hungry."

"Oh, Mrs. Purdy paid me to feed him while she was in Arkansas."

"That's *my* cat," Cash snorted.

"Tell that to the lady," the boy said.

"By thunder," Cash laid the hamburger near the boxcar, "that woman interferes in everything. I got to get back to the hotel, I want to talk to Bat Masterson."

The skinny boy's eyes widened. "That the famous gunfighter?"

"He used to be. He's a sportswriter now."

"The old West is about gone," the boy sighed.

"Maybe so." The thought depressed Cash as he walked back to his horse. Everything had changed, even here—women marching for voting rights and against men boxing. That just wasn't like Texans at all. Of course things hadn't changed much out on the ranches and he longed for those days when he rode across the prairie, rounding up stray calves. What had happened to him that he was living in a hotel in a crowded city and seldom seeing a blade of grass any more? "Necessity," he told himself as he mounted up. "Maybe someday, you'll be able to afford that ranch and leave this hated city life behind, but not unless you pull off this big fight."

He returned to his hotel room to wait for Bat Masterson.

Bonnie heard the sound of Cash's boots in the hall, then his key in the lock. She ran to pull the hankie from the keyhole, knelt and looked in. The gambler looked weary as he lit a cigar and took a comfortable chair. In a few minutes, she heard more bootsteps in the hall, then a knock.

She watched Cash get up, go to the door and open it.

"Good to see you, Masterson." The two men shook hands.

"Call me Bat." He twirled his cane.

"Want a drink?"

"Don't mind if I do, wash this Texas dust out of my throat."

Cash laughed. "One excuse good as another, I reckon."

As Bonnie watched, the two settled into comfortable chairs with their drinks and cigars.

"Well," Cash said, "you got any news?"

The other grinned. "I thought you'd give *me* some."

Cash shrugged. "Can't put on the match in Hot Springs."

Bat paused, his glass halfway to his lips. "I thought Hot Springs was a wide-open town?"

"I did too," Cash shrugged. "It seems there's a few respectable ladies and preachers there and Mrs. Purdy found them."

"That the prissy little thing I saw at the depot?"

Cash grimaced and nodded. "There's no one else like her."

"She's sure been the worm in your apple, hasn't she?" Bat laughed.

"That ain't the half of it," Cash griped. "She's also stealin' my cat's affection."

"What?"

"Never mind, it's just annoyin' that's all."

"Awful pretty gal," Bat leaned back in his chair.

Cash made a face. "Think so? I hadn't noticed."

The nerve of the man. She wanted to shout out, "You thought I was okay when you had me down on my back in the grass." Of course, being a randy stud, he'd probably take any female down if he got the chance, without even looking at her face.

"Well, she ain't exactly coyote ugly," Bat replied.

Cash snorted. "You'd have to put a bag over her

head to keep her from lecturing you on how to do it while you made love to her."

On the other side of the door, Bonnie fumed. She had a good mind to bang on the door and tell him what she thought of him, too, but she didn't want him to know she was eavesdropping. "Coyote ugly" was a term Westerners used to describe a girl so homely, if you woke up in a strange bed with a coyote ugly gal lying on your arm, you'd chew off your own arm to get away without waking her up. Damn men anyhow.

"Oh," Bat said, "I got news. Important person coming in on the train tomorrow."

"Who?" Cash perked up.

"John L. Sullivan himself, wants to see the fight."

Cash stood up, paced up and down. "By thunder, now that's more like it! I'll let all the newspapers know."

Bat stood up. "I have to tell you, people are losing interest, Cash. They're beginning to think this boxing match ain't gonna happen."

"It'll happen," Cash promised. "There's a lot of money ridin' on this. Oh, it may not be around Dallas, but I've just sent telegrams to the governors of Nevada and New Mexico Territory to see about havin' the fight there."

Bonnie took a deep breath. There was no time to lose. She had to get in touch with the ladies' clubs of those two areas to put a stop to this, plus protestors would have to be at the train station to meet John L. Sullivan tomorrow.

Bat twirled his cane, paused at the door. "If you can get the mayor and some dignitaries to the train station to welcome John L. without the protestors, that would be great."

"Don't worry, we'll kept this pretty secret. We'll give him the key to the city and get the men all excited about a great sportin' event before Mrs. Purdy ever hears about it."

"You going out?" Bat asked.

"Yeah, I think I'll go get a bite of supper, maybe catch the show at the Black Lace."

"It's good," Bat punched him in the ribs with his elbow, "when Fifi LaFemme turns her little round ass to the audience and shows those split drawers, the men sure go loco and yell for more."

"Yeah, Fifi has a nice rump," Cash agreed with a snicker and the two men went out the door together.

Gracious. Bonnie was completely disgusted as she got up from the keyhole and stuffed the hankie back in. "Men. They ought to be ashamed of themselves, ogling half-dressed women that way. Well, they weren't all like that. Herbert would never do such a thing.

She listened to the men's footsteps disappearing down the hall. Where had Cash been all day? Not in his room; not taking care of business. He had left the train station with Fifi. That's where he had been all afternoon. The thought made her grit her teeth. He'd gone from tumbling Bonnie in the grass to Fifi's bed. She wondered if he would say Bonnie had a nicer rear than Fifi's. Oh, the sheer gall of the rascal. More than ever, she wanted to ruin him; and it had nothing to do with poor Danny, God rest his soul.

Well, she had things to plan. She went to alert Reverend Tubbs and the local officers of the Lone Star Ladies about the arrival of that sporting man with the lurid reputation.

Then she drove back to the hotel, passing the Black

Lace as she went. The hitching rail out front and the whole street was full of tied horses and buggies. Evidently, Cash and Bat weren't the only two who wanted to see Fifi's nice rump.

Was that Herbert's rented buggy out front? No, Herbert wouldn't be caught dead in a lurid place like this. Besides, he had said he was leaving on a selling trip over to Abilene. She reined in and studied the horse. Maybe someone had rented the same buggy. From inside came music, laughter and hooting from men. It was almost dark and she ought to go back to the hotel.

She'd never been in a saloon before. Bonnie paused and listened to the music. Then curiosity got the better of her. What was it about Miss LaFemme's dancing that interested men so? This might be a place where the Lone Star Ladies needed to lead a protest march. She'd just peek inside and see what outrageous behavior went on.

Bonnie took a deep breath and pushed through the swinging doors. The place was dark and crowded with rowdy men, all drinking and smoking cigars. Men in derby hats jostled through crowds of cowboys in Stetsons and soldiers in blue uniforms. As she moved along through the crowd, men turned and stared at her. A slick-looking man with a red vest and a handlebar mustache came out on the stage and raised his hand for silence.

"All right, gents, here's what you been waiting for, Miss Fifi LaFemme lately of New York and Kansas City doing the cancan!"

The crowd whistled and clapped and stomped their feet. Every man's gaze was on the stage as the piano began to play "Ta Ra Ra Boom De Ay" and half a dozen pretty girls danced out onto the stage.

The men began to clap and shout, "Fifi! We want Fifi!"

Bonnie saw Cash and Bat Masterson sitting at a table near the stage. Of course he would be right up front. At another table close to the stage, there was a familiar figure. Bonnie blinked and stared at him.

About that time, Fifi LaFemme danced out onto the stage, kicking her legs high as the men roared approval. Then all the dancers turned their rears to the crowd and bent over, showing the back of their split drawers.

Oh, my gracious. Bonnie gasped, shocked speechless as the girls danced and showed their lace-clad rumps. The split-drawers left nothing to the imagination. Then they whirled and kicked high again.

Scandalized, Bonnie turned to run out when a familiar voice yelled, "More! Fifi, give us more!"

She moved to get a closer look at the man who was waving a handful of currency at the dancers.

"This is for you, sport!" Fifi grinned and danced closer to the man, coming down off the stage and into the audience while the crowd cheered. The man yelled and waved her closer.

Bonnie blinked and moved in for a better look. It couldn't be, but it was. Herbert. Fifi danced up to him and he leaned over and tucked the cash into the girl's garter while the men roared approval.

She had never been so furious and hurt in her life. Without even thinking, Bonnie pushed her way through the crowd to confront the chicken feed salesman. "You!" she shouted and she hit him with her reticule.

"Bonnie, dear, I can explain!" He threw up his hands to protect his head while she pummeled him with her purse.

The piano player seemed to see Bonnie and stopped playing; the girls stumbled to a halt. The men gradually grew quiet at the spectacle of a respectable woman in the Black Lace Saloon. She saw Cash McCalley turn with an exclamation of surprise, stand up and begin to make his way toward her. Everyone, including the chorus girls, gaped, open-mouthed.

She'd just made a terrible fool of herself. Hurt and angry, Bonnie turned and started out of the saloon, head high, tears blinding her.

Behind her, she heard Herbert pleading, "Bonnie! Wait! It's all a big mistake!"

She pushed her way out of the saloon. Outside, Herbert caught up to her, sniffing and wiping his nose. "It's a mistake, I tell you!"

"Mistake? I saw you, Herbert! Your tongue was hanging out like a hungry hound's and you were stuffing money in her garter!"

"But I can explain!" He grabbed her arm and they struggled.

"Herbert, let go of me!"

Cash McCalley ran out of the saloon just then. "You heard the lady, let go of her."

"Now who asked you to mix in?" Herbert sounded hysterical. "She's my fiancée."

"Not any more!" Bonnie sobbed and hit him with her reticule while he hung onto her arm.

"I said let go of the lady," Cash snapped and then he socked Herbert and sent him stumbling backward. Herbert sat on the sidewalk, whimpering and wiping blood from his mouth.

"Oh, don't act so gallant, McCalley!" Bonnie sobbed. "You're no better than he is!" Tears blinded her as she stumbled toward her buggy in the darkness.

"Bonnie, wait!" Cash ran after her, caught her arm, whirled her around.

"Leave me alone!" she struck out at him blindly. "I reckon you'll tell your friend, Bat, and this will be in the papers tomorrow so all the men can have a good laugh."

He stared down at her, thinking she had never looked so small and vulnerable and desirable as she did now. "No, I won't tell anyone, I promise."

"You promise? I can't trust you, you're no gentleman."

"I never claimed to be," he said, and wanted very much to take her in his arms; hold her, protect her. "Here, let me drive you back to the hotel." He caught her arm but she twisted out of his grasp.

"No. Hell, no!" Blindly, she lifted her skirts and struggled to get up in her buggy.

"If you'd let me help you—"

"Stay away from me, you bastard. You're as bad as Herbert is."

"At least I'm not a hypocrite," he pointed out as he watched her struggling to get up in the buggy.

"And for your information, I'm not coyote bait, either!" she managed to get up in the buggy, grabbed the reins.

"What?" He scratched his head, evidently confused.

"Oh, don't be so innocent! You can forget about a bag for my head, too, because you won't get the chance."

"The chance for what?"

"Don't play innocent with me. You know, you rascal!

Now hear this! I'll see you in hell, Cash McCalley, before I let you put on your bloody boxing match!"

"You said this was a matter of principle, not personal," he protested.

"Well, by God, now it's personal!" She snarled and struck out at him with her little whip.

"If you'd just let me talk—"

She slashed at him with her whip again. "I'll do whatever it takes to defeat you, you Scots-Irish rake!"

Herbert called, "Bonnie, I—I can explain—"

"Oh, shut up! Men!" Still sobbing, she slashed wildly at her horse with the little whip and the startled animal took off at a lope.

Cash stood watching her drive away. He regretted the hurt in those big blue eyes and he wanted to protect her, shield her, make love to her. And what she wanted to do to him was ruin him, destroy him.

Herbert stumbled over to him, wiping blood from his cut lip. "I wasn't doin' nothin' other men don't do."

"But not to Bonnie," Cash grabbed him by the lapel, "not to her."

"She's my fiancée," Herbert backed away.

"Not any more," Cash said. "You go near her again, I'll make you look like the dogs have had you under the porch. I'll whip you 'til you look like you tangled with a bear."

"I was just trying to better myself," Herbert muttered as he backed away from Cash's doubled-up fists.

"We've both hurt her," Cash admitted, "but she expected better from you."

"You ain't gonna get her," Herbert whimpered. "She hates you."

"Yeah, she does," Cash sighed. "Now get out of here before I hit you again!"

Cursing and wiping his bloody mouth, Herbert stumbled away into the darkness.

Cash turned and looked down the street toward the disappearing buggy. *I was just trying to better myself.* What had Herbert meant by that?

Fifi came out of the saloon. "What the hell's going on out here?"

She was the last person Cash wanted to see. "Nothin'."

"Nothin', huh?" She put her hands on her hips and looked down the road at the disappearing buggy. "Ladies ought not come into saloons; they sees stuff they shouldn't see. Herbert ain't the first man been caught where he wasn't supposed to be."

"That's true." Cash shrugged. "I felt sorry for her, though."

"She's trying to ruin you and you feel sorry for her? You been eating loco weed?"

He laughed ruefully and rubbed his bruised knuckles. "You're right, Fifi."

"You been fightin' for her? That sounds serious," Fifi said.

"Naw," he shook his head. "I been wantin' to hit that chicken feed salesman ever since I met him."

"And that's all it is?"

"Now what else?" Cash ran his hand through his mussed hair and picked up his Stetson from the brick sidewalk.

"Ohh," she smiled and put her hand on his arm. "For a minute, I thought you was goin' soft on me."

"For her?" he scoffed. "Never. I look out for Number One and I still will. Bonnie Purdy ain't gettin' between me and all that money I intend to make."

"Sure, Handsome." She wasn't sure he believed what he was saying, but she saw the way the chips were beginning to fall. Still she had to try. She ran her hand up and down his arm, loving this man. She had from the first time she laid eyes on him more than three years ago. Before that, she had been Clint Purdy's girl. "Hey, sport, why don't you come up to my room? I'll treat you good, you know I will."

She could tell by his expression he wasn't thinking about her. He was looking down the road again after that buggy. "Sorry, Fifi, I got things to do, plans to make."

She sighed. "Cash, there's a hundred guys in the saloon that would get on their knees for the offer I just made you."

"What?" He hadn't even heard her. He was still staring down the road.

"Never mind," she shrugged. "Okay, well, maybe I'll see you tomorrow."

"John L. Sullivan is comin' to town tomorrow," he said and brushed her hand off. "We're hopin' everyone will get excited about that and change their minds about the boxin' match."

"Yeah." She answered without enthusiasm. There were only two things on Cash's mind right now. His big boxing match was one of them. Sadly, she wasn't the other. Well, she would survive. She always did.

The fat manager stuck his head out the swinging doors. "Hey, Fifi, what the hell you doin' out there? Got some rich customers wantin' to buy you drinks."

"Sure. I'm coming." She blinked back tears as she

turned toward the saloon and swallowed hard. "'Bye, Cash."

"You mean, good night."

She shook her head. "No, good-bye. I know when I'm playing a lousy hand and have to fold."

"What do you mean?"

Men could be so dense. He hadn't realized it himself yet, but Fifi knew. She had already lost Cash to a girl who was too stupid or too strait-laced to appreciate a real man. He was Bonnie's for the taking and even he didn't know it . . . or maybe he hadn't admitted it, even to himself. She'd stolen Bonnie's man and now the lady was stealing hers. Turnabout was fair play, she reckoned.

Fifi took a deep breath, swallowed her sobs, pasted a smile on her painted mouth and went inside to have a drink with the rich customers.

Chapter Seventeen

It was still early the next morning when Cash rode to the railroad station to see if there might be messages for him. There were.

"By thunder, that woman is gonna ruin me!" Cash crumpled the telegrams from New Mexico and Nevada and glared at the telegraph boy. "Wilbur, I don't know how in the hell that Mrs. Purdy knew I was tryin' to set the boxing match there."

The scrawny boy backed away, shaking his head. "I swear, Mr. McCalley, I didn't tell her what you was trying to do. Matter of fact, last couple of days, I ain't talked to her at all. She's just come by, fed the cat and gone on."

Cash scowled. "*My* cat."

"She's got him where she can pet him now," Wilbur volunteered.

It was the wrong thing to say. "Prissy, civilized women!" Cash snorted and strode out of the railroad station. He mounted Dusty and rode back to the hotel, still wondering how that infernal, nosey girl was getting her information. Some of the hotel employees must be reporting back to her.

It was still very early in the morning and Cash went into the dining room to have steak and eggs. He looked around and said to the waiter, "Joe, how come I never see Mrs. Purdy in here havin' breakfast? I don't reckon I dare hope she's checked out?"

The waiter poured Cash a cup of coffee, shaking his head. "Nope, she's still here, but she don't never come into the dining room for breakfast; she likes room service."

"Oh," Cash grumbled and sipped his coffee as the waiter left his table. Come to think of it, he wasn't even sure what floor she was on; not that it made any difference. Now that New Mexico and Nevada had been crossed off his list of possibilities, just what was he going to do? This boxing match couldn't be canceled, he had a lot of money involved, and besides, he'd given his word to the sporting men of this state that Cash McCalley would bring them a world champion boxing match. Everyone in Texas knew that if Cash McCalley said a rooster could pull a train, you could buy your ticket and climb aboard.

He buttered a biscuit and thought about the important man who was about to arrive on a late morning train. John L. Sullivan was an ex-world champion and hundreds of people would turn out to gawk. "Includin' Mrs. Purdy and her protestors," he growled. "That is, if she's heard about it."

Cash had made a major effort to keep that information quiet. He'd hardly told a soul since he and Bat Masterson had talked.

Cash went upstairs to shave, glanced at his pocket watch. He'd better be getting back to the station. When he walked out of his room, he noticed empty dishes on a tray by the next door. "Some people too lazy to walk down to the dinin' room for breakfast," he muttered and kept walking. Just as he reached the stairs, he saw a familiar petite figure starting down ahead of him. She wore a dark blue dress, a bonnet with flowers around the brim and she turned when she heard his step.

He forced himself to be polite, although he was furious with her about blocking his New Mexico and Nevada bids. "Well, good mornin,' Mrs. Purdy, I didn't realize we were on the same floor."

She looked startled and he noted her eyes were slightly swollen and red. No doubt she had cried a bucketful over the humiliation of finding out about Herbert.

She gulped. "Uh, well, yes, I reckon we are." Then she hastened her steps as if eager to escape from him.

He hurried after her, decided he would not mention what had happened at the Black Lace, it would be too humiliating for her. "You and some of the ladies goin' shoppin'?"

"Maybe," she said and almost ran down the stairs.

Now Cash went down the steps into the lobby at a more leisurely pace, wondering why she was in such a rush. Could she possibly—? No, of course not, there was no way for her and her protestors to know about John L. Sullivan unless they had a spy working at the hotel or Bat had spilled the beans.

He got to the lobby doors just in time to see Mrs. Purdy getting into a buggy and driving away. At least she could handle a horse. Some women were so helpless, they wouldn't dream of driving a buggy themselves.

As per his instructions, Dusty had been returned to the stable for a good feed and rubdown and a buggy now awaited Cash. "I wish Mrs. Purdy was a little less independent and strong-willed," he muttered as he went out the hotel doors.

Of course, those traits were what made Bonnie Purdy different from other women. Would the little wench never give up and return to Shot Gun? Surely the Lone Star Ladies couldn't pay her bills forever.

On the other hand, he thought as he drove toward the train station, some of the women who belonged to that group were married to rich men and were willing to pay to support causes they favored. No doubt they saw Mrs. Purdy as a pure, unsullied Joan of Arc and would rally around her unless and until she fell off her pedestal. "Hmm," Cash thought, "if I could just tumble her off that pedestal. . . ."

Of course, that would be too rotten for even the worst scoundrel to consider. On the other hand, if he didn't figure out something quick, Mrs. Purdy and her bunch would ruin him and she'd have no qualms about that. "Sometimes an *hombre* just has to fight fire with fire." In his mind, a dastardly plan began to evolve.

As Cash reined in his rig at the train station, he saw Bonnie Purdy stepping down from her buggy. *Oh, no. Now what was she doing here?*

Herbert Snodgrass hurried to meet her. "Bonnie, dear," Herbert sniffed and tried to take her hand, "why won't you answer my messages?"

"Go away, Herbert. I can't deal with you now."

Cash sat in his buggy, watching. He had that sudden horrible feeling that she was one step ahead of him again.

Herbert was pleading with her. "Honestly, my dear, it's all a big mistake. I was in that saloon to spy on that promoter, that's all."

"Don't believe him, Mrs. Purdy!" Cash yelled. "He's in the Black Lace all the time, his tongue hangin' out like a hound dog."

They both turned and looked at Cash.

"Now," Herbert said to the girl, "would you believe that rascal over your own fiancé?"

Bonnie looked bewildered and uncertain. "I—I—"

"Don't believe him," Cash raised his voice. "I got no reason to lie to you."

She drew herself up proudly. "On the contrary, Mr. McCalley, you are the worst kind of scoundrel, and as for you, Herbert, I'll have to think about this."

Herbert was almost on his knees, trying to kiss her hand but she whacked at him with her reticule and tied up her horse. "I don't have time, Herbert. We'll talk later."

"He's a weasel," Cash called. "If you take him back, you'll be sorry."

"Who asked you to butt in?" Herbert whined.

Cash stepped down from his buggy and tied the horse. "Watch out, weasel, I socked you once before and you still got teeth to lose."

Herbert seemed to step backward.

"Stop this, you two, this minute!" Bonnie snapped. "We don't have time for these shenanigans right now."

It was then, Cash heard some commotion approaching and turned to look. It was a large parade, marching and singing. "Oh, no, don't tell me—?"

"You didn't think I'd let that old wastrel from back East arrive without a welcoming committee, did you?" Bonnie said triumphantly and headed to meet her faithful followers.

"I'd like to spank that sassy miss," Cash muttered under his breath, but there was nothing to do now but meet the handful of newsmen and sporting men who were gathering at the station to greet the famous John L. Sullivan. In the distance, the train whistled and blew smoke.

Up the block, Bonnie led her protestors with their signs. Reverend Tubbs marched beside her, leading the crowd as they sang hymns. "When we all get to heaven, what a great rejoicing there will be . . . "

"I'd like to send 'em all to heaven," Cash muttered. "Now how in the hell did Bonnie find out about John L.? I don't remember tellin' anybody but Bat Masterson and I warned him about keepin' it secret."

Bat Masterson stood in the station, scribbling furiously in his notepad. "Well, I see we got protestors anyway."

"Did you tell anyone?" Cash watched the approaching march, cursing under his breath.

Bat shook his head. "Only a few newsmen. It's too big not to share. How often does a famous man like John L. come West?"

"By thunder, we got a spy somewhere in our midst!" Cash said and glared at the approaching Mrs. Purdy and her crowd. Since it was a hot summer day, besides protest signs and banners, many of the ladies carried parasols to keep the sun off their delicate complexions.

"Is it him? Could that twerp be the spy?" Bat nodded toward Herbert who had just joined the front marchers, walking between Bonnie and Reverend Tubbs.

Cash shook his head. "No, everybody knows better than to trust Herbert. That little snake would do anything to worm his way back into her good graces."

Bat shrugged. "I'd say it served her right if she ends

up with him. Seems you should be thinking the same."

"Sure, I'll be happy if she's stupid enough to take him back." But he wasn't happy. Somehow, he thought Bonnie was too smart to believe the chicken feed salesman, but women could be awfully stupid sometimes . . . especially if they were worried about ending up alone. For some of them, *any* man beat no man at all.

The protestors were almost upon them and the train was chugging into the station.

"We'd better hurry and get over there next to the mayor," Bat said, "before the protestors take over the whole platform."

"What? Oh, sure." Cash had been too mesmerized by the defiant girl to think much further. Yes, he was going to have to do whatever it took to bring her down.

However, the protestors were heading for the platform, too. Cash and Bat had to push through the singing crowd to reach the train as it pulled into the station with a puff of black smoke and squealing brakes.

The train stopped, the conductor put down the steps. A big, pompous man in natty clothes with a diamond stickpin in his tie, now stood in the doorway of the car.

The mayor cleared his throat and stepped forward. "Oh, Mr. Sullivan, it is a great honor—"

"We're marching to Zion, beautiful, beautiful Zion . . ." sang the protestors as they pushed forward.

Cash groaned aloud and had to struggle to reach the train. Some of the little old ladies stomped his toes and elbowed him hard as he tried to break through. "Come on, Bat," he shouted.

"I'm tryin!" Bat yelled. "But the little old ladies are whacking me with their signs—"

"Who you calling old?" And a frail, elderly woman carrying a PEACE NOT FIST FIGHTS sign hit him across the head with her sign.

"Mayor," Cash shouted over the singing, "I think you'll have to give up on the welcome."

"I don't get to make my speech? But I worked on it for two days—" The mayor was obviously crestfallen.

"Let's just get Mr. Sullivan out of here before some of these little old ladies hurt him!" Cash shouted.

"We are opposed to violence!" Bonnie Purdy shouted and gave Cash a good whack with her sign.

That started a free-for-all. Sweet, gentle housewives and ministers of the Gospel swung signs and reticules. Newsmen and public officials were poked with parasols.

Cash elbowed his way through the combatants to the train. "Mr. Sullivan, if you'll come with me, I'll get you out of here!"

"Is it safe?" The big man stayed on the train, looking around at the fights and screaming people.

"I'll run interference for you!" Cash shouted back.

But once on the platform, the pair was besieged by little old ladies and preachers with their protest banners. Parasols and signs became lethal weapons in the fray.

"Good Lord," said the former fighter, "is Texas always this dangerous?"

"Only when you upset the righteous!" Cash shouted. "You ain't one of them back East liberals, too, are you?"

"I dunno; I'm Irish, is that the same thing?" John L. fought his way through the station to Cash's side.

"I don't think so!" Cash shouted back. "Come on, grab your luggage. I've got a buggy waitin'!"

They began to push back through the crowd.

"Hey!" Bat yelled, "Wait for me! I want some quotes!"

But by now, the crowd had realized the object of their displeasure was about to leave and were giving chase.

"Sorry, Bat, it's every man for himself!" Cash yelled and shoved his way through the singing housewives and preachers, leading John L. Sullivan out to the buggy. "Get in, quick!"

The two men climbed into the buggy with the protestors gathering around. The frightened horse reared and whinnied.

Bonnie waved her sign at Cash. "We'll stop you! There'll be no fight in Texas!"

Cash snapped the reins and the startled horse took off at a trot. John L. hung onto his natty derby and looked back. "That's the meanest crowd I've ever had to face and most of them look like grandmothers, except that pretty little brunette up front."

"That's Bonnie Purdy, the ringleader, and don't let her fool you; she'd stomp us flat if she got the chance," Cash said and kept driving.

"I'd say she's got something personal against you from the way she glared," the boxer said.

"That ain't the half of it," Cash admitted, "She'd like to nail my hide to a barn door, that's what."

"Oh?" the other man grinned. "I can imagine—"

"It ain't like that," Cash snapped. "Although I admit, I've tried. She's incorruptible."

The boxer laughed. "Any woman is corruptible . . . by the right man."

"Believe me," Cash said as they left the protestors behind in a cloud of dust and the hymns faded in the distance, "if I could, I would. Then her followers would desert her and this whole protest thing would die."

John L. winked at him. "With all this riding on it, I'd be tempted to try again."

"Naw," Cash shook his head, "she's a lady. There ain't no smearin' her reputation."

"We headin' out to the training camps?" John L. asked.

"Yep, thought you'd like to see what's goin' on, although I reckon the protestors will come out there, too."

"Surely most Texans don't agree with the protestors?"

Cash sighed, watching the road ahead as they drove. "Nope, Texans like a good fight better than anybody, but the protestors are vocal enough to scare off the powers that be into voting against it."

"Your little lady must have a lot of influence then; know a lot of important people to cause all this trouble."

"I don't think so," Cash shrugged. "She's just a small town librarian who's president of the Lone Star Ladies. I figure her organization pays her expenses to stay in town, but surely they can't do it forever."

The other laughed. "When women take up a cause, they will throw every penny they can get into it. Still, that lady wasn't looking at you like she was just trying to stop a boxing match."

"You're right," Cash nodded. "It's personal with her; *very* personal."

They were approaching Fitzsimmons' training camp now.

John L. said, "Where is this match to be held, anyway?"

Cash hedged as he drove through the gate. "Well, I'm still workin' on that."

The other looked startled. "You mean, after all this time, it ain't finalized?"

"As you can see, the protestors have been creatin' a lot of uncertainty, but I got me a good idea this mornin' that I think might work. I've sent a telegram to a friend of mine." Cash reined in and they got out of the buggy.

"Hmm, nice training camp," the old boxer said. "Must be a lot of money tied up in this event. If it doesn't go—"

"If it don't happen, I'll be back workin' as a wrangler, cleanin' out stables. Every dime I got is due to be lost."

John L. Sullivan looked alarmed. "You're a real gambler, I'll give you that."

Cash shrugged as they walked toward the barn. "If I'd known I was gonna have to go up against that stubborn little librarian, I might have not done it, but now there's nothin' I can do but take the bit in my teeth and run with it."

They went into the barn where boxers were working out and the old lion chewed a punching bag.

"Holy Mother of God!" said John L., freezing in place. "Is that a lion?"

Nero roared half-heartedly and returned to his ragged punching bag.

"He's harmless." The challenger paused in the ring and came over. "Welcome, John, we're glad to see you. You'll add some fire to this project."

"Good to see you, Bob." The older man smiled and looked around. "I just met the opposition."

"Oh, the ladies and the preachers?" The sweating fighter leaned on the ropes. "The one that leads them is out for Cash's scalp."

"Let's talk about something else," Cash snapped, "like how much money this match will make."

"Won't if it don't happen," Fighting Bob said. "What's that sound I hear?"

Everyone paused to listen.

Very faintly in the distance came the unmistakable strains of "We're marching to Zion, beautiful, beautiful Zion. . . ."

Cash cursed aloud. "That'll be her and her bunch, along with a bunch of newspapermen."

John L. looked more than a little perturbed. "Then let's get out of here. I've been poked with all the parasols I want today."

"They don't usually hang around long once they get Nero riled up and he starts roaring at them," the challenger said.

"We'll leave anyway," Cash said.

"By the way," Fitzsimmons pulled off his boxing gloves, "you still ain't said where this big match is going to be."

"Uh, any day now," Cash said.

"It's been weeks now," the boxer insisted. "I want to know in the next couple of days or I'm heading back East."

"It's gonna be a surprise," Cash said. "I'll know in a few hours, honest." He grabbed John L. by the arm and they walked out to the buggy.

John L. looked over at him as they walked. "You gotta clue where you'll hold it?"

Cash shook his head. "Not the faintest, but like I said, I just sent a telegram. That's my last shot, but it's a good one."

"You ain't gonna let that little librarian win, are you?" They got into the buggy. The sounds of the hymns and the brass band were louder now.

"Not even if I have to pull the dirtiest trick in the book," Cash vowed.

They managed to get past the protest parade with the little old ladies yelling "Shame! Shame!" and throwing dirt clods at them.

Cash took John L. back to the hotel, saw him checked in on the third floor.

John L. said as they started up the stairs, "Anything in this town to do at night?"

"They got cancan dancers at the Black Lace Saloon," Cash suggested.

The other man's eyes lit up. "You want to go tonight?"

Cash shook his head. "I got plans to make a'fore that Mrs. Purdy destroys me. You go have a good time. There's a blonde named Fifi LaFemme you'll really like."

The two men parted and Cash went to his room to think. Unless his friend, the judge, came through for him, all was lost. This was Cash's last plan.

About supper time, there was a knock on his door. "Cash, I got a telegram."

He opened the door to Wilbur. "Is it good?"

The skinny kid grinned and nodded. "Sure is. You keep your promise?"

"You know I will." Cash took the telegram, read it.

"By thunder, looks like we got something. I need to send a reply, Wilbur."

"Sure, I got my pad and pencil." The boy licked the tip of his pencil and made ready.

> *To Judge Roy Bean, Langtry, Texas. Dear Roy. Stop. Glad you agree. Stop. Hurry up the arena. Stop. Plan it for this coming Saturday. Stop. You'll make a fortune selling beer and grub to the spectators. Stop. Best, Cash.*

Wilbur stopped writing and stared at him. "But, Mr. McCalley, Langtry is in Texas, ain't it? Down near the border. You know the governor said he'd send the Rangers—"

"Well, I wasn't plannin' exactly Texas." Cash winked.

"Not Mexico?" Wilbur asked. "You know the president of Mexico said you couldn't—"

"I got a trick up my sleeve, Wilbur. Now you don't tell Mrs. Purdy about this if you want a free ticket and a chance to bet on the match."

"Me? Naw, I won't tell her. Them women, always tryin' to keep us men from having fun." He turned to go.

"You seen anything of Mrs. Purdy?"

Wilbur nodded. "As I came up the stairs, she and some of her protestors were just coming into the hotel. I think they went into the dining room for lunch."

"Okay, now get that message off, pronto." Cash gave the boy a silver dollar, nodded to him and closed the door.

Maybe he had at last outsmarted Bonnie Purdy. For the first time in weeks, things seemed to be looking up.

Chapter Eighteen

Cash had a lot of plans to make so he ran downstairs, grabbed a quick sandwich in the bar and stuck his head in the dining room. The place was full of hot, weary protestors, fanning themselves and drinking iced tea. Bonnie Purdy sat at a table with the Reverend Tubbs and Herbert Snodgrass. She looked very pleased with herself.

Herbert Snodgrass? Surely she wasn't stupid enough to make up with that little snake? Or maybe he had joined her table without permission. Cash would have thought Bonnie was savvy enough not to believe the chicken feed salesman after what had happened before.

Disgusted and annoyed, Cash returned to his room. By thunder, if she ended up with the sniffling Herbert, she damned well deserved him. Anyway, why should Cash care? His only interest in the petite girl was getting her out of his business so he could make some money.

Cash tried to think about boxing, but he kept seeing Bonnie sitting with that snide little salesman in the dining room. In a few minutes, he heard footsteps

down the hall and they paused next to Cash's door.
The man said something and the woman demurred.
Evidently, the man was hoping to come into the lady's
room. She was telling him to leave. Cash stood up.
*Was he going to have to rescue a lady from some ardent
swain?* He went to the door, listened. The voices
seemed familiar, somehow.

There was the sound of a slap and the man stomping away.

"Good for you, sister," Cash grinned. "You must be
pretty sassy to put him in his place like that."

The voices had been familiar; too familiar. A
thought crossed his mind. Naw, couldn't be. He
shook his head. He heard the sound of her key in the
lock as she went inside. So this was the person who
had kept Cash from renting the whole suite so Fifi
could join him? He could hear the woman walking
around in the room next door. Puzzled, Cash stood
up, went to the adjoining door and listened. Then he
noticed the keyhole.

A gentleman never looks through a keyhole, he thought.
Well, no one had ever called him a gentleman. The
temptation grew too much and he dropped to one
knee and peered through. There was something
stuffed in the keyhole to stop his peering. Very disap-
pointing.

Cash returned to his chair and his notes. There was
a lot to do even if his buddy, the notorious Judge Roy
Bean, took care of things on his end. Somehow Cash
had to let all the boxers and their personnel, the
newsmen and hundreds of fans know where to rendezvous without stirring up Mrs. Purdy and her
troops. He had to face the fact that there was no way

to do this without Mrs. Purdy's hundreds of resolute
ladies finding out and creating yet another protest.

Hmm, he thought and leaned back in his chair. If
there was only some way to discredit this Texas Joan
of Arc so that her followers would desert her. He
smiled, remembering her ardent kisses. If only he
could seduce the lady, publicize it so that the Lone
Star Ladies would be too disenchanted to rally to her
cause.

"You randy rascal, that's something no Texan would
do; deliberately ruin a lady's reputation. Besides, so
far, you haven't had much luck with her." Cash shook
his head. Women had always found him irresistible,
and it stung his pride that Bonnie Purdy had with-
stood his charms. That made her an even bigger challenge and with everything riding on the fight. . . .
What a rotten, villainous idea. Cash grinned even
wider. Yes, but could he make it work?

The next morning, Cash was up early and going out
his door when he saw a waiter with a tray at the door
next to his. The boy knocked lightly on the door.
"Room service."

Cash went on down the stairs, preoccupied with
everything he had to do. Langtry was a long way off,
so there'd have to be a special train available. How in
thunder could he alert all the eager men about where
and when without also alerting Mrs. Purdy's protestors? He certainly didn't want a couple of hundred
ladies with their signs and parasols coming aboard.
He wasn't too crazy about having the Texas Rangers
along on the train, either, although what Cash and

Judge Roy Bean had planned was going to keep the law from interfering.

He had a quick bite to eat in the dining room with John L. Sullivan, who wanted to talk about how high Fifi could kick her legs. Somehow, the subject of Fifi didn't interest Cash any more. "Listen, John L., you want her, you can take her back to New York with you."

"Aw," he made a dismissing gesture, "I already asked, she said she was in love with some bloke here in Dallas who don't care about her, but she ain't giving up hope and couldn't leave."

Cash shrugged. "That's her loss, then." He wasn't interested in Fifi's private life; she'd been some fun, but for some reason, he hadn't thought much about her in several weeks. The resolute Mrs. Purdy had occupied his mind.

He told John L. his plan, swore him to silence, then mounted Dusty and rode to the railroad station to see about a train. The officials warmed to the idea once Cash told them his plan. Unfortunately, booking the train pretty much cleaned him out. If he didn't sell a lot of tickets to the fight in the next few days, he was in big trouble.

Next he rode out to both fighters' training camps. "We got to keep this quiet," he warned them, "or we'll have protestors lyin' down across the tracks so the train can't roll, or at least fillin' up the seats so the spectators can't get aboard. We meet at the station at high noon next Saturday."

Then he sought out Bat Masterson and told him his plan.

Bat whistled with admiration. "It might just work."

"Not if Mrs. Purdy's protestors get on the train or try to stop it from pullin' out."

Bat rubbed his chin. "Now how do you figure to get the word out without the protestors finding out, too?"

"I got a plan," Cash nodded. "If I could just discredit Mrs. Purdy so that her ladies would scorn her—"

Bat snorted with laughter. "Discredit her? Sorry, Cash, I believe she is the most stalwart pillar of virtue I've ever met."

"Ain't she, though? But I'm desperate. In the meantime, start spreadin' the word and sellin' them tickets. Remember, special train Saturday at high noon."

Bat pushed his derby back. "So where's this mystery train bound for?"

Cash grinned. "That's a secret I'll tell you and the engineer as we pull out. Then it'll be too late to stop us."

"The governor's bound to have some Rangers on board," Bat argued.

"Won't do 'em any good." Cash lit a cigarillo, mighty pleased with himself.

"But a mystery destination?"

Cash shrugged. "The boys won't mind as long as there's plenty of eats and drinks on the train." He stood up and the two shook hands. "Now sell them tickets and tell all the men you meet about the fight."

Bat grinned. "Wouldn't miss it for the world. See you Saturday noon."

Over the next several days, Cash alerted all the newsmen, who promised to print only the barest details. Then he sent runners to every saloon in town to spread the word: "Be on the special train leaving at high noon next Saturday."

It was evening. He looked down the street at the Black Lace Saloon, heard the music, but Fifi, or Gladys, didn't interest him. He had a snack in the hotel bar and went up to his room, tired but satisfied. His plan might just work—but not if Bonnie Purdy managed to get hundreds of females to come to the train station to protest. In his mind, he imagined Bonnie Purdy doing just that. By thunder, she'd be ornery and brave enough to lie down on the tracks in front of the engine. He couldn't help but admire her determination, but damned if he was going to let her wipe him out.

He heard movement in the next room. Cash pulled out his pocket watch. It was later than he thought and the lady was probably retiring for the night. Curious, he stepped to the adjoining door, squatted and looked through the keyhole. This time, whatever had been blocking his view had fallen out. He had a good view. An attractive lady stood with her back to him, taking off her dark blue dress.

Only a rotten cad would watch a lady disrobe, but he'd been called that a few times. As he watched, fascinated, the lady stood there in a lace petticoat and corset. By thunder, the petite miss had a shapely back. Cash took a deep breath and watched, fascinated as she took off the petticoat and stood there in lace drawers and her corset. Then she turned around and walked across the room.

Well, I'll be damned. Cash cursed under his breath. No wonder the voices had sounded so familiar. Bonnie Purdy. Bonnie Purdy had the room next to his. How could he have been such a fool? Of course she had also been using the keyhole to spy on him and listen to his conversations, no doubt keeping one step ahead of him that way. Why, that little—! He was so furious, he wanted to bang on her door and give her a piece of his mind, but now she was taking a long, lacy pink nightgown from the bureau drawer.

Later he would think about his outrage and her trickery, he told himself, but now, he couldn't tear himself away from the view as she began to take off her lace corset cover and then her corset. Cash held his breath and watched, mesmerized, feeling sudden desire despite his anger. Mrs. Purdy had beautiful skin and a pair of the most perfect breasts he'd ever seen and he'd seen a lot of them. These were perfectly formed with pink rosette nipples. He felt his desire rise.

You fool, he thought, *she's your worst enemy. How can you be thinking how you'd like to make love to her?* But that was exactly what he was thinking. Was she going to take off her lace drawers? He waited, holding his breath. She turned her back, pulling down the coverlet on her bed and stepped out of her drawers. That had to be the nicest, roundest little bottom he'd seen in a long, long time. No, the most perfect bottom ever. She made Fifi look like a fat cow.

Then Bonnie picked up the pink lace nightgown, slipped it over her head and blew out the bedside lamp. Cash heard the springs creak as she got in the bed. He pressed his eye to the keyhole, attempting to see more, but the darkness of the room defeated him. He could only imagine Bonnie curled up in bed in that long pink nightgown.

Taking a deep breath, he got up and began to pace the floor. Desire struggled against anger in his heart.

On one hand, he had never wanted a woman as much as he wanted this one and yet, she was his bitter enemy, standing between him and the big jackpot he needed so badly. What to do? His previous idea seemed doomed to failure. Then he paused and grinned. "Cash McCalley, are you not the biggest ladies' man in Dallas, no, in all of Texas? Then think of the lady as a challenge."

So far, that hadn't worked and he was running out of time. He lay sleepless, making his plans. Or maybe he was sleepless because in his mind, he saw Bonnie in her long pink nightgown over that luscious body, just a few feet away on the other side of that door. What he was going to attempt was unthinkable for any Texan, but if it came down to a choice of ruining a lady's reputation to save his boxing match, he'd have to do it. He told himself that Mrs. Bonnie Purdy had brought this on herself.

Early the next morning, Cash dressed and went out into the hall just as the bellboy rapped on the door next to his. "Room service."

Cash stepped back so that he could not be seen. After a moment, the door opened a crack and he saw a dainty arm clad in pink lace reach around to take the tray. Then the door closed again.

The bellboy started to walk away, but Cash caught up with him at the stairs. "You deliver room service to that lady every mornin' about this time?"

The boy grinned. "Yep. Lady tips good, too."

"She always order the same thing?" Cash's mind was working.

"Yep. She don't even tell the manager; I bring it up automatically every morning."

Cash put his arm around the boy's shoulders. "Tell you what; here's five silver dollars."

The boy became suspicious but he took the money. "What do you want me to do?"

"Nothin'. Just tomorrow, don't bring up a tray, okay?"

"But Mrs. Purdy will be upset—"

"Oh, you see, I'm plannin' on takin' the lady out for breakfast tomorrow—"

"Mrs. Purdy don't ever go out for breakfast," the boy protested as they walked.

Cash grinned. "Trust me on this, kid. I'm not sure the lady will be wantin' breakfast. In fact, I think eggs and biscuits will be the furthest thing from her mind."

The boy paused. "Maybe I should check with Mrs. Purdy."

"Oh, no, no. Take my word for it and don't bring up a tray, okay? Oh, would you like a free ticket to the fight?"

"Wow!" The boy gasped as he took the ticket. "Yeah, I really want to go."

"Good. Now be at the train station Saturday; train leaves at high noon."

"All right, Mr. McCalley," the boy sighed as he pocketed the ticket. "I sure hope I ain't about to get in trouble."

Cash winked and patted the boy on the back. "Trust me, son, you ain't the one who's gonna be in trouble."

"What about the next day?"

"I'm not sure Mrs. Purdy will still be in town on Sunday," Cash said. "In fact, if things go right, she'll leave town without much fanfare."

"What?" the boy asked.

"Never mind. Now you go along now, I got things to

do." The two split up and Cash went down to the dining room and grinned the whole time he was enjoying his steak and eggs. Yes, that little wench was going to get what she deserved and if it was a dastardly thing to do, well, nobody had ever called Cash McCalley a saint.

After breakfast, he started searching for the scores of reporters who were in town to cover the big fight. Being newsmen, they were drinking their breakfast at the Black Lace Saloon. Thank God, Fifi was nowhere in sight. But then, she never got up 'til noon.

"Hey, Cash," Bat pushed his natty derby to the back of his head. "The plan still in place? I been telling it all around town. I hear tickets is selling like hotcakes."

Cash nodded and sat down with a satisfied sigh as the newsmen gathered around him. "Yep, boys, be on that train."

"Well, where's it going?" asked one.

"Can't tell you that," Cash said. "I can just promise you that at the end of that ride is that big fight y'all have been waitin' for."

"In Texas?" another asked doubtfully. "You know the governor has sworn—"

"I know what the governor says, but I think I've outfoxed him and all those protestors, too; once that train starts rollin'."

Bat lit a cigar. "Rumor's already spreading like wild fire. You can just bet Mrs. Purdy will have hundreds of her protestors at the station to stop that train."

"Now just suppose all the ladies got disillusioned with that pillar of virtue?"

The others blinked. "What do you mean?"

"I mean, suppose Mrs. Purdy turned out not to be the staid, upright person everyone thinks she is?"

"Oh, she is!" One of the newsmen nodded. "I tried to flirt with her some and she hit me with her parasol."

"That's Bonnie, all right." Cash sighed and a tiny bit of doubt joined the uneasiness in his brain. "Anyway, Bat, I need you and about a half dozen reporters to do something for me early Saturday mornin' that's gonna change everything."

"What you got in mind?" Bat leaned closer.

"Let's talk, old friend." Cash led him outside and told him his plan. "Don't tell the others 'til Saturday morning as you come into the hotel."

Bat shook his head. "Won't work; we all know the lady hates you."

"We'll see. It's my last chance of success so I got to try. Remember the room number?"

Bat nodded. "Dirty trick if it works."

Cash grinned to hide his own inner discomfort. "She deserves it. The whole boxin' match depends on stoppin' that lady in her tracks."

"Okay, we'll be there," Bat promised.

"That's all I'm askin'," Cash said. "I'll take care of the rest." He left Bat and then went out to check on his boxers. They were working out, jogging along the road, the old lion loping along after them. Cash rode next to them. Even Dusty didn't get excited about the lion; maybe he'd decided the old beast was harmless. "You all ready to catch that train?"

"You sure we can get away with this?" Bob puffed. "I ain't wanting to end up in jail."

"Believe me, we'll be out of the Texas Rangers' jurisdiction." He rode along beside the joggers.

"Well, now, if this train is going to Mexico, I ain't

hankering to end up in some dirty jail down across the border because the president of Mexico said—"

"I know, but the *Ruales* got no jurisdiction, either."

"Hmm," Corbett looked up at Cash as the horse jogged next to him, "what about all them protestors?"

"Let me take care of Mrs. Purdy and her bunch."

Corbett stopped and eyed him, still puffing. "I hope to hell you know what you're doing. That woman don't seem to be the type to back off."

"She ain't," Cash nodded in agreement, and was surprised to realize he felt a hint of admiration for the stubborn girl. "Now you just make sure all the boxin' equipment and your people is on that train."

"Can I bring Nero?" Fitzsimmons leaned over to pat the old lion.

Cash scratched his jaw. "Sure, why not? There might be a stray goat or sheep out there for him."

When Nero heard the word "goat," he roared and then panted in the heat.

"Okay, then, it's all ready except for one small thing and I'll take care of that," Cash said.

"What about Reverend Tubbs?" Corbett asked.

Cash said, "I heard he's out of town on a revival. He's turned his protestors over to Mrs. Purdy. Stop worryin' so much; I got an idea."

He said his good-byes and returned to the hotel in time for lunch. He had to put his plan into action.

Bonnie Purdy was there, lunching alone. Cash slid into the chair opposite her. "Do you mind if I join you?"

She frowned. "It appears you already have."

He gave her his warmest, most sincere smile. "I've come to apologize, Bonnie."

She was taken off guard, then she eyed him suspiciously like a little hen surveying a wily coyote. "For what?"

He tried to look contrite. "I realize now that I was wrong and that boxin' is a brutal sport that ought to be done away with."

Bonnie blinked in surprise and then studied him closely. Besides being the handsomest, most virile man she'd ever met, he was also the cleverest. Gracious, he could talk a preacher into giving him the collection plate. "Cash McCalley, I'd believe it would snow in July down on the border, before I'd believe you were truly contrite."

"Now, Mrs. Purdy, Bonnie, you know I don't know the meanin' of a big word like that. I'm just a poor cowboy, not a smart librarian like you."

He tried to take her hand and for a moment, she let him. His hands were strong and big and she felt so helpless and feminine. Then she remembered what a rascal he was and reluctantly pulled away. "Mr. McCalley—"

"Call me Cash." He smiled and leaned toward her.

She had forgotten he had such a square chin and sincere gray eyes. When she took a deep breath, she smelled the scent of some wonderful aftershave. "Mr. McCalley," she tried to keep her voice stern, "I have already heard the rumor that you have arranged for a train to take the boxing crowd to some mysterious destination."

He only looked deep into her eyes, making her feel flustered and confused. "What?"

"I said—"

"Oh, yes. I'm sorry, my dear, it's just that when I look at you, I forget what the subject is."

"That's ridiculous," she answered, staring back into

that handsome face. "We're discussing . . ." Now what had they been discussing? She wrinkled her brow in thought. "Oh, yes, about the boxing match—"

"I told you you had convinced me it is a brutal sport and I should call it off."

"I would no more believe you, sir, than I would believe that a raccoon wouldn't steal eggs."

He winced. "I'm sorry you feel that way, Bonnie, but I reckon I deserve it. I'll go now, but I wanted you to know that I apologize for whatever trouble I've caused you and hope you'll think kindly of me later." He started to get up and without meaning to, she laid a hand on his arm.

"Wait? Where will you go?" It occurred to her that she might be seeing him for the very last time and it left a void in her life that surprised her.

He looked down at her hand on his arm, put his big hand over her small one. "What does it matter? You've won and I'll be broke, but I don't care much."

My, his hand on the back of hers was warm. "Are you—are you really going to be penniless?"

He shrugged. "It don't matter. I used to be a cowboy."

"I know, Senator Farraday told me."

"Well, maybe I can go back to work on his ranch."

His sincerity was making her feel terrible. "I didn't mean to ruin you; wipe you out."

"But it appears you have." *Were those tears in those blue eyes?* "I just wanted you to know I'm sorry and about what happened in Austin and in Hot Springs, that was most ungentlemanly of me, and I'm sorry." He lifted her small hand to his lips and kissed it.

I'm not, she almost said, remembering lying on the soft grass with him kissing and caressing her. If someone hadn't come along the bridle path, no doubt they would have—

"Bonnie, are you all right?" He looked anxious.

She started. "Why wouldn't I be?" Surely to God he couldn't read her thoughts?

"Well, your face is scarlet and you're breathin' deeper. I thought you might be having an attack of the vapors, or something. I reckon this is good-bye—"

"Wait!" She looked around, wondering if anyone else in the nearly empty dining room might be watching. "I think we need to talk."

He shook his head and stood up. "No, I've caused you enough trouble and you've shown me the error of my ways. You've won, lady, but I admire your dedication."

"Perhaps we could go riding or something," she said, surprised at how reluctant she was to let him walk away.

"Oh, no," he shook his head again, "that would wreck a lady's reputation; to be seen with me."

"I'm feeling badly that you've lost all your money on this boxing match."

He smiled down at her. He had such white, straight teeth. "You've got a good heart, Bonnie. It's okay, though, I've learned to roll with the punches. As I said, I'll just do something else." He turned to walk away.

She felt terrible, now that she thought of it, that this man would be penniless and broke because of her. *Don't be silly,* she scolded herself, *isn't that what you wanted—to stop him in his tracks?*

But he is so likable, so charming, her heart said. *And as slick as a snake,* her brain warned. "Where—where are you going?"

He shrugged. "I thought I'd take Dusty for a little

jaunt out through that pretty meadow to the west of town."

"Oh," she said.

"And you can go rally your troops again," he said. "Oh, by the way, about the cat—"

"I feel badly about Kitty Tom," she admitted. "I feel like I've been stealing your cat."

"Doesn't matter. I won't even be able to afford scraps for him now, so he'll be better off with you."

Tears came to her eyes and she blinked them away. "I—I don't want people to say that not only did I break you, I stole your cat."

"What does it matter what people think? Well, good-bye, Bonnie. In spite of our differences, I've come to admire you these last few weeks." He turned and walked away, smiling to himself. *Had she taken the bait?* He'd know in the next few minutes. There was a lot riding on this so he hoped the old McCalley charm still worked. He was still smiling as he strode out of the dining room.

Chapter Nineteen

Bonnie stared after the tall man as he strode out of the dining room. She really hadn't given much thought about leaving him penniless and even though the rascal deserved it, she felt badly. *Be careful, Bonnie, he's probably just like Clint Purdy, only wanting . . .* but Cash seemed so sincere.

If indeed he was giving up on the boxing match, her work in Dallas was done and she could return to Shot Gun. *What would happen to Cash McCalley?* He'd said he might go back to work as a wrangler on Senator Farraday's ranch. She knew of another ranch, the Lazy S, that needed more than a wrangler—it was in bad need of a foreman. Maybe she should tell Cash and if he didn't hold any hard feelings over losing the boxing thing, he might be willing to take the job.

That decided, Bonnie left the dining room and went to the hotel desk. "Could you have someone bring around a good horse from the livery? I thought I might go riding."

"Certainly, ma'am." The balding clerk snapped his fingers for a bellboy.

The young Mexican stared at her strangely as he

was given orders. What ailed the young man? However, he only nodded and went off to get her a horse while she ran upstairs and changed into the blue riding habit. She remembered the last time she had worn this. She flushed as she picked a wisp of dried Hot Springs grass off the sleeve. Bonnie stared into the mirror as she adjusted her cocky little hat with its broken feather sticking out at an odd angle.

Everything in her warned her not to trust Cash McCalley any further than she could throw a barn, yet the rascal held a terrible fascination for her. And knowing his stubbornness, it was difficult to believe he was going to give up on this big project and just walk away. Unless he might be feeling the same mixed emotions toward her as she did toward him.

Gracious, why all this thought and turmoil? she scolded herself as she went downstairs and out the door to where a pretty black filly waited in front of the hotel. Bonnie mounted up. She would just enjoy a ride and stop thinking about that charming scoundrel.

She found herself riding west. It's just that the prettiest view is that little valley west of town, she thought. There's a few trees and that would be nice in this summer heat. She flicked the filly with her little whip, hurrying a little.

In a few minutes, she saw a familiar big frame on a gray horse ahead of her. Even as her brain warned her, Bonnie's heart skipped a beat. She rode up next to him.

"Would you like some company?" She smiled, sheepishly.

He appeared genuinely startled. "Why, Mrs. Purdy, it don't make me no never mind, but I reckoned I'd seen you for the last time."

Now she felt foolish. "I—I just thought I could use a little exercise."

"Of course. I must say, you've been a worthy opponent. Now that this is over, I presume you'll go back to Shot Gun and marry Herbert?"

"Marry Herbert? I don't think so. Frankly, I don't trust the man. He reminds me of Clint Purdy, only not as handsome."

Cash smiled at her. "Good. I would think you could do much better."

"And what about Fifi LaFemme?"

"Who?"

"You know who I mean."

Cash snorted. "Oh, her. She never really figured into my plans. Besides, she's lookin' for a rich guy and that ain't me."

Bonnie watched the path ahead of them as they rode. "About Fifi," she hesitated. "I—I suspect Clint was seeing her all the time he was courting me."

"Oh? What makes you so sure?" He glanced over at her, gray eyes full of sympathy.

Bonnie swallowed hard. "Because of something he said just before he left our hotel room on our wedding night."

"I'm sorry." His voice was gentle. "Clint had to be the world's biggest fool. If I had you as a bride, waitin' for me in a hotel room, damned if I'd be headed for the Black Lace and Fifi."

She must not feel warmly toward him. "It's—it's kind of you to say so, but I figured I didn't have what it took to interest a man, except for one thing."

He didn't ask about the one thing, he only shook his head. "Bonnie, if we had met under different circumstances—"

"You think we'd be friends instead of adversaries?"

He grinned and winked at her. "There you go with the big words again. These horses are gettin' lathered. We ought to walk them a mite."

"I reckon you're right." *Should she take this chance?* Her intellect said "no" but her heart screamed "yes."

He reined in and dismounted. "See that big tree and a little stream up ahead? We can water there." He came around and held up his hands to her.

"I can dismount by myself," she said.

"But with a man around, you won't have to."

And what a man, she thought. Every nerve warned her to turn her horse around and head back to the hotel. However, there Cash McCalley stood, all tall and wide-shouldered, holding up his hands. She took a deep breath and dismounted, letting him put those big calloused hands on her small waist. She wondered if he would try to kiss her and if he did, would she resist?

He only set her little boots gently on the ground and took her filly's reins. "Let's walk, Bonnie."

"All right." She was relieved that was all he wanted. She liked the way his deep masculine voice said her name.

It was a Texas kind of day; warm, a light breeze blowing with butterflies drifting and mockingbirds singing from the trees, quail calling from the brush.

"Ah," he sighed, "a day like this makes you feel sorry for the whole world that they ain't lucky enough to be Texans, don't it?"

"It surely does. There's no place like Texas."

He grinned at her as they walked. "Amen. What will you do now, Bonnie, I mean, now that your convention is over and I've surrendered about the boxin' match?"

She shrugged. "Like I said before; go back to Shot Gun."

"Work in the library?"

"No. It's closed while they build the big new one that a wealthy rancher has donated. Then they'll hire a full time librarian, or maybe two."

"Not you? That don't seem fair."

She wouldn't tell him the truth. "I—I don't mind. I always knew it would be temporary."

He glanced at her with those gray eyes, more like a peaceful Texas dawn than a thunderstorm now. "I didn't mean to pry. I was worried about how you'd make it without a job and figured it gets pretty lonesome all by yourself in a small town like that."

"I was wondering the same thing about you," she countered.

"Ah, well, I'm used to it; me and Dusty. I just never met a girl I felt I couldn't live without, and besides, I could hardly afford a wife."

"Some women wouldn't care if you were broke," she said.

"I got my pride," he said. "I can't ask no woman to live in a tumbledown shack and go without like my Ma did."

"Did she love your father?"

"Oh, yes." He smiled, his expression far away. "She was the ranch house cook and they managed by workin' hard. She always said she wouldn't trade Pa for the governor."

"Well, then, that's true love. It's pretty rare, I reckon."

They came to the trees and Cash tied the horses so

they could drink from the creek. "You want to sit a spell?"

"I—I shouldn't."

"Suit yourself." He shrugged and pulled off his coat, spread it on the ground and sat down.

"I didn't mean any offense—"

"That's okay, Bonnie," he nodded. "I reckon I had that comin' after the way things happened in Hot Springs. I just couldn't help myself that day."

Very hesitantly, she sat down on the edge of his coat and leaned back against the tree. "We mustn't stay long."

"We'll go whenever you want. I've enjoyed your company. In fact, I kinda hate to see your stay end. Never met a woman who could go toe to toe with me."

She reached out and put her hand on his broad shoulder. "To be honest, I don't quite know how to deal with you. We've been like two fighting chickens all these weeks."

He looked down at her. "I know. Damned shame to have wasted this time. Funny, every time I looked at you, I wasn't thinkin' about fightin', I was thinkin'— oh, never mind."

"What were you thinking?"

He shook his head. "Forget it. I can't stand to be laughed at." He stared off at the sun sinking lower on the Western horizon.

"I would never laugh at you, Jack," she said softly.

"I believe that is the first time you have called me by name. I like the way you say it." He looked bashful and a little awkward.

"I reckon I feel a little bit the same," Bonnie admitted. "If we'd met under different circumstances—oh, well, I reckon it's too late to think about that now."

"Yep. We'll both leave in the next day or two. Don't reckon we'll ever have reason to meet again."

She didn't say anything, but sighed deeply. She saw her future stretched out ahead of her; a lonely widow in a rambling, empty house with a bunch of cats; people in the little town surely feeling sorry for her. "I don't suppose you'll ever get to Shot Gun?"

"I'd be lyin' if I said I would." He shrugged and looked at her earnestly. "It's a long way from West Texas."

"Yes, I know." She had hoped he would say he would come to see her, but at least he was being honest. *Honest?* She tried to remind herself that this was Cash McCalley she was thinking about. The word "honest" was not in this *hombre's* vocabulary. Funny, he seemed so different now than he had been. The swagger, the superior attitude was gone. The bravado that made women's hearts flutter had been replaced by almost a shyness, a vulnerability that appealed to her.

"I reckon we ought to be gettin' back," he said. "I wouldn't want to ruin your reputation by keepin' you out after dark. Folks might talk."

"I imagine if my reputation were questioned—"

"I'd put a stop to that pronto, ma'am. No true Texan is gonna let anyone ruin a lady's reputation."

Be still my heart. Oh, how she had dreamed of a man who was a real man; a Texan who would fight like a knight of old for her. Now she remembered the night at the governor's ball in Austin and the way he had kissed her out on the veranda. She sighed wistfully.

"What's wrong, Bonnie?" He took one of her small hands in his two big ones.

"You'd really fight for me, wouldn't you?"

"Well, I'd say yes," he smiled ruefully, "but I know how you feel about fightin'."

"Gracious, it's not quite the same."

"It ain't? I mean, it isn't? You know, I always hoped I'd end up with a gal that would teach me to be proper so I wouldn't embarrass myself. I never had much education."

"I haven't either. I taught myself," she admitted.

"You must be smart then. You'd give a man some really smart kids."

She flushed to her toes, but he didn't seem to notice. *Was he asking?* No, of course not. She had been both fighting and denying her attraction to this man all these weeks. He was big and dangerous and charming, a true Texan. And hadn't she always said she'd never wed another Texan?

"Did I say something wrong? If I did, I'm sorry—"

"I—I was just remembering the governor's dance," she whispered, "and what happened in Hot Springs."

"I'm mighty sorry I was so forward," he appeared flustered and his face reddened. "I ain't used to dealin' with a real lady, just women like Fifi."

She ran her hand down his arm. Such a strong arm. "I don't reckon I know all the things that interest a man like Fifi does."

"Lady, I wouldn't trade that kiss on the veranda or those few minutes in Hot Springs for a hundred nights in Fifi's bed."

She didn't mean to, but he was so sincere and those gray eyes were looking deep into hers so she leaned into him and kissed him.

He seemed almost taken aback and then he took her in his arms and kissed her, really kissed her like she had never been kissed. "Bonnie," he murmured, "oh, Bonnie, you don't know what you do to me."

She kissed him deeper still, clinging to him, loving him, wanting him. She didn't care any more about the boxing match or anything else; nothing mattered but being in his arms. She felt loved and safe and protected as only a woman who has ever been embraced by a Texas cowboy can feel. "Jack, I—I can't fall in love with you."

"I know, darlin'," he said against her lips. "I'm just a no-count rascal, and not fit for a lady to love—"

"Don't say that, Jack. We don't have to be enemies." And she kissed him again, running her fingers along the cords of that strong, sun-browned neck and up into his tousled curly hair, pushed his Stetson off so that it fell onto the ground. Her tongue teased his lips and he opened them, sucked her tongue inside.

One of his big hands went to the neck of her blue riding outfit and down through the lace corset cover to her breast.

She gasped with pleasure as his hand cupped her breast so possessively and stroked there while his mouth took over the kiss, forcing her lips open. He caressed the inside of her mouth with his tongue.

She shuddered all over and clung to him, wanting what this big male had to give. "Jack, oh, Jack . . ."

"Maybe we ought to go," he murmured. "I know you're worried about your reputation."

She wanted to say, *Damn my reputation! I want to be on my back under you, feel you plunge into me, drive me wild in a way I've never known, rip the front of my dress open so you can taste my breasts.* Then reason came back to her. They were out in a field where someone might happen along and find them. "Uh, I—I reckon you're right, Jack."

She took a deep breath and pulled away, straightening her clothes.

His face was flushed and his gray eyes intense. "I know we got to stop," he said, "but damn, I never wanted anything as much as I want you."

She wanted him, too, wanted him more than she had ever wanted anything. "It'll be dark soon. We ought to go back to the hotel."

"Reckon that's right, Bonnie. I might be a rascal, but I ain't gonna ruin your reputation."

He was trustworthy after all.

She leaned over and kissed his cheek, loving him and trusting him, although her head told her she shouldn't. "I reckon you're right."

He reached to pick up his Stetson. "Much as I'd like to . . . well, never mind. We need to go." He stood up and reached to pull her to her feet.

"Yes, I reckon we must." She went into his powerful embrace. He held her close, kissing her in a way that made her breathless.

"I never lost to a better opponent," he grinned. "It makes the boxin' match not matter."

"I'm glad you feel that way." She smiled with relief. "I was afraid you wouldn't."

He brought the horses over. "Here, darlin'," he said as he lifted her up into the saddle. "Now you go on along, you hear?" He stooped to pick up his coat.

She smiled at him. "Jack, if I don't see you again—"

He shook his head. "Don't. I hate good-byes."

"Then *vaya con Dios*," she whispered. *Go with God*. She blinked back tears, blew him a kiss, turned her filly and rode away.

He stared after her a long minute as she disappeared into the distance. Then he mounted Dusty. "Little gal, you don't know it yet, but that boxin' match is set for sure!"

Humming to himself, Cash rode at a slow canter back to the hotel. He had no qualms about what he was going to do; he was a poor boy from West Texas and he had always lived by his wits and his charm. All was fair in love and war and Mrs. Purdy was trying to destroy the last little bit of wealth he had any hope of ever getting.

Besides, she had stirred his blood in a way no woman ever had and he intended to charm his way into her bed tonight. It looked to be a very pleasurable Friday evening. And in the morning . . . well, that was her problem, she ought to be more suspicious of men.

Cash rode into town, saw Bat Masterson crossing the street toward the Black Lace. He hailed him as he dismounted. "Hey, Bat, you got some of the reporters set up for the mornin'?"

Bat pushed his derby to the back of his head. "Yep, but it's a rotten thing to do, Cash."

Cash grinned. "Ain't it, though?"

"Suppose she changes her mind?"

"Trust me; I know women about as well as I know horses. That lady is destroyin' me. I got to save that boxin' match—there's too many people involved to let it die now."

"Okay. I'll see you in the morning, then. I have to say you're a lowdown, rotten skunk."

Cash shrugged. "I ain't never been one to worry about ethics. I worry about Number One."

"Ain't that the truth?" Bat grumbled. "I used to think there was something good in you."

"Don't give me no sermon when you're headed over to watch Fifi flip her skirts."

"True," Bat admitted, "but she ain't like that little Mrs. Purdy. Now there's a real lady."

"So what? What she is is a prim, fun-bustin' strait-laced widow who's out to ruin me financially and stop men from havin' fun. She deserves this."

"If you say so. See you in the morning." Bat nodded and walked off across the street.

Cash had a slight surge of conscience as he watched the reporter walk away, but he quickly squelched it. Humming to himself, he turned his horse over to a stableboy and went inside the hotel. He strode into the dining room and ordered a tray.

The waiter smiled at him. "Delivered to your room?"

"No, Joe, I'll wait for it and take it up myself. I want roast beef, some fresh asparagus, a fruit salad, some of those yeast rolls, chocolate eclairs and a bottle of champagne. No, make that *two* bottles."

The waiter scribbled furiously. "Entertaining a young lady tonight?"

Cash glared at him. "Now, Joe, that's none of your business. Just get it ready."

In minutes, the waiter was back with the tray. Cash took a whiff of the food. Oh, it was excellent, all right. And if he took it himself, he wouldn't be humiliated if she wouldn't let him in and he ended up dining alone.

Humming "After the Ball," he carried the tray up the stairs, paused at his door, unlocked it and carried the tray inside. He carefully closed and locked his door, then he went to the adjoining door and knocked softly. "Bonnie?"

No answer. He rapped again. "Bonnie, it's Jack. Maybe we could have supper together before we part forever."

On the other side of the door, Bonnie hesitated. This man had been her enemy for weeks now. Everything in her warned her that he still was her enemy, that he was no better than any of the other men she had known. Her brain warned her that she should not answer that knock or open that door. What she should do was ignore the man, go down to the dining room for supper and then lock herself securely in her room until tomorrow. Tomorrow she would get on a train to Shot Gun and never see Cash McCalley again.

"Bonnie? Are you there?" He rapped again.

With a sigh, she remembered that night on the veranda at the governor's ball and what had almost happened at Hot Springs. She could still taste his kisses from this afternoon. *Should she listen to her brain or her heart?*

"Bonnie, are you there? Please let me in."

She made her decision then. This might be the only memorable night of the rest of her life and it was worth whatever the risk she was taking. "I'm here, Jack." And she unlocked the door.

Chapter Twenty

He came through the door carrying a tray laden with good food. "I was afraid you wouldn't open the door." He grinned at her as he set the tray on a nearby table.

"I did have second thoughts," she admitted.

"We're just eatin,' that's all," he assured her. "And nobody knows. That's the reason I brought the tray up myself. Here, sit down. Let me pour you some champagne."

"Champagne? What are we celebrating?" She sat down and he popped the cork. They both laughed as the champagne bubbled over.

He filled two glasses and handed her one as he grinned. "That we're not enemies, in spite of everything."

"I must say, you're being a good sport about it." She took a sip and smiled. "The bubbles go up my nose. Gracious, I feel positively naughty."

"I'm losin' to a worthy opponent." He leaned over and kissed the tip of her nose.

She felt herself flush and took a big gulp of her drink. "I've never done this before."

"Do you want me to leave?" He turned toward the door separating their rooms.

"Oh, no. I mean, what's the harm? We're just having a little food and champagne—"

"That's right." He nodded and sipped his drink. "You like your roast beef rare or well done?"

She took another sip, feeling very daring. "I like mine well done. Oh, the asparagus and the salad look wonderful."

"I tipped the chef," he admitted and served her a plate. Then he took one and sat down across from her. The food was excellent. Every bite she put in her mouth was juicy and wonderful. She savored it.

"Here," he said, "let me pour you some more champagne."

"I really shouldn't have more than one glass."

He laughed. "If we don't finish the bottle, it'll be poured out. It goes flat and it's a very good year."

"Oh, expensive?"

He nodded and refilled her glass. "Yep, so it'd be terrible to waste it."

"In that case . . ." She picked up her glass and took a swallow.

He returned to his roast beef and she watched him, smiling. She liked him more than she was willing to admit. Jack was being such a good sport about losing. Well, she'd ask him later about taking the job as a ranch foreman. Of course, he was so proud, he might not want it.

"Finish up your food, darlin'," he urged. "We've got chocolate eclairs, too."

"I'm not sure I can eat another bite."

"Well, after a while, we'll bring in my phonograph

and dance. That'll make room for some dessert," he said.

"Oh, I'd like that. You're such a good dancer." She leaned closer, smiling and sipping her champagne. She was feeling warm and happy. "I'm sorry about the boxing match."

He shrugged. "Forget it. You win some, you lose some. I reckon you're right; it's a savage sport that needs to end."

"I'm glad you realize that. You're more genteel than I thought, Jack."

"I'll get the phonograph and we'll dance," he nodded and went into his own room.

It occurred to her that she had time to run to the door, close and lock it. That's what she should do, but did she really want to? In her heart, she wanted to share the rest of this bottle, dance close to him for an hour or so, and then it would all be over and to-morrow, they'd go their separate ways.

He returned to her room carrying the phonograph with its gleaming brass horn. "Not havin' any second thoughts, are you?"

Was she? The champagne was confusing her brain so that she only shook her head. "You've been such a gentleman."

He set the phonograph down on the dresser and cranked it up. "I've got some Stephen Foster."

"Have you got 'After the Ball'? I love that one."

"Sure, That's my favorite, too."

He put on the wax roll and set the needle. "After the ball is over, after the break of morn . . ."

"Here," he came over to her, "let me pour you an-other glass and then we'll dance."

"I really shouldn't have any more," she protested.

He poured them each another glass anyway. "By thunder, this calls for a toast."

"All right. What should we toast to?"

He thought a minute. "How about 'to no hard feelings for the loser to the winner'?"

"Of course," she said, looking at him. "Jack, you don't have hard feelings for me, do you?"

"No, of course not, but I want this to be a night worth losin' over."

"I'll drink to that." She drained her glass and stood up, a little wobbly.

"Here," he said, "let me start the music again." He went to the phonograph, wound it up and came back to take her in his arms. For a long moment, he just stared down at her and she tried to read the look in his stormy gray eyes.

"Is something wrong?"

"Huh? No, no, it's all fine. Let's not talk or think so much, let's just dance." He took her in his arms and she sighed as she rested her face against his broad shoulder and put her small hand in his big one.

. . . after the ball is over, after the break of morn, after the dancers leaving, after the stars are gone; many a heart is aching, if you could read them all; many the hopes that have vanished, after the ball . . .

They waltzed slowly about her room and she had never felt as safe and loved as she did at this moment in the big Texan's arms. "It's such a sad song," she whispered. "I never realized that before."

He kissed her hair. "What do you mean?"

"It's about something that happened at the dance; someone was betrayed and a heart was broken."

She felt him stiffen a second, then he shrugged. "It's just a song, Bonnie. Quit thinkin' and enjoy it."

"I am enjoying it," she sighed and rested her face against his shoulder again. "I could dance with you the rest of my life."

He kissed her hair again. "I want you to remember that tomorrow, after . . ."

She waited for him to finish, but he only held her tighter and danced.

"After what?" She paused and looked up at him.

"Nothin'. After we each go our separate ways tomorrow, I reckon."

"I don't want to think about that. I've been alone too long, Jack."

"Me, too." He sounded regretful.

They didn't talk for a long time, clinging to each other and dancing slowly around the room until the wax roll was used up and the needle made a clicking sound.

He pulled away from her and went to take the roll off. "We'll have some eclairs and then we'll dance some more," he promised.

"It must be getting late," she said as she watched him serve up the dainty dessert.

"Does it matter?" He handed her the eclair and refilled her champagne.

She took the plate and smiled at him. "I just hate for the time to tick away. I'm having such a good time."

"The best is yet to come," he said, "unless you decide otherwise."

She didn't answer because she was so uncertain and confused. Jack was letting her make the decision and that made him so different from other men. Why, he wasn't even angry that she had defeated him and caused him to lose so much money. She ate the chocolate and the whipped cream very slowly, savoring it.

He looked at her. "How's the eclair?"

"Delicious."

"You've got chocolate on your mouth," he whispered and he leaned over and kissed her, the tip of his tongue taking the swirl of sugar away. "Almost as delicious as you are, darlin'."

She set the plate aside, put her arms around his neck and laughed. "If I had known you were going to do that, I would have smeared the icing all over my face."

"Pretend you did," he murmured and he kissed her lips, her eyes, her cheeks.

"You're so silly," she patted his dear face. "After we dance, I want you to kiss me and kiss me some more."

"Lady, your wish is my command." He walked to the phonograph, looked at several wax rolls. "You want to hear 'Aura Lea' or 'Lorena'?"

"I like 'Aura Lea,'" she said.

He grinned at her as he wound the phonograph and set the needle on the wax roll. "Come to me, sweetheart."

With a smile, she complied, going into his arms and he held her tightly as they danced. "I think I love you, Jack."

He hesitated. "Don't say that, Bonnie."

"Oh." So he didn't love her in return, or he wasn't certain. "I didn't mean to obligate you."

"Just dance, okay?" He sounded annoyed and she wondered why. *Had she said something wrong?*

They danced a long time and she kissed the side of

his dear, sun-browned face. "Time for some more champagne," she laughed.

He stopped and looked down into her face. He seemed to be fighting some inner battle. "I think you've had enough. Maybe I should leave."

She shook her head. "Oh, no. We're having such a good time."

He hesitated, frowning, and she wondered if maybe he wasn't having a good time. However, he nodded abruptly. "Of course. Why not? Champagne all around. We'll enjoy tonight and not think about tomorrow."

She didn't want to think about tomorrow, either. She might only have tonight with this man and it was enough that he was hers until dawn . . . if she wanted him. They drank some more and danced again until she paused in the middle of the floor, her arms around his neck. "Kiss me," she whispered.

She could feel his warm breath on her face as his lips came down on hers ever so gently.

"I never dreamed it could be like this," he said.

I didn't either, she thought and surrendered to the kiss that probed deeper still. Now his mouth was hot and demanding, dominating hers as his big hands caressed her.

He swung her up in his arms, looking down into her face. "My enemy," he said and he didn't smile, "my adorable little enemy. I've wanted you since the moment I saw you."

"Oh, Jack," she swallowed hard, "I've wanted you, too. There, I've dared to say it."

The wax roll in the background had reached the end of the song and the needle cut into the roll as it went around over and over. She thought maybe she should mention it, but the look on his face, those intense stormy gray eyes told her that nothing mattered to him at the moment but her. And nothing in the world mattered to her but this man.

He carried her to the bed and lay her on it. Then he began unbuttoning her bodice. She noticed his hands were shaking.

"Here," she said, "let me." She kept her gaze on his smoldering eyes as she unbuttoned her own bodice and unhooked the eyelets of her corset so that her breasts were bared.

He gasped and sat down on the bed, and dimmed the lamp. Then he bent his head to kiss the rise of her breasts. "Oh, Bonnie, I never dreamed. . . ." Then his words were lost against her breasts. She felt the heat of his breath against her flesh and then his mouth sought her nipples. She had never felt such a sensation as she felt now with his lips caressing her there. She arched her back, offering him still more and caught his face between her two hands, willing him to kiss and caress her breasts until she was thrashing about, wanting more than this.

She reached to unbutton his shirt and noticed her own hands were shaking as she slid her fingers across his bare chest and the rippling muscles there. He sighed and pulled her up off the bed so that her mouth found his nipples and she bit him while he gasped and tangled his fingers in her hair that tumbled from its pins.

For minutes or maybe hours or an eternity, they pleasured each other with kisses and caresses and then she felt him stand up. "Bonnie, you should send me back to my own room, before—"

"No," she shook her head and reached for him. "No, I want this; I want you."

He took a deep, shuddering breath and began to unbutton his trousers. His gaze sought hers in the dim lamplight. "I want you," he said. "I must have you. I must have you now."

She reached to pull up her skirt and spread her thighs and he began to pull off her lace drawers.

"You are beautiful," he whispered and bent his head to kiss her there.

She had never had a man touch her there, much less kiss her, but his mouth felt so good and she spread her thighs even wider. Then he lay down beside her and kissed her again, his hands stroking her breasts and bare belly until she was shivering with her own need.

"Bonnie," he whispered, "oh, Bonnie."

"I love you, Jack," she said and pulled him to her.

"I need you," he gasped and now she could feel the heat and pulse of his big manhood against her flesh.

He had not said he loved her, but at the moment, she didn't care; she wanted Jack in the most primitive and carnal way a woman could ache for a man. She pulled him to her.

His fingers stroked her. "You're wet; so wet," he whispered and then he came into her.

He was big and for a moment, she wasn't sure she could take him. Then he put the strength and the muscle of his lean hips behind his hard thrust and went deep inside her. She almost cried out and then his pulsating manhood felt so good that all she wanted was more and more of him.

She locked her slim legs around his muscular body as he began to ride her, deeper, longer, harder until she was gasping and moaning under him. "Jack, my dear Jack . . ."

"Oh, God, Bonnie, darlin'," he murmured against her ear as he wrapped his arms around her, "I never had anything like this before."

She did not tell him she had never experienced anything like this before either. Her first husband had never aroused desire in her and Clint had never even bedded her. Yet nothing mattered now but that Jack satisfy her, riding her faster and faster while her eager body rose up to meet him, wanting what he had to give. He was an experienced lover, she knew, and he was waiting for something, holding back. Her own body wanted something, too, but she was not sure what it was. The crescendo was building, wanting more and more, deeper and deeper, harder and harder. She knew she was clawing at him, attempting to pull him inside her while he kissed her face and eyes and plunged hard and deep and sure into her very depths.

"Come to me, darlin'," he commanded, "just let go and come to me!"

"Ahh!" she gasped one last time, digging her nails into his broad shoulders and then she reached some previously unknown height, paused for a long, glorious moment, straining and then there was an exhilarating fall like tumbling off a mountain into a delicious blackness.

It seemed an eternity passed and when she exhaled in a long, shuddering sigh, it seemed to excite him and he began to ride her again until he gasped, paused and plunged into her one more time, straining to give up his seed. Then he collapsed on her and lay very still, breathing hard.

In the semi-darkness, she brushed his curly hair away from his face. "Jack? Dearest?" She kissed his cheek.

He seemed to come out of his faint and kissed her lips, her mouth, her eyes. "You; you're wonderful," he whispered. "I never knew it could be like this." He took her in his arms and held her close as he rolled over on his side.

"Me, either," she admitted and burrowed deep into his embrace. She had never felt so loved and protected in her whole lonely life. She could stay in his arms forever if time would only stand still. She began to weep.

"What's the matter?" He kissed her tears away.

"I—I want to tell you something; something I've never told anyone."

"It doesn't matter."

"No," she shook her head. "I think you need to know why I've fought you so hard on this boxing match."

"Because you're the president of the Lone Star Ladies and they expect—"

"No, it's more than that." She burrowed deep into the protection of his strong arms. "I've always felt so guilty about Danny."

He raised up on one elbow. "Who?"

"He—he was my brother; only a year older than I, and he knew how much I wanted to escape our awful life."

"And?"

She choked back sobs. "This is so—so difficult, but I have to tell someone; I can't live with it anymore."

Jack brushed her hair away from her face. "Don't, sweetheart."

"No, I must." She took a deep, shaky breath. "We were at the county fair and there was a boxing exhibition with a hundred dollar prize for the winner."

"Ohh," he sighed and nodded as if he were beginning to understand.

"The other man was so much bigger and I begged Danny not to fight, but he laughed and said 'suppose I win that hundred? And if I don't, there's a twenty-five dollar prize for the loser, that'll get you out of here, sis.'"

"Oh, God," Jack sighed and lay back down.

"I—I begged him not to fight, but the crowd egged him on and it seemed like so much money to a poor boy; he never had a chance."

"That wasn't your fault, Bonnie."

"Yes, it was. He did it for me and I can never forgive myself; never." She was sobbing now as he held her. "I used some of the twenty-five dollars for his funeral, then I took the rest, went as far as I could go. I ended up in Shot Gun, broke and hungry. That's when Hans Schultz offered me a job cooking and cleaning."

"It's okay, Bonnie," he soothed her. "I understand."

"Do you?" she sobbed. "Do you understand that I've got to stop every fight I can? There's too many young, poor boys getting killed or hurt because they need money so badly."

He hesitated, then held her close. "Yes, I reckon I understand you now, sweetheart." And he kissed her tenderly.

They both drifted off to sleep and sometime in the night he came awake and made love to her again and yet again. Then they snuggled down in the big comfortable bed and slept. She drifted off with a smile on her lips. Whatever happened, she had tonight and it had been an unforgettable one.

Just after dawn, she awakened and rose up on one elbow, looking down at him. He looked as peaceful as a young boy with his tousled hair. Very gently, she leaned over and kissed his cheek. He slept soundly and did not stir. "I love you, Jack McCalley, you rascal," she whispered. Only maybe he was not so much a rascal as everyone thought and maybe there was going to be a happy ending after all.

About that time, there was a sharp rap at the door. "Room service."

"Just a minute." She hoped there was enough breakfast for two as she reached for her lacy pink robe.

Cash lay naked with a sheet wrapped around his hips and now he stirred and looked puzzled. "Bonnie?"

She smiled and winked at the sleepy man.

Again the man's voice, louder this time. "Room service."

She started across the floor.

Cash sat up in bed suddenly. "Bonnie, don't answer that, for God's sake!"

"Why? It's just room service. Shh! Keep quiet." She paused, nodded to him reassuringly even as he grabbed for the sheet, trying to get out of bed.

"Don't answer that door!" He roared and as he stumbled out of bed, tangled in the sheet, he fell on the carpet.

"Shh! Be quiet. The boy won't see anything." She unlocked the door and reached around to take the tray.

Cash protested in the background, "No, Bonnie! No!"

At that moment, the door suddenly swung wide open throwing her back against the wall and men burst into the room. She shrieked as she recognized some of the reporters including Bat Masterson, with their pads and pencils.

"Get out!" Cash yelled at them and tried to get to his feet, thus losing the sheet.

"Look at him, buck naked!" yelled a newsman, scribbling furiously.

"Yeah, what a headline for tonight's papers: PROTEST LEADER CAUGHT IN LOVE NEST."

"Or BOXING OPPONENT GOES DOWN FOR THE COUNT UNDER OPPONENT?" suggested a tall one.

"Or how about: LONE STAR LADY KAYOED BY A NAKED GAMBLER?" yelled a third.

Bonnie screamed, "Get out! Get out!"

How had they known? Bonnie tried to push them out the door, but there was a dozen of them in the room now as Cash stumbled to his feet, wrapping the sheet around him.

"Hey, Cash," Bat yelled. "You're right! What a head-line this is going to make!"

"Hey, baby," another winked, "you want to make a statement?"

And then she realized the truth. She had been betrayed, very deliberately and carefully betrayed by the man she had loved. With all the dignity she could muster, she strode across the room, hesitated before Cash McCalley. "You rotten son of a bitch!" And she slapped him so hard, his head snapped back, the blow leaving red marks on his face. "Get out! All you rotten bastards, get out of my room!"

Chapter Twenty-One

The men suddenly seemed speechless as she strode into the bathroom and slammed the door. She locked it, then leaned against it, trying to hold back her sobs so the men outside wouldn't hear her. After a minute, she heard Cash McCalley ordering the reporters out and then the sound of his feet coming to her door.

He knocked. "Bonnie, give me a chance to explain."

"Did you plan this? Did you?"

"Yes, but—"

"Get the hell out of my room!" she shouted through her tears. "You've won and now you can laugh!"

"Bonnie—"

"Get out! I won't listen."

She thought she heard him sigh and then footsteps. She heard the door between the rooms opening and then closing.

She waited a long time before she came out. She had never been so angry and so broken-hearted. *How could she have been stupid enough to trust him?* He had only been out to destroy her. No doubt he was in his own room now, laughing up a storm and making plans for the boxing match. . What a blind fool she had been. It was her own fault for falling for him; she'd known from the start that he was a rascal, not to be trusted. *But if you truly love someone, you've got to trust and take the chance; hope for the best.*

She locked both doors, stared into the mirror. Her face was swollen and tear-streaked but the worst hurt was deep inside. Even now gossip would be spreading about what had happened. The reporters would have it in all the evening papers, of course, and Bonnie would lose both her reputation and her credibility. No doubt the Lone Star Ladies would also ask for her resignation, but none of that mattered as much as the realization that she had been deliberately set up and tricked by the man she loved.

Damn him, damn him for making her trust and fall in love with him. And to think, she had thought he might love her, but he'd only been thinking of money and his damned boxing match.

She washed her face, dressed and put her hair up. Cash McCalley had won. In an hour, the gossip would have flown faster than a telegraph message. Not only would the boxing match go forward because she would lose her following of protestors, but she would have to run a gauntlet of condemning stares as she left the hotel and caught the train while he would get sly winks and pats on the back from rowdy men. It wasn't fair, but that's the way life was.

Bonnie blinked back tears as she sat down at her desk and wrote a letter of resignation for the Lone Star Ladies. The vice-president might understand, but the others wouldn't. Then she took her little red, white and blue pin, put it with the note and licked the envelope. Finally she gathered her things and packed.

She did not want to go outside this room and face the scorn and criticism of all Dallas, but of course she had to. She must get to the train station amid the whispers that would be flying. No doubt even now half of Dallas had heard about her being caught in her hotel room with that naked, randy rascal. The rest would learn about it when the evening papers came out. Cash McCalley had done this to her so he could win. And she had thought he might love her as she loved him.

Now Bonnie picked up her little valise, took a deep breath, squared her small shoulders and left her room. Mustering as much dignity as she could, she went downstairs to check out.

Even the desk clerk seemed to be leering at her. "Checking out, Mrs. Purdy?"

She looked him squarely in the eye. "Yes. Please send a messenger with this note to Mrs. Ethel Wannamaker."

"Oh," he nodded. "Mrs. Wannamaker has already been here; left a note in your box. Here it is." He took Bonnie's letter, handed her the other one.

She opened it slowly.

Dear Bonnie:

Tongues are already wagging and I'm so sorry to tell you there's been an emergency meeting of the officers and Board of Directors of the Lone Star Ladies. I have been ordered to ask for your resignation. However, if it's any consolation, I think one night in bed with that lusty stallion would be better than a lifetime as president of the Lone Star Ladies. I envy you. Good luck.

Your friend, Ethel.

Bonnie smiled in spite of herself. "I'll need a buggy to the station."

"Yes, ma'am." The clerk nodded.

Was he smirking at her? People passing in the lobby and coming out of the dining room seemed to pause and look at her, then hurry on, whispering. Yes, before noon, it would be all over town. She went outside to wait for the buggy.

Two men passing by on the street yelled at one another, "Have you heard? The fight's back on. Get on the train that leaves at noon."

"Yeah? Boy, that Cash McCalley never gives up, does he? Where's the fight?"

The other shook his head. "Dunno, but I intend to be on that train."

"Me, too!"

Bonnie took a deep shuddering breath. Of course this had been carefully planned in advance, her seduction, her shame, so that Cash McCalley could make a fortune. By tonight, he would be a rich man from the ticket sales.

The driver came with the buggy, helped her in. "To the station, ma'am?"

Did he know? Was he smiling behind his hand?

"I—I need to stop at a store for a cat basket."

"A cat basket?" He loaded her luggage.

"Yes, there's a stray cat at the depot I'm taking home."

He nodded, helped her into the buggy and silently drove her to a general store. The people inside stopped talking as she entered and it seemed to her they gathered to whisper as she bought her little basket and left. It came to her that these citizens were all as condemning and closed-minded as she had been. Maybe she deserved a dose of her own medicine.

Let them talk. She put her chin in the air and returned to her buggy. The summer sun was very hot today, she thought as the buggy moved toward the train station. She noticed people turning to stare as she passed. Wasn't it amazing how fast gossip traveled? Her followers would be disappointed to hear she had weaknesses, too, feet of clay. Funny, she hadn't realized that until she'd fallen for that Texas rogue. She'd been so smugly superior, so haughty.

She got to the train station and looked around as she stepped down and the driver carried her luggage inside. "Why is there a crowd gathering?"

"The boxing match, ma'am," he nodded as he led her into the station. "Everybody's supposed to get on the noon special train."

Oh, Lord. She sighed, realizing she'd bump into Cash McCalley here and he was the last person in the world she wanted to see. He had hurt her like nothing had ever done before, except Danny's death. Tears came to her eyes and she blinked them away. Damn McCalley for making her care when he hadn't cared at all.

She left her luggage in the depot and now she walked along the tracks, searching. "Kitty Tom? Kitty, kitty."

The ragged orange cat stuck his head out from under a freight car and peered at her.

"There you are. Here's a bite for you." She had bought a little meat at the general store and she tossed it to him.

He ate it, watching her warily.

"You'd better let me catch you, Kitty Tom, if you're

ever going to give up your wild ways and have a home because I'm leaving in a few minutes." She moved toward the cat, but it backed away. "Here, kitty."

It flattened its ears and ran under the freight car.

"Don't you understand? I'm offering you love and a home. Isn't that important to you? Belonging somewhere?"

She took a couple of steps, but the cat ran. "Come back here. You're being a fool, cat. You don't want to be a wild stray all your life." She realized she wasn't going to be able to catch him. The tears welled and she bit her lip. "You're just like him!" she sobbed. "Just a wild stray, too stupid to take the love I'm offering."

She turned, blinded by tears, and went inside the station, bought a ticket from an old man she didn't recognize. "Where's Wilbur?"

"Oh, he's got the day off, ma'am. Going to the fight."

Every man in town was probably going to the big fight.

"When's the train to Shot Gun?"

"Less than an hour."

Bonnie got her ticket and checked her luggage, except for the cat basket. She would make one more try at catching the cat. She found a bench in a shadowy section of the station and sat down. No one seemed to notice her as the crowd of men grew larger. After awhile, a train pulled into the station, puffing and whistling. On the side of the cars hung a big sign. "Special excursion train to the championship fight."

Men seemed to be coming from every direction. They began to board the train as it stood in the station.

Herbert hurried past, getting on the train. He didn't seem to see her and she didn't call to him.

What a hypocrite, she thought, he who had pretended to agree with her. She was well rid of him.

She saw maybe a dozen Texas Rangers board the train. There were hundreds or maybe a thousand men jousting for a spot in the coaches. There were of course, no members of the Lone Star Ladies gathering to protest. Word had already reached most of them, no doubt, that their president was a disgraced hypocrite and not the paragon of virtue they had thought her to be. There was no way she could stop the fight alone and anyway, she didn't have the heart for it. Cash McCalley had defeated her in a way Danny's death, hunger and poverty never could.

As the minutes passed, the crowds of men became larger, bustling and pushing each other. No doubt the promoter would make an absolute fortune at the final destination because men were surely coming from all over Texas.

She kept to her seat in the shadows and watched as the champ and the challenger and all their people showed up, including old Nero, the lion. Among the noisy crowds were the men sportswriters who had invaded her room this morning. No one noticed her or spoke to her. Then the crowds grew so large that she couldn't recognize individuals any more, but no doubt Cash McCalley was among them, smiling with cocky confidence as he boarded and waited for the train to pull out, knowing he had won.

"All aboard!" the conductor yelled, "all aboard the excursion train!"

"Where's this train headed?" yelled a Texas Ranger as he swung aboard. "This fight better not be happening in Texas. The governor will have somebody arrested!"

"Now where it's going is a secret," the conductor shouted back. "You just get aboard and find out."

"We've been ordered to stop it if it's held in Texas!" the Ranger said as he climbed aboard.

Bonnie gritted her teeth. On that train somewhere was her betrayer, enjoying his victory. He'd make tons of money off this boxing match and that had been most important to him, important enough to shame and betray her.

The train blew a warning whistle. It was so crowded, men were hanging out the windows, laughing and talking. Then it pulled out of the station, puffing black smoke and whistling. She watched it leave, knowing Cash McCalley was on that train. She felt both sad and relieved when it finally cleared the station. In the distance, she heard its long drawn-out wail and the clatter of its wheels as it gained speed.

She got up and went to the ticket widow. "How long before the train to Shot Gun arrives?"

"Maybe ten minutes. Just be patient, little lady."

She went back to her seat. It was a big relief that in ten minutes she would be away from this city and back to her little town. When gossip finally reached Shot Gun, maybe the local people who knew her wouldn't care or wouldn't believe it.

"Meow?"

She turned at the sound. The big orange Tom cat stuck his head round the corner.

"Kitty Tom?"

The cat padded toward her.

"If you've changed your mind and you're going with me, you'd better come on."

"I wish I could." A tall man stepped around the corner and she looked up, startled.

She stared at the man, barely feeling the cat as it jumped in her lap. "Jack? What—?"

"I'm takin' a train out to West Texas. Thought I could get on as a wrangler there." He took off his Stetson and stood looking at her, twisting the brim. She had never looked so beautiful and so hurt as she did now. He hated himself for what he had done.

The anger and the hurt welled up in her as she looked up at him. "You rotten—!"

"I know, I know," he nodded. "And I deserve everything you think about me. I'm a tricky scoundrel. Even I'm ashamed of myself." He came over.

She put the cat on the bench and stood up. "If you come near me, so help me—"

"Don't worry, I won't." He ran his hand through his hair, looking miserable. "I didn't expect to see you again, but I'm glad I got a chance to tell you I'm sorry."

"Sorry?" She could hardy contain her contempt. "You've deliberately disgraced me, have everyone in town gossiping and all you can say about what you did is you're sorry?"

"I know it's not enough, Bonnie. Everything you thought about me is right; I'm a rotten sonovabitch."

A thought occurred to her suddenly. "Wait a minute. The excursion train has left, why aren't you—?"

"On it? I decided the money don't count for much, just as I realized even as you opened that door this morning that I didn't want you disgraced, no matter what it cost me."

"Don't give me that! You planned for those reporters to burst in—"

"Yes, I did." He admitted, shame-faced. "I reckon it don't count that at the last second, I had a change of heart and tried to stop you from openin' that door."

He had tried to stop her, she remembered now. "Why?"

He came over to her. "Because after last night, I realized that I loved you, loved you more than money or winnin'; loved you enough to protect you. You trusted me and I let you and Danny down."

She blinked in disbelief. "After all this, you aren't going to the boxing match? You'll lose a fortune!"

He shrugged. "Don't matter. I got just enough from my share of the tickets to pay my hotel bill and buy a fare for me and Dusty to West Texas. I realize I'm happiest out on a ranch anyhow."

She didn't know what to think. "But the excursion train; where is it headed?"

He smiled. "Down to Judge Roy Bean's town on the Rio Grande; Langtry, they call it. There's an island in the middle of the river. That puts it out of both Mexico and Texas' legal jurisdiction so the fight can happen."

How clever. She had to admire him for that and yet . . . "But you're not there, so you'll be left out of the money."

"Right," he nodded. "It don't make me no never mind. It's all I deserve for what I did to you. I just hope that someday you can find it in your heart to forgive me."

She stood staring up at him, loving him, hating him.

In the distance, a train whistled. The station master yelled, "Hey, lady, that's the train to Shot Gun coming in."

She nodded, still staring up at Cash.

The tall man looked ill at ease. "By thunder, I wish you'd say something, Bonnie. At least let me help you get your stuff onto the train."

"So that's it? You want me to forgive you and you'll get out of my life forever?"

He nodded, shame-faced. "What else can I say but I'm sorry and I wish I had it to do all over again? I know I can't expect you to forgive me, but I just had to see you one more time." He looked down. "You takin' the cat with you?"

"It's really *your* cat." She was trying hard not to cry.

"Aw, he'll be better off givin' up his roamin' ways. I'm sure you'll give him a good home."

"I will." She leaned over, picked up the cat, put him in the basket. "What—what will become of you, Jack?"

He smiled. "I like it when you call me that. Nobody but my Ma ever called me Jack. Well, I reckon I'll make out; I always do. Maybe if you'd let me, someday I might manage to save a little money and come visit Shot Gun. That is, if I can find work on a ranch out west."

In the distance, the train whistled again, closer this time. In about five minutes, she would be away from this rascal forever, this scoundrel who had humiliated and ruined her reputation, broken her heart.

She was leading with her heart again, but she loved him still. "I—I don't suppose you'd be interested in that foreman job I told you about?"

"After what I've done, you'd help me?"

She nodded, blinded by tears.

"You think they might really hire me?" He looked hopeful and toyed with the brim of his Stetson.

"It's a good job, the Lazy S," she said.

"That's a big spread, I hear." He whistled, obviously impressed. "With a job like that, I might could get married, settle down, just like old Kitty Tom there."

She glanced down. Kitty Tom was happily dozing and purring in his basket. She was outraged. "If you think I'd help you find a job so you could marry Fifi—"

"Bonnie, I wasn't talkin' about Fifi. I was hopin' you might—oh, forget it, it's a loco idea. I'd better head on out to West Texas, but I'll help you aboard; see you off."

The train was chugging into the station now.

It was her move. Did she dare gamble on love? It could be painful, it could hurt, too, but oh, the joy, the happiness was worth whatever it cost. Danny had loved her that much, she realized now, enough to risk his life to help her escape her dreary life. It had been Danny's decision to make; she needn't feel guilty any more.

She looked up at Jack, loving him, angry with him. He was a wild one, that was true, but he'd just thrown away his own big boxing exhibition and all that money because of her. Sometimes maybe a wild one could be tamed. She took his arm. "Jack, it isn't a loco idea. You can at least come talk to the foreman of the Lazy S. I'm sure you'll get the job."

He hesitated. "You know the owner very well?"

She nodded. She wouldn't tell him yet that she was the owner of the Lazy S, all one-hundred-thousand acres of it. Her first husband, Hans Schultz, had left it to her. The ranch and her money was what Clint Purdy had been after, he'd told her that in the hotel room right after their wedding. He didn't want her, he wanted her wealth to spend on another woman. Then he'd left her alone in the hotel on their wedding night to go to the Black Lace Saloon to gamble, and then was killed in that street fight.

Did she dare trust again? Somehow, she was sure Jack was different; her heart said he was. "I—I think you can get that job if you'd give up your wild ways; settle down."

"Settle down?" He hesitated.

"All aboard!" shouted the conductor. "All aboard for Shot Gun!"

She picked up her cat basket. "You've always been a gambler, Jack. Take the chance."

He took a deep breath and grinned at her. "By thunder, I believe you are the stubbornest, most contrary female I ever met, but I love you; damned if I don't! Okay, I'm bettin' that we can make it." He grabbed her and hugged her so tight, she could barely breathe. "Now come on, darlin,' I got to get my horse loaded."

"All aboard!" the conductor called as they rushed toward the train.

On this hot day, all the windows were open and people peered out, watching the little drama with interest.

"Hold everything!" Bonnie ordered the conductor. "This cowboy has to get his horse loaded."

The grizzled conductor peered at Cash. "Ain't you Cash McCalley? Why ain't you aboard the excursion train?"

Cash winked at the man. "Because I'm headed to Shot Gun with the lady—that is, if she don't change her mind."

"The lady won't change her mind, cowboy," she assured him and handed the cat basket to the conductor. Then she went into Cash's embrace as the people on the train hung out the windows and cheered and applauded.

Cash kissed her then, kissed her like he would never let her go and she had never felt so safe and protected as she did that moment in his arms. Nothing mattered but that she loved him and so she must trust him; forget and forgive him.

"Go load your horse, cowboy," she whispered. "And then come join me on the train." She had a private compartment, but he didn't know that. She was already planning on making love to him the whole way.

He hesitated, almost afraid to ask, but he loved her so. He didn't have much, but maybe with the way he loved her, it wouldn't matter. "Bonnie, I hope you won't mind bein' married to a poor cowboy."

"Not at all." She smiled and kissed him again. Later she would tell him he was going to be one of the biggest ranchers in Texas and that she was the rich donor who was building the big new town library. She whispered in his ear. "Hurry up, Jack, this train is ready to pull out. And you got some hard riding ahead of you."

He grinned down at her. "Yes, ma'am. I can hardly wait!" He ran to load Dusty in the freight car while the conductor helped Bonnie up the steps. In a few minutes, Jack returned, climbing aboard, taking her in his arms and kissing her as the train whistled and began to chug away from the station. "I love you, Bonnie."

"I love you, too, you rascal." And she returned his kiss, knowing that soon, in spite of everything, she was going to wed this Texan and marriage to him would be the most exciting adventure of her whole life. She could hardly wait.

Epilogue

Early Christmas morning, 1899

Bonnie shivered on the ranch's back porch, holding her baby girl close, all wrapped in a pink blanket. "Hurry up, Jack, it's cold out here."

Jack came out of the big ranch house, holding their little boy's hand as they walked. "By thunder, don't rush us. Our little man had to put on his new boots and Stetson before he could come out."

Little Danny looked up at her, grinning, the hat falling off. "Santa Claus brought them," he lisped.

"Well, imagine that!" She reached down and patted her son's curly head. He looked like his father, but there was something about his eyes, his expression that reminded her of his namesake, her brother.

Jack said, "Here, give me the baby."

Bonnie smiled and handed Annie to her father. "Gracious, she's getting heavier every day."

He grinned down at Annie. "You look like your Ma, even though you're named for mine; you know that, Little One?"

Baby Annie cooed.

"Okay, Bill!" Jack yelled, "Bring out what Santa Claus left in the barn!"

Old Bill, their retired foreman, all bundled up and grinning, came walking out of the big red barn. "Look what Santy Claus brought for a little cowboy." He led a small black pony, complete with a red leather saddle and bridle.

Danny had picked up his hat and now he jumped up and down, hanging onto his Stetson. "Santa! Santa!"

Bonnie said, "Jack, he's a little young for his own—"

"Naw, he ain't." He gave her that engaging grin and shook his head. "He'll be four in May and he and Sis there are going to own this ranch some day. They got to learn to ride. We'll get Sis one next Christmas, she'll be almost three then."

She smiled at him, loving him. What a great husband and father he had turned out to be, as well as a ranch manager. The Lazy S had prospered ever since Jack had taken over. Kitty Tom, fat and sassy, hopped up on the porch and rubbed against her legs. Spottie and her kittens gamboled and frisked around old Bill as he led the little pony across the frosty grass and up to the back porch. Both children squealed with delight.

"Good mornin', y'all." Bill tipped his hat and grinned at the children.

Danny jumped up and down with excitement. "Pony! My pony!"

From the kitchen wafted the odor of turkeys, brandied fruit cake, and pies baking as Rosita and her girls worked on the big holiday dinner.

Bonnie nodded. "Merry Christmas, Bill."

Annie craned to look, sticking her little head out of her blanket. "Pony?"

Jack laughed. "See? Next Christmas, we'll have to get one for her."

"Gracious, Jack, you spoil them so." She was smiling as she said it.

Old Bill grinned. "That's what kids are for. Besides, every Texas cowboy got to have a horse."

Jack handed the baby back to her, picked up their son and put him on the pony. "By thunder, he looks like he was born to ride."

"Well, I'm freezing out here," Bonnie said and held Annie closer. "You men go make a trip around the pasture and then come in for breakfast. There's a big fire inside by the Christmas tree and lots of gifts to open."

Jack pushed his Stetson back. "Gonna be a big crowd for dinner. Bill, we got your favorite—pecan pie."

Bill's weathered face smiled and he nodded approval.

Danny urged, "Ride now."

"I'll take him around the pasture," Bill said and started away, leading the pony.

Bonnie watched, sighing with contentment. "I'm so happy."

Jack put his arm around her shoulders. "Glad you finally found your brothers so they could bring their families for Christmas."

"I'd better warn you not to get into any poker games with Brad and Blackie when they get here," Bonnie said. "They used to be gamblers, you know."

"I'm a rancher," he smiled down at her and kissed the tip of her nose, "I don't know nothin' about gamblin'. Honey, you and Annie get back in the house and I'll join Bill in the pony walk. Then we're comin' in for breakfast and a cup of hot coffee in front of that big fire."

"Merry Christmas, honey," she whispered, her heart seemed almost too full to speak as she opened the back door. Kitty Tom, Spottie and the kittens ran in ahead of her.

"Merry Christmas, darlin', and here's to a good new century about to start." He kissed her then, almost squeezing Annie between them and the baby howled in protest. "Later," he promised and winked at Bonnie.

"Sure." She nodded and watched him stride out to the pasture where the delighted boy rode the pony. Later tonight, she would give her husband another gift, she would tell him she was expecting again early in the summer. A new century was a good omen for a birthday. Gracious, three kids were going to be a handful, but she was looking forward to a big family.

She paused in the doorway. "Ride em, cowboy!" she yelled to her little son.

Danny turned and waved to her, and for a moment, she saw her brother again in the child's eyes. She glanced up at the winter sky. "Isn't he wonderful, Danny? I know somehow, that you watch over us." The memories didn't hurt any more.

For a minute longer, she watched the old foreman and the broad-shouldered Texan leading the little black pony with the excited small rider, their breaths making smoke in the cold air. Then smiling, she carried her baby back inside to warm themselves before the big, roaring fireplace. Oh, it was going to be a great holiday!

To My Readers

If you're interested in the outcome of the famous fight, it finally happened on February 22, 1896 and was won by Bob Fitzsimmons in approximately one minute and forty-three seconds against opponent, Peter Maher. In the nine months of squabbling since the planning began in the spring of 1895, Gentleman Jim Corbett had gotten disgusted and dropped out.

True, the pastors' associations and groups of respectable women put pressure on the governor to stop the fight since boxing was illegal in Texas as it was in most of the other forty-four states. The dispute finally included both the presidents of the United States and Mexico as well as the governors of Arkansas, Nevada, and New Mexico. And yes, Bat Masterson and John L. Sullivan were also involved. Fitzsimmons really did own an African lion named Nero and his opponent, Corbett, kept a goat to provide milk for his baby.

While my hero and heroine are fictional, the actual gambler/promoter who put on the famous event was Dan Stuart of Dallas. As I told you, the excursion train from Dallas joined other trains arriving at Judge Roy Bean's tiny town of Langtry, on the Texas-Mexican border, where the fight took place. The Texas Rangers and the Mexican *Ruales* who had been sent to stop the fight decided that the middle of the Rio Grande River was nobody's jurisdiction. That decided, they settled down to watch the fight along with the other enthusiastic spectators. It may have seemed like a lot of fuss for less than two minutes worth of entertainment.

Here's a sobering thought for you to ponder: while John L. Sullivan fought the last bare-knuckled contest, men have continued to kill each other in the ring even while wearing gloves. Nearly five hundred men have died in boxing matches between 1918 and 1988. One, Benny "Kid" Paret, was fatally injured on television in a 1962 match against Emile Griffith.

I know some of you are going to write and ask about the popular movie: *The Life & Times of Judge Roy Bean*, starring Paul Newman. Sorry, almost nothing in the movie is true. If you are interested in the infamous judge, one can still tour his home and store. The state of Texas maintains the Judge Roy Bean Visitor Center at Langtry. Thanks to center supervisor Kenneth Fatheree for providing information.

I am also greatly indebted to a hilarious research book entitled *Dan Stuart's Fistic Carnival* by Leo N. Miletich, 1994, Texas A & M University Press, College Station, Texas, for the basis of this story, and I admit to have taken some liberty with the facts.

So what happened to the real people mentioned in this tale? Bat Masterson died at his desk at the New York *Morning Telegraph* on October 25, 1921. John L. Sullivan, who fought the last bare-knuckle championship fight in the U.S. and had lost to Corbett in

1892, tried running a saloon, went broke and took to the temperance lecture circuit. He died forgotten and almost penniless in 1918.

Dan Stuart was still determined to put on a fight between Corbett and Fitzsimmons and the two rivals finally met in the ring in Carson City, Nevada, on Saint Patrick's day, 1897. The fight was won by Fitzsimmons in the fourteenth round. Fitzsimmons died in 1917 in Chicago and is buried there. Corbett died in 1933 and is buried in Brooklyn, New York. In 1942, there was a movie made about Corbett called *Gentleman Jim*. It starred Errol Flynn. Both fighters were inducted into the Boxing Hall of Fame in 1954.

Jim's daughter, Rose Corbett Diamond, generously built a hotel and housed and fed the poor for free during the 1930s Great Depression in Galveston, Texas. Their son placed a bronze marker that still stands in the 300 block of Tremont Street in the historic section of Galveston, commemorating his parents' generosity.

Hot Springs, Arkansas, is the site once revered by American Indians for the boiling hot springs that whites later used for medicinal purposes around the turn of the century. To this day, the water coming up out of the ground is steaming hot. While most of the big bathhouses are closed now, the site is part of our national park system and interesting to visit. However, there was never a swimming pool at any of these bathhouses; the patients soaked themselves in regular bathtubs.

As far as music from the time period: "After the Ball" was the first song to sell over a million copies of sheet music and made its author very rich. "Aura Lea" was a very popular song during the Civil War and has the rare distinction of becoming a hit for the second time a hundred years later. Given new lyrics, you know it as "Love Me Tender," sung by Elvis Presley.

If you've been reading my other books, you know they all connect into one long, long saga that I first began writing in 1987. You've met Bonnie's older brothers, Blackie and Brad O'Neal before; Blackie in *To Tempt A Texan* and Brad in *To Love A Texan*. The Maverick and McBride ranch, where Cash bought his horse, Dusty, figured into two earlier books: *Comanche Cowboy* and *To Tame A Texan*.

For those of you who want to know which of my books are still available, go to your computer to contact kensingtonbooks.com or ask any bookstore that sells new books. They can check and tell you what can be ordered.

For the latest info about me and my books, see my web site at: nettrends.com/georginagentry or write me at: Box 162, Edmond, OK 73083. Please send a stamped, self-addressed #10 envelope if you would like a newsletter and an autographed bookmark.

So what story will I tell next?

The O'Neals have a cousin, a big, Texas cowboy named Waco; think John Wayne or Randolph Scott. It's 1864 and the Civil War is raging as Waco and his buddies ride up to a town in Kansas, planning to rob the local bank. Finding too many Union troops in the area guarding the town, Waco creates an alternate plan; they will kidnap the banker's twenty-year-old daughter, Rosemary, and hold her for ransom.

Little does Waco know that Rosemary is so spoiled and impossible that the banker is delighted to be rid of her. In fact, he not only refuses to pay the ransom, Waco may have to pay him to take the ornery girl back.

Of course, Waco and his buddies have no money, so they are stuck with her.

In the meantime, what is Waco to do with this rich, spoiled captive who is making his life hell? Plain, plump and stubborn Rosemary is desperate enough to escape to try seducing this tall Texan, although the sheltered girl knows nothing about men. What a pair of sparring, unlikely lovers this is in my next humorous Western tentatively titled: *To Seduce A Texan*.

Come Return To the Old West With Me,
Georgina Gentry